Mrs Fytton's *Country Life*

Mavis Cheek was born and educated in Wimbledon. She is the author of eleven novels including *Janice Gentle Gets Sexy* and *The Sex Life of my Aunt*. She lives in the English countryside.

Mrs Fytton's *Country Life*

MAVIS CHEEK

POPULAR ERROURS

OR THE
Errours of the people in
matter of Phyſick.

Infirmum Corpus Medici
Committe fideli

ff

faber and faber

First published in Great Britain in 2000
by Faber and Faber Limited
3 Queen Square London WC1N 3AU
Open market edition published in 2000
This paperback edition published in 2001

Photoset by Faber and Faber Ltd
Printed in England by Mackays of Chatham plc

A CIP record for this book
is available from the British Library

ISBN 0–571–22586–1

2 4 6 8 10 9 7 5 3

Acknowledgements

This book would never have been completed without a spell in the friendly purgatory of the Tyrone Gutherie Centre in Co. Monaghan, conducive, as ever, to that necessary combination of Hard Work and Hard Play.

for Angela, of course

and in loving, happy memory of her friendship
and her fun, Celia Hall 1949–1999

The seventeenth century marked the beginning of the separation of the place of work from the home . . . Once a woman lost the ability to support herself and her family through domestic activity centred on the household, she found herself very disadvantaged compared with men . . . women were in a weak position in the labour market.

SARA MENDELSOHN AND PATRICIA CRAWFORD,
Women in Early Modern England

I have yet to hear a man ask for advice on how to combine marriage and a career.

GLORIA STEINEM

Prologue

There is so little difference between husbands,
you might as well keep the first.
ADELA ROGERS ST JOHNS

When little Angela Lister, ardent reader, went up to Cambridge to read history in the late summer of 1976 with her Kate Millett and her Germaine Greer and her Andrea Dworkin tucked under one arm, and her nineteenth-century novels and Virginia Woolfs tucked under the other, and the bib of her dungarees containing the latest copy of *Spare Rib* and *Honey Magazine* and the *Guardian*, she felt she could conquer the world. And she might have done, had she not, a little later in the term, attended an informal debate between a large-hipped young woman in a loud floral frock (always a statement about something) and a tall, aquiline, golden-haired, scarf-flinging young man – no, *God* – in rusty corduroy.

The informal debate centred on the premise 'This house believes that Women's Liberation is righting some wrongs but also causing unacceptable levels of disruption in some patterns necessary to the good of society'. It was considered pretty revolutionary to have a man speaking against the proposition – though it did cross Angela Lister's mind that there was nothing revolutionary about it at all, really, because men had been speaking for women for thousands of years.

'Shall we go or shall we boycott?' she asked her friend Rosa.

Rosa said, 'If we don't go we won't know.' As Angela knew she would.

Honour satisfied, off they went to greet another piece of enlightenment in the new dawn.

1

Angela Lister leaned forward on her pew, her chin in her hands, and gazed at the God. And he struck her as so beautiful, so eloquent, so very right on, that she forgot to remember the point of principle involved, and instead, like so many of her sisters before her, she listened enraptured and did not interrupt him *once*.

The hips was for the motion, and it was also considered pretty revolutionary and a bit of a wheeze to have a woman defending the status quo. Angela Lister also thought – fleetingly, it is true – that this was less of an indicator of the scrupulously fair nature of Cambridge University's policy towards the new dawn, and more something of a gimmick. But the thought just fleeted in and fleeted on out again. For Angela Lister had seen, gazed and fallen in love.

The God caught her eye, somewhere between 'In a world of tall men, some women are tall, but men are always tallest' and 'Society penalizes women for their caring dispositions. Society must change to accommodate them.' And she smiled. That is the man I am going to marry, she found herself saying, with only the mildest of winces at the way it betrayed the legend on her T-shirt, which said 'The Personal is the Political'.

'Women have always been able to get what they want without aggression,' shouted the hips.

Angela scarcely noted the outrage. She was trying very hard to keep her face perfectly good-natured and still. Which, she was well aware, was how she looked her best.

Someone with very short hair and an androgynous mien called out and asked why the God felt obliged to argue the women's cause, and the God tossed his scarf and called back that he did not feel at all obliged only convinced, as a history undergraduate, that women had been given short shrift and men must help to put it right if they wanted to live in a happy and harmonious world in future.

'Fine words!' said the short-haired androgyne.

'I mean them!' said the God.

'Pah!' said the short-haired androgyne.

2

At which point Angela Lister stood up and said, 'You wouldn't be so down on him if he had long hair, a beard and sandals . . .' Which was, alas, quite true – since the men's support group to the women's circle comprised, entirely, doe-eyed men with a remarkable resemblance to Jesus as seen by the Pre-Raphaelites. Unfortunately, though they did much for feminist solidarity, they did not do a lot for female desire.

A look of appreciation passed from the God to little Angela Lister, who acknowledged it by continuing to look very good-natured and still.

A liberated husband, she thought, would be absolutely ideal.

She rushed off to the women's room with her friend Clancy's kohl pencil and her friend Rosa's peach lipstick and a territorial determination that, had it been quantifiable, would have dented any argument regarding the weaker sex. Angela Lister was in love. And she was going out there to get her man. And once she had got him, she intended to keep him. All this she knew in those first minutes of his entering her life. Her blueprint was fashioned at the age of eighteen.

But not for nothing was she a liberated young woman. And suddenly, very high on her agenda of the breaking down of traditional male and female shibboleths was the shibboleth that suggested a girl must wait around for a boy to ask . . .

She made it known in double quick time that she was Up For It. He appeared to be Up For It too. She carried off her trophy successfully and she congratulated herself that she had made the choice. But after she got what she was Up For – that is, a steady, faithful, sexual and intellectual relationship with a man who made her heart flip every time she saw him – she had the misfortune to find that her love deepened and widened and engulfed her. In fairness to the God, who turned out to be called Ian Fytton, he found that his love deepened and widened and all but engulfed him too. The all but being the important factor here.

At the end of their Cambridge days he had a first-class honours in modern history and a high profile as a potential anything you want, and she had an upper second. He was a bright, ambitious embracer of the world. He loved women, but best of all women he loved Angela; he loved wine and good red meat, and all the things that flesh is heir to when it has a bit of money in its pocket. And he absolutely loved and adored technology – the strange, new, ever-growing hydra that the likes of Angela Lister found alien and cold and requiring of the obsessional. But Ian Fytton's father, a businessman who loved his only son, knew the future. He lent him the capital to start his own computing business, and his son took it with eager hands. If Angela Lister thought they would travel the world together now their degrees were complete, she was quite mistaken. The Brave New World of business and technology was expanding quicker than bacilli on *ordure*. And Ian Fytton intended to be at the very heart of it.

She was twenty-one years old. There was a great deal of life left in which to travel the world, or end up with roses around the cottage door, once they had consolidated their future together. She promptly set about learning the vagaries of this brave new world. She took on the mysteries of computer software and won. Ian Fytton thought nothing of it. For women were the equals of men in their capacity to understand all things. It did not occur to him that while his delight in the subject came from, well, delight in the subject, Angela Lister's came from loving him. That was something he simply did not consider. Much, perhaps, as Pierre Curie did not bother to ascertain the true fount of Marie's dual obsessions.

Angela's parents, who owned a hardware shop in Reigate, were happy enough. If they had hoped she would come back and live with them in leafy Reigate, they did not say. They had given the girl an education and they were not silly enough to expect her to return to the past. They were introduced to Ian Fytton and liked him and did not ask too many questions about where their daughter intended to live. Which was, of course, with her man.

It was, Ian Fytton thought, very unfortunate that Angela became pregnant immediately they moved into their rented flat in Clapham. But Angela's genetic biology was working away. What Ian called a mistake, Angela privately called insurance. Now that she had a baby on the way, he would go out and hunt and bring back the kill for her and no other.

'Just think,' she laughed, 'when this one is off to university we will still be young ourselves. And we will be so rich we will be able to do anything... anything at all... Jean-Paul Belmondo is still fantastic, even now.'

'And so is Brigitte Bardot.'

Nevertheless, he expressed doubt about her ability to both be a mother and help him with the business.

'Rubbish,' she said, with her last vestigial memory of her history course before the sleep of pregnancy overcame her. 'Women always did work as well as have their families – farming or shopkeeping then is no different from running a computing business from home now. None at all.' And then she yawned.

'I'm only trying to protect you,' he said tenderly.

And she smiled. For somehow that sounded exactly and perfectly right. And so she slept easy.

They married immediately and had a four-day honeymoon in Venice. Angela had heard it was the most romantic city on earth. Which it was. Four days was all the time they could spare, because already the business was going crazy. Ian expanded the office out of the flat and into a couple of rented rooms in Hammersmith. Angela, although heavily pregnant, continued to work with him. He installed the systems, she talked people through when they went wrong and Ian was unavailable. She was still talking to an unsuspecting client on the telephone when Ian was in Huddersfield and her contractions began. Fortunately she had kept up – though intermittently – with her local women's group and there was someone to hold her hand until Ian arrived.

The baby, a boy they called Andrew after his grandfather, was born easily. The women's group seemed disappointed. Everyone could have sworn it was going to be a daughter. But Angela, delighted to be in control of her destiny, just smiled and planned ahead. She found a large, crumbling house in west London which would be big enough for both their home and their office. She would refurbish it herself to save money, and from these premises she would be mother to their child and partner in the business. Which was agreed.

'A bit pre-industrial revolution,' she said to Clancy and Rosa when they came to coo over the baby. 'But we're equals.'

When Clancy said, 'Whose job is it to clean the lavatory?' she pretended not to hear.

Finding the house was like a military exercise. All she wanted was something with three floors, six bedrooms (because the upper floors would be their living space) and a garden for their son. In whatever condition it came. Apart from that she was entirely without sentiment. And thus, very quickly, when Andrew was less than three months old, she found it. No. 13 Francis Street. Perfect.

She donned her old dungarees. Once they had been mere symbols of her political determinism; now they were its evidence. Here was true liberation, here was true breaking down of traditional gender roles. Ian learned not to be gallant as he watched his wife pick up the stepladders and trundle them upstairs, and he learned not to be embarrassed when he closed the door after her and went back to his desk. It was a joint undertaking, this life of theirs, and each did what they could. She hired a young woman who could look after the telephones and do simple office tasks, and also double as a mother's help.

Ian had no role in all this. Within their empire each had separate responsibilities. From each according to his ability. And hers. His job was to get out there and do what a man had to do.

6

She worked hard on no. 13 Francis Street, beginning with the ground-floor rooms, which Ian used as his offices. A small cloakroom was installed in the downstairs corridor so that visiting clients did not need to brave the big, cold upstairs and the scruffy family bathroom. The big, white, back kitchen was extended and fitted with double doors to muffle offending domestic noise, and a spiral staircase was driven through its centre, which made the prospect of caring for small children a nightmare. On the second and third floors there were the family rooms, all in dire need of care and attention. She dealt with those last. She learned glazing, tiling, basic woodwork and decorating and she felt that this great plan was unravelling just as it should.

Ian's business acquaintances began to compliment him on this superwife of his. He basked in the praise. And the business went on expanding. And then, as far as Ian was concerned, disaster struck. When Andrew was only seven months old, Angela became pregnant again. The following year she gave birth to Claire.

'Don't worry,' said Angela. 'I can handle it.'

And she could. She was young. Life was sweet, life was solid and life was happening just as she planned. Through the hard times she kept in mind the glowing grail of a future in which she and beloved husband had filled all life's pigeonholes and could fly away and do whatever they wanted. Every time she pricked her finger sewing up a curtain hem or got paint down the back of her neck from those high ceilings, she would smile to herself and say, 'One day, Angie. One day . . .'

While Clancy finished her MA in California, and Rosa got her first book commission to consider the !Kung, Angela went right on building up her world the way she wanted it. Claire was born, Ian was there by her side, and immediately after the birth Angela had her tubes tied. Mission accomplished.

When their office assistant and mother's helper left to have a baby, Ian tutted. Next time, he said, he would employ a man.

No danger of that happening then.

He did so. And Angela employed a part-time mother's help for herself and carried on. She was young, she had energy, she could fit her work in between the requirements of mothering and helping with the business. And – if there was any time left over – she used it to gradually make the rest of the house nice and warm and attractive to live in. What she managed to do in the way of soft furnishings with yards and yards of cheap mattress ticking would have filled a book by Conran. But one thing she knew – young as she was – and it was this: men go walkabout if they don't like what they get at home. When Rosa or Clancy came to stay and poked fun at her, Angela would whistle Tammy Wynette's 'Stand by Your Man'. With, as she would say, irony. But she adhered to the principles of Tony Bennett's 'Wives Should Always Be Lovers Too', as if Marilyn French had never been born: 'Hey, little girl, comb your hair, fix your make-up, soon he will walk through the door . . .' She might wink at her friends, but she also meant it.

Ian told her that he loved her, and that he admired her, and that he did not know what he would do without her. If she remembered that Henry II once wrote something very similar to Eleanor of Aquitaine before putting her in a château and throwing away the key, she dismissed it. Man might learn from history that man learns nothing from history, she told herself, but women do. She supported and was supported, she loved and was loved, she admired and was admired. It was enough.

She attended PTA and parents' evenings and did her bit for fund-raising events. She loved her children but, like her own parents with her, she knew that one day they must fly the coop and she was happy to let them go. The better they did at school, the freer they would one day be, and so would she and Ian.

Her local married women friends bemoaned the passing of romance from their lives. By the time most of them had two children of school age, the private pleasures of their marriages had long since faded against the brilliance of the domestic burden. Not so Angela. She kept down the cellulite and kept up (or down) the seductive underwear, and enjoyed it all for the game it was. Whatever she did now went into the pot for later. Ian Fytton could only look out of the window or up to the ceiling when one of his male colleagues bemoaned the passing of fun, romance and marital relations . . .

By the time Andrew and Claire began senior school, the office had long since moved from Francis Street to fine new premises further into town. Angela turned the house back into a complete family home again, so quickly that it was almost a conjuring trick. Let's get it out of the way, she thought. And she did. She worked with Ian three days a week and on the other two she did all the other things a mother and wife and business partner needs to do to survive. Now Ian employed a large staff of young men besides himself, and an unmarried woman of fifty to oversee the office side of things and to be his secretary. Young women came and went in the more menial areas and it therefore mattered not, as he said, when they left to get married.

At Angela's suggestion, they took on a partner. Ian agreed, saying he could do with the help and the extra capital. Angela nodded, keeping quiet about wanting the new working partner to take over for good, eventually, while she and Ian, finally unencumbered by their offspring, circumnavigated the globe. Still young and vigorous – just as she had always planned.

As the years passed, Ian went from love's delight in all she did to apparent awe of her capabilities. 'My wife,' she once heard him say to his new business partner, Bernard Ball, 'could easily have *been* a bloody rocket scientist. Put her in Cape Canaveral and she'd have an interplanetary probe on Mars by Monday . . .'

Angela smiled to herself. It was true, she would, if Mars be where her husband stood waiting. She never lost that memory of the God of the Cambridge Union and hot sex in small beds with mulled wine. It was there, waiting for them still, just below the surface, and they would find it again. The day was drawing near.

To fill up the evening and as a little additional interest she began to look hard at the financial papers and suggested, from time to time, where they might invest any small surplus. Ian could not deny her skill in this department either.

'I sometimes feel redundant,' he said playfully to her one evening.

'Redundant is it?' She smiled back, and hauled him off to the bedroom to redress such foolishness.

It was as well that these investments had been made. During the lean times of the early nineties not only did Ian's father die but his mother needed capital as the paternal business went to the wall.

'Well done, Angie,' said Ian, almost to himself, as they cashed in the investments she had once advocated. Partner Bernard slapped him on the back and congratulated him on his foresight in the matter of stocks and shares and he – rather awkwardly – took the praise as his due. Angela just smiled and said nothing.

'Where would I be without you?' said her husband again one evening as she slid back his shirt collar and massaged his tired neck.

Mrs Fytton senior was moved to a comfortable new house in Taunton, from where she observed the world with increasing sourness and immobility. Angela arranged for a daily companion and went down to visit her mother-in-law whenever she could. The children, now teenagers, refused. Angela withdrew their monthly allowances. The children, now teenagers, agreed. Ian saw this through a haze of firm and peaceful family discussion. He never interfered in the rows, or felt obliged to deal with a door slammed in anger. That was

Angela's department and she dealt with it – as in all things – extraordinarily well. Never once, in anger, did Angela say, 'You deal with this, I've had enough . . .' Though she asked his advice, of course. Her job, her *business*, was the family. His part in it was to be there for it and enjoy it. He played tennis with his son at weekends and he took his sweet little teenaged girl shopping occasionally and bought her and her friends hamburgers. They knew better than to give their father a hard time. Or their mother, mostly, come to that. She ruled the roost with a velvet glove covering a hand of razor wire. She even knew how to disengage the woofer from the hi-fi if they played the bass too loud. When their father was at home they behaved. Life ran as smoothly as a well-oiled clock. Whatever, in those days of digitalization, such an old-fashioned item might be.

Business colleagues and the men of the neighbourhood looked upon Ian with envy. They were working twice as hard as before in the harsher economic climate. They had wives who screamed and threw crockery when they were late home from the office. He had a wife who stayed late at the office with him or went on occasional business trips with him. Or who was waiting, powdered and painted, in his bed, when he returned. They had wives who were passing their sell-by dates, had hot flushes, cold sweats and neurotic syndromes. He had a wife who was still young enough – just – to be a floozie from the typing pool, with legs to match, and from whose clear eyes shone nothing but the light of admiration. They had wives who thought computing was as exciting and sexy as running an abattoir. He had a wife who not only knew what he did for a living but understood it, respected him for it and – if he was ill – could step into his shoes. Ian, when this was pointed out to him, found it quite hard to smile the smile of the Pantocrator. For some reason.

As the tough early nineties gave way to easier times, Angela still worked with Ian, but only for a day a week. The technology

– as he pointed out to her – was getting more and more difficult even for him to understand and he and Bernard really
needed another full-time partner. She acceded cheerfully.
Another working partner would make it even easier for Ian to
devolve when the time came. Of course, at the moment he
had to work flat out because the scars of the early nineties
were still healing. But they were on course . . . Definitely on
course . . . And Angela needed to give a little extra attention to
the children, who were in the process of completing their
GCSEs. David Draper – a lively Jack the Lad – came on board
with Ian and Bernard and the future seemed assured.

It was at this point that Ian said, very firmly, that she
should take some time for herself. He had two partners now –
and all the help he needed. She had paid her dues. Why not
release herself from the office entirely?

'Take me to Venice for a week and I might consider it,' she
said.

He told his secretary to fix it and a fortnight later there they
were. No longer staying in the unpretentious La Calcina,
hotel of their honeymoon and overlooking the Giudecca, but
in the Gritti Palace, looking down on the Grand Canal. Which
just about symbolized their every achievement.

In the course of the next seven days they screwed like rabbits, drank like fishes, ate like pigs and walked around the
city wrapped in their eel-like arms. Ian had kept his golden
hair and she had kept her twenty-five-inch waist. It was as if,
she thought, they had only just met.

'One day soon,' she whispered as they stared into the
moonlit waters of the Grand Canal. 'One day soon it will be
like this all the time . . .'

'Yes,' he responded firmly. 'Yes.' He was looking at the
water and he was thinking how lucky, how *very* lucky, he
was. He could not have achieved the half of it without his
wife. It was what he predicted at the Cambridge Union all
those years ago. All those years ago . . . He turned to his wife.
'Take a break,' he said, even more firmly.

She did not argue. A woman who seeks to control should make sure – just as with a girdle – that the control is well hidden and quite out of sight.

She stopped going into the office from that day forth. And she allowed dashing, dynamic David Draper to accompany Ian on their foreign business trips. Though she did take the one to Hong Kong for the handover. She too relaxed enough to enjoy an almost dowager status. Yes to Hong Kong, no to boring old Brussels and the flatlands.

Just as she felt safe enough to retire a little, to unplug herself from a world where she felt she must be one jump ahead.

Just as she sat back in her sunny garden, smiling and waiting for the final piece to fall into its correct place and Andrew and Claire to go off safely and happily to university.

Just as she thought, 'I am still only thirty-nine. Bliss. Brilliant. All is going perfectly to plan.' Recalling that 'Women! Take control of your lives' had once been her watchword in the seventies.

And just as she congratulated herself that, after all, the famous old adage set down by Robbie Burns that 'the best laid schemes o' mice an' men gang aft a-gley' says nothing of women, and only applies to small rodents and the male of her species . . . Something in the blue sky darkened above her.

But when she looked up and shaded her eyes she could see nothing.

Nothing at all.

Which perhaps, after attending that Cambridge Union debate, was her second big mistake.

For just at that precise moment, in a small, smart restaurant at 's-Gravenhage, a pretty little woman, attending a conference on Europe and dentistry, and wearing too-high heels, slipped and fell at the feet of a tall golden-haired man, who bent to help her up and who insisted (as she brushed the pretty little tears from her eyes, and shook her pretty little curls into place, and whose dainty vulnerability was written all over her round little figure and quivering little mouth, and who kept drawing her skirt hem above her sweetly rounded knee and rubbing it to show that she was being brave), who *absolutely* insisted, that she should join him and his colleague, David, at their table and have a drink until she was calm again. Which same David it was who winked and nudged him and said, much, much later, 'What's The Harm?'

Blue skies, on the whole, are never to be trusted further than you can see them.

Part One

April

If I can't have too many truffles, I'll do without.

. COLETTE

The day was a warm one. April gold. The sky was celebration blue. Clouds floated by like spoonfuls of buttery mashed potato, and the verdant grasses below them were all sparkling with dew. It was a harbinger of a day, a day of portent, a day of opportunity and possibility that was not to be missed. A heavenly day. The kind of day, surely, that Milton had in mind when he suggested one should 'Accuse not Nature! she hath done her part... Do thou but thine.' In short, it was a day upon which to get up, get out and get cracking.

Mrs Angela Fytton put her black thoughts behind her. Good, she thought, instead. Good. And she shook out her once-sleek hair until it was fluffy and wriggled her body, with its newly acquired half-stone and waistline that was an inch and a half bigger than it had ever been and all made entirely of chocolate, into something loose, floaty and cotton.

Good.

Her fingers hovered over her dressing table and her make-up bag. Hovered, clicked the familiar thing shut decisively, and moved on. Her feet slipped into flat, canvas shoes, once worn to besport herself during family holidays upon the beaches of Portugal. The T-shirt she pulled over her head had a distinct feel of slackness, the softness of many washings. Whatever else she was going to be on this heavenly day, she was going to be comfortable. *Very* comfortable. One might almost say At Last.

She looked down to where her little-friend-chocolate

protruded. She patted it. It gave her, she decided, the look of a naked Eve by Cranach or Memling, with that very female curve so beloved of the Northern Renaissance. She winced at the thought of the Art of the Flatlands. Had she only cared a little more for that and a little less for putting her feet up in the garden of life, she would not now *have* this new curve. Ah, well . . . She patted it again. Little-friend-chocolate. She refused to even consider the word plump. That new curve was female and it was art. Chocolate art. Testimony to pleasure. She had stopped the chocolate for now, but the sweet swelling remained. Good, she thought again. *Good*.

The something loose, floaty and cotton was a little creased, due to its having been squeezed to the back of her wardrobe for more years than she cared to remember. It was possible that she had worn it once or twice in the last stages of pregnancy with Claire. In which case that would be eighteen years ago. It had an elasticated waist. On a day like today, an elasticated waist – a slightly *perished* elasticated waist – was suddenly the most perfect sartorial requirement. It gave her the illusion – or was it illusion? – that she could breathe again.

Here you are, world, she said to the mirror reflection, pulling and releasing the elastic which slumped rather than snapped back into place. I'll draw no analogy from that, she thought, as she watched it sag. Oh no. This is the new me and it is comfortable, she thought. Very comfortable.

She had one last pull at the elastic. No restrictions, no constraints. After all those years of wifehood, workhood and motherhood, Mrs Angela Fytton let it all hang out. In fact, she stood there letting it All Hang Out so committedly that she was suddenly extraordinarily and wonderfully tired and almost picked up her copy of *Country Life* and got back into bed. But the beauty of the day, with all its challenges, beckoned through her window. A day to get up and go, she reminded herself. And taking her slight hangover carefully down the stairs (she had stayed up late, writing her last will and testament, which seemed, last night, to be a wise and holy thing to do, requiring much thought and Rioja), she prepared to venture forth. For if she did not, she reflected, as she closed the door of her vast Victorian semi and set off down the M3 towards the west in her new and zappy little three-door hatchback, she would scream. And the scream might never stop.

She negotiated the zappy little three-door hatchback down streets full of large cars containing baby seats, of houses with funny cut-out pictures stuck on to upstairs windows, of fat or thin, plain or pretty, pale or ruddy nanny-girls pushing strollers, with a vacant air. Little houses, big houses, clematis, wistaria and conservation, all the same: safe, secure, middle management or media moguls, top professionals or just starting out. Houses all cluttered with baby alarms, little bicycles, big bicycles, skate boards and the odd bit of dope tucked behind the biscuit tin.

With one bound I am free, she thought. The perished elastic lay about her waist as light and gentle as gossamer.

Good, she thought once more. *Good*.

2

April

Be plain in dress, and sober in your diet;
In short, my deary, kiss me and be quiet.

LADY MARY WORTLEY MONTAGU

The motorway was smooth, which was soothing, and not full at this time of the morning. She would be spared the knuckle whites of power-crazed sales reps and the merry quips of lorry drivers as they tried to run her off the road. She relaxed. Nothing like a nice long drive to give you time for sorting out the brain. Thinking. She had quite a lot of that to do.

She passed the crenellations of Windsor, the gravel pits of Slough and the amazing ugliness of Basingstoke. She could identify with Basingstoke. Once Basingstoke had been an innocent little market town, full of attractive byways and good will. Now it was a modernized, brutalized mess of misplaced planning. Somewhere beneath its ugly, post-war craziness lay the foundations of its goodly, ancient past. As, she thought, did her own.

The only difference between her and Basingstoke was that she might find hers again if she dug down deep enough. She could lift off the layers of what time had done and from underneath resurrect her old self. Poor Basingstoke, ugly hulk, was probably stuck like that for ever.

She drove past it, eyes fixed on the horizon. London never seemed to be quite far enough away until you reached beyond that point. When the children were growing up she would base getting away from it all on the simple rule that she was never far enough away from it all until she was too far down the motorway to turn back and save a forgotten tray of scones in the oven.

And did this rule of thumb denote a lively, imaginative mind? No, it did not. It was just that once she *did* leave a tray of scones in the oven when they were travelling to Ian's mother for the weekend. And Ian drove back in time to save them. The hero. They were inedible, of course, but not burnt. She rechristened them biscuits and set off with them cooling in the boot, because Ian's mother liked her daughter-in-law to cook her things. Well, you would, thought Angela, and she had certainly obliged. Ian was delighted with the way she obliged his mother. And she was delighted with the way her husband was obliged. Left to her, of course, old mother Fytton could have whistled for home-baking. But if her husband loved her the more for doing it, do it she would.

Well, she would not be cooking scones or biscuits for the dowager Mrs Fytton ever again, her being six feet under. Nor would she be cooking scones or biscuits for family consumption at home either. She had done her best over the years to star in the play called Family Life and personally she felt she deserved an Oscar. She had been mumsy in the kitchen, whorish in the bedroom, stylish in the world and efficient in the workplace. And now she was alone for all her pains. Curtain. No applause. Even on a glorious day like today, the little bubble of bitterness would rise. She wished it would not. Bitterness was a waste of energy. Bitterness pulled you down into the bog of despair. Bitterness fashioned those little lines around your mouth – the kind her mother-in-law once wore – and she was not going to let it win. All the same . . . Acting? *Acting?* Most women could take to the stage any day of the week and be convincing in any part written for them. She, Angela Fytton, certainly had. And just as with the actresses of her acquaintance, so there came a time in ordinary life when you were too old for the part. And a younger actress got it. There were just some rainy days you could not plan for. *Après toi le deluge . . .*

Truth was, despite the sorrow, there was something liberating about breaking out of that urban ghetto, that citadel of self-congratulatory private-sectorites pushing their nannied children into smelly little crammers so that the privileged brats could one day inherit the earth. And she included her own in that. Oh dear, yes, she did. Angela Fytton, she thought with shame, This Was Your Life.

Scone-reaching distance? No, Angela Fytton intended to live a lot further away than that. A lot. They could keep Francis Street and its environs. The barbarians were not at the gates, they were living inside the keep – and very comfortably too. But *she* was going to do a barbarian bit of her own and Visigoth off out of it. She put her foot down and exalted in the engine's tinny roar. It was wonderful, wonderful, to no longer drive a space wagon. So what if the horse she had backed had come in lame (the pity of it was that he had not come in minus his balls as well)? At least she was now free. To go wherever she chose. Beyond those scones. How a right-on liberated idealist, as she once was, could have become that nice Mrs Fytton with the high-flying husband and two sets of school fees she could scarcely tell. But she had. From now on she would have no more of it.

Mrs Fytton, Mrs Fytton, Mrs Fytton, she repeated in her head. She liked the name. It complemented Angela, which was too soft on its own, and it was considerably better than her maiden name, which was Lister and therefore rhymed too easily with blister – and anyway, since no name was anything but patriarchal, as she had spent so long telling the world in the seventies, it was as good as any other. Fytton. She never embraced the announcing of herself to complete strangers as Angela, and – despite those seventies – she still thought it a bit of a cheek when she received letters from women she had never met beginning 'Dear Angela' and signing themselves 'Naomi' or 'Ruth' or 'Portia'. A given name, Christian name, call it what you will, was the intimate passport of friendship, and friendship was precious. You earned it, you did not assume it as of right just because you were the same sex . . .

'Crap, Angela,' she said to the mirror. The reason she called herself Mrs Fytton was because it got right up the new Mrs Fytton's nose.

The road pulled her on. Away, away. Away from the bourgeois ideal and the brittle friendships of urban living. Now she was free, she observed that among the dilatory women of the middle classes a combination of intellectual and applied success was viewed as extremely suspicious. At best it was getting above yourself, at worse it was a separator – the modern equivalent of witchcraft. Instead of these silly women celebrating knowledge, they shunned it. They drove to Périgueux and avoided Angoulême. They stayed in Tuscany and avoided Florence. She had once made the mistake of mentioning Capri and the Villa Jovis and Tiberian reticulated brickwork in mixed company while wearing a clinging rose-pink frock and two days after her divorce came through. You could have heard a pin drop. Sorry, she felt like saying, sorry. It was then, looking into the hostile eyes of the assembled women, that the chilling notion occurred. Had she lived a few hundred years ago, a witchcraft trial would have been inevitable. And in our good Christian community too. Those eyes said they would definitely like to see her sitting on hot faggots. She was too young and too womanly to be single and live. 'Let not widows remain unwed lest they grow to prefer the state,' wrote one jolly philosophizing burgess in fifteenth-century Bristol. Nothing was ever new . . . Across those prating dinner tables the proud doyennes still dispatched the guilty.

She nearly hit the hard shoulder it made her so cross. So where did the fucking sisterhood go, then? Nobody ever said you had to look like the back end of a bus and think that Defoe was someone with whom you had Defight to be part of it. Besides, somewhere under that rose-pink frock were several lines of stretch marks, a couple of varicose veins and quite a lot of floppy bits . . . Perhaps she should have stripped off there and then and shown them. If Pliny berated the women of ancient Rome for honing their fingernails into talons, he should have leapt a couple of millennia and seen the women of modern-day west Londinium. Theirs came up spiky as gimlets to rip at the flesh of her tearful eyes, excoriate the tissue of her bruised, dumped heart. And she so innocent, so vulnerable, so-o-o . . .

That is not entirely true, now is it, Mrs Fytton? said the eyes in the driving mirror. There were a few *other* contributory factors, were there not? A few other factors that led to this excoriation that makes you bleed as you drive?

Well. Perhaps. Of course. A few . . . But I never, really and truly I never, ever thought that the old ways of the medievals persisted and that a new-made single woman must appear quiet, meek, humble and virtuous and keep her ankles covered. I thought we were all post-modernist feminists nowadays. I thought, I thought . . .

The eyes widened. There was something fiery in their lights. You thought, they said, wrong. That is only in magazines. Society still wishes to protect itself from the free woman, the loose canon, the wronged women who will not lie down and take it. Especially if she is anything over thirty and therefore beginning the road to wisdom.

I suppose it would have been all right if I had run down the road to *un*wisdom naked and cutting the heads off everybody's petunias and wailing like a Greek chorus before being carted off to a psychiatric unit?

That would have shown a thoughtful sensitivity to the situation, certainly. Instead of which . . .

What?

Instead of which . . . First time out solo and you stand accused of discussing the virtues of Apple Macintosh over IBM with a nice man from the local newspaper at David and Marcia's party while wearing fishnet stockings and a shortish leather skirt!

Bravura – I have legs like tree trunks.

Or the red satin minidress at your own party, with a little

help from daughter Claire's Wonderbra. Daughter Claire usefully absent and *not* consulted about either the loan or the appropriateness of wearing such a provocative garment.

Well, I *bought* the vulgar thing.

May I remind you that a 36-C cup is perfectly able to stand alone. Any more help and they'd have been strung round your ears. It was an action, a dress code *not* designed to make the ladies feel relaxed while the gentlemen gawped. Angela Fytton – wipe that smirk off your face . . . And it was unlikely, wasn't it, that dancing with their twenty-three-year-old builder at the Coopers' twenty-first anniversary bash would endear you further to the sisterly assembly?

It sure as hell endeared me to the brotherly one.

We are talking about the lost sisterhood. Smirk *off*, please.

OK. Maybe I did lick his ear a bit. But these things are surely acceptable for a newly dumped wife? It is called getting through. To be looked upon with kindness, with a sense of there but for fortune . . . No?

No. Shall I go on?

Oh no, thought Angela, suddenly weary, you do not have to.

She might just as well have done a Godiva down Francis Street with Finale tattooed on her bottom. So far as the be-ghettoed west Londinium witch-hunters were concerned, those knives, which they pretended were but pruning shears, came out sharp and strong. A woman who loses her husband, who discusses reticulated brickwork and who snogs a builder should be careful. Or leave.

Of course, if her husband had returned to her, tail between his legs, all would have been well. But he did not. She was left, small-waisted, big-titted, younger than most of the barbarians, high and dry and alone. If she had gone on with the chocolate and become gross – well, that might have made a difference, *might* . . . though you never could tell with the witch-hunters. But by then, by chocolate time, the little bit of London where she lived had already turned into an absurd replica of the school playground. If you play with her you can't play with us. Or it replicated something even more ancient, more sinister. It takes only one or two mad ones, like stinking lumps of tamarind, to sour the pot. So Clancy said, to comfort her. But then Clancy had moved away, now wrote for the *Irish Times*, and was allowed a fancy turn of phrase. And what, anyway, would Clancy know, being safely out of it nowadays with her nice husband, Jack, and her nice daughter, Philomena, and her comfortable Dublin life? And, by the way, how could Clancy and Jack have got away with calling their daughter *Philomena* and still have an apparently excellent relationship with her? The world, truly, was unfair in every respect.

When women turn against women they take the fascist approach. A Jew, a leper, a South Selma negro – or a woman in a respectable part of London with too much of something and no protector. Someone must embody the evil we feel we have in ourselves, she'll do. It was not hard to see where cruelty lay, just beneath the skin of civilization. Years ago, if they had not burnt her, they would have strung her up. And, just as in those far-off days, they would have paid no attention to her pleadings that she did not give Goody Grote a poisoned finger, so now what use was it to say, 'But I do not want your husband, I want my own'? Who would believe that – despite most of those husbands looking like advertisements for the immediate need for health insurance?

When Clancy, still living nearby, went blonde, everyone just said lovely. When Angela went blonde and met Lydia Curzon in Sainsbury's, she watched her practically hurl herself in front of her twinkly and semi-decrepit husband, lest he be in need of saving from the golden curls . . . Lydia Curzon had not spoken to her since. Clancy, on being taken to task for this by Angela, said, 'Yes, but I'm blonde and plain and I write about the history of things like the vacuum cleaner.' As if it explained everything. Perhaps it really did . . . How depressing.

And so Mrs Fytton, travelling west on this beautiful April morning, donned the armour of compromise. She was not on her way to war, she was retreating from it. If she negotiated terrain that fetched her up further than scone-burning distance, she knew she would be safe. Country good, town bad. That was the way of it. Like the plague-beset victims of yore, she was fleeing to the countryside and health. To a place where she would not be thought a witch but a wise woman. She re-read Goldsmith's *Deserted Village* with a manic gleam in her eye: 'Ah! Sweet Auburn . . .' Indeed. And now, with the countryside whizzing past her windows, she began to recite, ripping it out at the sweetly clouded blue and those trembling verdant grasses.

'A time there was, ere England's griefs began . . .'

'Please yourself,' she said, to a rapidly retreating winged speck in the sky. She began to sing it, and even more loudly, more defiantly. When they were small, the children used to plead with her not to sing to them on long car journeys. 'Don't sing, Mummy,' they implored. Now, in a moment of joyous liberation, she gave it all she had got:

'When every rood of ground maintained its man;
For him light labour spread her wholesome store,
Just gave what life required, and gave no more:
His blest companions, innocence and health;
And his best riches, ignorance of wealth.
. . . de dum de dum . . .

I still had hopes, my latest hours to crown,
Amidst these humble bowers to lay me down . . .'

Presumably, if every rood of ground maintained its man, might it not also maintain its woman? Whatever a rood was.

Simplicity she was going for. Back to basics. Just a housewife. How wonderful.

Peace at last.

She accelerated. If that blue sky above was anything to go by, it was a day for finally finding the right humble bower. Mrs Fytton, she repeated. Mrs Fytton goes to the country. She smiled a not altogether Sweet Auburn! sort of a smile. And Mrs Fytton it would be. Ian, beloved husband, now beloved ex-husband, would have two of them to contend with. There might now be another Mrs Fytton, a younger Mrs Fytton, who was not six foot under like the sour old dowager Mrs Fytton (more's the pity and that could be arranged), but she – quite frankly – could go and piss up her leg. This Mrs Fytton, the first Mrs Fytton, was keeping that name. She had a use for it and both church and civil said that she could. She tooted and waved at a passing lorry. Mrs Fytton she was and always would be. Strong in her armour, free to do whatever she liked, able to leave behind those silly female pygmies and, like poor Goldsmith, after a youth of labour seek an age of ease.

She might even get her husband back. In fact, she fully *intended* to get her husband back. For Mrs Fytton the First was not going down this route without a plan. Most definitely she had one. And it was a *corker*.

When it was clear that Ian was not coming back, she was told by a counsellor to get on with her life, and she had tried. Getting on with her life was, she felt, justifiably interpreted as finding and keeping another bloke. After all, she told herself grandly, that was the only thing she lacked.

She had therefore tried, and she had, somewhat ignominiously, failed.

She did not see why she should try any more.

She had put a lot of effort into her marriage.

A lot of spadework.

A lot of manure.

So why

should she

end up

eating dirt?
And besides,
she really
and truly
still
loved him.
Ian.

If they weren't castigating her, those London folk, they were *pitying* her. It was hard to say which was worse. In her little bit of west London, pity had begun to spread all over her like measles. A woman alone and incapable. *Pity* from the man at the garage, who showed her exactly how to use T-Cut to get a real shine. As if she had either the time or the inclination to want a shiny car. 'I just want to swap this space wagon for something nippy. Got it?' He looked at her even more kindly. Women! Always changing their minds.

Pity from the doctor's receptionist, who told her that Prozac got *her* through, while smiling happily upon a small boy drinking the daffodil water. 'And it still is,' she added proudly. 'I'd never have known,' said Angela.

Even the postman, George – a part-time poet and fond of calling himself a man of letters (oh, the wit of these people) – said to her, 'You can get too fond of your own company, you know,' with a sad little screw of his eyes. Fuck me, she thought, unusually aroused, philosophical jewels sharding through her letter box from the bloody *postman*! And when she retorted that, as a matter of fact, she was really very enamoured of her own company, it being loyal, affectionate, quite sexy and totally in tune with the things she enjoyed, he shook his head, as if she were tripping down the path of madness. And probably went off to talk to the man at the garage.

It was in that very same doctor's waiting room, with the eyes of the sympathetic, be-Prozacked receptionist upon her, that she had flicked through one of the superior women's magazines, only to find that its editor, reeling from the statistical news that 40 per cent of women of child-bearing age considered themselves celibate, asked in a headline, 'And where does all that sexual energy go?' Like a hypochondriac, Angela Fytton read this and felt a terrible clutch at her heart. 'Failed again' echoed through her shrinking brain, and she immediately switched to *Country Life*, the magazine that seeks not the depth of one's psyche.

Too late. Despite the fact that she was attending the surgery only for her tetanus booster, she imagined all that sexual energy whizzing through her system, imploding her energies, drying out her knee joints, draining off her hair pigment, creeping round her retina to suck away the sight. A gammer, a harpy, a crone – a.k.a. Mrs Angela Fytton of Francis Street in the town of L—, in the year of 19—, in the process of decomposing.

Did all human beings need to shag on a regular basis in order not to go crazy? Like the old-fashioned idea that if men didn't get It on a regular basis they went off pop. Or became serial rapists and paedophiles. Now – hello, equality – were women getting the same treatment? Post-feminism, it was imperative to have sex. No sex for some time meant imminent disaster. This way to the loony bin, via infanticide, kleptomania, peculiar eating habits, hemlock for hubby and all those other well-known things the average potty, sex-starved female is heiress to. Never mind that some of the most dangerously peculiar women she knew were having lots of sex all the time and imploding all over the place. To be seen to be unshagged was definitely outer darkness.

'All that sexual energy' indeed. She vowed never to pick up that particular magazine again. *Country Life* was much better. And much more useful. For wasn't she here, on this beautiful spring morning, because of it?

She changed into fifth gear, glad to be nearing the end of the motorway now, and overtook a silver Saab. Cars for boys, she thought grandly, and nipped on, allowing her brain to expand once more to its true and mighty size. You see, it got to you if you weren't careful. At least, once upon a time, women had the right to say no. Now they seemed to have the right only to say yes and make sure the world knew about it. She suspected it was the same for men too. Otherwise why would rock bands, as she had read, have to put shuttlecocks down their trousers when performing? Her stunned mind went walkabout for a moment. A shuttlecock? Why a *shuttlecock*?

She glared at a distant lone donkey in a field. Sex was not, she told it, the problem. Sex was always out there if you wanted it. Even if you had two heads and a third eye, there was always someone, somewhere, advertising for just that combination. Of course they were. You just had to believe in yourself. If George Eliot could get a man of thirty-nine when she was sixty, after being told by at least two suitors that they rejected her on the grounds that she was too ugly (one hoped she head-butted them out of the room with that remarkable nose of hers), then anyone could do it. Celibacy as failure? Not at all ... No one, male or female, needed to be without sex if that was what they wanted. But it was not sex that people sought, not really; it was love. She had loved every minute of loving her husband and being made love to by him. There was never a time when it was not a delight to welcome and be welcomed into his arms. And frankly, when you had known *that* the prospect of a quick shag with someone as a way of dealing with 'all that sexual energy' was wholly unedifying.

On she primly drove.

No, the country with its promise of peace beckoned and was best. No need to worry about where the sexual energy was leaking out once she had established herself in the pastoral. She would be too busy with her half an acre and a cow, or whatever it was. She'd buy a book. She'd hire a man. She nearly swerved into the outside lane ... No, no, she would *not* hire a man. She would do it all herself. And she was bloody well going to enjoy it. Of London, truly, Mrs Fytton, aged forty and a half, had had quite enough.

She would grow old there gracefully. Learn to live without benefit, or oppression, or cosmetics or hairdressers. Unless

31

there was a way to do it in the self-sufficiency method. Berries or crushed newts or something. Women have always known how to get what they want in the looks department. In Newgate did not Moll Flanders keep her teeth pearly by rubbing them on her hem every day with a little soot?

Her spirits rose as the car sped further and further away from the horrible place, London. London, which contained more lunatics of the male rampant variety to the square mile than anywhere else on earth. This was a fact. Rosa, living in Buenos Aires, might say that she'd got them all down there, but she was wrong. Clancy might say that, according to the local mavourneens, they were all over in Dublin, thank you very much. But she also was wrong. Even Elizabeth, an escapee from west Londinium like herself, but for quite different reasons, now up on some Outer Hebridean isle, could sometimes be a bit short about the male aspects of the community, but since this largely comprised her husband and a few goats, and since her views on the subject directly corollated to the state of their marriage, this was somewhat suspect.

Puzzled, they reminded themselves that it was still largely the women who brought up the next generation. 'So why,' they wondered, 'is the next generation of husbands and lovers not appearing to get any easier?'

Angela, pondering her own experiences back on the market, shrugged and said, 'How can you redirect the next generation when you are still defending the barricades against the first?'

'It is not a battleground,' said Rosa gently.

'I know,' replied Angela, just as gently. 'And Stalingrad was just a little dust-up between mates . . .'

The Lunatic Swains were definitely, *definitely*, clutched up in her small bit of west London. Solipsistic this might be, but Angela was sure of it. If the nastiness of the neighbourhood pygmy witch-women was silver-medal standard, the lunacy of the male rampant was gold cup for the championship . . . This was the bit that the counsellor left out when exhorting her to get on with her life. What she should have added was: and preferably in a nunnery.

'Perhaps you are setting your standards too high?' said Elizabeth, who was obviously back on her husband at the time.

'Ah, yes,' said Angela, 'you are probably right. I will instantly become a visitor at the Scrubs. Sure to find someone that way . . .'

'Angela!'

'Elizabeth!'

'Angela, that's not what I meant.'

'Oh, very well then. Holloway.'

Mrs Fytton's Swains. How Ian curled his lip as each one went down like a nine-pin. 'I cannot bear to see you getting so hurt,' he said. Trundling back to his bint.

Bear to see? Bear to see? She watched him go, too stricken to object.

Strange, she thought, how the vocabulary changes emphasis according to situation. Ian's 'cannot bear' was on a direct par with son Andrew's statement, during his summer holidays, that he was 'desperate to get a job'. 'Desperate' was used interestingly here. 'Desperate to get a job' comprised lying in bed until about 11.30 and then stumbling about for a bit before embarking on a fruitless amble around the immediate locale with several of his mates, calling in to shops on the off-chance and no doubt frightening the proprietors rigid with their gangling six-foot clumsiness, their menacing inarticulacy and their shuffling gait of the young homeless. 'Give us ten pounds, Mum. There are no jobs to be had anywhere.' 'Anywhere' in this situation was also an interesting variation on received meaning. Anywhere, apparently, could also mean 'this small bit of London in which we live'.

Just to be fair, and not to imply that the sorority was hanging back in the matter of the changing shape of the English language, daughter Claire's linguistics were also interesting. To pick one at random, 'it's doing my head in' could be said of anything from the introduction to the household of cheaper shampoos to the imposition of a five-minute rule for the telephone – both of which were quite likely, in daughter Claire's head-done-in state, to contrive the failure of all three of her A-levels and a permanent place under a blanket outside Woolworths.

Now she knew that it was an inherited trait. Husband Ian's 'cannot bear' was in the same class. Meaningless. Though she wanted to believe it, how she wanted to. But subtext. What he actually meant by 'cannot bear' was that it made his life difficult having an upset dumped wife. Apart from making him feel guilty, which detracted from the quality of life within the bosom of the new bint, Ian's heart was not entirely free of her. He was not entirely averse to jealousy when she was happy with another man. She had seen that. She knew him well enough to read him. She did not need to lean across the table and say that the new man in her life had the genital equivalent of a Polaris Tomahawk stationed in his underpants, she had merely to lean back and let her eyes go secretive and misty. Something old and primal, she supposed. He would come and call and sniff it out, like a confused dog.

But unfortunately her experiences with the new swains were so unerringly awful that to pretend was useless. No one could say that, after Ian, she had not tried. But if Dorothy Parker was right about 'Scratch a lover and find a foe' she should come on down to west London. Never mind *scratch*. In west London it was 'put the slightest, softest finger pad of pressure on the *skin* of a lover and you will find yourself availed of the entire Napoleonic retreat, Gallipoli, and assorted extracts from the Somme and Dunkirk . . . with artillery. Something to do with loss of empire and the lack of big-game hunting probably. No other outlets but the snare of the signal of a wiggling piece of skirt (gloriously into battle) and the fury of being captivated by it (retreat with guns).

As a married woman she was so protected from it all. It made her shiver every time she thought now about the

Houses of Parliament and the male majority who ruled within thinking about sex every six minutes. Could that be true? If it was, then the only compulsion she could liken it to as an experience was the number of times you thought about peeing when in the last stages of pregnancy. And then you had the excuse of the baby's head or bottom or tender little foot on your bladder. Male politicians had no such excuse with regard to their wobbly bits, unless they had called into Cindy the Whip for a quick trussing *en route* for the House. Which, she was not surprised to read in Cindy the Whip's autobiography, was not unknown.

But rare.

Which meant, God help the planet, that most of the assembled parliamentary representatives did it *spontaneously*. One minute the Chancellor of the Exchequer was holding up his Treasury case and spouting about family allowances, and the next he was in the mental grip of a lurid coupling that might or might not include goldfish. That, she thought, must be the point at which he reaches for a glass of water. She imagined sex peppering every single debate in Parliament, like perforations in a colander: whale hunting with harpoons – congress in wet suits; pregnant prisoners wearing shackles – Vaseline, leather and whips; the European Union butter mountain – *Last Tango in Paris* and what Marlon did with half a pound of unsalted . . .

Recalling that particular piece of filmic legend, her heart contracted with grief. It was after borrowing the video of *Last Tango*, on the pretence of its being a cinematic milestone (her) and the perfectly honest desire to see a woman buggered (him), that Ian turned to her, or – to be fair – peered round her heaving buttocks, and suggested it would be nice to have another baby.

What?

The children were teenagers. Freedom was in sight. She was thirty-six and crisp on the matter. 'You want one, you go and have one,' she said.

He looked surprised (apart from a little daft), peeking between her legs like an anxious gynaecologist. Well, he *was* surprised, unsurprisingly surprised, because until that moment she had denied him nothing. She knew how to get and keep a man and it was not by saying no to things.

He scowled.

I have spoiled him, she thought, as she watched little willy die. Another baby? My plans, my hopes, my dreams, she thought, amid a lathering of Lurpak.

'Come on, baby,' he wheedled. He could wheedle her like nobody else. But this time – for the first time – she denied him.

'Ian, I have had my tubes tied.'

'But you could always have them undone.'

That her delightful, high-flying businessman husband should suddenly discover an interest in gynaecology astonished her.

'No,' she said. And she continued to deny him. Now the pain of the mistake of it cut her in two.

She clutched the wheel and slowed a little. That was the thing about long car journeys – there was nowhere to hide your brain.

Last Tango in Paris, it was.

Oh, go butter those scones, woman.

Despite her sterling efforts, he remained flaccid for a week.

If a mind-reading alien wandered in and rummaged around in their respective brains, what terrifying, terrifying madness would be revealed . . .

The Swains. The Swains. Mrs Fytton's Swains.

Lunatic, Lunatic. Lunatic all.

Time to let the swains bubble up to the surface, be considered, and be dealt with for once and for all. Nothing like a motorway for dealing with the grimmer side of the cranial filing system. The Swains, then. And let that be a lesson to her. Shadows of the past, be they gone.

3

April

His mother should have thrown him away and kept the stork.

MAE WEST

She was now but half an hour from her destination. Just time to bring them out, one by one, those Male Lunatics Rampant, shake them and put them back in the drawer marked Unnecessary. She slowed the car and took her mind to those first painful days when she was free and when, mindful of the counsellor's advice, she was on red alert and prey to the first Volpone who came along with wandering hands and a soulful light in his eyes.

Sheep are renowned for looking sympathetic, especially if one announces the name of a well-known fox to them, and she was just passing fields and fields of the woolly creatures. All looking very sympathetic indeed. Volpone, she repeated, opening the window and calling out to a field of chomping ewes. 'VOLPONE!' Sometimes lunacy is catching.

Victor.

And a lesson that one should never take up with a bloke with a vanquisher's name. What with his innocent smile (hiding foxy teeth) and the soulful light and the wandering hands, and her being a trusting sort of a person who, as a happily married woman, had read her Fay Weldons as if they were fairy tales, she was not prepared for the killer instinct of the average small-female-game-hunting male. Not his honey tongue, not his seductive and quivering external equipment – not his lunacy. And certainly not her vulnerability to it.

She looked into Victor's eyes and read there kind understanding and pleasing desire. It was one in the morning on the pavement outside the Chelsea Arts Club. She was too drunk to even see a taxi, let alone hail one. He took her hand, which she so willingly proffered, and led her down the garden path. She fell through her front door; he picked her up and looked at her all night with tender light of love in between bouts of electrifying orgy. She went on reading the same ocular tenderness until all her little feathers were quite smoothed, not a ruffle in sight. Until she could say the name Ian without weeping or kicking the furniture. Until she could believe, yes, believe it was that easy.

At which point the ocular message from Victor became cloudy. She read panic, suddenly, when she suggested normal things like going on holiday together ('Ah, well, um, oh, I'm not very good with holidays as such') or meeting her children ('Ah, well, um, oh, I'm not very good with children as such') or actually getting out of the house in which he still lived with his divorced wife and two dogs ('Ah, well, um, oh, I'm not very good at living on my own as such . . .')

He did not feel ready to commit.

'Commit?' she said. 'Commit? You managed to commit yourself to having your dinners cooked for you while you watched the mud-wrestling or the pogo-stick championships or whatever it was. You managed to . . .' And then she shrugged and backed off. 'Ah, well, um, oh, I'm not very good at dealing with inadequates as such.' With which she marched out. And then marched back again. And then marched out again, until she was worn out with it all and suggested he could find a most useful route away from her by travelling very fast, and in circuitous mode, up his own bum.

She telephoned Ian one night after this, pushed beyond endurance with the loneliness, and he came over. For about an hour he sat with her in the kitchen, sipping whisky, talking about the children, even laughing. All very ordinary, all very gentle, the anger dispelled in the comforting of her need. She loved him all over again. She hoped he would stay, and almost believed that he would suddenly realize what a mistake he had made in leaving her. Then he said, quite easily, that he had to go. Casual. It had become casual between them. He even squeezed her arm and gave her a hug. She smiled and nodded at him and let him out of their house, and watched him scurry over to his car and drive away. It was, she felt, like watching your own shadow depart from you. Shortly after this he asked for a divorce. Pragmatism said to her there was little point in refusing.

And then – quite suddenly – Ian remarried. So swiftly after the divorce that it was as if a bereaved had married the mortician. He took his bride-to-be (little, blonde, helpless Miss Fang the Dentist from 's-Gravenhage), and Andrew and Claire, out to Sydney for the wedding. Clever. Very clever. The children were thrilled. New dad, new wife, new presents.

Thrilled.

His wife, now ex-wife, Angela, lay in bed sipping port and lemon (she had – she'd convinced herself – a sore throat) and rang everyone she could think of. Some of her old political fire surfaced, but it was hazy. She told them all that it was just a pose of a wedding and organized so they could dance on the bones of Aborigines.

'That's my girl', said Clancy, if a little vaguely. And she changed the subject.

Rosa congratulated her on getting such a generous settlement. Why? She had earned the money too. She remained in a huff for three weeks until she realized that the only person it hurt was herself.

She told her parents about the divorce, defiantly, but her parents, now retired, were very disappointed. Their golden girl had lost the golden boy and the golden life. After all they did for her too. She must have brought it on herself with all those dungarees and what not. Thanks, she muttered as she left. After that she scarcely went to see them. And they never came up to see her. Old people became very selfish. How she longed to be old.

She needed lost Victor so badly during that *annus dreadfulus* in her life that she used to wander along his road in case he might pop out and see her and say, 'Hi – let's get married as well.' All she saw was a dog turd or two, and she was driven mad enough to stare at them on the pavement near his house and wonder if she could possibly identify them as coming from Tipper and Tansy . . . If not, maybe he would still come out at midnight with them slavering on their leashes for the coyly named canine bowel activity 'Walkies . . .'

The sheep and the hawthorns had now given way to fields of free-range pigs, or whatever you called them – organic porkers? She must get her terminology right if she was going to be part of the agricultural scene. She looked down at her map. Not far now. She would be quick in the dispatch of her chilling memoir.

Angela, all legal links with Ian severed, gritted her teeth, behaved with dignity and found a new job doing much the same as she had done as partner to her husband – but now she did it for their friends Joe and Gracie, who also installed systems. Dignity went out of the window when Ian actually wrote her a stiff letter saying he felt it was a bit much for her to go and work for a rival outfit. She immediately wrote back to Ian, saying, '*Au contraire*, my duck, but *you* are the rival now . . .'

Then Joe and Gracie gave a party. And she met Leaky. 'Call me Leaky,' he said, with that devastating crooked smile. She'd often wondered since if she would have felt different had he said, 'Call me Norman,' but he did not. 'Leaky,' he said, grinning down at her like Gary Cooper on stilts. And her heart went Blip! Lust flared, thank God, pain was pushed to the outer darkness, and she knew she was saved.

He looked like a Leaky, she decided (putting the notion of drips firmly out of her mind). He was long and rangy and hands-in-pockets and dangerous lopsided looks. He dealt in fine old vintage cars. She just said, 'Mmm, mmm – I love old cars . . .' And tried desperately to name one. 'Lamborghini!' she almost shouted eventually.

He nodded as if it were a great truth. 'Did you know,' he said, 'that there are spare parts for cars like Lamborghinis still available in places like Honduras and Poona?'

'Fascinating,' she said, over and over and over again.

Then she talked about lying in bed reading Austen or Tolstoy or Hardy by night.

And he said, 'Fascinating,' as if it was. She managed to imply that she was lying in bed reading *alone*.

Ian's new wife was pregnant; Claire and Andrew were disgustingly delighted – 'a sister, a brother . . .'

'*Half*-sister, *half*-brother,' she reminded them curtly. But 'ooh ooh, aah aah' they went. Vile renegades. To be shunned. Not that they noticed. So Leaky arrived just in time.

Call me Pandora, she thought. Hope. But she forgot that Pandora was burdened with all the ills of the world for her trouble.

Then one evening when she had gone to the theatre with Gracie to see Carol Churchill's *Top Girls*, Leaky turned up in the foyer. 'Hi, darling,' he said. 'Decided to come along too . . .'

He barely spoke to Gracie. And the discussion afterwards was hampered by neither of them wishing to offend Leaky. Who said the play was interesting, but unresolved. At which Gracie raised an eyebrow and Angela felt uncomfortable. It was many things, but it was not unresolved. It said very firmly, and in a very resolved way, that it was hard being a woman in a man's world and that you had to make sacrifices in order to succeed on masculine terms. That, in her book, was pretty resolved.

She said, 'Marlene gets to the top after abandoning her daughter, her class, her femininity . . .'

'Don't give me all that silly nonsense, Mrs Fytton,' he said, smiling at her tenderly and patting her cheek.

Gracie blinked. Is there anything worse than reading Ditch This Person in your friends' eyes and not having the courage to do so?

'Goodbye, Leaky,' she wrote. And she booked a holiday to coincide with when the baby was due. There was some satisfaction in seeing Claire and Andrew's innate selfishness at work, for despite the thrill of 'Ooh, a sister' and 'Ooh, a brother' they wanted a holiday too. Despite Ian asking them to be around for the event, they declined and came to Crete instead.

It may have been then, in that moment of revelation regarding her children's naked selfishness, that she began to form the tiniest little embryo of an idea . . . Whose fruition she was bringing about in this mistress plan of moving to the country. The one which would bring Ian back to her like a fly to sweet glue. Women, take control of your lives! There were many other ways to skin a cat, she thought, with a haziness matched only by her historical commentary on the bones of Aborigines. At least, if it failed, there would be no one who knew her to see.

Now she was driving along small, hedge-lined roads. Passing wistaria-clad cottages and ruddy-bricked farmhouses, proper, safe, untouched by London madness. She went slowly, enjoying the peace. And she smiled. That moment of rebellion – that moment when Andrew and Claire stuck out their teenaged lips and said, 'No,' to their father – was sweet, sweet, sweet . . . She remembered sipping her Olympic Airways gin and tonic and praying that the baby came on time. They had only a fortnight.

She gave Ian the wrong hotel telephone number so that he could not contact them as the proud father. Her children discovered the windsurfing and the nightclubs of Crete and never looked back. Well, certainly not at her lying on the beach. But there, in the warm blue waters, paddling around the lacy edge of the Med, she met Otto. Unpartnered Otto, who was there with his family of two grown-up children and assorted grandchildren. And who had a ground-floor bedroom in their villa. An accessible ground-floor bedroom.

So that was all right. A few stolen trysts, a few nice relaxed mezes washed down with the local paint-stripper. Quite a lot of paint-stripper. And bingo – the beginnings of a light-hearted relationship. Neither Andrew nor Claire noticed if she slept in the villa on account of the fact that they were never back to sleep in it themselves. She felt happy again.

Otto, from Hamburg, was a translator. Short, bald, creative, stylish, a little ponderous but nice. Fifteen years older than she was. Long-divorced. He did nice things like trailing along the beach to find her and producing a bucket of icy water full of beers. And despite the myth, he had a sense of humour. He once crept up behind her while she lay on a sun-lounger, threw his towel over her and said that it was the traditional way for a German man to bag a woman. He then produced yet another bottle of very cold paint-stripper and two glasses. He was so thoughtful.

'Haf lap-top, vill travel,' he said, smiling cheerfully. Within two months of their Cretan idyll, Otto had decamped from Hamburg to a small flat one tube stop away. She might have been flattered, instead she was horrified. The bell-like poetical words, 'What the fuck did you do that for?' fell from her lips. He was terribly hurt.

'Sorry,' she said. 'Sorry, sorry, sorry.' She must not give him the baggage of her previous experiences. He was new, he was kind, he loved her (he said) and he was *German* – different from the English men of her acquaintance; continental men were much less screwed up. She gave him the benefit, put her anger to one side and forgave the encroachment. In a way . . . it was nice. The thoughtfulnesses were still there. Including, rather oddly, the coolers of cold beers and the ice buckets of chilled wine. Rather a lot of them.

Within three weeks she discovered that he had a nasty little problem called alcohol.

First he slid under a pink-tableclothed restaurant dinner. Bringing the pears in marsala down with him. Then he crashed his car. Then he crashed her car. Then he clung to her fence railing one night singing what was possibly a Bavarian love song, until she came out and hauled him in. He promised it would never happen again.

He did it two nights later and he called her a whore for not letting him in. She called Ian. Ian rang the police. The police came. There was something about their smiles as she stood shivering in her pyjamas on her front step at three in the morning that made her realize it was still a man's world. Something in their smiles that said he was a bit of a rogue and she was a miserable cow to keep him out here. Which balance may have been helped by the way Otto clung to the officers' arms and told them he 'Luffed zem all *and* his liddle strudel dumpling . . .'

Angela was free once more. Ian told her she should stay that way. She thanked him for calling the police and said he should mind his own business. He said he bloody well intended to mind his own business, but he couldn't if she kept ringing him up about lunatics. She did not apologize. She had spent a lifetime protecting him from the ills a husband and father is heir to. No more.

She watched his back as he walked down her path and closed the gate. She saw him turn as if to wave, think better of it and walk away. She heard the car accelerate. And she knew that she still loved him. She still loved him because she had fashioned him. As he had fashioned her. What she saw was her twin leaving.

It was then that she had three revelations, each one quite as disturbing for Angela as a Pale Horse, Seven Seals and several Pillars of Fire.

First, she decided that she would move away to – as Goldsmith so sweetly put it – 'Dear lovely bowers of innocence and ease . . .' She would go and find a lovely bower of her own, a little plot, a humble cot, and turn her back on this miserable urban world.

Second, she suddenly remembered the naked selfishness of

Andrew and Claire about the birth of the new baby – a boy (who very kindly arrived in the world two days after they arrived in Crete and thus did Ian have twelve days of going up and down a very greasy pole trying to track them down to tell them. Good, thought Mrs Angela Fytton on learning this. *Good.*) And that it is the hallmark of adolescence and young adulthood to be the last gasp of supreme self-focus to the point of cruelty before it must wither on the vine of adulthood.

And third, she realized that she had spent all her married life absorbing the brunt of life. Ian, given a bit of a brunt to bear, would not know he was *born* ... And neither would Little Miss Fang. Not if she, Mrs Fytton the First, left her teenagers behind for them to play with ...

Thus, telling no one of her plans, she set about doing just that. The end of Ian's happy little universe was well on the way.

Yes, it was a battleground. Yes, it was Stalingrad. And yes, she would give not an inch in the fight.

She stopped the car beside a little pub called Ye Olde Black Smock – all mellow bricks and well-kept woodwork and rainbow tubs of primulas – with a stream running by. Perfect. She picked up the estate agent's details from the seat beside her. She was nearly there and she had a feeling, a very strong feeling, that this one would be *the* one. Something told her that everything about it was just right. Like Goldilocks and the porridge, she had tried a few, but this one, this one ...

She jumped as a yapping veteran of a sheepdog ran out of the pub door and up to the car. 'Staithe Road?' she called out to the owner.

'Round the bend,' he replied, rather appropriately.

Good, thought Mrs Angela Fytton. *Good.*

4

April

If she had scarcely bothered with the purchase of Francis Street, she savoured this new choosing now. The property was called Church Ale House and if it looked good on the estate agent's sheet, it looked superb in reality. A foursquare Georgian house, as neat as a child would draw, with three upstairs windows and two windows and a door with a porch on the ground floor.

The heavy brass knocker, in the shape of a fist, was loud against the sturdy, panelled door. She had a terrible, frightened feeling that beyond this door she was lost. Even the knocker sounded triumphant. Footsteps echoed on an uncarpeted floor, a dog barked and the way was opened. Here we go, she thought. Here we go ... For some reason her heart was beating as loud as any village girl on a first date.

'Mrs Fytton,' said Angela. 'From Pinnocks, the estate agent's.'

The woman wiped her palms down her faded floral pinny before shaking Angela's hand. Angela liked faded floral. Angela liked pinny. Faded and floral and pinny was light years away from west London witch-hunters daywear. Faded and floral and pinny allowed you a bosom, hips and simple acceptance of the march of time. I will have faded, I will have floral, thought Angela, as she marched through the door to her doom. 'Let the rich deride, the proud disdain,' she thought, 'these simple blessings of the lowly train ...'

She smiled, very brightly. 'May I come in?'

The woman did not smile brightly back but merely said, 'Yes.'

Angela turned to take one more look behind her. At the bricked path mossy with age and flanked by cottage-garden beds bright with daffodils and tulips, just beginning to hint with the green of summer plants to come. She could imagine, later, the lupins and hollyhocks, the sweet Williams and the scented stocks. Even now one or two dozy-looking bees hovered about in the sunshine, hanging precariously off bowing tulip heads.

'Thank you,' she said crisply, when the door was closed behind her.

'This way,' said the woman.

'Thank you,' she said again. It was all she could do not to throw her arms around the woman's neck and weep tears of joy on to the pinny front. If it is true, she thought, that you only know you have been sad when something makes you happy, then here is the moment. I am happy again. Or on the way to it. For the worst thing about sorrow is that it takes away all relish. And this place she was going to relish. She could feel it in her new-warmed bones.

'I am Mrs Perry,' said the woman shortly. She did not look very delighted about it.

And Mrs Fytton followed, wiping her car-clean shoes carefully on the mat, though the hallway was stuffed with wellington boots and piles of newspapers and assorted outdoor accoutrements that made the odd bit of dirt from a passing shoe mere grains in the desert sand.

The woman had fairish, greyish, fading hair, sun-dried skin and a figure that deserved to be called comfortable. She might have been sixty, she might have been eighty; it was hard to tell. I shall be like that, thought Angela, staring at her back view as she strode off down the long, bare-boarded hallway. She was curiously lopsided. One side of her hips was definitely less rounded than the other. Country ways, thought Angela vaguely. Inbreeding. Rickets. But her mind was already engaged, if not enchanted, with the house itself.

'I'll put the kettle on,' said the woman over her shoulder. 'And then we'll start.'

Angela said a very bright, 'Oh, yes,' and went on noting, in an interior-magazine way, that the floorboards were broad and even and certainly eighteenth-century or older – maybe elm; she daren't hope for oak – and perfect for polishing up. That the walls were grubby white-emulsioned plaster, that the ceilings were of medium height but not oppressive, and that it was certainly the kind of symmetrical Georgian house in which any Jane Austen heroine would be comfortable. The sort of house in which you would pop on your sprigged muslin and hope for a visit from the squire's eldest son. Instead of a dull-eyed young duster-seller purporting to be homeless and likely to break your windows if you refused to buy.

Why was it, she wondered, that the so-called Age of Enlightenment seemed so enchanting to her and others of her sex? Why was it that Austen-land still captivated female hearts when Jane herself would have told them, very firmly, to buzz off with their stupid yearnings? Women were oppressed in those days. Women died young. Women were not free. Women lived in the landscape, but if they wanted to go for a walk in it they either needed permission or were considered wayward and faery weird. And as for Austen-land's near neighbour Brontë-land . . .

She stood still, momentarily captivated by the perfect scale and symmetry of the hallway and its adjoining rooms, before scuttling onwards and returning to the past. As for Brontë-land, it was just the same. Rochester meeting Jane Eyre on the road does not think, 'What-ho, out for a little jolly exercise, then, dearie?' No, he thinks she must be a non-human flitting about the countryside. Normal women stay in. You had, she reminded herself, to be careful about getting too romantic about the past . . . But then again, there used to be *rules*. You might not *like* where you were, but at least you *knew* where it was.

She smiled. Unlike first appearances in Church Ale House. For, as they progressed towards the back of the house, all symmetry vanished. Odd little windows and doorways began to appear, high up, low down, narrow and rounded. And now they seemed to be walking down a wedge – a wedge with rooms and bits added on like a child's Plasticine model. The house was beginning to go out of shape. The Age of Enlightenment gave way to the Age of Mongrel in building terms – bits tacked on higgledy-piggledy with no thought for form.

'This is unexpected,' she said.

'It gets older as you go back,' said the owner, without turning round. 'The front bit was added when they bought more land. In the golden days of farming. Or one of the golden days. But fortunes come and go. They sold it all again eventually. We had the local history society making noises about the place once.'

'Interesting,' said Angela brightly. 'This round window must be a later addition, then.'

'Oh, yes, they liked their windows,' said the owner. 'Put them in all over the place.'

Angela stopped for a brief moment and peered through the roundel at the sunshine and warmth beyond. She could almost hear the sound of chattering and laughter as the earlier occupants of the house donned their holland aprons and went about their tasks. Mrs Perry went on walking.

As the owner she was not exactly doing her bit. Unless, thought Angela, it was double bluff and she was just being cool. Somehow, looking at that back view, she doubted it. Mrs Perry's back view looked just about as free of fancy as you could get. Nevertheless she tried again.

'Even in the Age of Enlightenment the women still had to stay in the house for most of the time, didn't they? I mean, they couldn't just go wandering off. No wonder they liked

49

big windows . . .' she finished lamely. 'Or small ones.' She peered through the roundel again. Part of her, like Alice, wanted to step through into that other world.

'I dare say,' said Mrs Perry, without turning round.

She walked through a low-arched opening and down a step. Angela followed her guide's lopsided bottom reluctantly, down the step and along the much narrower passageway beyond. There was nothing of eighteenth-century harmony in the layout now. Ah well, she decided, coming back up to date, no one wore sprigged muslin nowadays, they just threw it over a pole and let it drape artfully at the window. As for the benign squire and his sons, or a charmingly attentive Colonel Brandon on the neighbouring estate, they would never come a-calling in these modern times, being too busy helicoptering up to town for meetings with their London-based business consortium and dining out at merchant banks.

They turned a narrow corner and went through a glass-paned door into a large and sunlit kitchen.

'I see what you mean about windows,' said Angela.

Someone, perhaps understanding how much time is spent in these regions, had set in two enormous twelve-paned windows which were almost ceiling to floor and looked overwhelming and odd in the otherwise irregular space. Angela had to blink away the romantic image of a red-cheeked cook making her fruit tarts while the sprigged young mistress sat blushing at a pair of striding boots in a foursquare parlour. Something very peculiar seemed to be taking place in her psyche, she observed nervously. And it appeared to be love. A very dreadful, not-to-be-ignored urge to possess. She had felt it only once before, with Ian. With the children it was entirely different. When she looked upon them, newborn, she knew that she *did* possess them. The whole future process with them was one of letting go. The whole future process with Ian was one of trying to keep hold of him. She touched the rough whitened plaster of the kitchen wall. She still was.

She shivered. Could she actually do this thing? She considered her children. They were part of her, warts and all, like her feet or her ears. They still had a lot of growing up to do before they became fully human. A lot. She remembered, for example, last year, when she had had flu. She was nursed by the two of them. If you could call it that. God knows where the deferential, caring children of yesteryear had gone, but they were certainly not living in no. 13 Francis Street. Death would have been infinitely preferable. Capital Gold (old pop music for old people) with the radio placed just out of reach. Judgement of Solomon regarding a particular pair of jeans when her head – yes, she had been sure of it – was the item that was splitting in two. They'd be all right in time . . . Part of being supermother was realizing when to let go. Part of being superwife was knowing how to hold on.

She stared at the ancient flagstoned floor. Mrs Perry looked at her questioningly. 'Bit messy,' she said as a cheerful statement of fact.

For a moment Angela was startled. Did she mean her life? And how did she know? Was she a mindreader? Then she realized it was addressed to the room, not her. 'Neat kitchen, dull life . . .' she said glibly. And she thought what a good, wholesome countrywoman Mrs Perry was in her floral pinny. I'll bet *she's* never even looked at another man, let alone been privy to the world of adultery . . . Best go easy on such thoughts, though, just in case the woman *was* a mindreader. Country people had their ways. *She'd* read her Thomas Hardy.

She leaned against a wide and ancient table, set around with battered wooden chairs, and tried to avoid thinking how Shaker they were. Not Shaker, Angela. Battered. Got it? 'How old is this bit?' she asked, looking up at the slopes and slants of the ceiling. She would not have been surprised to see a sign above the old stone sink warning the house's occupants about the dangers of the Black Death: 'Now Wash Ye Olde Hands'.

Mrs Perry shrugged. 'Old,' she said.

'Yes, but –' Angela shrugged. 'Three hundred? More? It must be a lot older than the front.'

'Five, six . . .' Mrs Perry also shrugged. 'Who knows?' She jerked her thumb. 'There's a well out there they say is Celtic.'

Angela's heart went bump with love again. Mrs Angela Fytton, at home in her garden, perches on her Celtic well.

'In the *garden*?' she said as casually as possible. 'An old well in the garden?'

Mrs Perry looked at her with something vaguely akin to pity. 'Where else?' she said.

'Well, *quite*,' said Angela, feeling an urban fool. 'How lovely – all that pure water.'

And then the first edge of humour crept into Mrs Perry's faded blue eyes. 'With the churchyard just above it. Below body level. Which tells you that the church was built after the well. Which we all know anyway, given what we know . . . No thought for anybody, the church in those days.'

Angela tried to look as though a few bodies draining through her water supply were neither here nor there. Mrs Perry did not look convinced. Perhaps she really was fey.

Just in case, Angela tried to clear her mind of anything compromising. Like giving a twenty-pound donation to the anti-bloodsports lobby. She wanted this house so badly that if Mrs Perry had said, 'We like setting the dogs on little fluffy infant fox cubs and dipping our newborn babies in their blood afterwards,' Angela would have wished her mind, if Mrs Perry was able to read it, to say, quite unequivocally, 'Of course you do – things are so *different* in the country . . .' Rather than reflect the more worrying conundrum of people in red coats with hunting horns saying that they just enjoyed a good day out and scarcely ever found one of the blighters, while other people in red coats with hunting horns said that it was the only way to keep the foxy numbers down . . .

'I think foxes are *very* overrated,' she said out loud.

52

Mrs Perry looked at her strangely. And then, as if making up her mind to humour Angela, she said, 'I don't think my hens would agree.'

'No,' said Angela brightly.

Hens. Of course there would be hens. She tried desperately to remember what they had been talking about before the consideration of foxes. Graves? Death? Hunting? Football? *Football?* Why should she think of football?

Mrs Perry said, 'It probably serviced this place once.'

Football? thought Angela. *Football?*

'The old vicar banned dressing it.'

Football? Dressing? *What?*

Mrs Perry, who may or may not have read her mind, added in a kind voice, 'For the well.'

Ah, the *well*. That was it.

Celtic well.

Celtic football club.

The green and white hoops of the football club.

Just try reading my mind, she thought. It could be dropped behind enemy lines with its code-breaker and still not be unscrambled.

'You mean this could be as old as –'

'Alfred and the cakes,' said Mrs Perry informatively. 'Here.'

Angela gazed around her. 'Not actually in here?' she whispered hopefully, looking around for the hearth.

'No,' said Mrs Perry, quite kindly in the circumstances, 'in Somerset. Alfred hid in Somerset. It was somewhere round about here that he played his harp in the Danish camp and did all that wandering.' She looked thoughtful. 'It was always a good site. Of course, most of the land's gone now. But I don't doubt there had always been some kind of place to live in on this part. Protected from the Levels, you see, by the hill. And with the well and the stream.'

She gave Angela a bright smile. The kind of smile a schoolteacher might bestow upon a foolish but keen child. 'I suppose Alfred might have used this kitchen – or the one before it – or even the one before that. No one could say he didn't, now, could they?'

Angela was still blushing. How could she have thought King Alfred actually sat in this room? She smiled as sanely as she could at Mrs Perry and slid over towards one of the windows.

'Lovely,' she said, staring out unseeing. By the time she looked around she had composed herself again. Sod Alfred. Sod burnt cakes. And sod the foxes. She wanted this house. And she wanted it just as it was. She had seen enough Smallbone kitchens and Pogenpohl bathrooms in her time. And the final madness of her London neighbours, they of a gazebo that dare not speak its name, throwing a party to celebrate the completion of their poky little conservatory. 'It'll be the new en-suite next,' she said, making Ian laugh.

Don't, she reminded herself. *Don't* . . .

Mrs Perry gestured with her square, red hand. 'Well, then. Kitchen,' she said. And, crossing to the other side of it, she opened another door and said, 'Pantry. Which I don't mind admitting I shall miss.'

'Where are you moving to?' asked Angela.

'Taunton,' said Mrs Perry. 'Near the town centre.'

'That's where my mother-in-law used to live. One of those newish houses up on the hill as you go in.'

'No more hills for me,' said Mrs Perry firmly. 'I want it flat with my hips.'

Angela eyed her hips. Gout? she wondered. Old hunting accident? 'Um,' she said.

Mrs Perry filled the kettle while Angela tried not to think of all those graveyard bones adding flavour. The kettle had once been white and now – from a distance – looked as if it had been stylishly marbled in Conran shades of grey. Next to it was a bowl of dark brown eggs – the kind found resting on straw in the better class of delicatessen – and these too looked as if they had been enhanced by art. Sepia art, with feathers and pretty little smears of shit. Everything looked as if it had come from Divertimenti's rustic department. And on the central table were an upturned loaf of bread, a scattering of crumbs, a half-full bottle of milk, three used mugs and a pair of very dirty red plastic gloves. Oldenburg among the Vermeers. She sighed, reaching out and touching one of the gloves despondently. There was no one to share the visual joke with now . . .

Several of Angela's inner organs contracted painfully again. *She* wouldn't keep him, that new one. *She* couldn't keep him. She couldn't and she wouldn't because – she tried to think of a why. Because – death knell of love, the modern equivalent of rings round the bath and crusty socks – *she*, the silly young cow, second Mrs Fytton, sent him out *jogging*. One of the things she always admired about her husband was his cheerful indifference to sport – whether watching it or performing it. Now he was jogging and pretending to like it. Men of Ian's age either died or moved on when that happened to them. The scales would soon fall from his bulging, sweat-filled eyes as he hurtled around Wimbledon Common like a demented Womble. It crossed her mind, when he first told her about it, that she might drive there early one morning, catch him on the homeward run and lean out of the car window with a cool drink and an adoring look of surprise. But good sense prevailed. It would not do to illuminate his foolishness. If she wanted him back, then she wanted him back with his self-esteem intact. And, under the circumstances, she was not altogether sure she could keep from laughing. Send him jogging, would she?

Good, she thought, smiling like a serpent. *Good.*

She removed her mind from the erotic consideration of her ex-husband's sticky, sweaty body embracing her across an empowering Vimto and focused on a large red and black object. She knew she should restrain herself but it was too late.

'Oh, an *Aga* –' she gushed.

Mrs Perry looked at her as if she had just admired a dead cat. 'I'll show you round while the tea brews, Mrs Fytton.'

Country people, Angela reminded herself, do not *admire* Agas – they *cook* with them. 'Thank you, Mrs Perry,' she said. And, changing the subject – rather cleverly, she fancied – she added, 'Brews is a funny way to describe something non-alcoholic, isn't it?'

Mrs Perry said, 'Everything brews in the country. It's all the same – wines, ales, medicines, teas –'

'Oh, the ancient arts,' said Angela. 'Wise women . . .'

'Well, I don't know about that,' said Mrs Perry, then she nodded. 'But women *were* the brewers once, so I'm told.'

Angela was just about to ask her the origins of the name Church Ale House when Mrs Perry said, 'Talking of age . . .' and crossed to the window ledge. She picked up a handful of little white objects which, just for a very bad moment, Angela thought might be teeth.

Teeth? Fine. She gritted her own as Mrs Perry took her hand and tipped the objects into the palm. They were roughly square, very smooth, a pearled yellowy white, about a quarter of an inch thick. Angela ran her fingertips over them and rattled them together.

'Know what they are?' said Mrs Perry.

Angela was about to suggest upper front molars, but after her orgasmic spasm over the Aga she kept quiet. She shook her head, stared into her palm and hoped that whatever she held there had been very well washed.

Mrs Perry took one and held it up. 'Roman mosaic chips.'

Angela blinked. 'No . . .' she said.

Mrs Perry nodded. 'Daphne Blunt told me. I dug them up in the garden. Or the rabbits did.' She put them back on the window ledge and shrugged once more. 'So who knows how old this place might be?'

'Tesserae,' Angela said in amazement.

'That's the name. They turn up occasionally. So there must have been something once. This house has seen a lot of changes

– bits built on, bits pulled off, money made and money lost. I don't suppose the plot has ever been idle.'

'Bit like life,' said Angela.

The woman nodded. She patted the teapot. 'And now,' she said, 'you'd best be looking around, I suppose, since you're here.'

5

April

Well! some people talk of morality, and some of religion,
but give me a little snug property.

MARIA EDGEWORTH

The tour began with what Mrs Perry called the parlour, to
Angela's delight. 'The parlour,' she repeated to herself softly
as they travelled towards the front of the house, their footsteps clumping and creaking on the fine, bare boards. Not the
lounge, not the sitting room, but the *parlour* . . .

On the way Mrs Perry paused and opened a door with half-
lights. 'The utility,' she said. 'Washing machine, freezer, sink
– you know.'

Angela said that she did.

'And where the dogs sleep.'

'Ah yes,' said Angela, thinking with pleasure of three baskets labelled Victor, Leaky and Otto.

'The estate agent called it the utility. I call it the old wash-
house. And before the war it was the still room. The *first* war,'
she added.

Angela nodded knowingly, wondering what the hell a *still*
room actually was, as opposed to a moving one, but she did
not ask. She was never very good at showing her ignorance
and she didn't intend to do so now. After all, she had a history
degree; she knew how to look things up.

She peered over Mrs Perry's shoulder. The room was big
and cold with stone walls, a grubby little high-up window, a
well-trodden flagged floor and a small half-glazed door leading to the garden, a door so small in proportion to the space
that it looked like an Alice in Wonderland opening. A hen

peered in, head on one side, comically querying its outer exile. It pecked at the glass and Mrs Perry rapped her knuckles to frighten it away.

'They can crack this old glass, silly varmints,' she said.

Angela was thinking that it would make good office space. Ian would need office space. 'Hens are funny,' she said, to cover her smile.

'The parlour,' said Mrs Perry eventually, pushing open a panelled wooden door that creaked. 'This and the one opposite are the best rooms, and the two above.'

'Georgian,' said Angela.

'Must get that hinge oiled,' said Mrs Perry. She had obviously been saying it for years.

Double aspect, thought Angela, maybe sixteen foot square, original fireplace or as like as damn it, two good windows overlooking the front shrubs and holly hedge, probably good boards under the carpet, two doors – maybe original – certainly nicely foursquare and fitting. Not a central heating pipe in sight. And good light. Pinch me someone, she thought, pinch me.

She went over to a window. Mrs Perry's curtains, pulled carelessly aside, were velvet, once a rich olive green but now faded to the colour of gooseberries. Where do you get velvet like that? wondered Angela. As if she had read her mind again, just at that moment Mrs Perry tugged at them and said, 'I'll leave the curtains. There's a bit of life left in them yet. They came from the Hall when it was sold. One of Archie's aunts made them. I remember seeing her sewing them when I was a girl.'

'How lovely,' said Angela.

'Ruined her eyes,' said Mrs Perry.

'Ah,' said Angela, realizing she must distinguish sentimentality from happiness.

'No electric then, mean buggers,' said Mrs Perry. 'And all the girls sewed. Servants' rooms didn't get electricity till the Abdication.' She pulled back the curtains at the other window.

'They forgot.' She smiled grimly. 'Apparently. And no one complained. Knew their place then.'

Angela imagined giving her daughter a needle and thread and a candle to sew by. 'They certainly don't now,' she said.

'Good job,' said Mrs Perry.

Celia Johnson, thought Angela suddenly, *Celia Johnson* . . . That is the kind of person I shall become. I'll have a black bicycle and a wicker basket full of library books and a wide-eyed innocence for an innocent world in which I'll be surrounded only by good, honest folk who do right in the end.

'Doesn't seem to be doing much good,' said Mrs Perry, looking out of the window.

Celia Johnson gave a little ring on her bicycle bell and rode off. Angela returned to the present. 'What?' she said.

Mrs Perry pointed and Angela followed the line of her fingers. Strung between two trees and hanging from a thin wire were several dead carcasses – possibly birds, possibly rodents, possibly not.

'Does it really frighten them off?'

Mrs Perry shrugged. 'I never thought so,' she said. 'I'd have thought that animals just saw other dead animals as food. Only humans would understand it as a warning.' She shook her head and smiled that grim smile of hers. 'Not so long ago it was folk rather than vermin. There's been a few - of those strung up round here.' She nodded her head directionally. 'Up on the hill. And not so long ago either. My grandmother said her mother had seen a hanging.' She gave Angela a straight look. 'That's where your ancient arts could get you. My mother made lotions and potions and left me all her recipes. And her mother's. But if you'd called her a witch she'd have spat in your eye. I must look them out.'

The second room, with another window on to the garden, had the same proportions.

'My mother used to say the house was like an old duchess, with everything carried at the front. We don't use this as a dining room. Shame really . . .' She went over to the window and pulled a crumpled, faded chintz curtain further aside. 'It's got the best view of the house – this and the bedroom above it,' said Mrs Perry. 'Front and side view. The Mump and the church.'

Angela stroked the old chintz as gently as if it were a cat. She perched on the window seat and gazed out and thought of Goldsmith. All these years she thought she was a pragmatist and now here she was, a romantic.

Near yonder copse, where once the garden smil'd,
And still where many a garden flower grows wild.
There where a few torn shrubs the place disclose,
The village preacher's modest mansion rose.

'Royal land,' said Mrs Perry. 'Never to be built on.' She came and stood by Angela. 'And we own that field at the side. That's not part of the sale. We want to keep that. Lord knows why we want to keep that . . . the peasant in us, very likely. You don't get rid of all your land.'

'Can it be built on?' Angela's mouth went dry.

'Not while we own it, it can't,' said Mrs Perry firmly. 'Too much building in my opinion.' She looked about the room, as if for the first time. 'Panels need a coat of paint, fireplace needs unplugging . . .' She crossed to one of the cupboards beside the mantelpiece and opened it. 'There's a bit of damp in this one. Are you a do-it-yourselfer, Mrs Fytton? Archie and I are *not* . . . as you will have noticed.'

Angela thought of all her years of paint pots and wood finishes. And shook her head. Not this time, she thought, not this time.

'What are the neighbours like?' she asked.

'You've got the new vicar. *Not* married. Plays the guitar . . .' Mrs Perry pulled a face. 'And a couple I don't know very well beyond him, weekenders – boys away at Frome Hall, they *board*.' She sniffed. 'Both solicitors in Bristol. Rudge, their name is. Never see them really. Then on this side –' she pointed westwards – 'you've got Dave the bread, who delivers.' She shrugged, as if arguing with herself. 'Well, saves making it.'

Angela nodded.

'His wife, Wanda, does weaving and craft things. Beyond him the Elliotts. Some sort of writer he is, and his wife and children – three under six, I ask you.'

Angela tried to look as if she had never had two under two.

'And further up the lane you've got the history woman, Daphne Blunt. Swears by olive oil and doesn't like fat bacon.' Mrs Perry turned to Angela and said, as if in deepest sympathy, 'A thin woman. Very *thin*. Interesting, but likes to poke her nose . . .'

'Ah,' said Angela. 'Aren't there any true locals, like you?'

'Not many,' she said, apparently without sentiment. 'Most of them have moved into sensible accommodation. We've still got Sammy with the pigs up that hill.' She pointed beyond the window and her eyes softened. 'His place is right at the other end. The eelers still come in. You can see the eel beds from the church. And then there's old Dr Tichborne and his wife down there.' She pointed again. 'They were born and bred round here, but grandish. I remember my father taking off his hat to *his* father when the car went by, just after the war. And she came from the Hall . . . which got pulled down to make room for the road. They've a niece who's set on marrying an estate agent.' For some reason she looked a little flustered at this last. 'Well, anyway . . . Now, the bedrooms.'

They mounted the stairs. Creak, creak, creak.

'It doesn't mean anything. Just age. I creak myself some days.' She opened a door and smiled at Angela as she did so. 'You will too one day . . .'

They walked into what Angela supposed was the main bedroom. Master bedroom, as the estate agent's details described it. Mistress bedroom from now on. And eventually – why? – master and mistress bedroom, she supposed. A branch or two of an outside tree came right up against the window, but the view was clear. 'You can see the church and the vicar's garden from up here,' said Mrs Perry. 'The church land comes right to our boundary hedge at the back.'

But Angela was looking around the room. She wanted everything in it: Mrs Perry's high brass bed and the ancient white piqué bedcover, the brass rail that held up the old blue and white striped curtains, the dusty fireplace with its faded tissue paper stuffed into the flue and the gas taps that still poked out of the wall. Next to them were electric wall-lights: imitation shells made from Woolworths Lalique. Modern by this house's standards, probably fifty years old – ugly then, somehow quaint and delightful now. It was all too much, like eating too many sweets. A setting from *Country Life* entitled Rural Chic.

The next bedroom was darker because the tree stretched across the window. There was an enamel basin set into an enamel stand with an enamel bucket below. She smiled to see such an old-fashioned vanity unit. Once she would have wandered around making notes about improvements. A shower here, a second bathroom there. But now she felt she *knew* these walls, could relax into them. The floor sloped slightly, the bed looked high and lumpy – essence of bed, much as Van Gogh painted his. Looking around, she doubted if there was a true right angle in the place.

'Don't use it much,' said Mrs Perry, ushering her out. 'Third bedroom,' she said, opening another panelled door.

In this little bedroom there were the original window shutters. Just for a moment Angela imagined some dimpled owner of cap and ringlets peering around. She went over to the window and pushed them. They were fastened down but workable. Behind her, and oddly out of joint, were bunk beds.

'For the grandchildren,' said Mrs Perry. '*When* they come. Of course, they're nearly grown up now. But that's why the shutters are fixed. Didn't want them pinching their fingers. They're useful though – keep out the draught. Have you got children, Mrs Fytton?'

'I have two.'

'How old?'

'Eighteen and nineteen. Boy and a girl.'

Mrs Perry stared at her.

'I had them young,' said Angela. 'I wanted to.'

'I had mine late,' said Mrs Perry. 'Daughter. Moved to Bristol as soon as she could. And I don't blame her . . . Two sons, but nothing for them here. Long gone.'

They came out into the corridor. 'One more bedroom,' said her guide, opening a door. They peered into a small-windowed, sloping-ceilinged room almost bare of furniture but piled high with cardboard boxes. Mrs Perry looked at them and sighed. 'Have to start filling those soon.' She closed the door firmly. 'Now, just the old sewing room, and then that's it and we can have our tea.'

'Imagine having a whole room devoted to sewing,' Angela said.

Mrs Perry looked at her with sharp look again. 'It's the lightest place upstairs. And it was work. Everyone sewed on the side. It wasn't called needle*work* for nothing. My own grandmother was such a needlewoman that they'd send over with stuff from beyond the Quantocks. And *her* mother did some of the lace trimmings for Wells when the Queen and Prince Albert visited. I had a little bit put by in a box somewhere.'

They went down a short corridor. At the back the house was a hybrid of half-landings and diversions, with all sense of eighteenth-century rationale gone. Angela thought it was the same with life. You put all your balanced bits at the front for the world to see and kept the muddled accretions of a lifetime out of sight.

Mrs Perry opened the door on to a small room with bare boards and bare walls and full of dazzling sunlight streaming from its one huge window. But if Angela had hoped to see a couple of mop bonnets nodding over fancy stitchwork, she was disappointed.

'Not much sewing room in here now,' said Mrs Perry wryly, indicating the mountains of agricultural magazines, cardboard boxes full of yellowing papers, unappetizing bric-à-brac. Above it all sat a glassy-eyed stuffed stag's head. In much the same condition as herself, Angela thought.

Mrs Perry sighed. 'Archie,' she said. 'Another good reason for moving. Since we got rid of the last few milkers, he's started going to car-boot sales. Only he brings back more than he takes.'

'Now, here's my pride and joy. The bathroom.'

They entered.

'Two outside walls to it – Archie never thought – but we've got one of those electric wall-heater things –' she made a mime of pulling at a corded switch – 'and that does all right. It's the only room we did up.' She touched the avocado suite with reverence. 'Before this it was Saturday night in front of the fire.'

Angela decided to concentrate on the velvet curtains, gooseberry green like the room below. In a *bathroom . . . velvet*? Caption for *Tatler* photograph: 'Angela Fytton chooses velvet for the family bathroom . . .' She had the grace to wince.

Mrs Perry's eyes softened as they had done at the door of her old room. 'I shall be sorry to leave this bathroom,' she said. 'You only need curtains for the cold, not because you're overlooked. That's why I've got these thick things up.' She touched the velvet and dust flew about. 'It's all got too much for me,' she said softly and more or less to herself. Then she pointed. 'You see, the trees outside hide everything. Even in the winter. The holly and the yews protect you. If it ever gets hot, you can sit in the bath with the windows wide open and enjoy a chat with the birds. I might miss that.' She touched the edge of the big, ugly sink. 'If we'd only had more time and the inclination, we'd have put in more improvements like this,' she said wistfully.

Angela, who had never quite understood the philosophy

behind Zen and archery before, now got the idea. For just as the arrow flies truest when you detach yourself from the act and let the spirit guide you, so she heard her own voice, coming from somewhere she did not know she had visited, saying, 'I'll take it. I'll pay the full price. And you can leave behind anything you don't want. *Anything.*'

Now she felt wonderful. Shriven. Purged. Born anew. It was, indeed, as delirious as the moment of acceptance of a lover. Yes, she was saying. Yes.

Mrs Perry's mouth went into that thin line again. 'Oh,' she said. 'I thought the agent would have told you. It's already sold. He's buying it.'

Angela Fytton, embarrassment notwithstanding, immediately burst into tears. Of sorrow. And of rage. 'Then why the bloody hell did he send me here if he's going to buy it?'

'Ah no,' said Mrs Perry, 'that was the *other* agent who sent you ... Tea?'

They sat at the table with the milk bottle and large brown Betty between them. The brew was dark brown and the biscuits were ginger snaps, which they both dunked. A couple of hens came tottering in and Mrs Perry shooed at them absently. Then, from beneath a bench on the far side of the room, there was a stirring and a low groan or two, and the unmistakable sound of a fart. Jesus! thought Angela, it's a drunk. But it was an ancient Labrador who slithered out, padding thoughtfully towards the hens. Relieved, and from the deeps of her disappointment, Angela watched. They stood their ground, those poultry, defiant, heads cocked, aware of the ginger snaps that were so near. The dog pushed on, his nose coming within inches of their feathered scuts. Still they remained: determined, brave, resolute. Robert the Bruce had a spider, thought Angela, I have sodding hens.

'Mrs Perry,' she said, 'I will pay more.'

'Mrs Fytton,' came the reply, 'those are town ways.'

The hens squawked and rose on their silly wings, but still

66

they did not get out of the Labrador's way. Any other buyer, she knew, would butcher the place. The very things she wanted to conserve would be thrown away.

'This estate agent,' said Angela, 'you know what he'll do. He'll buy it, do it up and sell it for a fortune.'

'That's up to him,' said Mrs Perry, pouring again. *'We* don't want to, that's for sure.'

She put the teapot down and gave Angela a straight, if slightly weary, look. 'It's over. Time moves on. Does it never occur to you town folk that we country folk might like the look of what you want to leave behind? It's not very comfortable living here and it never was. You should think about that.'

'What? Noise pollution, air pollution, shops that don't know you?'

'Shops of any kind. And air pollution means some form of transport. We used to have a railway station *and* buses to connect us to it. Noise is a part of the price you pay for still being included in the human race. What the common agricultural policy began, BSE just about finished. Along with politicians up in London telling us what we can and can't do. They should try telling a young lad of sixteen that he can go out on the withies for a living but he can't make a bob or two for the hunt.' She sniffed. 'Anyway, what withies are there left nowadays?'

Well, *quite*, thought Angela, wondering what the hell a withy was and putting it in the box marked still room.

Mrs Perry took a packet of cigarettes from her apron and offered one to Angela, who, in distraction, would have taken a brier pipe.

'My family was from around these parts for a very long time and I'm the last. It's the same with Archie – apart from his old aunt in the home over Shepton way. My family did dairying and were blacksmiths for generations.'

'Blacksmiths?' Angela was enchanted.

'Blacksmiths,' said Mrs Perry, a little irritably. Her hostess struck a match. Angela bent to the flame. Mrs Perry looked up. 'But oddly enough, Mrs Fytton, the latest farm models do not require shoeing. It was all over when they stopped the hunt. I ask you . . .'

Angela hoped her eyes looked back clear of the guilt of that twenty-pound note. 'Must have been a hard life,' she said.

'It was. But when I look at my daughter I'm not so sure. We women were better off here on the land in some ways. It was hard work, but it was your home. What husband in his right mind is going to have a dairy herd and a pig unit and leave his wife? He's a fool if he does. Risks everything. Whereas the towns . . . well.' She leaned back and gave Angela a very straight look. 'Country women had more independence than you think in the olden days. And time. It was the seasons that dictated, not clocks.'

Angela said defiantly, 'When I am here, I shall adopt the ways of the country and go at the season's pace.'

Mrs Perry ignored this with as much contempt as Canute poured upon the notion of sea-control. She shrugged. 'Well, it's over now.' She leaned forward and looked into Angela's starry eyes. 'It is not a romance, Mrs Fytton, the life. And I can't say I'm sorry it's over. Leastways I'll never have to go up that hill in midwinter to rescue some damned stray beast. Or get my hands frozen to the churn. Or worry to Archie's coughing.' Suddenly she banged the table with the flat of her palm. Angela jumped, and so did the hens, which ran scattering. 'Get out, you lot,' said Mrs Perry, quite good-naturedly. But they lingered by the door, still eyeing the biscuits and the dog alternately. They showed no fear. Just for a moment Angela felt like putting her head on one side and clucking too.

'Well, I want what you don't, Mrs Perry,' she said defiantly. 'Sanctuary and a bit of history. Ancient and modern.' She tried not to think of the avocado suite.

'If you want sanctuary, you need a church,' replied Mrs Perry quite sharply.

'Immunity, then,' said Angela, suddenly understanding what Virginia Woolf meant when she wrote the word in her diary. 'I want immunity, protection, safe harbour, peace.'

'It's a lot to ask of a house, Mrs Fytton.'

'I know,' she said. 'But as soon as I saw this house I knew it was right. Like a lover.'

Mrs Perry looked at her. 'Do you think those give you peace, Mrs Fytton?'

Angela realized that it was not the language for a pure-bred country wife. She changed the subject. 'Why is it called Church Ale House?'

More tea was poured. The cigarette was sucked.

Mrs Perry said, 'They used to brew the church ale here. Daphne Blunt says it would have been done by an ale-wife once upon a time. Apparently it was women's business but it made them too independent.' She laughed. 'There's always been good profit in drink. Anyway, it was celebration stuff. Church ale, bride ale. Before God and the priests said they mustn't.'

'Was that recently?' said Angela, thinking of licences, regulations about the marketing of comestibles and Women's Institute jam.

Mrs Perry shrugged and looked amused. 'Depends what you call recent,' she said. 'Not bad in country terms. Three hundred or so years.'

Angela smiled uncertainly. *Was* she being played with?

'Look,' said Mrs Perry, suddenly serious again, leaning forward and stabbing at the air with her cigarette. 'There isn't enough good in folk to go round as it is, without us climbing on the bandwagon. I haven't got straw in my hair when it comes to gazumping. First come, first served. It has to be so. I want doesn't always get. I wish it was you, but it isn't and that is that, Mrs Fytton.'

I want doesn't always get. No, she wanted to cry, it does *not*.

She remembered. How she thought he must be ill because he looked so white and so shaky and so crumpled. He sat on the settee and she beside him, but when she reached out to touch him, he pulled away from her and she suddenly knew. There was a kaleidoscopic tumble of images and memories in her head, a sudden realization of jigsaw pieces that never quite sat true. He is leaving me, she thought. Just as he said, 'I am leaving you.' And when she said, 'Don't go,' he said, 'I must.' She said, 'What about the children?' He said, 'Don't make this hard on me.' So she didn't. And he went. He closed the front door so quietly that she could not be sure he had gone. Then she called his name. And the house was suddenly empty, like a body without a heart. Which left her sitting on the settee thinking, So that's how people *really* speak in this situation. Instinct told her to preserve some dignity. He would never come back if she showed him how deep the wound went. He would be too afraid.

Well, she was not going to give up on this house in the same way she gave up on her marriage. She adopted the same bright-eyed pose as the hens. Dangerous, expectant. Mrs Perry brushed some crumbs from the table for them and they pounced. No waiting, no politesse. That was the way. Say what you want and hang around until you get it. Mrs Perry tapped the dog's nose out of the way as he came scuffling among them, and the hens, as if taking their cue from her, made a series of runs at him, their little beaks flashing like flick knives. He immediately slid back under the bench.

Exactly so, thought Angela.

'How long have you been married, Mrs Perry?'

'Forty-seven years.'

'Happily?'

'Well, I –' Mrs Perry looked flustered.

'Sorry,' said Angela. 'That was very rude.'

'This and that,' said Mrs Perry. 'But we made a good team.'

'Oh,' said Angela. 'I was dead romantic about it all.'

Mrs Perry raised a wispy grey eyebrow. 'I was the opposite. Archie's family were glad when I accepted him, me being strong and sensible. And so were my mother and my aunts. Of course, I swapped the dairy and the forge to only go half a mile over the hill to work with Archie's mother, so she couldn't complain. We did the milking, of course, and the eels, preserves and cider – which were their three sidelines. When you've gutted eels and stoned plums and washed bottles for a year or two, everyone is inclined to want you to stay around.' And then she stared out of the window towards the hill and the pigs.

Now that the hens had quietened down she beckoned, with a low whistling noise, to the bench. Out came the dog, meek and happy. She bent and scratched behind its ear. The hens stood quietly to one side, tap, tap, tapping at the cracks between the flagstones. All, it seemed, were waiting.

'Women can be your worst enemies,' said Angela.

Mrs Perry looked perfectly noncommittal.

Well, thought Angela, what would she know? 'Do you know, Mrs Perry, I once tried to go down to Greenham Common to take some food and blankets and stuff – and they wouldn't let me on the minibus with my son. Because he was male.' She paused. 'He was six.'

'No,' said the woman, suitably surprised.

'Yes,' said Angela. 'Six.'

Something suddenly dawned on her. 'Mrs Perry,' she said, 'I'm sorry. I realize you won't know what Greenham was.'

Mrs Perry raised her eyebrows.

'It was an American base, for nuclear weapons, close to London. Women made a peace camp there and cut the wire and did a lot of material damage and hassling and held vigils to make the army and the police understand the women weren't just a passive load of skirts but were political, fighters . . . The women were spat on, reviled and despised. But they stayed there for years, some of them, and lived in the most appalling conditions – tents that were constantly being torn down by the authorities – snow, wind, rain, frost – no facilities of any kind except what a few kind locals offered. They were really brave.'

'Ah,' said Mrs Perry.

Angela shrugged. 'It was just a little moment in history. And in women's history. And then – pouf – it was over.'

Mrs Perry nodded. 'Women did a lot in the war too,' she said. 'But they knocked you straight back afterwards.'

'Of course they did,' said Angela vaguely. 'But *six*. I should have known after that.'

There was the sound of a car driving on gravel. 'Oh,' said Mrs Perry, standing up. 'That'll be Dave the Bread.' And she went out of the back door, pushing it open with a smart smack of her hip. The small one. Now Angela realized what caused the lopsidedness.

The hens followed Mrs Perry, rushing and squawking. The dog did not move. Angela stroked his head. Time, she thought dreamily, makes door frames drop. And then, even more dreamily, she thought that once she was installed here she would allow herself the same privilege. Why, she could drop all over the place. Buttocks scraping the floor, belly swinging low as a chariot, and hiding it all under swirling elastic-waisted rustic skirts while she beamed at the world . . .

Mrs Perry returned, followed by a large man dressed for the part in a white coat and white baseball hat bearing the boast 'Dave the Bread'. Angela tried not to look at the baseball hat.

'Morning,' he said, smiling at her curiously. He had a strong south London accent. Ah well. Despite that, he held a big square rush basket in front of him from which floated a yeasty, tantalizing smell. He put a large square white loaf on the table, and then Mrs Perry pointed to a currant one.

'That too,' she said. 'As I've got a guest.'

Angela put out her hand. 'Mrs Fytton,' she said. 'I'm hoping to move in here.'

'Good, good,' said Dave the Bread. 'Family?' he added hopefully, obviously seeing a many-loafed bill. He hovered, eyeing the teapot.

'Goodbye, Dave,' said Mrs Perry.

'See you again,' he said, and left very reluctantly.

'Yes,' said Angela. 'Yes, you will.'

'Go on,' said Mrs Perry, sitting down and cutting away at the loaf. She pushed a piece of the speckled soft white bread across to her. No plate.

Great, thought Angela stoutly. No plate. Tentatively, she brushed at the table top with her hand. There were a lot of deep grooves in the table top – a *lot* . . . Natural bacteria, she told herself, *natural*. She broke a piece of bread and put it in her mouth. It was soft and stuck to her teeth – insubstantial, like those clouds. She preferred to think of it as 'bread like thistledown' and to imagine it on a hoarding showing rolling green hills and sleepy distant hamlets . . .

Outside the hens squawked and scratched at the door and the Labrador groaned in its sleep. Sunlight streamed through the kitchen window, making the air so warm that Mrs Perry opened the door again. Bash, bash went her hip. The hens eyed her.

'I have nothing for you,' she said.

Angela was amazed to see them turn and run away, with the fowlesque equivalent of dark mutterings. Fight your corner, she wanted to say. Stay and fight your corner.

She stared out into the garden – the neat back lawn leading down to the stream, the old trees bowing – the very picturesqueness of it seemed too good to be true. 'That is exactly the kind of view you would expect in an old-fashioned English murder mystery,' she said. 'Everything on the surface looking peaceful and contented, while underneath it seethes with evil and murderous intent. Just why are those roses growing so energetically, my good woman? What is buried beneath them? Just *what* have you used in the soil?'

Mrs Perry looked perplexed. 'Compost,' she said. 'Though it's true Archie piddles on it.'

Angela stared with embarrassment. 'Really?' she said, thinking that Archie was probably senile.

Mrs Perry nodded. 'It's the best way to bring your compost

on. He very seldom uses the one indoors. You're supposed to say the name of your enemy while you're doing it – to make him rot.'

'No!'

'Yes.'

Angela laughed, immediately christening her own proposed compost heap Belinda. 'Perhaps he's called the compost heap after one of your admirers.'

Mrs Perry looked *extremely* uncomfortable and quivered in a scarlet blush.

'I'm so sorry, that was quite tasteless,' said Angela. How, she asked herself, could you?

'Your compost is very important,' said Mrs Perry.

'Oh, it *is*, it is,' said Angela effusively. 'So important,' and she just about managed to stop herself from adding, 'Mmm, mmm, *compost*,' and licking her lips.

The hens came pattering in like overflounced tap-dancers.

'What will you do with these when you go?' she said.

'The pot,' said Mrs Perry shortly.

Angela looked suitably careless. 'But I could have them if . . . I mean, I've never looked after hens but I'm quite sure I could learn.'

Mrs Perry did not look up. She nodded. And then, as if to herself, she said, 'And then there's the bees.'

Bees? thought Angela. Oh, fuck. But she just shrugged as if she and Brother Adam of Buckfast were as one, and said, 'Bees are so vital, aren't they? Honey, candles, that sort of thing.' She remembered her Sylvia Plath. 'Bee boxes. Hunting the queen.' Who said good art must be useless? 'Brood cells.'

'You might like a sip of my mulberry wine,' said Mrs Perry, obviously impressed. 'I know I would.'

Mulberry wine, thought Angela, mulberry wine . . . 'From your own – um?' She wasn't entirely sure what mulberries grew on.

'We have the oldest tree by a long way round here. Went in

before Queen Victoria, they say, and mostly we get more than we know what to do with.'

Angela looked doubtful. Chinese heavy embroidery and worms came to mind. 'Mulberries?' she said cautiously. 'Lovely.'

'Think of it as medicine, Mrs Fytton,' said Mrs Perry affably as she poured two small tots of ruby liquor into tiny glasses. 'That's the tree out there. They say that after the mulberry tree has shown green leaf there will be no more frost.'

Angela went to the window and immediately gave a little gasp. Behind her Mrs Perry laughed. There was no doubt about it, the trunk with its two central boles looked like a gigantic male back view – rough and muscular as a half-hewn Michelangelo and just as naked, with vast sinewy arms reaching out west to east and barely shadowed with tiny soft green leaves.

Mrs Perry chuckled. 'Some see it straight away and some never do,' she said.

'Did it grow like that?' asked Angela.

Mrs Perry looked bothered by the question. 'Not exactly,' she said delicately. 'The bit you see was done a good hundred years ago.' She smiled and pushed the little glass of red liquor along the table. 'Mulberry and rosemary tea,' she said, 'is supposed to restore – er – vigour.'

Angela said, 'Oh,' went pink, and resumed her seat. She looked at the glass hesitantly.

Mrs Perry said, 'I don't think mulberries on their own have any particular force in that department.'

And again Angela wondered if she was laughing at her. 'How do you know all these things?' she asked.

'It's passed on. Mother, daughter, grandmother.' She shrugged. 'It's the country for you.'

'Yes,' said Angela. And she suddenly giggled. 'Even the trees.'

'All promise and no delivery,' said Mrs Perry, looking firmly at her glass. 'When you see it from the front. It was got at. By Archie.'

Mrs Perry held her glass up to the sunlight, where it glowed like a ruby. 'It's supposed to have once been a white fruit that got stained by the blood of a pair of murdered sweethearts. According to our history woman.'

But Angela was already far away, imagining herself slipping out in the moonlight to stroke those rippled buttocks; or winding and spreading herself within its arm; or reaching up to bite the fruit so that the juice ran down . . .

The dog was pushing the Perry pinny up over the round knees with its nose. 'He wants a walk,' Mrs Perry said.

Angela tried to look at him fondly. Go away, stick your head up your bum and let me finish, she thought, hoping it was true that dogs had extrasensory perception.

The dog eyed her. No doubt about it, he knew. Any more from you, she transmitted, and you'll go into the pot too. No Sheherazade could have felt more desperate, she thought. I am telling this story to win.

Angela put down her glass and continued. 'Well, to cut a long story short, my husband met a pretty woman who wanted a baby. Just when we were almost free again, he falls for the oldest trick in the world. Young, blonde, with size four feet. Shafted by my own sex. First there was the Greenham group, who shafted me because I *had* a child. Then there was this Belinda woman, who shafted me because I didn't.'

Mrs Perry said wryly, 'The one thing about the old days is that you had no choice in the matter. Bit of a relief in some ways. If you lived.'

'I want to come here to a decent, honest community where I can rebuild my life. Please.'

Mrs Perry stood up very quickly. She was embarrassed. 'I must take this dog for a walk.' The dog came rushing over to her as she reached for his lead.

Miserably Angela downed her wine. So she had lost, then?

'I do understand,' said Mrs Perry kindly. 'But I won't break our promise. The man has made us an offer fair and square.'

She held out her hand. 'Come again, Mrs Fytton,' she said. 'Will you do that?'

'Why?' said Angela aggressively as they walked off down the path together.

'Come in three weeks' time and the mulberry will be in leaf,' said Mrs Perry at the gate.

Angela turned. She traced the words in brass – Church Ale House – and looked back along the path to where the breeze moved through the boughs of the tree. She fancied it was waving at her. I will not go and look at the front of it until I *own* it, she thought.

She knew now that the ruddy-faced cook would have been making *mulberry* tarts, of course, while the fantasy ladies of the house wore the product of the worms in which to eat them. And what had the Roman women who lived here worn? Or eaten? And what did the Saxon matron use to make the cakes that Alfred burnt? How she wished she could be a part of that whole cycle – the timelessness of Mrs Perry's own connections, her innate happiness drawn from a sense of belonging. That was what she lacked. Now she no longer belonged anywhere. She could have belonged here, but someone with shiny shoes and insider knowledge was buying it. Nothing short of an act of God could prevent the sale, and God was unlikely to have a gap in his schedule, given the state of the world.

She watched Mrs Perry set off towards the hill where the pig man kept his pigs. Angela heard her say, 'If you chase those pigs again you'll be on the lead properly.' The dog walked soberly by her side. Even at a distance the old woman was looking very thoughtful. Angela slowed as she went past, and waved.

The woman turned. 'By the way,' she called, stopping for a moment and leaning on her stick. 'Thank you for the explanation, but I went up to Greenham Common myself, to see my daughter. She was living in our old tent.'

Angela opened and closed her mouth, but no sound came out. 'Oh,' she said eventually. 'I just thought . . .'

'We don't all have straw in our hair, Mrs Fytton,' said Mrs Perry, quite kindly under the circumstances.

'Well, no, I never –' began Angela, but Mrs Perry cut her short.

'And anyway, I have a bit of an apology to make to you. Carol, my daughter, was probably one of the women who banned your son. She was a stinker about all that.' Mrs Perry paused and shook her head and smiled. 'Until she had her own family. Both boys. Did I laugh when they came along . . . "There's two of the little so and sos," I said when she had them. "Now what?"'

'Into the pot?' said Angela.

Mrs Perry laughed and turned to continue her climb.

Angela leaned despondently on the steering wheel. The horn went off. Fuck, she thought, as a bird of some sort rose from its cover with a great hullabaloo and piercing, menacing look. Mrs Perry's look was not dissimilar as she tried to calm the dog.

'Like you,' Angela whispered on the air, 'I wish to be good. Just like you.'

Mrs Perry waved her stick and continued on up the hill. The pig pens glinted in the sun. 'Next time,' she called, 'I'll show you the bees.'

She thought of her perfect and elegant home. And she knew she was sick of that too. Two bathrooms indeed – who needed them when one avocado suite would do?

O luxury! thou curs'd by Heaven's decree,
How ill exchang'd are things like these for thee!

She sobbed. Her stomach churned. She stopped the car and got out. Pigs, mulberries and the warmth of the sun made her queasy. She apologized in advance to the profusion of cow parsley – about the only country plant she knew – at the foot of that ancient hill and threw up as neatly as she could. When she was a child and had wanted something very badly, it made her literally sick with longing. As she bent double she was aware that this was serious, this was very serious indeed. She felt possessed. She threw up again. She waited, watching the hill. And she had to stop the car several times in the lane before finally driving away.

Afterwards, she thought of those medieval heretics who, when given the Host, were depicted as vomiting forth their furious little devils. She wondered if she had been given a form of Host by Mrs Perry and was finally vomiting Ian out. Rather amusing to think of him as a little, black, wriggling, yapping creature furiously waggling his forked tail as she exorcized him.

She drove slowly back along the lane and took one more yearning look at the house before setting off for home. The beauty of the day made it all the more poignant a leave-taking. She wondered, not daring to hope, if by the time she came down again there might have befallen some wondrous divine intervention. After all, it was the sort of thing you could expect from this pure and spiritual place called the Country.

6

April

Dave the Bread took off his cap and threw it down on the scrubbed deal table in his own kitchen. He then walked over to the rubbish bin, fighting his way past hanks of yarn and a vat of scented, liquid candle grease, and pushed several crumpled packets and papers down further into its depths. Wanda, his wife, wearing a flowing ethnic frock, was busy removing the labels from old washed jumpers she had purchased from various jumble and car-boot sales.

'It would be stark staringly obvious,' he said irritably, 'if someone came into our kitchen at this precise moment and noticed what's hanging out of our rubbish, that I have just unwrapped several out-of-date currant and honeybran loaves from their supermarket wrappings, heated them up and sold them as of my own making.'

'I doubt it,' said Wanda comfortably. 'Can't see the wood for the trees round here. Brilliant stroke, putting them into the oven for a moment or two before going out.'

'Brilliant is as maybe, but I told you to burn the wrappers.'

'Ooh, sorry,' said Wanda, putting a coy hand to her lips and batting her eyelids like a naughty schoolgirl. 'Do I get a smack?' Wanda knew the drill. She pouted.

'Come here,' he said, and, grabbing at her substantial buttocks through the flowing, elasticated skirt, he pressed himself through the folds.

'Ooh, let me put the scissors down first,' she squealed, 'or I'll do you an injury.'

They heard the roar of a passing car, an unfamiliar roar, and looked out of the window. Dave the Bread removed his hands from his wife's nether regions with a regretful squeeze. Very occasionally a motorist stopped for directions and it might be taking the bucolic image a little too far to be caught *in* full yokel *flagrante*.

Instead he patted his wife affectionately and touched one of the misshapen, felted garments that lay over the back of her chair.

'My, my,' he said happily, 'your weaving looks really authentic. Bloody awful and authentic. And the knitting,' he added, as he sank his teeth into a bath bun. 'Clever girl.'

Wanda pushed her bosom back down under her Tyrolean bodice and went on with her label-removal.

On the table by her side was a spray of woad (genus *Isatis*) plucked from the garden, and next to that a vat of weak Dylon solution – cornflower blue – into which she dunked each delabelled woolly and then attacked it with a dolly tub. This gave every garment a suitably similar tonal quality, the unmistakable stamp of English homecraft, as if it had been dragged through mud by the local Puritan lobby to remove any relation to the colourful singing beauties of wayward nature. She sold a large number of them at country sales and car-boots. Sometimes, unbeknownst to her, and to the purchasers, she sold them back to the original owners, who wore them proudly to the Friday night ceilidh, where, between bouts of incompetent fiddling (Patrick Parsons originated from Watford and was enthusiastically self-taught) and very confusing calling (Una Parsons, once a low-pass-rate driving instructor from St Albans), they would point out the virtues of such simple, handmade garments. It was, as they said, the kind of thing that brought them down here. Back to basics. Quality of life. A handmade, hand-dyed, pure-wool sweater in any of those Bayswater shops would have cost three times as much.

Those who came to Tally-Ho Cottage walked past the woad patch to reach the front door. Ergo, if they saw a vat of blue, they assumed it was natural bounty. The spray of woad was placed on the table in case they sneezed on the path and missed the growing clump. It was the same with the lavender and rose bushes for the scented candles. She grew them right by the pathway also, and bought the oils from Boots. Sometimes she just melted down cheap scented candles from the market. By careful addition of colour, as with her weaving, she could produce candles that smelt horrible, were coloured like a baby's nappy and made everyone think they were entirely good for you. Not for nothing had Wanda Crow been an actress; she knew all about props and illusion. She had married the sparks from her last production, in which she played the back end of a goose, and given it all up. Given all what up? she sometimes asked the mirror.

She blew her husband a kiss.

'Happy?' he said.

'Never more so,' she replied. 'My best performance yet.'

They smiled contentedly.

'Thank God we left London.'

Dr Percy Tichborne pretended not to hear the tinkling little bell that was the summons for lunch. Just another moment or two, he said to himself, and readjusted the binoculars. It was only April, *April*, and yet the vicar was doing his exercises again, in a fetching little box and nothing else, because he thought he was hidden by the vicarage ilex. Well, to be fair the good doctor had told him as much. 'Totally private,' he said. 'The trees hide everything. Even in winter.' And the vicar, being a young man of God, believed him.

'Ah, but not from up here, my beautiful young Crispin,' breathed Dr Tichborne, and peered all the harder as those pale, stretched limbs pushed up down, up down, up . . . The dark red hair flopped and rose, flopped and rose, over that high freckled brow, and the perfect white teeth gleamed as the vicar grimaced in his striving to do press-ups worthy of God. Had the good doctor crept closer, he might have heard the muttered underbreaths of the vicar saying, apparently, 'No, no, no . . .' to some unnamed temptation as he pushed himself to the absolute limit of endurance. No flagellant upon the road to Compostela could have given his God more in the line of keep-fit.

Somewhere to the side of his vision, Dr Tichborne was aware of a little car stopping by the wayside at the foot of the hill and a woman getting out, apparently in deep contemplation of the foliage. She appeared to be in some kind of distress as she bent double. He might have focused on her if the vicar had not suddenly appeared to get cramp and roll over on to his back, clutching his leg. He did that yesterday too. The doctor's heart skipped a beat. Perhaps he was badly injured? How he hoped so, how he *hoped*. He could be very tender with that knee . . .

The little bell tinkled again. It sounded irritated. Dr Tichborne slid the binoculars back into his desk drawer. He longed, yet again, to be lying there, upon that very patch of dappled grass above which the vicar swung himself so rhythmically. To feel the heated breath, the sweep of that auburn hair upon his face, the brush of those barely contained manly bits as they bounced back and forth above him. If he could, he would, he swore, be the very turf upon which the vicar brought that virgin belly down.

It was not, said Dr Tichborne to himself as he descended the stairs, his fault. If the Anglican church saw fit to send a young single man of thirty-two to watch over St Hilary's, what could they expect? An *unmarried* young man of thirty-two, for heaven's sake. One with the body of an angel, the flaming hair of a god and the brain of an innocent young warrior. What is more, the doctor reminded himself, one who could recite the poetry of Gerard Manley Hopkins, play the guitar, kick up his heels at a ceilidh, hold the hand of a dying parishioner for half the night without once looking tired and, on top of it all, charm his wife into parting with some of her loot. What a cocktail to serve up in this vacuous hamlet. He reached the dining-room door, readjusted his expression to one of benign absent-mindedness and entered.

'You seem a little flushed, Percy,' said Dorothea. She was seated at the dining table, looking cool and austere in white, her hand still resting lightly on the little silver bell. The crucifix she had asked for as a wedding anniversary gift glittered on her board-like chest. All she needed, he thought sourly, was a wimple and she'd be a full nun. She went back to her plate of thin toast and the *Anglican Herald*. Dorothea fasted until one o'clock each weekday. Dr Percy Tichborne saw no reason not to follow suit. They must, he thought regretfully, looking at his wife's pale, even complexion, live the healthiest lives of any late sexagenarians in the area. So much for her supposedly dicky heart. I wonder, he thought, as he so often had since the advent of Crispin, what love and sex are like in combination?

If ever a man regretted marrying for money it was he. What you do when you are young, he thought, brings its heaven or hell eventually. He ran his hand over his bald dome. Experience, alas, is a comb that life gives you when you no longer have hair . . .

'Has something excited you?' asked his wife disapprovingly.

'I thought I saw a couple of siskins,' he said.

'Coniferous woodland,' she said, without looking up, 'only.'

'Oh well –'

'It was probably a pair of tits,' she said.

'Anything but,' said Dr Tichborne beneath his breath. And then winced as the little bell was rung again.

The young Dorkin girl entered, looking, Dr Tichborne thought peevishly, as if she had just had sex with some scrambled eggs.

'Fresh toast for Dr Tichborne,' said Dorothea, continuing to read, 'and scrambled eggs.'

He looked at the straining grey-white blouse with its open

84

buttons, its peep of grubby brassière and the gouts of un-
cooked eggs strewn about it.

'Just toast,' he said.

'Oh, but Sandra has been practising,' said his wife.

'So I see,' said Dr Tichborne.

Sandra gave him a lascivious smile. It was her mother's
ambition that she should marry a rich old man. Everybody
knew that Dorothea Tichborne had a delicate heart and could
go at any time. Everybody knew that Dorothea Tichborne
was ready to go at any time. Had been ready, so Dr Tichborne
thought, since before she married him, if their wedding night
was anything to go by. In which case, thought both Mrs
Dorkin and Dr Percy Tichborne, why did the wretched
woman take such great care of herself? She longed for
heaven, so why not go there? It was only a question of the two
strands connecting (only connect, thought Dr Tichborne pas-
sionately from time to time) and she would be gone. He could
then throw himself into a Grand Passion at last – with all the
comforts of riches to surround it.

In the watchful eyes of Mrs Dorkin, mother of Sandra, he
would then be a desirable widower. Mrs Dorkin had had her
eye on him in the old days for herself and went at him at quite
a lick with hot pants and thigh boots. But he stayed faithful to
his wife. Since it was not to be, she now claimed him for the
next generation. Her daughter had all the trappings of
entrapment: Mrs Dorkin had fed her on cream and butter and
eggs, bathed her face with eyebright and rubbed her with
whey since she was a little thing. Now there was nothing little
about her. She was perfect fodder for an old, rich, lonely man.
And they didn't come any richer hereabouts than the doctor,
said her mother with a wink. And lonely. Since the Dorkin
girl made the beds, she knew perfectly well that Dr Tichborne
and Mrs Tichborne slept in separate rooms.

Her mother said that what she and Sandra were about was
traditional. You sent a village girl up to the big house and the
squire first seduced and then married her. It was in every book

Mrs Dorkin had ever read. Which was not a lot and among which Thomas Hardy's Tess did *not* feature. Sandra would persevere. 'You marry him,' said her mother, 'and once you're married you can have your true love on the side.' Mrs Dorkin laughed. That was traditional too. 'Whoever he is . . .'

Sandra was thinking of him, her true love, now, as she idly stroked the soft pink flesh of her throat and hummed a happy hymn. 'Eggs, then, is it?' she asked. 'And how many would that be?' She leaned over the table at Dr Tichborne. Any other man would be forced to answer 'Two,' but he said, 'One please,' and sipped his orange juice.

In the weedless garden of the Rudges' house a snail slithered across the newly flagged path towards a bed of tender, delectable young polyanthuses in very bright colours. It stopped on the way to sniff and lick a little blue ball that also smelt delectable, about the size of a baby pea, lying in its path. 'Lick, lick, lick,' said the snail. And then it pulled a face. 'Yaroo,' it said. And exploded. A blackbird flew down and swooped upon the glutinous mess, pleased to find a quick takeaway for the family instead of one of those all-in jobbies that took for ever to crack open. Off he flew, gliding low along the road, narrowly avoiding being hit by an oncoming car. The glistening poison, so deftly dispensed by the little blue slug pellet, attracted his youngsters and his own dear wife, as he flew into view. He dropped it into the nest for his wife to serve up. 'Yum, yum, Daddy,' they chirruped, and ate it all up. After which they went remarkably silent.

The Rudges liked the peace and quiet of the countryside at weekends. When they first purchased Brier House they cut back their yew hedge into a long, thin perfect rectangle, cut down several badly placed trees, removed the ancient briers that grew there willy-nilly and from which the house derived its name, and generally gave themselves a tidier aspect to look out on from their new conservatory. It went pleasantly quiet after all that. They commented in amazement at the number of old nests they discovered in the course of reshaping the garden. Like Centre Point, the Rudges told some of their London visitors, for they had lived near its high-rise shadow before they left Fitzrovia. Now, loving the silence as they did, given how hard they worked in their law practice in Bristol, it was all to the good that the chorus of birdsong had diminished in their garden over the last couple of years. As, indeed, had the trails of the snails . . . And the toads. And the frogs. Even the breathy wings of butterflies seemed to be silenced and still. All, in their own way, had once made such a frightful din.

When the Rudges first came here from London, weekenders visiting with them would marvel at the rural cacophony, taking great pleasure in it. But the crows and rooks were ugly and loud, and the blackbird and the song thrush were piercingly insistent, and the toads and frogs croaked ceaselessly during the mating season, and, as the Rudges said as they waved their friends goodbye, those departing guests didn't have to listen to it every weekend. Well, well – something had sent these noisy elements on their way and it was very nice indeed to have a bit of peace.

Lucy Elliott stared out bleakly from the window above her sink and draining board. She wanted to sit in the sunshine and read a book, or listen to the radio, or have her nails polished by some visiting beautician and masseuse. She wanted to have flying lessons. Like Craig. Or faxes from her publisher saying how well the reviews were going, when they weren't. Like Craig. She wanted to be able to walk into the house on a Friday night, having been in London since Tuesday, and say, 'Hi, guys,' to the children, who were already tucked up in bed. And then have sex once the children were asleep. And then fall asleep herself. Like Craig. She did not want to be here at the sink, which had got blocked again, wondering if she had enough fish fingers to go round and afraid that she might be pregnant once more. Unlike Craig.

'We'll have a lovely idyll,' he said to her when he moved them all to the country. And then he buggered back off to London whenever he could.

'Let's have another baby,' he said, 'and see if we can't get a girl.' They got Esmond. 'Cyril Connolly might talk about the pram in the hall,' she heard him say to his agent, 'but I've got three . . . How can you expect me to get it in on time?' Overhearing, she wondered what would happen if she was six months late with the dinner.

Lucy Elliott pushed the plunger one more time with great strength – a strength which, she felt sure, came from heaving toddlers up hill, down dale, in and out of the car, the bath, the swing. Unlike Craig. A great gout of greeny-black matter flew up and hit her smack in the eye. Lucy Elliott burst into tears. She threw down the plunger, went over to the telephone, then heard the first wail of two-year-old Tommy, followed by the first wail of three-and-a-half-year-old Esmond, followed by the stamping of five-year-old Jamie on the stairs.

She picked up the telephone and tapped out a number. As she waited she thought, God bless the countryside for helping its mothers to keep their children at home and safe. If she had won and not Craig, they would still be in Weybridge, where there were pre-school playgroups and where children were certainly in full-time school by the age of four and a half. But a writer should not live in Weybridge, or anywhere remotely like it, said Craig. A writer must live where his Muse responds. No one ever, according to Craig, had a Muse that responded if they lived in a place like *Weybridge*.

'What about J. G. Ballard?' she answered with spirit. 'He lives in *Shepperton*. He's wildly successful.'

Unlike Craig.

The wails increased. The phone was answered.

'Millie's All Staff Agency,' said a nice, female voice.

'I want a live-in mother's help please,' said Lucy Elliott. And she thought, I want a very ugly one. Unlike Craig.

As she waited for the woman to take down her details, she

glanced at the hill and saw one of her neighbours striding upwards, a dog prancing at her side, a stick in her hand, comfortable and at one with the climb, pacing it as Lucy had still to learn to do. If she went out for a walk, it was with three children and the fear that one of them would do something to cause a tragedy while her eyes were on one of the others. I am thirty-five, she thought, and I walk like that old woman. What is to become of me? Fear clutched at her, as it so often did if she took a minute to think about anything beyond fish fingers. For the thought that always followed, What's to become of me? was, If Craig ever leaves me.

'We have a Dutch girl,' said the voice. 'Available at the end of the month.'

'Is she pretty?' snapped Lucy Elliott.

'She's from The Hague,' said the voice, as if that was an answer.

The vicar, fresh from his shower, limping a little and wearing his groovy blue dog-collar shirt and black jeans, slipped through the lych-gate and noticed the hinges were coming away. He skirted the gravestones and went to the side of the church. Looking up towards the dangerously crooked weather vane, he stared into the face of an old gargoyle and remembered that he was having tea with Mrs Tichborne. He apologized for the graceless thought, though the carving, like so many, did look uncannily like her. Not surprising, he supposed, since her family connection with the area went back hundreds of years.

His eyes went dreamy. He would make that the subject of his sermon at the family service on Sunday. He would string his guitar around his neck, talk about little and big and their place in the world, remind everyone that no matter how humble or how great, they all had a role in the scheme of things. That you should value what you had. And then sing 'Me and Bobby McGee' – the perfect anthem for such a theme. He started to hum it to himself:

'I took my harpoon out of tee dum tee red bandana
And was blowing dum while Bobby dee dum dum ...
Tee tee tee dum dum dee slapping time
I must learn the words –
Nothing ain't worth nothing but it's free ...
And I'd give all my tomorrows for a single yesterday ...'

'Ooh,' said a voice behind him that instantly made him think of very full, if very grubby, brassière cups. 'Well, if it isn't the vicar singing.'

He did not turn round. The limp melted away. He fled.

Puffing, he entered the church, hoping it would remove the lingering sense of that warm and unwashed skin. Inside it was still and quiet and empty. Too empty. He must set about changing that. He blinked away the muddled image of a Madonna and a milky breast from his mind and crossed himself. He conjured up the face of St Hilary's benefactress instead. He hoped Dr Tichborne would join them today for tea. He was always friendly and supportive, with his encouraging little smiles and his pats on the hand. Otherwise it would be hard going. Mrs Tichborne was set on spending a lot of money on a vast memorial tablet to her father, Sir Peter Devereux, and it was the Reverend Crispin Archer's job to get that money spent on something more urgent, more temporal. Like refurbishing the church hall and some heating that worked. Not for himself – *he* did not mind suffering for his witness – but he could hardly persuade his parishioners that turning blue with cold was useful. If God had sent them the potential for central heating, then they were obliged to use it. And in a church hall they could have playgroups, Sunday schools, quiz nights, youth clubs – and he could play the guitar. Though quite how he was going to persuade Mrs Dorothea Tichborne to drop the ancestral marble and pay for a range of requirements including a pool table instead was beyond him. Despite the fact that the memorial tablet to Sir Peter (RIP 1988) was highly questionable, since his great moment of glory was to stand up in the House of Lords and declare that one could not make an omelette without breaking eggs in response to a reminder that his family money came from a rollicking slave trade in Bristol.

Unfortunately the vicar's predecessor, the octogenarian Reverend Dr Bertrand Stokes, was keen on memorial tablets, genuflected both at the sanctuary light *and* at the appearance of the only remaining Devereux, though she was now called Tichborne, and never complained about wearing three pairs of long johns even in May. He was in a retirement home for nearly deceased clergy now – very bad arthritis and what was referred to by the staff in a whisper as *kidneys* – but his spirit seemed to be lingering on. Mrs Tichborne was always knitting him something beige and reading to him from Bunyan.

The vicar went over to the old squint and peered above it. Daphne Blunt, the history woman, had been busy. Gradually fragments of an early medieval fresco were coming to light. He peered even closer. And then he smiled. There was the Devereux face again, though this time attached to one of the newly revealed little black devils and spewing out the Host.

Strangely, at that precise moment of looking at the face of the vomiting devil, like a note of assent from God, he distinctly thought he heard the sound of retching from beyond the church gate. Just his imagination, he supposed. He must learn to rein it in. As he must learn to rein in everything else.

Behind him the church door creaked open.

'Ooh,' said a familiar voice. 'Ooh.'

Daphne Blunt sat in the Black Smock sipping half a Guinness and reading a book of Celtic symbols. 'Swans are solar symbols in later Celtic belief,' she said aloud, 'and ravens and crows represent battle.'

Nobody paid much attention to the pronouncement. Daphne Blunt was a single woman of marriageable age whose sole interest seemed to be in the past. She had been found, once, in the ladies' toilet, on her hands and knees, pulling up the lino.

She had been seen, once, sitting on top of the church with the workmen when the roof came off, and she was forever digging and poking and scratching her way around. Reading out loud to herself was small beer and they left her alone.

'Unsurprising,' she went on, to nobody in particular, 'if you consider that these traditions came from observations of nature. Swans are beautiful, graceful creatures of light – and ravens and crows feast on the dead. Why, it's as plain as the nose on your face.'

Daphne Blunt buried her own substantial Afghan nose back in the book. What she needed was a friend. Who took an interest too. But she'd have to make do with addressing thin, thin air.

Mrs Dorkin delivered Daphne Blunt's ham sandwich. The ham came from Sammy's pigs, the bread from Dave's basket. Absent-mindedly, and as usual, Daphne picked out the ham and left the bread. Halfway through chewing she gave a snort of irritation, to which nobody paid attention except a pair of tourists blown off course from the Bath trail. 'In the Polden Hills hoard there is a harness brooch with a symmetrical tri-partite design which could be interpreted as a face.'

The assembly went on with their beer and conversation.

'Rubbish,' she snorted, like a dragon. 'It's two confronted hippocampi . . .'

The assembly remained unmoved.

'Hippocampi?' said the passing Mrs Dorkin.

'Sea horses.'

'Ah,' said Mrs Dorkin, picking up the plate. 'Want your bread?'

Daphne Blunt shook her head. 'Fabulous creatures to the Celts,' she said. 'Rare as crystal.'

'Like till death us do part,' said Mrs Dorkin acidly. Think-ing both of the absconded Mr Dorkin and its infuriating opposite in old Dr Tichborne and his wife.

'Well, I wouldn't know about that,' said Daphne Blunt. The study of history, in Daphne Blunt's opinion, was quite enough for any woman.

Mrs Dorkin looked on the girl with pity. If she made something of herself she wouldn't be bad-looking. Apart from that nose. But catch a man wanting baggy overalls and boots and a woman who was always up a ladder or digging a ditch. She might have said something casually along the lines of how a face or hand could be much improved by dairy products rubbed well in, but just at that moment a car, passing the open window, braked very noisily.

'It's that black cat from Tally-Ho,' said Mrs Dorkin, peering out. 'And that's the car that was at Church Ale House earlier on. The woman does look very upset. Don't know why. She didn't run over Blackie at all.'

7

April

A bachelor never quite gets over the idea
that he is a thing of beauty and a boy for ever.

HELEN ROWLAND

When she reached the lower ridge of Mump Hill, Gwen Perry turned and stared down at the ribbon of road and the receding car. She gave it a wave just in case. Above her, in this sharp afternoon sunlight, the mysterious Burrow Mump, possibly built as a fortress for Alfred and possibly not, stood out like a huge polyp on an otherwise smooth cheek. It was said to house the Burrow Devils and, given the way of things today, thought Mrs Perry, they would all be laughing and shaking their forked little tails with glee.

She turned away and continued to climb. 'You can keep its ancient powers,' she said to herself. 'I'll take a bit of Christian town comfort now.' She struggled on. 'I've done with the old pagan pull, thanks very much.' The sun was hot and high in the sky, the air heavy with the warm smell of pigs and grass. She became quite out of breath and reminded herself, very loudly, that it would be an easy level walking distance to Sainsbury's once she moved into the Taunton bungalow. And that'd do her . . .

'Talking to yourself?' said a voice nearby.

She jumped, looked up and then smiled. 'I am,' she said positively. 'And who better to talk to?'

Sammy held out his hand to pull her up the last of the slope. Though white-haired and stooped, he could summon a surprising strength.

'Still got a bit of the old muscle left, then?' she said, taking his outstretched hand, and she went a little pink.

'You should know,' he said, and winked.

The smell of pigs was at its strongest up here, though by no means unbearable. She took a deep breath. 'Sweet,' she said, 'almost.'

He did not let go but pulled her to him and steadied her.

'Hands off now, Sammy,' she said, suddenly sharp. 'That was a long time ago.'

He laughed, showing several gaps in his teeth, and knocked his cap back further off his head. 'Best of the bunch,' he said.

She moved back from him and stared at his face. 'I wish you'd wear your plate,' she said. 'You look much better with it in.'

'If I'd known you were coming I'd have worn my plate,' he half sang.

'Stop that,' she said, but she was laughing.

'Oh, I can't be doing with it,' he said. 'It stops me whistling.'

They stood in silence for a while. The sun seemed to grow hotter. It glinted more fiercely along the metal ridges of the pens.

'You could fry an egg off those,' she said disapprovingly.

'They'll cool off by tonight.'

'Used to be wood and straw.'

'Easier to clean, these. And you can move them around.'

'Individual apartments, all mod cons.' She laughed 'They look like little air-raid shelters,' she said.

Sammy squeezed her bottom. 'Wouldn't fit in one of those now, would we?' he said, not expecting an answer. 'Better before all this scientific stuff when a sty was a decent size. When a fellow could lie himself out full-length *and* fit a woman on top of him . . .' He pushed closer to her, squeezing her a little harder.

'Sammy,' she said, mildly warning.

'Gwen,' he said. He did not remove his hand. 'Remember the sow's name?' he said, looking at her wickedly.

'I do,' said Mrs Perry. 'It was Renata, after that actress –'

'Singer,' said Sammy.

'Oh yes,' she said.

'Oh yes,' he said softly too. His hand crept under her skirt and stroked the top of her thigh.

'Sammy,' she said warningly, but he did not take it away. Very gently she guided his hand back from under her skirt. They were silent again.

'Anyway,' he said thoughtfully, 'pigs is in the past.' He ran his stick gently over and along the back of an oblivious creature as it snuffled in the earth. 'Weather, wars and the gentlemen of the party couldn't do it, but they've wiped us out with their rules.'

'Never liked rules, you,' she said.

'Common sense,' he said, 'dressed up for a party. That's rules.'

'Not all of them,' she said.

'They're welcome to the lot of it. Polishing their Land Rovers . . .' He spat. Then he smiled. 'Nice to break a few, though,' he said. He squeezed her again.

The Labrador sniffed around and then settled down on all fours to watch and wait for any pig that might come wandering by, but they were far over the other side of the hill where it was cooler. Even the rabbits seemed asleep.

Eventually Sammy said, 'So, you're definitely off to town, then. I shall miss you.'

'It isn't bloody Timbuktu,' she snapped. And then apologized. 'Sorry, but I've got something irritating on my mind.' She turned and twisted her body away from him. 'Do you mind leaving my bum alone?'

'I do,' he said.

She laughed and took his hand, then put it back again as if, after all, it was a comfort.

'The thing is, someone came to see the house today and wanted it and I had a feeling that I wanted her to have it. You know how you get?'

He laughed. 'Well, I know how *you* get. But in the pub last night Archie was doing drinks all round and said it was sold.'

She made an irritated noise, said 'Archie' impatiently, and walked a little further across the grass slope. She stamped her foot and slapped at her thigh. 'It is sold. Or damn nearly,' she said. 'And we agreed there'd be no funny business. First come, first served. And I'm one for keeping promises.' She looked at him fondly. 'As you know.'

He spat out a piece of the grass he was chewing by way of comment.

'Do unto others,' she said. 'It's the best way.'

'Not nowadays,' he said defiantly. 'No one keeps a bargain if they can do better. Promises get broken all the time. Houses, government quotas, marriage vows . . .' He spat more vigorously.

'Come on, Sam,' she said quietly. 'That's enough.'

She stared down at the road. The car had stopped again. She shook her head in annoyance and threw a twig for the dog, who went running and scudding down the hillside after it. She sighed, watching the dog's tail bob and weave. 'I don't suppose for one minute that estate agent will back off,' she said.

'Can't blame him for that,' said Sammy.

'I don't,' she said. 'All the same, I don't like her to be disappointed.' She turned to him and gave him a questioning smile. 'I know one thing that might change his mind. And it's harmless.' She whispered into his hairy ear.

He listened, then smiled. 'You always were a devil,' he said. 'On the quiet.'

'So are most of us.' She nodded at the road. 'Which she'll discover if she gets down here . . .'

The dog trotted back and sniffed forlornly. They ignored him.

'What's it worth if I do?' he said, pushing even closer.

She pulled away and patted his arm. 'Your seat in heaven, Samuel Lee. Maybe.' She looked at him hard. Touched his face where the cheeks were sunken. 'Who'd have thought it?'

she said. And for a moment her eyes looked at something that was long ago. She touched his cheeks again. 'I do wish you'd put your plate in.'

He said. 'Fat lot of good a seat in heaven is.'

She laughed. 'Where's the harm? Will you do it?'

He winked. 'Old times' sake, is it? When?'

'Soon,' she said, and she whistled the dog. 'Tomorrow.'

'Archie'll complain.'

'Let him,' she said, looking back at Sammy, her face suddenly hard. 'He never complained about anything else.' And she stomped back down towards the house.

Angela Fytton looked at the shiny holly leaf, stolen from the hedge of Church Ale House, now winking, deep green, in the palm of her hand. Like the woman in *Our Mutual Friend*, she could wear it sewn into her petticoats as a permanent mortification, if it would do her any good, bring her any nearer to her goal. And if she wore petticoats.

I shall do what I can to spread good in the world in future, she said that night into her pillow, beneath which rested the holly leaf. And if you let me have Church Ale House I'll live the rest of my life with honour in the cause of good. Sadly, she felt completely safe with this great promise. The Perry woman was clearly beyond corruption. So she could lie here in her London bed and be as pious as she chose. She would never have to live up to her promise.

Her son had put the woofer back into his hi-fi. She lay there wondering whether to get up and remove it – yet again – but she just could not be bothered. Somewhere else in the house she heard Claire on the telephone. It was two in the morning. Ah well . . .

Archie sat up in bed and nudged his wife. 'Did you hear anything?' he said.

'Like what?' she asked innocently.

'Like banging?'

'It'll be those Travellers,' she said. 'They'll be fixing their vans.'

'At midnight?'

'It's a bright moon,' she said.

Archie decided not to go into it any further. 'Did the solicitor send the stuff?' he said.

'What stuff?'

'Should have been here today.'

'I know.' She smiled contentedly to herself and settled back down to sleep. Beneath her pillow an envelope crackled.

Out in the moonlight Sammy Lee pushed another piece of wood into place and stood back to admire the structure. Get six in there easily when he'd finished. Just for a week or two his pigs would have to squash up a little and not take so many baths. He set to with the hammer again, whistling under his breath and thinking that one good thing about being on your own and growing old was that if there was no one to go a-wooing, you no longer had to put your false teeth in all the time. And if that was all he could come up with, he decided, it was a very sad day. He made the covered part of the sty secure and waterproof. Just in case.

8

May

The trouble with the rat race is that even
if you win, you're still a rat.

LILY TOMLIN

Alan Bushman, of Pinnocks estate agency, winked at his soon-to-be-wife Camilla. She tossed her mane of blonde hair in response. Like a fine young filly, he thought, pleased. Somehow, he had always known that a Camilla completed the picture, squared the circle, iced the cake. Girls called Camilla were bred not born, and that she, O joy, out of all the suitable young men in her milieu, should choose him was a piece of fortune in which he daily rejoiced. His transmogrification was almost complete. Once the bond was tied with the well-connected Camilla, he would be serving Château Margaux and sausages along with the rest of them. The moment she said, 'I do,' these people would be his sort too. He could see it now, the pearly white paper, the engraved lettering, Mr and Mrs Alan Bushman, Church Ale House, Overstaithe, Somerset. He sighed. Mission accomplished.

Where to live had been a tricky one. His deceased father, so Bushman junior maintained in a wonderful fabrication, had lost his shirt, in the shape of the family home in Berkshire, to gambling and fast women. So no shame there, then. He almost believed it. But it did leave the tricky matter of the marital home. He could hardly move Camilla into a semi in Taunton. It had to be the country. And it had to be convincingly *potential*. And it had to be cheap. She was, after all, the bearer of a few drops of Devereux blood – the last – and though considered a little weak in the head, she would require decent stabling. Then Church Ale House came on the market and there was the answer.

Of course, it had disadvantages. It needed extending, but he had the right contacts to smooth the path for that. And there was no land to speak of – maybe an acre and a half in all – but the Perrys would probably let him buy the adjoining field eventually. That would give them what could very properly be described as the paddock. For the ponies. When the children came along. And a pool room for him in the outbuildings. He would call it Camilla's project, the house. And she would spend her dowry on it. Or her father would.

Today, for the first time, he would show his intended her future home. The big surprise. She loved surprises. Practically whinnied over them. He had won, he had won. He had crossed the social divide and he would never look back. In six weeks' time she would say, 'I do.' As an estate agent, he knew the pitfalls of counting your chickens, but now, contracts almost exchanged, he could hold her back no more.

'Darling, it is time that you saw our future home.'

She practically galloped across the room to hug him when he told her.

'Oh, yummy,' she said. '*Yummy* . . .'

'Yes,' he said. 'It will be a project for you. A great big project, darling.'

'A project,' she repeated, tossing her head again and again to show her pleasure.

She might have added 'At last.' After school her parents, a little at a loss, sent their daughter on a design and deportment course in Kensington. One, as she proudly pointed out, that *included* flower-arranging. She had never actually used the skills learned, but he could now honourably persuade her to make Church Ale House her very first commission. Somerset was particularly cool about planning permission. She could bash it about to her heart's content in the name of interior design – thereby drawing a veil over the fact that he could not possibly afford the otherwise required alternative, which was to employ a real one.

Now, here they were, rounding the bend of the Mump Road, on this glorious late spring day, and Camilla had her hands over her eyes as per instructions.

'Don't open them yet,' he said, pulling in by the old holly hedge at the roadside. He would install an electric gate.

He switched off the engine. And he sniffed. And then Camilla sniffed. And then Camilla, still with her hands over her eyes, said, 'I smell piggies,' rather anxiously. 'Do you?'

And Alan Bushman, though betrothed to her, very nearly said something extremely curt in reply, since to *not* smell piggies, given the density of the piggy smell, would have required removal of the entire nasal area.

He sniffed even harder and got out of the car. He very nearly gagged, the air was so rich with the scent of continual porcine dumping. He went up to the gate, sniffing like a bloodhound. The smell was stronger somewhere to the left of the house. He walked along the side of the hedge, still with his nose in the air. And when the holly hedge ended and the field began, he saw whence the rich, disgusting smell came. There was a sty full of the creatures and they seemed to have taken a leaf out of the Entala warriors' bible – to wit, covering yourself in excrement wards off evil spirits. He stared. One or two of them stared back, equally impolitely. But since he carried nothing in the way of a bucket or stick for either of those twin delights of feeding or ear-scratching, they soon lost interest and resumed rooting.

It would have been quite difficult for any passing phoneticist to distinguish between the grunting emanating from the piggery and that emanating from the viewer of the piggery. Both had an inhuman quality. Though to be sure, the grunts of the former held a quality of contentment quite absent from the noises made by the latter.

Still grunting, Alan Bushman gripped the old five-barred gate and stared into the field. The sty had the look of age about it. Yet he knew very well that when he last viewed the property, no such sty existed. He looked about him. Not a human soul in view. He returned to the gate leading to the front door of Church Ale House. Passing his car he saw Camilla, still sitting with her hands over her eyes. Irritation rose. 'You can open them now,' he said, less kindly than usual.

She crept out, looking about her fearfully.

'Darling,' he said, 'your future home awaits.'

'But the *smell*,' she said. And she appeared to gag.

'Temporary.' He waved his hand confidently. And opened the gate. And strode up the path. And banged very, very hard on the front door.

Which was opened, eventually, by the owner's wife. Who informed him that her husband was *not* there. That she owned just as much of the house as *he* did. And that people could do what they liked with their own property until the ink was dry, she supposed. And so saying, the three of them made their slow way around the house.

Every window was open. Every door was ajar.

On remonstration, the owner's wife said, 'What smell?' And then, 'Oh, you get used to it.' If she had told them that these pigs not only had wings but took passengers, they could not have been more sceptical.

'Sammy Lee's pigs are champions,' said Mrs Perry innocently. 'It is very traditional. He's been using that field for hundreds of years.'

Even Camilla, reckoned to be a couple of gemstones short of a tiara, blinked at this.

Mrs Perry realized that she had become a little carried away. 'His family, that is.'

Camilla's eyes were large and wet above the scarf. You have let me down, was what Alan Bushman read there.

'Mrs Perry,' he said, 'could we cut across the red tape? My fiancée and I would like to purchase the field, along with this lovely old house, and I can offer you . . .' He named a tidy sum. 'Without the field, I'm afraid the deal's off.'

Mrs Perry smiled at him with complete understanding. 'Don't you worry. I'll have a word with him,' she said. 'Now, how about a little nip of my mulberry wine and a ginger snap?'

But the couple declined. Indeed Camilla, keeping the scarf pressed to her nose, declined very forcefully, pressing her free hand into her stomach area and making a little gulping noise.

Mrs Perry gave her a kindly smile. 'Ah,' she said, 'expecting, are you?'

Camilla shook her head violently and, for want of any better way to communicate, crossed her eyes.

'We are not yet married,' said Alan Bushman, with dignity.

From behind the silk and Givenchy came a guttural yawp that indicated that there might be something up with his use of the term.

Yet . . .

In the car Alan Bushman closed all the windows and put on his best cheerful voice, the one he had discovered he owned many years ago when, on showing a client around a spanking new barn conversion and closing the front door a little briskly, the entire lintel, arch and lodestone had fallen in on the potential purchaser. To which his quicksilver response was, 'What luck. I'm sure they'll lower the price substantially after that.' To which the client's quicksilver response was entirely unrepeatable.

Now to his wife-to-be, much as one might inquire of Jackie Kennedy if, despite all that, she thought Dallas a pleasant town, Alan Bushman said, 'Darling Camilla, isn't it the best house in the world?'

And she, whinnying through her scarf, with a depth of voice he had not known she possessed, just said, 'Drive . . .'

Archie Perry received a letter from A. Bushman. Archie Perry wrote a letter in reply. You might give up the house, he thought, but you never gave up all the land. Not if you can possibly help it.

He then walked down to the letter box by the side of the road and, coming back, rested himself on the five-barred gate, gazing at the pigs. Sam was losing his grip too, then? He had never let his pigs get in such a mess before. Perhaps that old eye of his was roving again, even now. His father had said it to him, and his father before: Never trust a pigman. Should have listened. But she'd be safe with him in the bungalow. At last.

Of Alan Bushman and the lovely Camilla they heard no more. And neither, quite rightly, shall we.

9

June

Angela sat between two highly articulate furniture removal men as the van rumbled its way down the motorway. Having exhausted the subject of castration for paedophiles and the usefulness of bombing the Chinese in the matter of regaining Hong Kong, they fell to more domestic subjects.

'So,' said one, 'moving, are you?'

Angela felt the usual female helplessness in the face of such a question. She longed to say, 'No, just fancied a day out in a furniture van.' But instead she said, 'Yes,' and stared fixedly down the road to the west. When you needed the muscle of men, it was no time to start playing around with wit. You bet, she thought, that out there on the savannah, 15,000 years ago, no woman in her right mind would have made anything but humble obeisance until she'd taken delivery of her dripping lump of meat. It was, she supposed, the same oil driving the masculine engine that takes a wench out for dinner, fills and refills her glass, and then nods sagely at her confident pronouncements on the benefits of shooting all cripples on sight until he's successfully got his leg over. She had let the paedophiles and the Chinese go without a murmur. Why object to anything else? So Angela Fytton merely stared on, smiling and silent.

'Wouldn't get me moving down there,' said one.

'Nor me,' said the other.

'Country people are nicer than town people,' she began.

The driver looked at her peevishly.

If she wanted her furniture delivered without incident, she thought, she must stay humble. 'It's such a lovely day,' she added lamely.

'Very backward they are, in the country,' said the young one.

She closed her eyes and pretended to doze. About her mouth played a little smile of reverie. One might even construe it as *smug*. When in doubt, drift off into a pleasing memory. So she did.

She was smiling and remembering the dinner at which she announced her impending move to Church Ale House to her ex-husband and her children. These latter, bang on developmental target, were currently the wholly self-centred fruits of her womb. She chose the Depot, on the river at Mortlake, useful if it all got too hot and she needed to throw herself in; close enough to home if she was made to walk back. A distinct possibility. For they assembled like three innocent little carefree skittles ready to be bowled over.

Once seated, the first thing Ian said was, 'You've put on weight.' The second thing he said was, 'It suits you.' The thrust of which latter did not ease the delivery of the former. She was riled. But she let them be served. She let those happy skittles chat for a while and eat their first course in peace.

Only when they were halfway through their *confit de canard* did she begin.

'I am moving to the country. To Somerset.'

Ian looked unimpressed. Nothing would come of it. Like her notion to go and live on a Greek island, or to move to Venice and write a biography of Tintoretto's wife.

('His *wife*?'

'His wife.'

'But why?

'Why not?'

'Because it's the *painter* they'll be interested in!'

'If Virginia Woolf can write about Elizabeth Browning's *dog . . .*')

Of course she never did. His ex-wife was a brilliant pragmatist, not a cultural radical.

He smiled placidly. Dear Angela, what a good wife she had been. He had tried to be as generous as possible in the settlement because he respected how much he owed her. He could not help falling in love elsewhere. And that was, really, that. But he was still fond of her, very fond of her, and she was still the mother of these. He looked at the two great teenagers fondly. They were going to be terrific, terrific. And he got on with them really well. He was looking forward to having more children. Only this weekend, in one of the supplements, he read that he was genetically programmed to do so. And with a younger mate. It was biology. So it was odds on, really, that if Angie didn't want any more he might look elsewhere. Not that it had been conscious at all, but it did help to know that it was in his genes and older than time. It wasn't his fault he couldn't have children himself. He rather envied women. Women really were wonderful. He had always thought so. But it was, still, a man's world. He'd employed enough women and then lost them to their pregnancies to know that. If you wanted continuity in the marketplace, get a man. Once he might have denied this; a few years into his own business and it had dawned. Not everyone was as able as his ex-wife. What a juggler she had been. Frighteningly good at everything. Frighteningly. The new one was very fluffy in comparison. Dear Angela.

Angela returned the smile. 'I really thought I had lost it,' she said. 'And then – well, it was a miracle. I went down a second time and – hallelujah – it was mine . . .'

With, she must confess, a little drop taken, she began telling them all about Church Ale House. It was more than a little drop, she now realized, because she kept referring to her purchase as 'O Lustworthy Place' and squinting suggestively at her ex-husband as if it were a brothel. Smiling placidity gave way to arousal. Ian looked – quite satisfyingly – alarmed.

Good, she thought. *Good . . .*

She watched the waiter clearing away the plates as she told them about that second visit. The drive down had been so mournful, and the day so full of drizzle and grey, that she arrived feeling damp and cold and miserable. The owner opened the door with a smile like the sun and told her that her lovely home, O Lustworthy Place, was back on the market. It was hers if she still wanted it.

'The Gods take care of the good,' she said, fixing Ian with a look.

He continued to watch the waiter.

'Well, I just threw my arms around Mrs Perry's neck and hugged her so tight that she staggered back into the wellingtons and old newspapers and assorted livestock and nearly fell over them.'

She waited for them to laugh. Nobody did.

'Well, quite frankly, I could have kissed her to death,' said Angela. 'Because she gave me back some happiness.'

The waiter having withdrawn, Ian immediately began studying the menu. The children looked embarrassed. Happiness is a strong word on a parent's lips.

'Ian?' she said. 'What do you think?'

He looked very directly back at her, eyes suspiciously reflecting nothing in the candlelight, refusing to respond, saying instead, and perhaps more belligerently than he meant, 'Well, what was wrong with it then, that the others pulled out?'

Mrs Fytton of Church Ale House would conduct herself as genteely as a daisy.

'Well?' he said. 'What?'

'The pigs,' said Angela, 'I believe.'

That told them.

Her family had never been ones for singing *en troupe*, so it was a miracle of pitch and unity when they all managed to chorus '*The pigs?*' together.

She very nearly broke into song herself with a bit of Gilbertian stichomythia:

'The pigs?
Yes, the pigs.
Not the pigs?
Yes, my pigs.
How can you say you own such things when you have
never owned such things?
They're my pigs, they're my pigs, they're my PIGS!'

Instead she sat there smiling. The Mona Lisa with a ring of
confidence.

Ian said, 'Pigs, Angie?'

'Oh, not *my* pigs,' she said. 'I've only got bees and hens and
eels on their way to Sargasso.'

'Pigs, Mum?' Claire was trying to be calm.

She looked at her son. 'Pigs, Andrew,' she said, just so he
would not feel left out.

She thought he looked slightly amused. But perhaps it was
only a constriction of the lower intestine. He had been like
that as a baby – you never knew if he was pleased to see you
or had wind. She smiled at him anyway. His face froze again.
Why did her children not know how to even *smile* at her?

'Yes,' she said firmly, 'pigs. Apparently the previous prospec-
tive owners couldn't stand the smell. Which is quite ridiculous,
because the dear little things are on the top of a hill far enough
away and there is only just the very faintest tang on the air. So,
thanks to the porkers, it's mine. Anyway, I think it was all meant.
The owner was probably a white witch. You know, ancient
forces drawing me back to my roots and all that . . .'

Ian snorted. 'You were born in Reigate.'

She looked at him superiorly, aware there was a halo
around him of some sort. Afterwards she realized this was
because she had drunk so much, but at the time she took it as
an omen. 'Not that sort of roots,' she said. 'I mean experience
and identity.'

Her daughter looked at her blankly. Andrew was staring
straight ahead at a very bad painting on the wall. She

thought, Oh, how the longest revolution has failed, remembering her own politicization at that age. Why, when she was first pregnant she had to be sent home from a sit-in because her advanced condition made it just too uncomfortable to sleep on bare floors. Ian had been very supportive over that, taking the remaining women blankets and wine and coffee, shouldering his way past the sneering police. Where did all that go?

To the marketplace, she supposed. Come to that, where did all those women in blankets go? Not to the marketplace? Clinging on to the cliff face of life by their fingertips while the next generation of little blonde plastic persons in power miniskirts hit at their knuckles with a hammer and pinched their husbands *from* the bloody marketplace, she supposed.

Ah, ah. Well, well. Life was like childbirth. If you told women how hard and painful it was really going to be they would never attempt it. So far, for her success in life, she had been served with a pair of children who could scarcely shit unless she both reminded them and paid them to do it (her own fault), and a husband who'd run after a little bit of skirt (whose fault – testosterone's?). Love–forty.

She looked at her family. Somerset, she went on to tell them, is representative of anywhere rural really. Could be Yorkshire, could be Derbyshire, could be Norfolk. Somerset, she went on to tell them, is full of honest, caring folk, real and vibrant nature, past and present history. She was getting back in touch with a time when women had a place very firmly marked out for them – in brewing, in preserving, in dairy-making, in hens and goats and – yes – *pigs*. And they didn't have to bloody do EVERYTHING and still look like a supermodel

'Back to my roots,' she reiterated. She saw Claire's puzzled eyes staring at her hair. 'Not those roots,' she said, exasperated.

'Well,' said Claire, 'they are showing through a bit.'

'*The roots of life*. Those honourable, ancient ways.' She looked at her ex-husband in triumph.

He looked back at her. 'Not having a washing machine, then?' he asked.

Andrew smirked. So did Claire. Angela did not respond. Instead she broke into Goldsmith:

'O luxury! thou curs'd by Heaven's decree,
How ill exchang'd are things like these for thee!'

'Have some water,' said Ian, quite affectionately.

It was at that point she realized she must be careful. If she said such things they would put her in a home and freeze her assets. So she just smiled sweetly and said that she hoped her children would continue to call her home theirs. But in Somerset. Non negotiable. A *fait accompli*.

Ian, pouring her water, said, very quietly, 'And whatever happened to Women's Liberation – all your ideas of equality? *The Times*'s top 100 companies without a woman chairperson among them,' he mimicked.

She was stung. 'Whatever happened to yours?'

'Oh, *purleez*,' said Claire.

So Angela contented herself with saying, 'Women's rights have done well enough. Not brilliantly, but well enough. You can legislate for those. But Women's *Liberation* comes from within. This will be liberation. Free to do whatever I like within the annals of time without feeling guilty.' She slumped a bit then. Knocking out a sentence as complicated as that took a huge effort in your cups. She wasn't entirely sure it contained a subject and predicate. She regrouped. 'Anyway, we've been let down, we mothers with children –'

'Mothers usually do have children,' said Ian, half amused again. 'It's one of the qualifications.'

'Oh, ha ha,' she said. 'Anyway – it has let us down.'

She raised her glass to the unsmiling stare of Andrew, the rolling eyes of Claire, leaned back luxuriously and sighed. 'And I am also a dumped wife. And you have got away with it, Ian Fytton. New home, new wife, new baby . . .'

He had the grace to look uncomfortable, which was something, she supposed. Personally she didn't feel uncomfortable, she felt heartbroken and enraged.

'In olden times if a *woman* willingly committed adultery she was put down a well with a large stone around her neck. Or tied to the whipping post at the edge of the town for any passing sadist to chastise. If a *man* committed adultery he was told off – but he couldn't help it because women were lustful creatures. You know, the vampire-vagina, the devil's gateway. *Plus ça* bloody *change* . . . If the woman with whom he committed adultery was not willing – that's to say, if he *raped* her –'

This was too much for Andrew, who stood up. 'I'm going to the toilet,' he said.

'Lavatory, dearest,' she said automatically. 'If he *raped* her, she had to pay a fine to her feudal lord for her loss of value . . .'

'And?' said Ian.

She filled her glass very slowly, almost drop by drop. 'Not a lot has changed.'

'You're not down a well or tied to a whipping post.'

Her eyes were brilliant, she knew, because she could feel them moistening. 'No?' she said, far, far too bitterly. '*No?*'

'Go on about the house, Mum,' said Claire eventually.

Andrew returned and sat down. He looked very pale. She longed to put her arm round him and say it would be all right. But she couldn't promise that. This was not a grazed knee. It was a decision she had taken entirely for herself, about herself. It was in a way – a rejection. Her son shrugged at her smile. There was about his mouth that same line of disapproving resistance that lay around Ian's. Very possibly its source was the phrase 'bloody women'. Well, he must learn to paddle his own canoe. He was nineteen, for God's sake.

She smiled at Claire instead. Who glowered. One day, my little bird, she thought, one day you will know.

'Now, shall I go on?'

The skittles nodded, suitably receptive to information.

'I arranged this dinner in your honour, mostly,' she said to her ex-husband. 'Because this move of mine will affect you

113

quite a lot.' She said this composedly. Really she wanted to run wildly round the restaurant like a goal-scoring striker, hugging everyone in sight.

He looked at her, puzzled.

Firmly retaining the image of herself down a well with a stone round her throat and him above, looking down, smiling, while fondling a toothsome maid, she made it *very* clear. It would affect him because, despite his having remarried and become a new father, he was also father to these two children sitting here. They should have been suspicious at her use of the term *children*, since most of the time nowadays she pleaded with them to grow up. But they were not. This was still fantasy land; still Tintoretto's wife and it will come to nothing.

We'll see about that, she thought. And so saying, looking at the three skittles, she took a deep breath and prepared to roll that ball. But the skittles refused to play. At the mention of new fatherhood Ian suddenly perked up, Church Ale House forgotten. He took from his pocket an envelope of photographs, which he dealt out to Claire and Andrew amid squeals and gruffs of delight. Instead of launching into her moment of glory, Mrs Fytton, genteel daisy, sat through long delighted descriptions of baby Tristan (*Tristan!*). She sat through long delighted reminiscences of Australia and the wedding and how Binnie –

'Who's Binnie?'

'Belinda.' Ian's wife.

'Ah,' she said. 'I did not know you called her that.'

Smile, sip, smile, sip.

'Sounds like a plastic rubbish sack.'

In future, she decided, she would think of the woman as a bin-bag. Or a victim of her own gender, she added vaguely.

'I want a wedding like that.' Claire was acting as she once did when stroking someone else's Barbie-at-the-Ball gown.

Binnie, apparently, though already pregnant, looked so great, made everyone laugh, danced the night away ...

Whatever happened to children loathing their stepmothers?

'I used to have a twenty-five-inch waist,' said Angela to thin air. 'Once. Until very recently actually.'

'I can't get into her clothes,' said Angela's wonderfully soft and rounded daughter.

It was. It was sodding Barbie. Only this time her wondrously soft and rounded daughter did not so much want to own the doll as be it.

'Yes, yes,' said Angela, whose resentment grew at each new Binnie attribute because she was paying for the meal and because it was supposed to be her evening and because no amount of agony aunt consolations along the lines of 'Try to be glad if your old partner remarries someone your children admire because it helps them' made her feel any better about La Bin-bag and the cherubic Tristan. If she wasn't still sucking up to God following God's major reversal of her fortunes concerning Church Ale House, she might even have wished a six o'clock colic on the babe. That'd sort *all* of them out.

'Yes, yes,' she interrupted. 'But what about pudding, folks?'

'Remember when we went surfing at dawn and Binnie managed to –'

'LEMON CHEESECAKE sounds good,' said Angela.

Andrew, no longer pale and no longer in need of the bad painting, said, 'The surfing was really great. Can we go back there, Dad. Can we?'

He sounded, this son of hers, as if he was ten. She felt disgusted and had another glass of wine.

'Or ZABAGLIONE,' she shouted, not managing the word at all well.

They ordered.

'Tristan's cutting his teeth in a very interesting way,' said Ian, with total seriousness.

Angela waited for Claire to say, 'Euchh! Dad, *PUR-LEEZ*,' but instead, meretricious fruit of her womb, she said 'Really?' and leaned closer to hear.

Even Andrew affected to look interested, though Angela-the-mother knew his mind was still somewhere in the surf of Bondi Beach.

'Aah,' murmured Claire sweetly, which went through Angela like a knife. 'Aah – how many has he got now, then?'

Ian said, 'Two,' as if it were a double-first from Cambridge.

No one was paying any attention to her. She tested this by saying, 'You both had a full set by the time you were two weeks old.'

Neither of her two little Judases noticed, and the father of Tristan carried on. Apparently the Bin-bag, who was a dentist, thought she could write a paper on the subject.

Angela felt oddly unliberated towards her. 'She'll be lucky,' she said with tremendous satisfaction, 'if she has time to pick up a pen.'

At which all three of the skittles gave her quite a look.

'Oh, Mum,' said Claire. 'You're so *critical*.'

Critical? she wanted to say. *Critical?* This woman stole my husband and behaved in all kinds of devious ways and you call me *critical*? There, it was out, free at last in her mind, and fuck the sisterhood. 'This thing is bigger than both of us,' the small blonde plastic woman trading under the name of a rubbish sack had had the nerve to tell her. To which Angela had responded shrilly, 'So – we're not talking about my husband's cock, then?' before showing her the door.

'It's not being critical,' she said, as mildly as possible. 'I know what it's like to try to get anything done with a little baby. That's *all* I meant . . .'

She said no more. Gather ye rosebuds, my children, she thought, sitting back and eyeing them as they rattled away to their father. For soon it will be as ashes in your mouth. A little muddled, she agreed, but her bruised and failing ego felt considerably repaired.

Ian said, very nicely, 'Your mother was very, very good at it all. I'm actually having to be hands-on with this baby. Not like with you.'

Somehow it sounded like a failing on her part.

'Ah,' said Angela, 'did you miss all the mess, then, darling?' And she picked up Andrew's spoon, dipped it into the zabaglione and gave it to Ian. 'You can catch up now if you like.' And she laughed. It did, indeed, seem a comical idea.

'Mum,' hissed Andrew. 'Be quiet.' His expression distinctly said he wished his mother was on the moon.

Be quiet, the boy says. Unable to think beyond his perfidy, she said, 'Andrew, don't speak to me like that.'

She fixed him with her gimlet eye. He fixed her back with his. This was perfidy indeed. 'I'll have you know, my son,' she said loudly, stabbing at the table top, 'I used to wipe your bottom.'

All three pairs of eyes were fixed on her. As indeed were several pairs of eyes from the neighbouring tables. And the waiter's.

In the eighteenth century, she thought, you really would go in fear of Bedlam if your family looked at you like that.

'Oh, Mum,' said Claire, in a voice that put her in imminent danger of being smacked. 'Oh, *Mum* . . .' And she slid Angela's glass away.

Angela promptly slid it back again. That is quite enough of Bondi weddings, the wonders of milk teeth and Belinda Warren's Profession, she decided. No more delays. She rolled that ball.

'So, I'm moving to Somerset,' she said.

Ian nodded, dipping into his zabaglione. 'You said. When?'

'Three weeks' time.'

'WHAT?'

A strike. A veritable strike. All three stilled their spoons. If she was inclined to smirk it was, she told herself, only fair.

'Well, three and a *half* weeks to be exact.'

'And where are *we* going to go?' asked Claire, all forlorn.

Andrew was staring at his mother as if she *was* the bad painting now. Ian's eyes were fixed, glazed, spoon half to his lips, the zabaglione dripping from it in plops like yellow tears.

'It's got four bedrooms,' she said. 'Five if you count the sewing room. You'd like the sewing room...'

'Sewing room?' Claire's eyes went very round.

'But only one bathroom.' This she directed at her daughter. 'One.'

'How long have you known about this?' asked Ian.

'About six weeks,' she said. 'You can speed things up beautifully if you have a good solicitor. I didn't want to worry Claire and Andrew while they were preparing for their A levels.' She did not add, 'Or in Andrew's case *re*-preparing for them...' Perfect cover story. Why, she could have been a spy.

They continued to stare, mouths open, exactly like figures in a very depressed Aunt Sally.

'Francis Street sold very quickly. As they do. Didn't even need to put up a board.' She smiled, humouring. But they were not to be humoured. She eyed her daughter and her son with the faintest touch of malevolence. That'll teach you to pay absolutely no attention to anything going on around you, she thought. 'You always said you hated living there...' She shrugged. They could not stop her, no matter how they tried.

'You cannot do this,' said Andrew.

'Oh, come on,' she said. 'It isn't as if I've murdered anyone.'

They continued to stare at her. Murder, it seemed, would be more acceptable.

'But it's our gap year, I don't want to be in Somerset,' said Claire.

'Nor do I,' said Andrew.

'But I do,' said Angela.

'I want to be in London,' said Claire.

'So do I,' said Andrew.

'But I do not,' said Angela. 'In Somerset I shall be a good person and a busy person, and I shall be good to others and back to my roots...'

'Oh, you and your roots,' said Ian, which he really shouldn't have. If ever a man flapped a red rag at an enraged bull cunningly disguised as his ex-wife, it was him.

'*And* manage my own small patch. Women have always been allowed to do *that*, at least. Even the aristocratic lady of the manor, who was supposed to lie around like a lily in her chastity belt, was allowed to dispense alms and grant favours. Of course, I could take the veil, but I think I prefer just moving to the West Country in order to facilitate this. I can't do it in London because everyone is entirely horrible, and half an acre and a cow would cost the earth.'

A flash of the old Ian again, amused despite himself. 'Isn't it seven acres and a cow?' he asked, quite fondly. 'I think they've worked out that you need at least that in order to sustain life.'

'Well, there you are – imagine trying to get that lot in Holland Park . . .'

'Yes,' he said, almost – *almost* – laughing. 'I see your point.'

She knew he wanted to say that she was plastered. But he was also amused – and shrewd – and controlled himself. He had finally realized that he was not dealing with the rational and he put his red rag away. If he had so much as tried again with 'What about a little water, dear?' she would probably have upended the bottle over him. She loved him for that judgement. She nearly reached out and wiped a little speck of yellow from his chin and *told* him she loved him for that. But she let him speak. One day she would tell him that she still loved everything about him. Including dribbling.

'You're being a little on the selfish side, Angie,' he said, calm but gritting his teeth. 'Surely you could wait a while?'

'Nope,' she said. 'And don't call me Angie.'

She raised her glass to him in an unmistakable gesture of defiance. Her version of the Hemingway spit. 'I'm going, Ian,' she said. 'And no one will stop me.'

The penny, it seemed, suddenly dropped. Ian finally understood the full implications of her actions. She was going to Somerset. From the look of his son's stony eyes and his daughter's Bouchette at Hanging Rock, his children were not. The penny that had dropped was the one regarding his being *their* father as well as father to the advancedly befanged Tristan.

And being their father meant that he still had responsibilities in that department, were they to find themselves homeless in London, so to speak. He had the exquisitely alert sensitivity of a drowning man. He knew. She leaned towards him and said, 'Now do you see why it will affect you so much?'

'No,' he said firmly. 'I do not.'

The children were staring at her.

Her ex-husband was staring at her.

And it was at this precise and precious moment that she knew she would break him. And once broken, she would have him back. To mend him again.

'You cannot,' he said.

'But I have.'

She knew her children would not follow. And you, my wandering husband, she thought, are in for a terrible shock. Claire and Andrew, your children, are teenagers. And they are completely horrible at the moment. Worse, they are completely horrible without knowing they are horrible. There is nothing malevolent in their behaviour. They are – just for the time being – a complete walking disaster area. And they have nothing else to do for the next year and a bit but lie around watching television. Watch this space: Binnie, the multi-molared Tristan and those twin guns of gross insensitivity, our children, with you somewhere in between. All under the same roof. And not mine.

'Well,' said Angela, 'if you two don't want to come with me to Somerset, you'll have to find somewhere else to stay in London. After all, your exams are over. I'm sure you've done really well, so it's only for a year or so. Then you'll be off to university.'

'You could go this year instead,' said Ian to them, clutching at the proverbial straw.

'*Dad*,' they both said, 'we're on our gap year.'

Angela sipped from her glass daintily and licked her lips. 'Now,' she said, 'who do you know with a large enough house in London to put you up?'

The Aunt Sally eyes, or two pairs of them, swivelled in Ian's direction.

'Just wait a minute,' he said.

'Ian,' said Angela, with a wonderful smile and a raise of her glass, 'you and *Binnie* have such a lovely big house. All that garden . . .'

'But, Mum,' said her two offspring, once more in unison, 'it's in *Wimbledon* . . .'

'Well, that's London, isn't it?'

If Claire's lip came out any further it would throw a shadow. 'Hardly,' she said, and kicked at the table leg as she used to do in her infancy.

'Claire,' said Angela warningly, 'don't kick. And anyway, as you keep telling me – all of you – she, *Binnie*, likes you both so much . . . And you her. And then there is child of the tooth fairy, Tristan. It seems an ideal solution. I'll miss you, of course.'

Ian finally replaced his spoon. Angela sensed an imminent explosion and rushed on. 'So let me know as soon as possible and I can let the removal firm know about your things. I'm very happy to take them with me. Very. If you want to come. And you'll just love the house – I know you will. It's miles and miles from anywhere, but there's a church and a vicar who plays the guitar and some lovely country walks. Now, when will you come down and see it?'

'But it's *Somerset*,' they both chorused.

'It is,' she agreed, smiling.

'And you're our mother.'

'I am. And I always will be.'

The fuse then blew.

'It's another of your blasted men, isn't it?' said Ian savagely.

'*Au contraire*, my duck,' she said. 'It is the exact opposite. It is Mrs Fytton alone.' She looked at her children. 'Unless you two would like to change your minds?'

But she knew she was quite, quite safe . . .

The removal men brought her back to earth.

'What's tickling you?' said the driver.

She realized she had been chuckling out loud.

'Families,' she said firmly. 'Mine in particular.'

'You can add mine to the list,' he said with feeling.

'And mine,' said his mate.

The van turned into the Mump Road.

'But at least,' said Angela proudly, 'at least I have made my escape.'

The men both looked at her suspiciously.

'Now the children are grown up,' she added quickly and dutifully, mindful that there was a lot of furniture in the van, a lot of heavy furniture, including the blessed piano. Why she had brought that, she really did not know. She couldn't play and Claire and Andrew's stumbling Grade Three hardly made the bringing of it worthwhile.

She pointed to the house. 'That's it. The one with the holly hedge on the left.'

The older driver pulled up at the gate and took a look, squinting at her beloved new home critically.

'Is that it?' he said jumping down.

She followed him. Standing to face him on the road. New beginnings, she reminded herself, and placed her hands on her hips in what she hoped was the manner of an earthbound peasant woman.

He looked back at her and curled his lip contemptuously. Moving to the country, in his opinion, meant acreage.

'It's not very big now, is it?' he said scathingly.

The younger man jumped out of the cab. He too stared at the house and he too was derisive. 'Not big at all,' he said positively. 'Not at *all* big . . .'

'Well, you wouldn't want it up your nose for a wart, now would you?' she said sharply, having had quite enough of good behaviour.

After the men had left and she had arranged the basics, she went out into the garden. After all, she had the rest of her life to decide where the cutlery should go.

The summer evening's light was just beginning to fade. First she walked up towards the top of her garden, passing the Celtic well, which was overgrown and ordinary-looking. Some previous incumbent had fashioned a rough wooden cover, which made an ideal place to sit in the late evening sun. She tried to peer over the blackthorn and the yews behind the well, separating her from the churchyard, but they were too dense and shadowy. She ran her hand over their metallic leaves and heard flutterings from within – mice or birds, and not taking kindly to being woken. A few apple trees, the remains of a small orchard, were set behind a straggly japonica hedge, which was covered in marble-sized growths. Mrs Perry had told her they were quinces. 'Oh, good,' she said to the hard little fruits. For she was full of enthusiasm for her stores and looking forward to spending a lot of time in that kitchen, communing with the past sisterhood of selves. She was not entirely sure what you did with a quince, but she was entirely sure she could find out.

Beneath the apple trees the hives sat quietly, like miniature tower blocks, and she kept well away. Sammy the pigman was to come and show her how to deal with it all and until he did, she knew better than to mess with the community. She whispered a hello and walked on. You were supposed to talk to them. She'd read it in a book.

The adjoining Perry field was covered in tufted grass except for an ugly brown churned-up patch close to the hedge, and she wondered what had caused it. But it was none of her business. Just be thankful, she told herself, that they kept it. And then she went over to the wicked mulberry. She paused to run her hand down its curious trunk and then peered round to the other side. Archie had certainly done a good job. All promise and no fulfilment indeed. But despite the paucity of its frontal endowments, the fruits were coming on, the pale green clusters flushed with a faint pink. Mine, she thought, touching it again. Mine. She put her face close to the rough bark and kissed it.

The day's heat had lessened and the air was damp and cooling with evening dew. She crossed the front of the house and walked down towards the ramshackle outbuildings, pinching at the lavender bushes as she passed. They had been knocked about by the removal men and the scented pellets lay scattered on the path, sending up their heady mixture of peppery mint as she bruised them with her feet. A bit like a bridal path, she thought, except you couldn't carry yourself over the threshold.

She found a broom down near the hens, an alarmingly witch-like broom made from twigs and a knobbly stick, and she began to sweep. The hens clucked and ran around suspiciously, pecking at the lavender and looking understandably surprised when they ate a bit. She had no idea what to do with them. Mrs Perry said you put them away for the night. What she did not say was how you got them into the henhouse. She could hardly offer them mugs of cocoa and plump up their pillows. They were probably as wayward as night-time children and sulked and ran about. She swept on, building up to it. The first battle. She would probably fail.

She swept until all the bricks were clear, and she would have swept until Domesday, enjoying the sense of possession, the sense of being on her own. She had never been on her own in the whole of her life. It was oddly pleasant.

Suddenly she was aware of silence. Complete silence. She looked up at the deepening sky, around her at the darkening garden. Silence. Where, then, were the hens? She walked around the house again and back down the path towards the henhouse. Still silence. No clucking and scattering at her feet. She tried a few little clucky, clucky, clucky noises. Nope. Perhaps they had run away? And she had let them go. On her very first night. Were they like pets, then? Had they decided to leave now their owner was gone? Did they in some way *know* how incompetent she was likely to be? Her confidence

124

waned in the silence. This, surely, all of it, was the stupidest, most irrational mistake of her life . . . She stared bleakly at the empty pathway, bent to peek under the leafy shrubs, scanned the verges beyond her gate. Nothing. She walked down the path, making sad little clucking noises. No reply. Zilch. She sighed. She stopped and peered hopelessly into the gloom of the henhouse. And, lined up, looking at her sleepily from their perches, six pairs of weary eyes met hers. The odd comfortable sound of hen-crooning floated about. Little *poulet* noises that said they had all had quite enough for the day, thank you, and could she please bugger off and let them get some sleep. She tiptoed away, closing the door, slipping the bar into place, feeling quite as emotional as if it were a nursery. If anyone who shouldn't came near her chicks, she'd put a hex on them. Goodwife or not.

A bicycle stopped and a woman, fair-haired, sharp-nosed, leaned against the gate.

'I'm Daphne Blunt,' she said. 'Not going to mess this place about, are you?'

'I'm Angela Fytton,' she said, 'and no. Though I might have to do something when my husband joins me. But that won't be for a while.' She enjoyed the sound of the words 'my husband' on her lips again.

'And you know about the Alice Sapcotes?'

Angela shook her head. 'Who's she?'

'You've got eight of the best cider trees at the back. Alice Sapcotes. Very ancient.'

'Hens, bees, cider, eels . . .' Angela put her hand to her head, feeling a little dazed by it all.

'Don't worry. You just put them in sacks and someone from Burrowbridge adds them to *their* Alices. And there's not much eeling now.' She remounted her bicycle. 'But we always slip one into each of the cider barrels. Gives it body.'

The trouble with the country, thought Angela, is that you never know if they are laughing at you or not.

For safety's sake she changed the subject. 'Seems strange to be talking about cider in a place called Church Ale House,' she said, tracing the name on the gate.

The woman began pushing off. 'Glad you're not knocking it about,' she said. 'Sorry to disturb. See you again.'

Angela went in. The house was a shambles of her own furniture, the stuff she had not sent to the London auction rooms and the Perry's cast-offs. Somehow she had to make a fitting order out of the chaos, which was a suitable metaphor for the rest of her life. Welcome to ye olde countryside, Mrs Fytton, she said to herself, picking her way around the boxes.

That night she slept in a goosefeather bed. Exceptionally soundly.

Part Two

10

July

In their role as agriculturalists, women produced the bulk of the country's food supply. The entire management of the dairy, including the milking of cows and the making of butter and cheese, was in women's hands, and the women were also responsible for the growing of flax and hemp, for the milling of corn, for the care of the poultry, pigs, orchards and gardens.

ANN OAKLEY, *Housewife*

Church Ale House proved to be much like a lover. From seeing and wanting and finally, rapturously, being clasped into its warm, responsive arms, it gave up its mysteries one by one. Some of which were not entirely easy to accommodate.

On the first night Angela woke in a puddle of cold fear to hear the tap, tap, tapping of evil fingers on her bedroom window. Insistent evil fingers. The old spirits, she told herself, expecting to die and thinking that if she survived, which was not very likely, she would string a bulb or two of garlic around her neck in future. She wished the image of Wuthering Heights would remove itself from behind her screwed-tight eyes, along with the creeping certainty that some Somerset Heathcliff had torn some Somerset Cathy from her coffin and left her unhappy spirit to roam the Levels. Half fainting with fear, she got out of bed and tottered to the window only to find it was the tip of a branch of the mulberry tree. A mulberry tree, no matter how romantically fashioned, can lose its charm at four in the morning. And she had not cared very much for its wine either.

The violence required in using her hip to open and close the back door made it less a rustic piece of gym equipment and more a painful imposition. She was now so sore and bruised on both hips that she could never remember which one she had bashed it with last. So much for symmetry and seductive boyish contours. If anyone did come along and catch her in her underwear, all they would think was that she'd been severely battered by a violent dwarf. And the bathroom – even in summer heat – was cool to the point of coldness, and damp. The howl of the vixens (as Sammy told her) kept her awake, and the lowing of newly bereft cows made her want to cry. The tap water had a reddish tint and left bits in the bath, and the roof rattled when the wind got up (which, despite the balmy summer, seemed a frequent occurrence after lights out – more disturbed spirits, she supposed). She could also hear a certain kind of scrabbling above her head which she was assured was nothing, but which she knew, for certain, was four-legged, came with a long tail and bred. And what with tractors and animals and grain dryers and a one-note church bell, the idea that the countryside was a quiet haven of peacefulness was laughable . . .

But yet, but yet . . . On a brilliant, still morning, when the smell of grass and the scent of an indescribable country something was in the air, she was never happier. What was the rust-red of a little tap water when her heart had once run pure blood? She was a betrayed woman on the mend. Loitering over the green of it all, as Goldsmith would say. Pausing on every charm – the sheltered cot, the never-failing brook, the decent church that topped the neighbouring hill, the hawthorn bush with seats beneath the shade, 'For talking age and whispering lovers made'. And finding in each day's challenge some sort of happiness. Her eyes held the permanent glaze of romantic stupefaction as she surveyed her domain.

She learned that if you turn everything that happens to you – from fusing the lights to getting mown down by a passing bicycle – into a positive, then the world becomes positive. In the course of finding the fusebox she discovered a wooden crate full of old medicine bottles that would clean up beautifully. And the rampant bicycle was ridden by the charming young vicar, who, after dusting her down, said that he would be delighted to take away all the stuff she no longer wanted, for the poor of the parish. She spent so much time putting the stuffed stag's head on the jumble pile, and then removing it again, that she began to read a hint of accusation in its glassy eyes. Do you want me or not? She was tempted, but rose above. It had no place on her walls. Dorothea Tichborne purchased it as a gift for the Reverend Bertrand Stokes, so that he could look upon it and remember the days when men were men and even a stag knew its place. Thus did everything negative contain its positive.

The hens were easy. They tended not to sleep in, but they were comparatively easy. No rushing around trying to get them out of bed and on to the bus each morning. No demands for fivers. No saying Weetabix was their absolute favourite in the whole world, and then a week later asking, 'Why are you giving me this disgusting stuff, Mum?' If she tottered down at eight o'clock to make tea, they were already up, let out by Sammy, who disapproved of lying-in (unless, presumably, it was for farrowing), pattering on the path, staring through the windows, tapping their beaks hungrily at her. This, she found, was excellent therapy, since she let fly with a stream of obscenities about where they could go and what they could do when they got there, which set her up nicely and calmly for the rest of the day. I have not come down here to shed one stricture for another, she told them, and continued to totter down at eight.

But in the end, the hens won. She learned to adjust her clock accordingly. She learned that ten o'clock was not a bad time to fall into bed at night, which meant that half-past six was not a bad time to get up. Amazing. Astonishing. But not bad. Of course, she had made the mistake of telephoning friends at odd hours, like seven-thirty in the morning – forgetting that *she* might have been up for an hour but they had not. As Clancy said one Saturday morning, in that inimitable Yeatsian way of hers, 'Ah, fuck off, will you ...'

She excused herself to her friends. She needed, she said, time to make it work. One day she would invite everybody down here and then wouldn't they marvel at her country life? 'I could give them *coq au vin*,' she said loudly. 'Quite a lot of it . . .' The hens scarpered.

From Wimbledon there was silence. Which suited her for the while. Two could play at that game. The exam results were fine, they told her. More information than this she neither asked for nor was given. To her suggestion that they come and see the place, there was miffed refusal. She would capitulate eventually and break the disapproving silence, but just for the moment she had enough to think about. Occasionally, as she was washing floorboards or polishing windows, it did occur to her how very pleasant it would be to get a tearful phone call along the lines of, 'O mother, we are so sorry that we undervalued you all these years. How wonderful you really were. How sorry we are not to have taken your side in the divorce. How horrible Binnie is and how ill-behaved her child. Please forgive us and let us come and stay with you. And may we bring our father, who cries for you each night.' Which was about as likely in the early days of their moving to Wimbledon as any of Sammy's porkers taking a sudden and elevatory interest in aerodynamics.

It took her a while to come down from her romantic rural cloud. For the first couple of weeks each discovered egg was like a great wonder – she would feel its warmth and smoothness in her hands and gaze at its rich brown shell as if it were a mighty miracle. She also apologized individually to whichever hen she thought had laid the thing. 'Sorry,' she would say, and add helpful things like, 'But you wouldn't want all those children, now would you?' She was having just such a conversation one morning when Dave the Bread called. He obviously overheard. She bought a currant loaf by way of proving her sanity but neither of them could quite look each other in the eye for some days. She gave the loaf to the hens, who looked at her witheringly.

Dave told Wanda and Wanda said, 'Good. If she's that sort of person she'll be wanting corn dollies' – in bulk from Taiwan – 'and bog myrtle sheaves' – fashioned in Wellington by Tibetan refugees – 'to decorate her house.' She reckoned that if you were alone you probably *did* talk to things like hens. At which Dave the Bread rolled his eyes. 'What – about *birth control*?'

When Dave told the vicar that he'd caught the new owner of Church Ale House talking to her hens, the vicar said, 'So did St Francis.' But when the vicar called on her and she was working in the garden and he saw her cooing, so lyrically, over a delphinium – 'Oh, you're so blue and tall and strong and strokeable, you beautiful, beautiful thing . . .'– he crept away, somewhat shaken at the passion of it all and trying not to think of the Dorkin girl.

The vegetable patch was another treasure trove: she found little fir-apple potatoes, beetroots, carrots and other hidden things. At first every dig took an age because each time an edible anything came up, she would clasp it and hold it as if she had just given birth to it herself – smiling into its little eyes and admiring it for several minutes. It took a while to get used to the idea and to fling handfuls of young parsnips and shallots about, heedless of their miraculous nature. She also, on Sammy's advice, made a rough plan of what went where. She did not know why she had to do this, and he did not yet tell her, but every time she discovered something, down it went on her grubby bit of paper. At the end of each day, when he passed her gate, she would show it to him, like a hopeful child, and he would, if he acknowledged it at all, just grunt. Not surprisingly, given his calling – though it was to be hoped he drew the line at eating potato peelings and being scratched behind the ear with a big stick. She put herself doubly on her guard against clucking. All the same, she found herself doing it from time to time. It was irresistible to see the hens stiffen and stare in complete amazement as she clucked her way past them with the broom.

Sammy had been asked to look after her and, in his unbowing way, he did. She swallowed her pride. She who had never felt challenged by anything in the domestic department, decided to be grateful for his skills. You did not, she realized, pick up the way of the rural from an overnight reading of *Country Life*.

But the Fytton Enlightenment was gradual, with several embarrassing moments on the way. The most blushworthy of which occurred during these vegetable garden proceedings when she – in full view of Sam the Pig and wishing to display her at-oneness with nature's bounty – pounced on what she took to be a stalk containing baby cabbages, eulogizing about the perfection of their form and who would have thought these little brassica globes would one day be the size of footballs? To which Sammy replied laconically, 'No one. Being as how they're Brussels sprouts.' Well, she thought defensively, *well* . . . How would a girl from Reigate know about such things? Cabbages came from *shops* . . . Did he know that pineapples grew on the ground? He looked at her blankly and shook his head. Mistake, Angela, she told herself. Big mistake. Anyway, she only knew because she and Ian had once visited a plantation in Thailand owned by one of his clients. Where did *that* Angela Fytton go? she asked herself, not unhappily, as sweat poured from her digger's body.

Sammy was also very helpful with the hives, though she, like Sylvia Plath, felt mean beyond Scrooge to feed the poor things on pale sugar while stealing their own sweet gold. She would have suggested giving them something a little more exciting in return, like maple syrup perhaps, but after the incident with the sprouts she was inclined to say less, listen more.

'Did you know,' she said, as they carried out this sugary thievery, 'that everyone thought the queen was a king until the seventeenth century? Virgil. Even Shakespeare – "So work the honey-bees . . . They have a king, an officer of sorts . . ."'

'Daft,' said Sammy Lee.

Which proved you did not need much in the way of words to make an oral historical point.

Apart from their vegetables and the hives, the Perrys left much that was desirable in among the dross which went to the vicar. The white piqué bed cover, the bed itself, the curtains she had coveted, even the scrubbed (now) kitchen table remained. But one item above all else pleased and informed her. It even told her, at last, exactly what a still room was. Once she knew, she retracted her decision to turn it into Ian's office. It was wholly woman's domain. And it would wholly be hers.

The item that pleased and informed and told her about the still room was a gift from Mrs Perry. It was, apparently, something about which she had thought long and hard before deciding it should stay with Church Ale House. She herself no longer had need of it, but it had served her well in its time. Her own daughter had shown little interest, and Mrs Perry doubted she would even remember its existence when the time came and she was laid in the earth.

'I'll leave it in the parlour on the round table you admired. Like the house, it belongs to you now. Good luck, Mrs Fytton.'

'Why, thank you, Mrs Perry.'

Somehow, at that moment, she felt that Church Ale House really was hers.

11

July

Books succeed,
And lives fail.
ELIZABETH BARRETT BROWNING

She found it in the parlour, as promised. The gift, the desirable item that came with the Perry blessing, was wrapped in old brown paper and labelled with her name. A note said 'This memorandum book was started by Maria Brydges, on the occasion of her marriage and just after the front addition was added to the house, when the farm was doing well. It has the original recipe for mulberry wine. We have left you the last three bottles. I have also left you my mother's recipe collection. Good luck and God bless.'

Gingerly she put her hand into the packet and drew out what looked like a book that had burst. Its disintegrating mottled brown and pink and black covers were tied neatly with black sateen tape to keep all the loose pages safe. And there were a lot of loose pages – some looking as if they had been written yesterday, some as if they had been written a thousand years ago. She opened it at random, very carefully, to a page of closely written script headed 'Nothing is done that has not been done well', a saying apparently given to the world by one Mother Julian of Norwich. She squinted at the small, tightly packed and perfectly formed hand that had written beneath the tag:

All within has been prepared with great care and a proper attention to economy and accompanied by important remarks and counsel on the arrangement and well-ordering of the household. I have taken the instruction from my dear Mamma, and her Mamma before her. Take the good of the past and add to its store with the benefices of our modern world. It is your duty to be a Good Wife.

This was dated 1807 and it was Maria Brydges's job description, a working tool, her manual. She found a section dated 1837, headed 'How we live on what we eat', scripted in Maria's hand. There was little in the tone of it to suggest the meek little woman-at-home. This is my world, it seemed to say, and you can't take my domain away from me.

It is curious to note man gathering his sustenance all over the world, how in the search for it he fishes and hunts, rears flocks and herds, ploughs, sows, reaps, goes headlong into anxieties, rises early, lies down late and wears out and renews his strength. There is no land too stubborn for him, no sea too deep, no hill too high, no zone too burning hot or freezing cold, no bird too swift of wing, or beast too wild that he will not find it out; roots, plants, fish, flesh, he has stomach for everything. In accordance with these facts, we find men all over the world acting instinctively. Except perhaps the Englishman in India, who will change not his habits despite the anxious persuasions of his wife, and who eats too much meat for the climate, turning yellow and sickly ...

Reading this essay on good eating habits, Angela remembered how she felt when she was first up at Cambridge and she saw a re-run of the first moon walk. How, when Neil Armstrong said those famous words, 'One small step for man, one giant leap for mankind,' she had filled her mouth with chocolate creams in a valiant move to make one small love-handle for woman, one gigantic spare tyre for womankind. No women tread here, she had thought sadly, switching off the television set. And she had sighed with frustration.

What did they think women did all day in history before consciousness-raising groups wrote them back in? Lay around mutely in caves drinking gin? And that moon walk was in the last gasp of the valiant sixties. Here at the end of the century the world still turned on an establishment upholding the feudal law of fraternal primogeniture.

Chocolate creams were the best compensation she knew for such iniquity. Though she did feel a little squeezing of the heart arteries from time to time at the thought of what a fighter she was once, and how it all seemed to get lost beneath the canopy called Real Life.

At least Maria Brydges had the excuse of a century and a half of gender-biased linguistics. Whereas only recently, when Angela went to register with a doctor in Taunton (kindly old Dr Tichborne was no longer practising), she found a pamphlet published on hypothermia which began with the words, 'The first thing to do for the patient is to make sure he is well wrapped up . . .'

'So, no hypothermic women there, then?' she said loudly to the receptionist, who had seen it all, every kind of nut on offer, and did not react. 'Or if there were,' she added, 'you could safely leave them out in the cold.'

So what was new?

She played the old consciousness-raising trick on Maria Brydges's text to bring those cave-dwelling, gin-sodden mutes back into the picture. It still worked. Maria would certainly have been shocked to her stays.

It is curious to note woman gathering her sustenance all over the world, how in the search for it she fishes and hunts, rears flocks and herds, ploughs, sows, reaps, goes headlong into anxieties, rises early, lies down late and wears out and renews her strength. There is no land too stubborn for her, no sea too deep, no hill too high, no zone too burning hot or freezing cold, no bird too swift of wing, or beast too wild that she will not find it out;

roots, plants, fish, flesh, she has stomach for everything. In accordance with these facts, we find women all over the world acting instinctively . . .

A couple of thousand years of that kind of affirmation, she thought, and we girls wouldn't be chewing our finger-ends worrying how to manage our homes and children and careers. Or beatifying the rare woman who managed it. A very good rule of thumb was that if you had to single out a woman in any argument you had already lost your case. As in Queen Elizabeth I or Margaret Thatcher. *Rara avis*.

You could also use it to point out the absurdities of gender behaviour. Some texts just did not reverse.

Except perhaps the Englishwoman in India, who will change not her habits despite the anxious persuasions of her husband, and who eats too much meat for the climate, turning yellow and sickly . . .

Hardly convincing, the idea of a rigid-backed lady with a face like custard ploughing her way through the roast beef of old England while her abstemious husband nibbled a biscuit and implored her to go easy on the slices.

Well, well, this was no time to ponder upon the mighty fist of language. She turned the pages very carefully. This was a time to concentrate upon the tasks ahead. So, what exactly *was* a still room? She found it described in the memorandum book. In no uncertain terms. Which was when she decided that Ian should have none of it.

Solely the housewife's domain. The apartment for your jams, jellies, preserves, chutneys, liquors should be cool, of even temperature and free from damp and draught. Keep it clean and wholesome and check the contents regularly. You are best to entrust this task to no one but yourself. If there be any sign of mould, gently boil up the contents of the jar anew. Brandy papers may be used and should be changed every six month. Keep not any of your containers up against the walls for they may be damp.

It would be so.

She remained in the parlour, surrounded by half-empty boxes, wholly absorbed in Maria Brydges's wisdom. The household journal represented everything inherent in the Goodwife – her memoranda, recipe book, blessed herbal, book of housekeeping, gardening, goodwifery, neighbourliness, mothering, nursing and virtually the curing of souls – and it seemed to Angela, at the honourable age of forty or so, that it held information much more useful to her now, woman to woman, than her raised-awareness meetings in the seventies. At this ripe old age she dared to say that she was much more interested in learning how to bone a chicken than in finding out what her own untrussed innards looked like.

She was overcome by a sudden desire for jams and jellies and preserves to inspect and brandy papers to change and the delight of tasks which should be entrusted, guiltlessly, to no one but herself. She wanted, suddenly, to be allowed to be supreme in one thing. To say, like Maria, 'My world – this is *my* world.' How refreshing after those designer wives and hopeless nannies and halfway house-husbands with this season's designer accompaniment of a baby on their backs, wittering on about weaning. Show me one house-husband, she thought, who rinses out milk bottles or makes tea in a pot or does any of those thousand and one small, light tasks that drive you nuts, like cleaning the rubbish bin, boiling the flannels, wiping sticky door handles, which no one ever notices unless you stop doing them. And I'll show you a hundred others blessed with brilliantly incompetent sparsity.

'Um – darling . . . Um, how do I separate an egg?'

Not on the floor, usually.

'Um – darling . . . How do I iron silk?'

Not at a temperature likely to melt steel, usually.

And quite right too. If they were looking after the baby, they were looking after the baby. And that was what they were doing. Looking after the baby did not mean wiping down door handles or rinsing out milk bottles. It was all about *focus*. Women now had lost theirs. Maria Brydges had focus. She could, and she did, decide what was important – and what was not. And she never underestimated the importance of anything that she felt was important to *her* . . .

Wrote Maria:

> I never did love my dear husband more than when I see him *carve* so handsomely . . . He is cool and collected and assists the portions he has carved with as much grace as he displayed in the carving of the fowl . . . Whereas Mr Porter, my sister's husband, becomes suffused with blushes and perspiration and persists in hacking and mangling the fowl while liberally be-spotting the linen with good gravy . . .

That was love all right. High-born or low-born, if you found yourself looking sentimentally upon your man's carving technique, then there was no doubt – as the Queen of Scots said of Bothwell – you would follow him around the world in your shift too. Probably even troubled Mary must have occasionally forgotten the True Faith and the Catholic Crown and sighed as she watched her warlike border lord cutting so capably at the capon. Just like the humble Mrs Maria Brydges after her. Maria, it seemed, knew nothing of political correctness but she *was* quite unblushing about what would now be a seriously mockable but increasingly fashionable offence . . . Celebrating the maleness of the male.

For there *was* something very comforting even for Angela about the memory of Ian sitting in front of the turkey on Christmas Day and taking charge of the brute. After all, she had eyeballed its bleary eyeballs in a shop, taken it home, investigated its entrails more closely than any woman should have to investigate anything's entrails, given how many of her own were just waiting to drop. She had then restuffed the gaping wounds with two kinds of stuffing, the chestnuts of which *alone* had driven her practically demented in the peeling thereof, and stumbled out of bed at some fucking unearthly hour on Christmas morning when even the *children* were still asleep, so that she could shove the horrible thing into the oven. It was hardly surprising, then, that she felt a joyous pride when some other bugger had the jolly task of cutting the thing up. Maria, I'm with you, she thought.

She was all for Women's Liberation, always had been, always would be, but let some ardent feminist come up to her in the supermarket and suggest that she should abrogate responsibility for the turkey a little earlier in the proceedings and she might, just, spit in her eye. Separate an egg? Iron silk? Buy, cook and present a Christmas turkey? What planet were they living on? Putting the finished turkey in front of your spouse while you finally abrogated responsibility for it did not seem a particularly reactionary or treacherous thing to do. Maria Brydges had a point. And yes, she did like to watch the family, all expectant, while the elegant thin slices were handed around . . . If she'd had a Mr Porter spraying the gravy everywhere and throwing mangled lumps on to plates after all *her* care and attention, she'd have been just as critical as Maria. She dared to say it now. Indeed she would.

As she turned the pages she was aware of looking for a Big Truth in all this. Aware that this was the end of the millennium and aware that, unlike her counterparts at its beginning, at its end she had no spiritual focus. She wanted one. It was as simple as that. She turned another page and read, entranced, 'Be sure to look well every morning to your pickled pork and hams.' She sighed to have such things.

Nature's Prozac. *Country life . . .*

12

September

*One cannot help wondering how medicinal herbs came to be selected
from those with no healing properties, and it can only be surmised that in
those far-off days in the childhood of the world, when man's guiding
interest was his never-ending quest for food, every plant was
tested by a method of trial and error . . .*

FLORENCE RANSON, *British Herbs*

[When woman's guiding interest was her never-
ending quest for food, very possibly, too]

If Mrs Fytton the First ever thought about that manipulated
group of residents in far-off Wimbledon, it was only with a
fleeting twinge of guilt and a lasting sense of celebration. She
just wished she had done all this a great deal sooner. In particular, before Extraordinary Little Mouth was born. There was
something about the existence of him that took away some of
her pleasure. Not because it threatened her, but because he
was born and he was innocent. As much as those wicked little
chubby dimpled things could be said to be innocent.

On the other hand, despite having almost no contact with
them, and therefore no real confirmation, Angela Fytton
could feel in her bones that Ian and his beloved Binnie were
beginning to feel embattled. Andrew let slip, though Claire
never would, that Ian had shortened a long business trip
because Binnie was stroppy about it. Andrew let it slip
because he wanted to go surfing in Cornwall and his father
had told him to stay put and care for his brother and stepmother.

'I ask you,' said Andrew.

'What about you, Claire?' asked Angela. But Claire refused to say anything of a disloyal nature. Being female, she knew the power of psychological warfare. Thank God I have a son too, thought Angela.

Ian was due to leave at the end of this month. Now the fish will begin to fry, she thought. Now she will see what it is really like.

Good, she said to her half-scrubbed still room. *Good. Good. Good.*

Meanwhile, life at Church Ale House was settling into place quite nicely. The mulberry tapping on her window scarcely invaded her slumber, the rustling in the eaves was but nature's way. She could go to bed at night (which she did) and wake the following morning (which she also did) and decide her future by the hour, by the day, by the month or by its eternity. She could take her early morning tea and sit in the shade of the garden (which she did) and let the day and her mind happen as they would. Or she could wander the lane, stretching her arms to the golden morning, and saying hello to any of the assorted neighbours she might meet. No one seemed to take any notice of whatever she was doing, except in the most glancing of ways. They were all just good folk going about their business. And she was a good woman going about hers. Which was to grow, garner, bottle, infuse, ferment, dry, preserve and even claim kinship with Demeter in her pursuit of country matters. The honey flowed, the Perry vegetables were ripening, the Perry fruit canes were bearing fruit, the mulberries dark and swelling and the apples firm on the bough. Even the quinces were the size of a baby's fist now. What more could a good woman want? Except, perhaps, a husband, of course. Sometimes she forgot to even think that.

One September morning, the sun warming her soil, the hives silent, the hens content and her car gathering cobwebs in the outhouse, Mrs Angela Fytton, late of London and now of

Church Ale House in the county of Somerset, sat on her Celtic well making decisions both great and small, in between sips of tea. She could no longer sit beneath the mulberry tree since the fruit was inclined to drop and cover her with ruby wounds. She ought, she knew, to gather the crop and begin the wine. It was time, according to Maria's instructions, and the recipe was very clear, but something – she was not sure what – held her back. She patted the tree's buttocks now and again, but that was as far as she got. There was just something about that sawn-off stump round the other side that she found unamusing and unpleasant to behold.

On this September morning (which also happened to be the date of her wedding anniversary, though no one had marked it, except her, and why should they?) she held her ever-ready notebook on her lap and a pen in her hand. It was a particular day, she said to herself, and therefore she would mark it with something special, even if no one else did. How many people carry silent anniversaries at which they may no longer legitimately make merry? Well, bugger that, she decided, it was still her wedding anniversary and she *would*. And she wondered what there was that she could add, like past owners before, to the fabric of Church Ale House to mark the occasion. Maria Brydges had added the front addition. Angela Fytton would do something likewise. Nothing so grand, of course. But something. She chewed her pen end. What? And where?

She threw out the little wicked voice that popped into her head saying, 'Build a bloody swimming pool, of course . . .' She could imagine Daphne Blunt's face if she announced that. But there had to be something. And she took a deep breath full of the aroma of sun on soil. She breathed in again – taking in the scent of roses, the rich, sun-warmed smell of orange blossom, the pulse of sweet William. But something was missing. And she suddenly realized what the something was: thyme, sage, parsley, bay, sweet cicely, mint, savory, tarragon, marjoram . . . She had no herb bed. Apart from the bushes of lavender and an enormous, straggling bush of rose-mary by the front door, there was nothing. Gwen Perry kept her few herbs in pots by the door and these had gone to grace their sun-trap patio. A herb bed she would have.

There must once have been a herb garden, because Maria Brydges recorded moving it in the memorandum book, along with the sketch of her new design, which was round and seg-mented, like an orange.

My sister Cressy and I did dig the round and I have let the new herbal bed be nearer to the house so that the kitchen girl can gather them fresh and still be seen. Otherwise she will run from her work and linger all the time, and encourage the sexton's boy . . . I have moved the what-not up to the top, where it always was kept, and away from the well too.

Later, when she told Sammy, he came out with the longest sentence he had so far uttered in her presence. 'The midden,' he said. 'That'll be why the nettles grow well up there. Time was we had nettle beer, nettle tea, nettle tops with our din-ners, and even fed them to the cows. Nettles mean good, rich earth.' He wandered up to the top and kicked at the soil with his heel. 'A good place,' he nodded.

'How big?' she said, for this was not clear from Maria's drawing.

'Big one here. Small one here.'

'Why two?'

'Main bed all laid out nice and pretty, and small bed out of the way where the roots can be dug up and let grow again without spoiling the looks of the other. Otherwise it gets knocked about by all that digging over.'

He approved of siting it up towards the hives. 'Means that even on dull, windy days, the bees can reach good nectar and pollen. You have thyme, marjoram, lavender, rosemary, chervil and plenty of bergamot – bee's balm – and you'll get golden-yellow honey full of sweet flavour.' He paused.

Angela waited.

'Be a lot of digging,' he said doubtfully.

'I'm strong,' said Angela.

He nodded. 'Maybe,' he said. He gave her a look that did not altogether fit in with the look of a garden adviser. It had a touch of kindness about it. But only a touch. 'And you'll be wanting love-ache and heart's-ease, then,' he said.

'Not necessarily,' she said, returning the look.

He nodded. 'As you like.'

'I wouldn't want much lovage,' she said firmly. 'It's too strong.'

That look from him again. But he was impressed.

Plant only a little lovage (loveache). It will go a very long way and is very strong and can be most unpleasant.

Presumably Maria needed no such cure for love's pain with that elegantly carving husband of hers.

'If you want medicinals, you've got to make a place for comfrey, betony, aconitum, poppy, belladonna . . .'

'Thank you,' she said shortly, desperately trying to untangle his dialect and keep up with jotting the names in her little notebook.

'You've got woody nightshade already, in the hedge there . . .'

'The belladonna?'

'No. Different.' He smiled. 'Woody nightshade. Felonwort. Draws poison. Other name's bittersweet or the comforter. Suck the stalks.'

She made a note of this and wondered if there was anything in the memorandum book to explain further. He looked at her again. Just as if he knew everything.

'I'd get the love-ache and heart's-ease in first,' he said.

The nettles and the dock, and all the other growing stuff that she could not name, eyed her beadily. It was their domain. To begin all over again would be quite an undertaking, but since none of the women who lived here before her would have thought twice about it neither would she. And once the herb beds were established she could gather them and dry them, or make decoctions, just as Maria Brydges had done before her. She would ask Dave the Bread to ask his wife if she could have lessons.

She watched a globally warmed, unseasonal white butterfly settle on a nettle head. She knew she was supposed to kill it because it was after her cabbages, but she had not got to that murderous stage yet.

Sammy had said it would only take one cabbage eaten through and she'd be convinced. 'Same with foxes,' he said contemptuously. 'Nice little beggars till you've seen a henhouse when they been visiting. If you're doing herbals you want great Valerie round the coop. That'll stop him.'

She said demurely, 'Thank you. I'll make a note of that,' putting the extraordinary picture of some tank-like female parading round the henhouse to one side. She saw him dart a quick, amused look at her notebook and the segmented diagram she had copied from Maria Brydges.

'Stinks like death underfoot,' he added, and waited for her to write that down too. She did. 'Not red-spurred Valerie,' he said. She wrote. Sammy was playing the country sage to the letter. 'Likes wet feet.' She did not write that bit down. He'd be suggesting wellingtons next.

'When my herb beds are finished,' she said, 'I hope they'll be as good a working arrangement as Wanda's. That's my goal.'

'Wouldn't be hard,' he said wryly. 'You do it your way. Let her do it hers.'

'I might ask her for advice.'

'Ask me.'

She closed the notebook. Enough was enough. 'Tea?' she said. 'And one of my fruit biscuits?'

To the pulp of any kind of fruit, put the same weight of sugar, beat them both well together for two hours, then make them into forms, or put them in paper cases, and dry them in a cool oven; turn them the next day, and let them remain until quite dry, then put them in boxes.

True, she had cheated on the beating time – by about an hour and fifty minutes – but they looked good to her. He took one bite and asked if she had any of Dave the Bread's Old Somerset butter biscuits.

Back in the garden, offended about the biscuits, she said, 'Did you know that once upon a time women did most of the medicine and curing. It was part of their job. And then you men came along and took it away . . . Or called it witchcraft.' She looked up at the Mump. 'There were probably a few of them strung up there.' She could not resist copying Mrs Perry's knowing words.

'Really now?' he said. 'No. I didn't know that at all.'

Their eyes met. Somebody was laughing at somebody.

'You better tell the bees first,' he said. ''Fore you go digging. Always tell them everything. Then they won't be offended and they'll stay.'

That bit was probably true. She watched him walk off, an old man, slightly stooped and slow. What did he know of love-ache?

She went up to the hives, hoping the bees liked herbs. She was still very cautious with them. Mrs Perry told her they stung you only for a reason, unlike wasps, which will sting you regardless. This was encouraging until she realized that 'a reason' could well be incompetence. However, she persevered, with Sammy's help, and began to like their black faces and yellow and black stripes and the extraordinary noise of their industry when she put her ear to the hive. Sylvia Plath called it their 'furious Latin'. But she never went so far as Sylvia in saying aloud, 'They can die, I need feed them nothing, I am the owner . . .' It was not to the bees, but to the miscreant husband and selfish children that she should be suggesting – metaphorically, of course – that they could die and she would feed them nothing. No more bits of her. Well, not for the time being anyway.

She had finished turning the fresh-scrubbed, newly painted still room into a cool white shrine and had begun stocking it. In it she placed the three bottles of mulberry wine, radiant as rubies in the light, and the first of her preserves and stores, as well as a row of golden jars of her own honey. Every time she looked at them her heart swelled with love, as if they were yellow-haired babies asleep in their cots. Most of the honey went to a shop in Taunton which collected it exactly as they had done with the Perry honey, but nevertheless she had achieved it. Money rattled in a tin box. At least the hives were giving something back to her.

With the still room now finished, she would turn her attentions to her wilderness outdoors. She would give something back to the earth and create new herb beds to tantalize those bees. Verily Demeter herself could not have felt more proud.

Fytton honey. When Ian returned she would spread it on the soles of his feet.

13

September

Be you wise and never sad,
You will get your lovely lad . . .
And if that makes you happy, kid –
You'll be the first it ever did.

DOROTHY PARKER

While Mrs Angela Fytton of Church Ale House in the county of Somerset was stomping around in wellington boots as she dug her new herb gardens, her ex-husband was tiptoeing around, treading on eggshells, in his large, well-appointed family house in Wimbledon.

A state of anxiety that Mrs Belinda Fytton of South Common Road, Wimbledon, in the county of Surrey (now defunct) found oddly conducive.

A husband who is so angry with his ex-wife that he has gone from mild guilt to being unable to speak her name without spitting, combined with a husband who cannot do enough for his current wife to compensate for the arrival of his two large teenagers, is quite a nice mixture to have around the place, decided the Second Mrs Fytton. For while he was in that unnerved condition she felt less anxious herself.

Less anxious about her complete loss of mental faculties, about her limp, morning wakening when she could not be sure she had ever been asleep and immediately thought about going back to bed that night, about the permanent smell of old milk that she was sure hung about her, though Tristan was supposed to be giving up the breast. And – deeper and darker than all of these – about her complete lack of libido. While her stepchildren were there, and perceived to be imposing so much, Ian just wouldn't dare raise the matter (or anything else) of a sex drive. If he liked his sex (and he did, which was how she got him), he loved her more. Of that she was quite, quite certain. He always said that he liked her vulnerability. After all, at their first meeting she fell down in front of him. Well, here she was, vulnerable in the extreme. Therefore, as long as Claire and Andrew did not actually bounce Tristan down the stairs, or assault the cleaner with handguns, she accepted the situation. She was wholly dependent on her husband now. And she didn't care if she never did another stroke of root canal or bridgework ever again. Ian liked her vulnerable? Binnie would oblige.

For his part, Ian scheduled his business diary so that he could be around and not travelling the world as he used to do, and he kept up the jogging, which was good. He kept it up because he was anxious to stay youthful and fit, and she encouraged it because he got so puffed that there was very little energy left over for even *remembering* conjugal rights. And if he looked like faltering, she had only to hint that perhaps he needed to slow down at his age to send him off with even more determination to make an extra circuit around Wimbledon pond. And just in case the lowering effect of all this worried her husband, she hid all newspapers and magazines that mentioned Viagra. She did not want him to even *think* about restoring what early morning vigorous exercise and the arrival of his children had so successfully kept at bay. In short, the advent of Claire and Andrew had, like their father of late, hardly penetrated.

Besides, it was a very large house. Chosen – originally and in that sweet, innocent far-off time when Tristan was no more than a small fluttering bump, and Binnie still raced around the bedroom saying 'Catch me' and 'You can have me' – so that one day Binnie could have her own practice on the ground floor. There were acres of pale, fawn carpeting and three floors of spacious rooms and not even a nanny living in because, when she and Ian had discussed how things would be once this new baby arrived, when they were cuddled up on the white linen sofa together, on the white sheepskin rug, staring into the real fire and making their plans, life seemed so perfect that the very idea of an intrusion on their privacy was unthinkable. Ian, bearing in mind his past experience, did not feel they needed a nanny to live with them at all. Maybe a good, reliable cleaning lady, but who wanted strangers on the stairs each morning? It all came naturally to mothers anyway.

Binnie, hands clasped happily around her tiny fluttering bump, agreed out of love for him. She would go back to work eventually, she supposed, and then they would need someone more vocational. But that was a long way off. As long as Ian rearranged his working schedules so that he was based at home most of the time, they could manage perfectly well together. And the cleaner would be useful. Cleaners always were, thought Binnie vaguely. They therefore found and employed one crisp, clean young woman, of Christian principle, called Trisha, who came four days a week and kept the house like a new pin. It was all going to be fine, just fine.

As for Ian, well, it was a new sensation to feel needed. The former Mrs Fytton seemed capable of conquering everything – even his job, if he had let her. As for fatherhood, why, he had scarcely ever changed a nappy. Things would be different this time. This time they would be a team. So they thought as they sat, in happy harmony, in front of their living fire. Before Tristan. Before Andrew. Before Claire.

Of course, now that the baby *was* here, Binnie wanted a full-time nanny, a full-time masseuse, a full-time chauffeur and anything else you could think of. But she persuaded herself that two young adults who both loved their new little brother would more than compensate. Truth was, though Ian was doing very well, he was not Croesus, and with paying off his witch of an ex-wife and supporting his elder children, money was not infinite. Binnie kept quiet about this since she did not want to remind him that she could, if she chose, earn a good whack herself. She just didn't want to. She was just too, too tired.

'The house is large enough to absorb two young adults,' she said sweetly to her husband. And he, who had been very afraid of her reaction, loved her the more. That scheming, malicious wife of his down in Somerset who had gone through such a run of men and *still* remained alone to haunt him would find that he was made of stronger stuff than she was. At last.

'Why,' said Binnie, 'you have only to close the door of your own bedroom and you are at peace.'

Binnie thought endlessly about closing her own bedroom door, and having her own relaxing bath, and getting into her own soft and silent bed. Even in rare moments of mental alertness, Binnie did not stoop so low as to think that Ian's ex-wife had brought the situation about with any ulterior motive. What ulterior motive could there be? Indeed, the prospect of Ian's ex-wife leaving London for the remoter parts of Somerset was a very pleasant, very wise one. The further away she went, the better. She feared her predecessor much more when she was a short car ride away. But stuck out in the wilds of beyond with hens and hives and all those other nutty things she owned, what possible threat was she? What possible damage could she do? Binnie, in her new fragrant guise of motherhood, reinvented herself as a lily-clad Madonna, above intrigue herself and therefore seeing no evil in others. She was just too tired to think anything more complex or devious.

Ian just thanked his lucky stars and went on jogging and walking on eggshells. He even felt the stirrings of something called Being Masterful.

Claire and Andrew's worldly goods arrived in Wimbledon, as they themselves did, two days before their mother's departure and three days after their last exam, when they had just about recovered from their hangovers. Tristan spent a lot of happy hours crawling in and out of the boxes as they were emptied and left strewn about the house. Trisha kept her mouth clamped in a very thin line as she went about the business of making sure the baby did not become packed into one and mistakenly left out for the rubbish men.

Eventually, a week or two on, the very last box was unpacked and carted round to the side of the house, found to be empty of baby and removed for disposal. And gradually the house came back to something approaching normal. Within reason they could play their hi-fis, within reason they could invite their friends to visit, within reason they could treat all the facilities of the house as if it was their own home. This was no revelation to them. Before they moved, their mother told them that from now on it *was* their home. 'You have two homes,' she said. 'Wimbledon and Somerset. But Wimbledon is the *home* home.'

'I suppose,' said Claire.

'It is . . .' said Andrew.

'If I were you, I'd suggest you open proper accounts and have credit cards and everything,' she said. 'Now you are grown up.'

Sudden amazement. Their mother had refused, categorically, to let them open accounts and have credit cards when they lived with her. Life was looking up.

And while they were contemplating this dizzy joy, Angela said, 'Oh, I do hope you'll come and live with me. Won't you? Please . . .'

And she read, after the pound signs and the amazement, another set of signs in both her children's eyes that, loosely translated, said, 'Not on your nelly.'

'I suppose you've got lovely big rooms?' she said.

They nodded. 'Huge.'

'Ah,' said Angela, with as much regret in her voice as she could muster. 'Ah.'

Their rooms were perfectly designed and decorated. Pale amber for Claire, pale turquoise for Andrew. With those perfect, perfect expanses of fawn carpet. They had nothing in particular to do for the whole of that fifteen-month period. And they felt that, after the strain of studying for so long, they deserved a bit of time and freedom. And credit cards and accounts with overdrafts. Those were the facts.

'Good job I got those rooms decorated and finished,' said Binnie, congratulating herself, at least, for *something*.

'Ye-e-s,' said Ian. He recalled the moment that Tristan chucked up his carrot purée over the white rug in the sitting room and how Binnie sat looking at it as if it were a hanged man for several minutes before bursting into tears and running to her bed. 'They are lovely rooms, and they are very lucky children,' he said. 'And you are wonderful.'

Just in case he was getting fruity, Binnie went to run a bath.

If she loved the idea of bed, this new mother-Binnie, she equally loved her bathroom. Even though it opened off their bedroom, she thought of it as her own and Ian tended to use the one down the corridor. All the paraphernalia of her womanliness was stacked and scattered in her en-suite. No baby stuff lined the shelves, no baby stuff dripped and dribbled down the tiled walls. It was her inner soul, her temple of femininity, her private sanctuary – full of the expensive stuff brought back by Ian from his business trips, as once a Prince of Fairy Tale would bring his Princess trophies from his travels and ask for nothing in return. Certainly not humping. Romantic love. Lancelot and Guinevere. No other favour save to adore. She loved it in there. In there she was safe.

Soon Ian was going on his first protracted business trip abroad since Tristan's birth. Binnie had shortened it to her satisfaction and was now quite relaxed about it. She had two teenagers to help her, the Christian Trisha, and she would *not* have to spend all day worrying about conjugal rights.

'You can bring me some more Patou,' she said, before vanishing up the stairs. 'Please, darling.' And, from the safety of the kitchen doorway, she blew him a pretty kiss.

He responded with two smacking noises made by his own lips that yearned to get themselves around more than just thin air. But with the advent of Claire and Andrew, good as they were, he knew better than to push home even the slightest of enquiries about when, exactly, that side of things might resume. He tried to remember when it resumed with Angela. Not long, he thought. But then, he also thought, with deliberate lack of gallantry, she was always gagging for it, and he wondered, as he tapped the words Belinda and Patou into his organizer, why she couldn't go out and get someone to be getting it from now. He was rather sorry for his gibe about her past lovers. If she only *would* remarry, then everyone could breathe a sigh of relief. Marriages ended all the time. New ones began. It was the way of the world. She'd looked so forlorn – first time ever – the night Otto got drunk that he had been very tempted. Only for a moment, of course. But if she was hooked up with someone else, it would make life so much easier all round.

The phrase 'gagging for it' suddenly re-entered his mind. Along with a picture of his ex-wife in a pose to fit the tag. He closed the organizer with a snap. Bloody woman. He was very fond of her, of course he was, mother of his children, companion for twenty-odd years. But if she thought she could break him, he'd be damned. For some reason he suddenly found himself calling on Jesus. O Jesus, he said to himself, O *Jesus* – if you make this one work I vow I will never be tempted to stray again. Not even for a one-nighter. Which is all it was going to be with Binnie. At first. He was still quite puzzled how he got from that to here. But he had, and he would not, he would never, ever again.

He remembered how, when he was still married to Angela, his colleagues came in to work saying that Her Indoors had had a go last night about their never contributing anything to the running of the home. And how he stayed silent because his own amazing, extraordinary, talented, clever, unbreakable, inviolable, unshakeable, capable star of a wife – whom he loved and adored and who weighed the same then as on the day he married her – *she* never said a critical word about it.

Just smiled. And handed him a glass of his favourite wine. And asked him intelligent questions about the day. And turned willingly, always willingly, towards him in bed each night if he required it. He longed to agree with his colleagues – to say that he too knew how a wife could undervalue a husband – to say that he needed a drink before going home sometimes and who didn't? – to be welcomed into the club of the hard-done-by and misunderstood. But he waited in vain. Much as he waited in vain for her to need him in any important sense. The one time he felt he was valuable was when she gave birth. Then she held on to him and really needed his strength. Twice in a marriage is not enough. And anyway, he'd been late for the first one. Apart from that, she made him feel like a king. It was wearying. It was relentless. It was false. And it was very tedious to live up to.

Fleetingly, he began visiting an alarming woman called the Virago, who tied him up for fifty pounds and told him he was bad. Something like 35 per cent of British males liked some form of bondage, he'd read, and he could almost understand why. Abrogation of all responsibility. The chance to be weak. He loved it when she snarled at him and spat out the words, 'Can't you do anything right?' But after a few visits he just lay there in that small back room in Bayswater and felt like a prat. 'You don't get it, do you?' said the Virago, untying him regretfully.

'No,' he said.

There was, he realized now, somewhere in between the two. And he had found it in his adorable Binnie when she landed so prettily and helplessly at his feet. Why, she'd had to import a special chair all the way from Canada for her practice, because the others did not take the patient down low enough. Little Thing.

Well, while his Little Thing was in her bathroom and Claire and Andrew were out, the baby asleep and the afternoon sun still warming the patio, he would have a beer. He went to the fridge, but where he had put half a dozen bottles of his favourite Czechoslovakian there were now none. Ah well, he'd have a warm one. He went to the store cupboard beneath the stairs. Two empty six-packs lay crumpled in the darkness. He felt something rising in him that he had never had cause to feel before. A rising bubble of pure rage directed towards his son. And he didn't mean Tristan.

Just then the puzzled voice of Binnie called down the stairs. 'You'd better get me some more Eau de Joy bath oil too, and some Calvin. Lotion and foam. They both seem to have vanished...'

He began to run up the stairs. If he could persuade her to take a little lie-down with him.

Her voice trailed off as the napping Tristan woke, too early, too early, from his post-lunchtime nap. Thoughtlessly, Binnie was standing right outside the nursery door.

Ian felt a rising bubble of rage yet again. And this time it was not for either of his sons. Someone in Somerset came to mind.

September/October

Three or four families in a country village
is the very thing to work on . . .
JANE AUSTEN TO CASSANDRA

No, Angela Fytton, in her simple busyness, did not miss her children at all. Her children were like a bunch of temporarily mislaid keys, about which you can say comfortably to yourself, 'Well, I had them when I came in last night, so they must be somewhere and I'm sure they'll turn up eventually.'

Much more pressing than her children's continuing huff was the end-of-summer activity beholden upon the owner of Church Ale House. The gathering of the apples for collection, the last of the garnering of vegetables for storing or bottling, the picking of fruit and the making of quince jam and jelly. The mulberries she abandoned to the birds, for she really did not care for the taste. The birds were more than happy to oblige and cleared the tree. As the first leaves began to fall she found herself avoiding the sight of that poor frontal stump and wondered, again, about Archie, who had caused it so much damage, and why. And why the sight of it affected her so much. Best get on. Didn't do to think.

By now she had learned to pluck a still-warm egg from under a sharp-eyed layer without so much as a by your leave, and she had so many that she looked up Maria Brydges for the pickling of them. Maria Brydges was her customary firm self: 'Procure only the best white wine vinegar. This can be obtained by dealing with a respectable tradesman upon whom you can depend.' Angela got hers from Boots the Chemist in Taunton, which seemed a reasonable compromise. She spotted Wanda at the other end of the shop, but she flitted away before Angela had a chance to speak. Which was a pity, because Angela would have liked some advice. Wanda was checking out the opposition, she supposed, since she was down by the herbal remedy section.

Lots to do, then, much to keep her busy. And when it was all done – when the winter set its seasonal seal on activity – she would give a party. At which she would finally get to know her neighbours really well and feel, at last, that she was good enough to become an established part of the place. Before she introduced her newly returned husband to them all.

She had the occasional fantasy about remarrying in St Hilary's. Though she was not altogether sure how the Anglican church felt about divorcees remarrying each other. Now *there* was a nice theological problem. The church seemed to be full of them. All the fault of the patriarchs, Daphne said, for not letting women in. If women were the law-makers there would be a lot more pragmatism. So said Daphne. Angela was not so sure. Remembering her west London witch-hunters, she thought the female of the species might be even more likely to put a stone round your neck and throw you down a well, or join in heartily at the whipping post. Daphne said it was divide and rule. At which point Angela gave up. Keep busy, she told herself. That is all you need to do. And it was. The pleasure was sustained. And if she did not – if she took a moment out to enjoy the strangeness of her rural surroundings – well, that was always a pleasure, and interesting too.

Craig Elliott, taking his customary stroll past her garden and up the hill, leaned over the gate, not for the first time, squeezed her hand and told her that she looked perfect in her garden – so fresh, so pretty, so inspirational in the light of this new opus of his with which he was having such trouble. He looked up at the hill and back at her, and his eyes were very friendly and kind. Then he squeezed her hand, smiled once more with his crinkling, periwinkle, friendly, handsome smile – with just a tinge of sadness around its edges, she detected – and said breathily, '*Inspirational* . . .' and squeezed her hand once more.

She was flattered and she blushed.

He then wiped his hand across his brow and shook his head in despair. 'It does not get any easier,' he said.

'The Muse?'

He looked at her sorrowfully. 'The au pair. She just does not fit into our lives.' He closed his eyes with the pain of it. 'She is a great, lumpen noisy thing to find on the stairs in the morning, and I must have quiet. And beauty, come to that.'

'Poor Lucy.'

'Poor both of us.'

That saddish little smile again, before he strode off towards the hill. He turned, once, waved his hand and called, 'But you have cheered my day.'

What a nice man, she thought. From a distance you could almost think his wellingtons were a gentleman's riding boots. And she blushed again.

'Perpendicular,' called Daphne Blunt from the top of her ladder, stretching her elegant Afghan neck and pointing with her long Afghan nose. 'The tower is anyway. Otherwise a good screen and *very* good bench ends.'

Angela ran her fingers over the low-relief of the pew carvings to her right – a boy holding a candle, two choristers with books, two curvaceous girls holding branches, an old man humping a sack, a woman with trailing cloak and flying curls carrying a flagon.

'You've got Faith, Hope, Charity and Time, the Virgin and Child, and the Five Wise Virgins down the left hand side –'

'And this one? On the right?'

'Well, I *think* that's very local. The Blessing of the Ale. Although it might just be a harvest procession, but it looks like winter to me – cloaks and caps and things. I haven't done enough research on it yet. The woman with the flagon might be a saint or mythical woman, or she could be the ale-wife, and if it is then she lived where you do now. Fancy doing a spot of brewing? Church ale was very special. It was sold off to the locals to raise money for the church and its charity.'

Angela laughed. 'I've got enough to do, thanks.'

'I know what you mean,' said Daphne, looking at the half-cleaned wall. 'You can't get a machine to do restoration. Thank God.'

'Amen,' said Angela automatically.

She went over to the ladder and peered at the emergent wall-paintings. They were crudely drawn, in black and red outline, a jumble of disproportionate cartoon shapes – men in flowing, striated robes; weird creatures that were half devil or half snake or half dragon or peculiarly imagined lion or bird; decorative patterning; wild, leaping flames . . . Heaven above, saved souls in the middle and hell below. 'Are they very old?'

'Late fifteenth, I think. Difficult to tell. Whitewashed over in the name of the Puritans,' said Daphne. 'And I think –' she pointed around the tops of the arched walls of the nave – 'that on either side, below the clerestories, there were more paint-ings, of the Seven Corporal Works of Mercy and the Seven Spiritual Works of Mercy. It was fairly common to remind the congregation of the charitable and worthy things that got you into heaven. You can just see the shadow of one there, where I gave it a brushing.'

Angela peered. She could see, faintly, a series of shapes. 'Only just,' she said.

'Oh, they'd have been bright as a cartoon when they were first done. That's "To Clothe the Naked", I think. And then over there –' Daphne pointed – 'is "To Bear Wrongs Patiently". It's all an instruction manual for the way to do things properly.' She returned her Afghan profile to the work. 'I think they might be in for a shock when I get round to that lot. Clothing the naked usually meant that you gave the clothes off your own back. We might yet see a Devereux patronness in the buff.' She laughed. 'And bearing wrongs patiently was not above showing a saintly wife being beaten and looking as if she was positively enjoying it.'

Angela felt a shiver down her spine, though whether it was the chill in the church or the thought of such brutality she was not sure. 'What happened if they fought back?' she asked.

'Best not ask,' said Daphne Blunt. 'Anyway, those won't get uncovered for a month or two. These are taking the time. Dorothea Tichborne's paying. She just might get a little bit more than she thought she was getting, that's all. She wants the glory of the family name restored in the shape of this place. Which her family built.' Daphne looked up sharply. 'Or rather put up the money for. It was the peasants and local craftsmen and masons who built it. Always makes me laugh the way they talk of this king or that queen having built something.' She pointed to the face of one of the devil figures emerging as she cleaned. 'Little people had their ways of getting back at big people. Look at this – it's a Devereux face. And the stonemason had a *very* big grudge.' She pointed up at the roof. 'Have a look at some of the gargoyles outside and the carvings in these bosses.' She picked up her torch. 'Funnily enough,' she said, concentrating the beam on the hell section of the wall, 'the ones that have lasted the best are the devils.'

Angela peered. It was so. Especially the devil spewing out the Host.

Daphne's laugh rang round the church, making the pigeons on the roof outside flap their wings and coo irritably. 'Gave them an extra coating of whitewash,' she said joyfully, 'to be sure of getting rid of them, but it meant they were only protected all the more . . . That's some kind of metaphor, I suppose. The more you try to eradicate something, the harder people hold on to it. Nothing like having to fight for something in order to value it.'

Angela nodded. In the torch-beam she could indeed see a very strong resemblance to old Dr Tichborne's wife. 'She's a good woman,' she said.

'She's pious,' said Daphne, 'which is different.' She laughed again. 'I love history for the jokes it plays. Nothing is ever what it seems. It's all conjecture and interpretation.' She turned back to the wall and continued cleaning.

'Let me know if you come up with anything about the ale. I'd be interested,' said Angela. But Daphne, engrossed again, just nodded. 'Well,' said Angela, taking her cue, 'I've got to get back and start my digging.'

'Digging?' The Afghan nose came up, sensing scent.

'I'm putting in a couple of herb beds. With Sammy's approval,' she added wryly.

'Where?'

'Up at the back. Near the hedge.'

'Let me know if you find anything interesting,' said Daphne. And then she added, as if striking a bargain, 'And I'll look out what I can about the ale ceremony.'

Angela thanked her and walked back up the aisle. She stopped by the bench ends on her way out. If the woodcarver held any grudges they were not apparent. The virgins all looked as dainty and silly as medieval virgins were supposed to, while on the other side the woman with the flagon was a mature, full-bosomed beauty in a stylishly swirling cloak. She certainly did not look like a saint.

Nevertheless, she was reminded of those seven corporal acts of mercy and decided, magnanimously, that she too would be charitable. Busy and charitable. As women have ever been known for their charity. Therefore, what she wished on Binnie was not death or pain or serious misadventure. It was just a very pleasant single-parenthood. That was all. Nothing wrong with that now, was there?

But something along the lines of Faith, Hope and Charity made her uncomfortable. She resolved never to make the acquaintance of baby Tristan.

No matter, she thought. Busy, busy, she thought. And put the irksome feeling to one side.

From the lych gate she looked up at the gargoyles.

Why that's outrageous, she said. Outrageous.

Angela was standing in the Elliotts' kitchen, having found one of the children's toys in the lane. Lucy Elliott's eyes were pink-rimmed, with the customary shadows of pale lilac beneath them. 'You're in luck,' she said. 'The oldest two have gone on the Sunday school outing with the au pair and the baby's asleep.'

'How's the au pair?' asked Angela.

'Large,' said Lucy Elliott happily. 'Very *large*.'

She handed Angela a cup of coffee and sat down as if she wanted to lie down.

'Craig's working?'

'Craig's working,' Lucy Elliott agreed, looking oddly suspicious.

'He's very dedicated.'

'He is,' agreed his wife.

'He gets on with things.'

'He does.'

'Creative types do, I suppose. I've just been in the church. Daphne Blunt's really getting on with things too.'

'Hah!' said Lucy Elliott, the manner of which implied that getting on with things so far as she was concerned was as likely as the moon turning blue. She said wistfully, 'I used to play the piano in there sometimes. Before number three came along.' She gave Angela a despairing look. 'I was a professional musician, you know. Played all over the world. I used to find playing the piano very relaxing.'

If ever woman was born who looked like she needed a bit of relaxing, this was she.

'Don't you still?' asked Angela.

'Oh no, not now. We don't even have a piano. The noise –' she lowered her voice and raised her eyes to the ceiling. Above which sat Craig Elliott, struggling, as he'd told Angela earlier, with his new novel.

'You must borrow mine,' said Angela. 'It's quite a good one.'

'No,' Lucy Elliott said firmly.

So firmly that Angela was surprised. 'I could have it tuned for you,' she said, 'if that's the problem. I'd need to have it tuned anyway. You and Craig could come over ...'

'No,' said Lucy Elliott, even more firmly. 'Craig is extremely busy. When he's not in London.'

'Come on your own. Please do.'

'Perhaps,' said Lucy Elliott, in a voice that meant she never would. She really was being unnecessarily unfriendly.

'It would be good for the thing,' Angela persisted. 'Really it would. I was told that pianos, like pearls, should not be left untouched for any amount of time ... They flatten and die.'

At which, Angela was astonished to see, Lucy Elliott let two silent, gigantic tears go plop on to her chest. So it *was* the piano she missed.

'Well, the offer is there any time you want to take it up,' she said.

And a soft and friendly voice from above said, 'Do I hear our Church Ale neighbour down below?'

'Goodbye,' said Lucy Elliott hurriedly.

Angela went.

'When are those kids of yours coming down?' asked Dave the Bread, as he dropped off a lovely warm loaf and asked her to admire his tie-dyed shorts. Bright yellow. Saffron, he said.

She had a vague feeling that you needed several acres of crocuses to colour a small pocket handkerchief, but when she said this to him he just smiled mysteriously and said that Wanda knew how to get the best out of even the smallest of things ... And he winked with such startling wickedness that she immediately wondered about the contents of his saffron shorts.

'When they're ready to come, I suppose,' she said. She told him about the herb gardens and the box of old medicine bottles. 'All shapes and sizes, and some of them probably as old as the century. I thought I might come over and get some advice from Wanda about the decocting side of things,' she said.

'Ah well. Ah well,' said Dave, backing away oddly. 'She's very busy doing the pink muslins,' he said. 'Beetroots and secrets . . . You know Wanda. Better not disturb.'

It was a similar situation to Lucy Elliott. Every time Angela made an overture of friendship, it was – though not unkindly – rebuffed. She'd been trying to have a cup of tea with Wanda for weeks. Angela often wondered if behind those closed doors and steamed-up windows, Wanda was really doing what she said. Was she dyeing muslins or making corn dollies and bog myrtle wreaths, or was her secretiveness because she was making a witch's brew or magicking up potions with incantations? Once or twice, cycling by the gate of Tally-Ho Cottage late in the evening, Angela distinctly heard the sound of cackling from within.

And Wanda not only looked very mysterious; Wanda *acted* very mysteriously. The last time Angela had met her on her bicycle in the lane had been very disappointing. Feeling quite proud of her newly acquired country knowledge, she wished to try it out on the expert.

'I've heard that yarrow, witch hazel and willow is a good tonic,' she began, all friendly-like. Wanda nodded furiously. 'Oh yes, it is, it is,' she said, and started pedalling away. 'Perhaps you could help me identify them . . .' But Wanda was too busy. 'Could you draw them for me, then?' she asked. 'So I can find them on my own.' But Wanda had a sore finger. 'Split a woody nightshade berry and bind it on,' Angela offered, remembering the additional information found in Maria Brydges's method of physick. 'They're very good for sore fingers, felonwort meaning whitlow or abscess healer – but I expect you know that.'

It was then that Wanda looked at her most witch-like and shifty. As if she knew something that Angela didn't. Angela longed to enter into those ancient ways and mysteries. But she understood. A wise woman keeps her sources to herself.

'Only a suggestion,' she said. 'Probably quite wrong. You'll know best.' And Wanda, nodding furiously again, began pedalling off. 'I'm not sure of the proportions,' called Angela. 'Of the yarrow, witch hazel and willow . . .' In her billowing clouds of tie-dyed muslin, Wanda looked like a large concentration of vapour, speeding away. 'For the tonic?' said Angela. 'Thirds,' called Wanda over her shoulder. 'And take it in water three times a day.'

Angela was surprised. Very surprised. According to Maria Brydges, it was supposed to be a health-giving rinse for the hair.

Witchcraft was tempting. If she could only get into Tally-Ho Cottage for more than ten seconds, she would ask Wanda outright for a potion to dribble into Ian's tea. Or an amulet to slip beneath the pillow. Perhaps she'd ask Dave about it now. He'd know when it was the right time to call.

'I've been trying to see Wanda for weeks now,' she said to the hovering Dave. 'I tried to catch her in Boots, and in the lane, but she always flying, isn't she?'

Dave nodded. 'Busy little bee, my Wanda,' he said.

'And how is her finger?' asked Angela.

'Ah,' said Dave. He looked at his watch. 'Got to get back for the oven,' he said. 'My biscuits.'

'I can give you some interesting old recipes for biscuits,' she called after him, but he was off, speeding down her mossy path in a welter of patchy yellow and hairy thigh.

He gave her the thumbs-up from the gate and was gone. Only the warm, inviting smell of new bread remained. Clearly, in the matter of getting to know her neighbours, she must be the one to break the social ice. Her party could not come a moment too soon.

Angela had not yet called upon the Tichborne residence. Whenever she saw the benign old doctor out with his binoculars, he smiled at her kindly, and she smiled back and said something polite about bird-watching before passing on. It was unsurprising that they socialized so little, his wife being, so she had heard, something of an invalid. Mrs Tichborne scarcely ventured out and looked so proper when she did that Angela felt it wise to wait to be introduced. She did, however, surprise herself and begin to attend church. Evensong. It just seemed the appropriate thing to do, given that her new home was so bound into the tradition. She liked to study the pew ends while the vicar did his stuff. All part of being in the country and being good, she thought. Looking away from the devils quickly.

To fill up the uncomfortable time between entering the church and the beginning of the service, Angela strove to - look as if she knew what she was doing. Just like everyone else, she wished to appear able to have long, private, interesting chats with the Almighty while on her knees and to look as if the Almighty were answering her back. Because He or She was certainly answering all the other assembled kneelers back in earnest. You could tell, she thought, by the rapt look on their faces that they'd got a hot line to heaven. All except her. 'Listen, God,' she said. 'If you are up there and offended, I apologize. You know I don't really believe in you, but – well – here I am and there you are. And when in Rome – well, no, not in Rome any more, not since Henry VIII and little Edward, but when in the country you do as the other country dwellers do, so I'm here as part of my social duty. You do not have to say anything . . .'

God duly didn't.

She attended Evensong because she had tried the morning family service only once and once was quite enough. At the family service, the vicar played his guitar, exhorting everyone – Lucy Elliott, her new Dutch au pair and her three fidgeting children; Mrs Dorkin and the Dorkin girl (who were surprisingly pious and sometimes attended Evensong as well); two very spotty youths in plastic biker jackets who stared, silent throughout, at the Dorkin girl's striking frontage; Dr Tichborne alone in the Devereux pew; and

Wanda, who, with her stage skills, kept them all in tune – to clap their hands and join in and sing! After which you had to kiss everyone.

And as if that was not embarrassing enough, at the exhortation to kiss everybody, she watched the extraordinary spectacle of the Dorkin girl practically elbowing a very speedy Dr Tichborne out of the way to reach the vicar, while the two spotty youths followed in hot pursuit of the Dorkin girl and appeared to think that church-kissing was just a longer version of the word 'grope'.

Evensong was an altogether calmer experience. Both the Tichbornes attended, and there was absolutely no kissing, hand-clapping, 'Wow!', 'God!' or hymn-singing of anything but a traditional nature. This service brought in Sammy and St Hilary's ex-incumbent, the Reverend Bertrand Stokes, who was driven there and back in a taxi paid for by Mrs Dorothea Tichborne. The sight of St Hilary's ex-incumbent attempting to genuflect to both the Holy Host and his aristocratic one was painful to behold, despite his being held in firm support by the taxi driver. Lucy Elliott came alone, keeping her eyes closed throughout, even when standing for the hymns, and Angela sat at the back feeling more sinner than celebrant. The Rudges would have come, but they always had to head off back to Bristol on a Sunday evening to avoid the traffic.

Daphne Blunt never came to services. As soon as the doors were flung open ready to welcome the sinners in, she slipped out of the side door and away. 'Too much bad done in the name of religion for my liking,' she told Angela. 'I'll care for the fabric. The witness can take care of itself.'

On this particular September Sunday after Evensong, the great and the good, in the person of Dorothea Tichborne, finally condescended to be introduced. For some reason best known to himself, Dr Tichborne was under the mistaken apprehension that Mrs Angela Fytton of Church Ale House in the county of Somerset was a recent widow. And for some reason he seemed to find this quite cheering. He beamed at her as they approached. 'Death is but a tavern on the way,' he said, as if he were wishing her a happy birthday. 'Time heals. Very quickly. Quite often.' He turned to his wife.

'And prayer,' added Mrs Tichborne. To which the bright-haired young vicar, hovering behind them by the church porch, said a very cheerful 'Amen'.

Dr Tichborne, showing more of the mettle that Angela had last seen fending off the Dorkin girl on the altar steps, then responded surprisingly by repeating the words 'Time' and 'Amen' with such passion, and such a look of fire directed at the vicar, that she thought he might have gone Shaker. Partic-ularly as the vicar's apparent response was indeed to shake, before suddenly hurtling off in the opposite direction, his cas-sock flapping above his jeans and cowboy boots, looking over his shoulder and down the path towards the gateway, fearful as if the devil himself were after him. Old Dr Tichborne eyed him very sadly. Angela felt sorry for him. There was, despite its joyous rural undertow, some oddly unfriendly behaviour in the country.

'There now,' said Mrs Dorkin disappointedly, as she and daughter Dorkin, and daughter Dorkin's considerable chest, leaned over the lych-gate. 'Never any time, that one.' She gave the girl a little dig in the back with her knuckles and, accordingly, the girl puffed herself out even further in the manner of a very well-fed pouter pigeon. Mrs Dorkin winked at her and said very loudly, 'Well, it's time my girl was bap-tized at any rate.' She gave Dr Tichborne a cocksure look. 'Can't get married in church without . . . now can you?'

Dr Tichborne took one look at the female swellings of his young servant girl nestling among the lichen and the ivy, and closed his eyes.

Mrs Dorkin looked upon the gesture and saw it as reward for all her efforts. She knew that look. It was unbridled pas-sion, as the books would have it, unbridled passion if ever she saw it. One day daughter Dorkin would not only have made her bed, but also be invited, urgently, to lie in it. Like the Lord, who governed over all of St Hilary's and Staithe, Mrs Dorkin looked upon her handiwork and was pleased. *Well* pleased.

Smiling beneficently upon the world and those rosy breasts in which she invested much hope, she tucked her daughter's arm into her own and gave it a yank. The nestling pair, so rudely pulled from their bed of lichen, bobbled about a bit uncertainly and then returned to their rightful place, before their owner and her mother made their way down the lane. From behind they were like a pair of ships in full sail, with their petticoats fluttering, their hips rolling, their dazzling golden curls flying in the summer breeze. Mrs Tichborne looked and saw the devil walking beside them and clutched at her crucifix.

'I am settling in very well,' said Angela. 'Thank you.'

'Good, good, good,' said Dorothea Tichborne. But her mind was on saving her servant's soul. Baptism, she thought, was the answer. A good deed to lighten the darkness. 'I must speak to the vicar about Sandra's baptism,' she said, with unaccustomed vigour. And with surprising agility she shot off in search of the fleeing cassock.

As, it must be said, did Dr Tichborne.

Thus an invitation for Mrs Angela Fytton, putative widow, to the ancient Devereux, now Tichborne, seat was not forthcoming.

After her customary Sunday evening stroll up one side of the Mump and down the other, Angela returned home. Once back in her own garden, on the other side of the yews, she found the vicar taking a tremendous interest in the faint stars that were beginning to appear in the evening sky.

'God's jewel casket,' she said.

The Reverend Crispin Archer looked strained. He was staring up at the stars for guidance but all he could think about was quite the wrong kind of heavenly body. There was a faint chill in the air, a hint of autumn.

'Would you –' She hesitated. 'Would you care to slip through the hedge and come in for a glass of mulberry wine?'

She had never seen such gratitude. At least the vicar was socially inclined.

In the gloaming, Sandra Dorkin leaned on the vicar's front fence and waited and dreamed. He must return to the manse at some time and she wanted to thank him, in the warmest way possible, for agreeing to baptize her. As her employer pointed out, a girl of nineteen, be she ever so pure, must have sinned a little on the way.

Angela faced the vicar across her kitchen table. She sipped the red liquor very slowly, determined to like it. The vicar appeared to like his very much indeed. The first one went down without, apparently, touching the sides.

'An adult baptism is interesting,' she said.

'Yes,' he said miserably. 'Our esteemed benefactor thinks I should give a full submersion, on account of all the sins accumulated. She's very taken with the idea.'

'That seems logical,' said Angela, forcing down another sip of the red stuff.

'I favour just a little trickle on the forehead,' he said mournfully.

'You're the vicar.'

Odd how the irrefutable seemed to cut no ice.

He nodded, still mournful.

'Cheer up,' said Angela. 'After the ceremony you can play your guitar and we can all hug and kiss.' She gave a gesture of solidarity. 'Mix the old with the new. Like your sermon this evening. You could use the water from my well – if there is any. We can dress it,' she added vaguely.

Dress it. Undress it. He winced. Full baptism. He winced again.

She refilled the vicar's glass but not her own, which she pushed to one side. 'Do you know,' she said, 'I can't go on pretending any more.'

The vicar looked at her. If another one was about to declare herself he would take himself off to a mission hut. 'What?' he said cautiously.

'This wine,' she said. 'It's horrible. And I'm not going to make any more of it. It really *does* taste of worms. I should be making church ale instead. And selling it to raise money for St Hilary's.'

If she had wanted encouragement, she received none.

'Like in the olden days?'

But the vicar merely remained looking distracted.

'Have some more,' she said, and poured out the remains of bottle number one. 'It really is filthy.'

The vicar could not agree. Indeed, he felt it had just the right poke to it. When he slipped back through the yews later, he clutched the two remaining bottles. I will donate them to the jumble, he said to the silvery night, before stumbling through his back door and undressing, rather awkwardly, in the dark. Though there was no need, for the Dorkin girl had grown bored with waiting and, when the two youths in plastic biker jackets came along, she went for a walk with them up over the hill and down among the pig huts. But he put the bottles in his own cupboard all the same.

The next morning Angela went off to post a card of the Glastonbury Thorn to Claire and Andrew. It was a survivor like herself, she thought. She also thought that a postcard would mean Ian and Binnie would see it. She made it as joyful and celebratory as she could.

> I am so enjoying living down here. Everything is working really well and I want you to come and try my Fytton honey, and see my herb bed, and eat my vegetables and preserves and pickles and make a breakfast of my eggs [she added 'hens' to the eggs, imagining some coarse wit if she did not]. So please come and visit me or stay with me soon, before the winter sets in. Or come

then. I really want you to meet everyone, especially Sammy, who is wonderful. No more now. Too tired from digging. Love Mum.

Coming back from the pillar box she met Rika in the lane.

'Ja, ja,' beamed the scarlet-cheeked au pair over the heads of the three screaming Elliott children, and then kissed them, one, two, three, so that they screamed even louder. They were wielding little nets, looking as picturesque as a field of poppies, Angela thought. Coming closer, however, she saw that they were beating each other over the head with them.

'No, no,' said the kindly Dutch girl as the children turned their attention to her own prominent bottom. And she gave each one in turn a pat on the head that nearly flattened them.

Whereupon they burst into tears and she hugged them to her substantial chest and made them cry even louder.

It was hard to know if she was several petals short of a tulip or highly intelligent, but whatever she was she was remarkably impervious to the tyrannies of children.

'Time to go home,' she said.

Angela walked with her. 'And are you enjoying it here?' she asked.

'No,' said the girl. 'I mean – time to go *home* . . . I miss my parents. I miss my friends. I miss my *beer* . . .' She rolled her eyes. 'Oh, the *English* beer. So weak, and it needs salt . . .' She shrugged. 'So, I go home. Mr Craig has bought me a ticket already.'

From an upstairs window, Craig Elliott looked down, crinkled his eyes and waved. He looked a much happier man. Did Angela imagine it or did he kiss his fingertips to her? She imagined it, of course. He was surely kissing his fingertips to his screaming children.

She went a little further on, and looked over the wall of the Rudges' garden, where nothing was stirring, not even a bird. And she was tempted – oh, wasn't she? – to ask their gardener, who came from miles away and drove a very shiny car, if she could borrow the petrol Rotovator before she began digging her herb beds. Cutting and slashing and clearing the nettles and other growing things had been tiring enough, without the thought of taking a fork and shovel to the ground as well. A Rotovator would relieve the pain of the effort quite nicely.

There again, it would also churn up and destroy anything in its path. But she was tempted, very tempted. Nevertheless, as she leaned there, looking down on the perfect, silent garden where not a leaf lay out of place, not a chewed petal drooped or an aphid glowed its green among the leaves, she was overcome with a desire to dig her own soil with her own two hands. Another line of Plath's floated into her head:

Perfection is terrible. It cannot have children.
Cold as snow breath, it tamps the womb.

No, no. If Daphne could do what she did with her own bare hands, then so could she. She had promised herself to go slow, with time, with the seasons – and so she would. Anyway, she might find something really interesting. A jewel from King Alfred's crown, perhaps. She smiled at the memory. A girl could dream . . .

She heard the latch of the Rudges' side gate. Someone was about to come out. She gave the Rotovator one last, yearning look before picking up her skirts and running back along the lane before her courage failed her.

She stopped by Sammy Lee's gate. How lonely he must be, she thought, looking at his silent, dark-paned cottage. And how sad never to have loved even once. Or maybe how sensible. He stood in the sun, leaning against his porch, a cup in his hand, a thin cigarette between his lips, and she supposed that was contentment. She looked at his cabbages and felt an odd sensation which she realized was envy. He had set jam jars of beer in among the rows of vegetables and they were full of bloated creatures who'd died smiling and ready to face that eternal hangover in the sky. She had not believed him and was at her wits' end, practically hearing the munching from her garden every morning. A beery demise, though, was fitting. It seemed an appropriate death to deliver as the owner of Church Ale House.

'So it does work,' she said.

'If you use the right stuff,' he agreed. 'No use putting Kestrel lager down for them. Even a slug knows what it likes.'

'Maybe I *should* make my own,' she said, pointing. But if she thought he would laugh she was wrong.

'See those,' he said, pointing to trails of greenery running through his hedge. 'Wild hops.'

She went back home. But she was definitely, *definitely* thoughtful.

'Keep busy,' continued the theme in her head. Along with 'Wild hops, wild hops, wild hops'.

15

October

The Original Witch
will pick up the switch
and turn off the lights
in the steeple's sight.
She will laugh, Ha Ha
She will laugh, Ho Ho
And the walls will go
just like in Jericho.

MAIGHREAD MEDBH

According to a Brydges ancestor, who had borrowed the text from the Puritan lobby, there was but one way for a good woman to conduct her life.

> The Goodwife is like a merchant's ship, for she bringeth her food and her nourishings for the heart, soul, and temporal body from afar . . . Thro her Wisdom and Diligence great things come by her; she Brings in with her Hands, for she putteth her hands to the Wheel . . . She overseeth the ways of her household . . . and eateth not the Bread of Idleness.

Angela took up the challenge regarding the Bread of Idleness wholeheartedly and commenced digging. Bread of Idleness, she thought scathingly, just about summed up those decadent, privileged women back in London with their cut-price Filipino skivvies and their trips to the hairdresser's. Bread of Idleness was certainly not for *her*.

She donned an old pair of Andrew's shorts and an even older T-shirt and told the mirror that the raggedy-looking creature with scratches on her arms (from the brambles) and red patches all over her legs (from the nettles) and a nose that looked as if it had been at the port (from being at the port) was indeed a Goodwife. She shoved her feet into Perry welling-tons, found a few grips for her hair and took up her spade and her fork. Looking around at the bright October day, she felt a rush of self-satisfaction. Who knew what treasures she might unearth as she cut into this ancient soil? If there were Roman tesserae, there might be Roman coins. If not Alfred's crown, then perhaps a helmet or a sword. If there were shards of medieval pottery, then might there not be silver plate?

She set to with a will, imagining it would all be done by sundown. Sammy, when she suggested this to him, shook his head. Just dig, he told her. So dig she did.

Thinking about it again, later, and up to her elbows in dry clods and nettle stings, Angela Fytton had a sudden urge to partake of the Bread of Idleness rather strongly. She was also less inclined to think that paying Filipinos to do *anything* in the way of alleviating the domestic burden was reprehensi-ble. Indeed, at one particularly warm moment of soil-turning, had a passing Filipino tottered by her holly hedge she would have hurled herself across their path and clutched their bloody ankles and *begged* them to take a turn with the spade – aye, offering well *above* the minimum wage and a free cut and blow-dry at a salon of their choice too . . . But it was an urge that passed – possibly because a Filipino did not.

She fought back. And it was the strangest thing. After all those years of keeping her brain in several different compart-ments, of having her mind on one thing while aware of an impending six others, where lists were required and strategic planning was a must, where managing the early years of having very little money gave way to swimming lessons and dinner parties and stocking the freezer and seeing the teach-ers and remembering to kiss away a hurt (including Ian's), or what required an apology, to have the right change for the bus on a Monday, to get Ian's train tickets for Tuesday, to have a six-page document translated into Japanese by Wednesday, to check catalogue copy and buy birthday cards on Thursday, to talk entertainingly through dinner to a junk mail expert from Stockholm on Friday, attend school sports and buy a new fax machine on Saturday, to listen to piano practice and go to the BMX track on Sunday ... Then tip into bed early and read a bit of a Booker winner. Fall asleep after establishing that they were not going to have sex. Fall asleep quite often during sex, if they were. And begin the whole thing again the next day ... doing it all out of fear that if she let one ball fall, one juggled plate crash to the ground, the whole works

would fall

apart –

which,

she now found,

it did not.

Ian had fallen.

Not her.

Digging, concentrating only on digging, with every justification for doing digging and *only* digging, was wonderful. The masculine focus, she thought, the envy of every woman born of woman. That focus, the security that what you are doing is entirely valid, full of worth, and that you may do it to the point of excellence. Your job, your role, your thrust. This, she felt, was Digging for Victory in the modern sense. Though she was still not entirely convinced that if a passing Filipino ...

Occasionally she stopped to draw breath and lift her eyes up to the hills, whence, so the Good Book advised, cometh her strength. And it did. What she saw made her happy. The glistening pig huts winking beneath a cloudless blue sky, the flicker and swoop of a confused late butterfly as its wings caught the light, all the beauty she beheld as she let her eyes sweep downwards to the flatness falling away to the west. The church with its Perpendicular tower and its soughing ilex, the manse beyond, the other houses ringed round about in this tight little community . . . How lucky she was to have come among such good people.

Sweet Auburn! Yes indeed.

She hoped that postcard would choke them.

Few items of interest emerged from the digging as the day progressed, not even more Roman teeth. The bits and pieces that she unearthed, Angela put to one side for Daphne to have a look at when she called. Despite this disappointment, at the end of the day, standing with a cracked cup (she did not have the energy to find a whole one) of elderflower tea (dried and sold by Wanda) in her hand and surveying the completely dug-over soil of her new herb beds – her day's achievement – she raised the cup. To liberation, she said. She felt *great*.

Next morning, of course, she was not quite so sure. Her back would hardly allow her to get out of bed. And then Sammy came along and tested the soil and said she would need to turn it all over again before she could even contemplate digging in the compost. She laughed and nudged him, thinking it was a joke. He pulled on his chin until she stopped laughing. Liberation did not seem quite so joyous. Neither did the masculine focus.

Another day of digging ensued, and Sammy was quite right. More lumps and clods appeared in what she could have sworn was soil made smooth as flour the day before. Dig, dig, dig. It was as if someone had slipped them in during the night. She worked until dusk, when Sammy came by. He nodded, rubbed a bit of the soil through his fingers, nodded again. One more, he said. And went on his way.

Barely able to make it to the kitchen table with her shop-bought gin and shop-bought tonic and refrigerator ice and foreign lemon, held in hands that looked as if they were taking part in a tribal-marking contest while attempting to grow an early crop of potatoes in the fingernails, she opened Maria

182

Brydges's book and found the herbal section. Too late now, of course. She should have made it up beforehand. Next year she would be able to create it all from her own garden. Even the juniper hung down from the church hedge and it was already full of ripening berries. Meanwhile, she would take the recipe to Wanda and see if she would make it up for her. Friendly-like.

RUB FOR BACKACHE

- 10 drops lavender oil
- 10 drops thyme oil
- 5 drops juniper oil
- 10 drops pine oil
- 18 drachms infused St John's Wort oil

A drachm, so the Lexicon explained, was three scruples, which was excellent news. How simple, after all, those London recipes where the initial list of ingredients was complicated and exotic enough to cause a minor safari and at which she always felt it was so vital to succeed.

URBAN HORS-D'OEUVRE

- Take three pounds of purple-flowering asafoetida, gathered from the foothills of the Himalayas
- a pinch of Winnipeg mace
- four ground mandarin roots
- half a dozen mackerel eggs
- coconut vinegar to blend

  Cook for fourteen hours in a Savoy runnel-pan and spread on thin slices of toast *brangee*.

  Serves 96

No more of that, she thought, pleased.

Tomorrow the cider apples would be collected and the last of the honey would go. And then the days would lie fallow until spring. Or so she hoped. To everything there is a season, she reminded herself. Winter is the dead, dark months. She was quite glad about that. Maybe her back would recover by spring.

And then, half walking, half crawling, and clutching her tube of Ibuleve, she betook herself up the creaking staircase to the avocado bathroom, the colour and style of which, she realized, she could not have cared less about. Nor the velvet curtaining. Nor later, the white piqué bed cover. Because every muscle in her body hurt. Except, miraculously, her heart.

A tumbrel of well-rotted pig muck was delivered, very silently, after she had crawled off to her bed. It was there in the morning, refusing to go away, in full view of her bedroom window when she limped and gasped her way over to pull the curtains. The hens were eyeing her cheerily from the dug-over soil, as if to say that this was more like it. Pinching all the worms, little buggers. 'Shoo,' she called from her window. 'Put them back.' Apart from anything else, she did not really like the idea that her beautiful brown shiny eggs would be entirely created out of horrible pink-grey wriggly worms. There were some matters of a country nature upon which she would prefer not to dwell. Sheep's and cows' bottoms, for example, when you had crawled behind them on your bicycle for a mile or two, were inclined to give you a rather jaundiced view of your own gynaecological mortality.

The Ibuleve practically winked at her: 'Hi, baby, see you later . . .' But as the misty morning gave up its vapour to the warmth of the autumn sun, she got into the rhythm of it. What had once been just a large, irregular patch of scrubby lawn and nettles and rotting newspapers and boxes of this and that, now began to look like a rich Christmas pudding of a mixture, just ready and raring for plant life. Sammy was right. You could see that it was now as well fed as any rosy infant, as fertile as any teeming womb. And like any well-fed, rosy infant, she thought, remembering her own two, a little frost would do it no harm. So Sammy said. The real planting would begin next spring. She looked upon it with great satisfaction. It looked fine. Beautifully dug over and neat. A perfect pair of circles, she had made. With the aid of string, wooden pegs and Sammy Lee's patience.

Sammy nodded in approval. 'Now let the rain come,' he said. 'Weather's been too hot and dry. It's turning for autumn now. You'll get your last sunny day tomorrow. Go in and have your tea.' He looked about him. 'I'd say you've earned it.'

She was sipping tea and looking through Maria Brydges's household recipes for a way to use up the excess beeswax. Although she offered it to Wanda, Wanda declined the gift. It was as if she thought that by accepting it, she would be required to give Angela something back. Like information. Angela screwed up her eyes, half amused, half irritated. The woman was certainly keeping her wisdoms, and her teapot, to herself . . .

> The best blacking for preserving boots and shoes, and
> which makes them perfectly watertight, is the following:

take of yellow wax one ounce and a half,
of mutton suet, three ounces and a half
horse turpentine, half an ounce
ivory black, three ounces

> Melt first the wax, to which add the suet, and afterwards
> the horse turpentine and ivory black. When the whole is
> melted remove from the fire. Use cold, rubbed on to a
> warmed brush.

It made her think, irresistibly, of gleaming black boots on a well-turned pair of calves. She thought again of Craig Elliott and the warmth of the pressure of his hand and, in a confused way, wondered what his calves might be like in well-polished boots. Before she could move from that to ringlets and ripped bodices, she shook her head free of the picture. Ian had been away far too long. She hastily turned the page. And there it was. The recipe for church ale, copied out in Maria Brydges's neatly perfect hand. With a postscript at the end:

This last was writ by Doll Caxton, whose brew was once known and which I set down in the hope it will not be misconstrued.

When hops are purchased, let them not be packed too loose in the sacks, for that does them no good. Gather what wild hops you have room to dry, for these will add a lightness of flavour, a freshness and bitterness that will do the ale well.

In the choosing of a malt it should be of a pale colour and broken into a coarse meal, not ground too fine. Good malt is known by a simple test, namely, by chewing it. If well made it will be nearly as sweet as sugar, delightful to the smell, mellow-tongued, of a round body and a thin skin. In short, it should have all the properties desirable to a woman.

Angela immediately rang the vicar and told him that she would be very happy to re-establish the old institution of church ale and that the profits would go to St Hilary's. He was suitably grateful and she felt full of love for the world.

Until she remembered that tomorrow was Ian and La Binbag's wedding anniversary. And despite herself she could not help wondering how they were marking *their* event. Marking hers with the herb beds had seemed so propitious; now it seemed like just another emptiness beside the idea of having him lying there in a real bed beside her. Well, she wanted both. That was it. Both. Herb bed and marriage bed. Why not?

She stared up at her ceiling with glittering eyes. The last time she talked to Claire on the phone, she heard Tristan cooing away in the background, banging something, and she could imagine the something clutched in a chubby little fist and being held out to delight his father as he walked through the door. Snapshots of other people's domestic lives hold too much poignancy, she said to the sloping ancient walls and her shadow that drooped there. 'Make it their last anniversary, please.' And the misery of it caused a pain that hurt considerably more than all her shrieking muscles put together. No amount of scruples could rub that one away.

She telephoned Rosa.

'Domestic homily number 346,' she said, across the crackling wires to Buenos Aires, still reading from the memorandum book. '"If you grate a nutmeg at the stalk end it will prove hollow throughout." According to Maria Brydges.'

'Who?' said Rosa. 'I can't hear you properly.'

'"Whereas the same nutmeg, had it been grated from the other end, would have proved sound and solid to the last."'

'What?'

'"Therefore, always check your potential husband for his stalk and grasp him from the other end."'

'It's a bad line,' Rosa said.

'I said, Next time I get hold of Ian, I won't hold on so tightly to the stalk.'

There was a pause. 'Angela, I think you should come out here for Christmas'

'Rosa, it's only just October.'

'Come.'

She agreed.

Dr Tichborne said, 'My love, I think our vicar is right, you know.'

Mrs Dorothea Tichborne said, 'If old Mr Lee can come three times a week and not mind the cold, then I think the youth of the parish can be asked to do the same. And if they want a club, what's wrong with Sunday school?'

The vicar said quickly, 'It was extremely kind of you to pay for the hinges and the fixing of the church gate. Here is the bill.'

Mrs Dorothea Tichborne picked it up and looked at it through her spectacles. The flesh around her lips puckered as she checked the calculation silently.

Dr Tichborne longed to leap across the table, take the paper, tear it up and throw it in her face and then turn to Crispin, eager-eyed, respectful, cursed with a patron of nun-like disposition and a purse of steel, and say, 'Have anything. Take it all. And take me too.' Instead he said, 'More tea, vicar?'

Oh, the perils of marrying for money. He should have known that the reason most people have money is because they keep it. He held the teapot, stared at Crispin's adorable curls and waited.

Dorothea said, 'Seventy-eight pounds seems a great deal.'

The vicar said, 'The hinges had to be made.'

Dorothea pursed her lips, said that it was, after all, to the Glory of God not to let the sheep into the churchyard and signed the cheque. 'And now,' she said, 'my father's memorial . . .' She rang the little bell.

The Dorkin girl arrived. She was wearing a raspberry-pink angora jumper.

The vicar's hand shook, rattling his cup in its saucer. Dr Tichborne reached over and patted the offending hand lightly (O soft, white skin) and gave him a look as if to say, 'Together we will win through.'

The leather case containing the mason's drawings was requested. The leather case containing the mason's drawings was brought.

'Do you feel the cold, Sandra?' asked Dorothea Tichborne.

Sandra ran her floury hands lightly over her pink-clad body. 'Oh no,' she said, and leaned over and rubbed the same hand of Dr Tichborne's that had so lately patted the vicar's. 'See?'

Dr Tichborne did. So did the vicar. They saw both the hand, and the way Mrs Tichborne's mind was working.

'Well, there you are,' said Dorothea, watching the Dorkin girl sashay from the room. 'No need for heating, now, is there?'

'I would not,' said Dr Tichborne with distaste, 'say that our servant girl is normal. She always seems to be *over*heated.'

The vicar bit quickly into his seed cake lest the words 'Hot stuff, hot stuff, hot stuff' fell from his mouth.

'Vicar?'

He gave a little nervous bow. 'Mrs Fytton has suggested making and selling church ale. For our funds. Specifically to be used to heat the church.'

'Then let her,' said the last remaining Devereux dismissively.

'Ah, the widow's mite,' said the doctor.

'Might what?' asked Dorothea, already poring over the drawing of the marble catafalque.

'Be lonely,' said Dr Tichborne happily, yearningly and quick as a flash. 'Do you get lonely, Crispin?' And before he could stop himself he leaned forward, looked into those sweet, sweet eyes, and said, 'We could play chess.'

'I'm not very good.'

'I could initiate you.'

The word hung between them. Old Dr Tichborne nearly fainted at the thought.

'Which reminds me,' said Dorothea, 'we must think about Sandra's baptism. A full immersion, I really do feel, would have covered the sins. But, alas, she is far too large to fit into the font.'

'Indeed she is,' said the vicar.

'Which is a very great pity.'

The vicar did not look entirely in agreement with the sentiment. But Dr Tichborne nodded vigorously.

Mrs Tichborne looked over her spectacles at the vicar. 'Nevertheless, she should suffer. *Cold* water in the font, I think. To cool the blood . . . Unless you can think of a way of getting all of her in?'

The vicar hoped to God that God would forgive and that to all others his mind remained a private place. What was going on in there was terrible . . . *terrible*.

Old Dr Tichborne gave him another cheering smile.

'Our new resident at Church Ale House,' said the vicar quickly, to calm himself down, 'is very keen to participate in the affairs of the community.' He thought, afterwards, that there might have been a better way of putting it. Affairs was such an ambiguous word. 'Not only does she intend to reinstitute the ale on our behalf, but she has offered us the water from her well for the – er –'

'Good, good,' said Dorothea. 'That will lend an air of gravity to the proceedings. The baptism, vicar, will take place sooner rather than later, I think. And you will give Sandra some careful instruction.'

The vicar swallowed. His eyes watered.

Old Dr Tichborne was full of sympathy for the afflicted. It would be a rotten job, most unpleasant. He thought of the new resident at Church Ale House. Free. Free as air. 'Such a very merry widow,' he said.

Both pair of eyes looked at him uncomprehendingly.

So, tomorrow was Ian and La Bin-bag's wedding anniversary, was it? I'll show them, thought the former Mrs Fytton. I shall become a pillar of the local community. And with that somewhat comfortless item of rhetoric, she went for a walk to catch the last of the fading light. If Sammy was right and the weather was about to change, then there would be few opportunities in the coming weeks.

She headed off towards the eel river, behind the Tichbornes' house. This was where the best wild hops grew. She could now, quite proudly, identify the pretty pale green *Humulus lupulus* at any stage of its development. At the moment they hung like fragrant ochre lace. She crushed one, smelt it and nodded with satisfaction. They were coming along very nicely. One more day of sun, Sammy said. She would leave them one more day then.

Bread of Idleness, she thought, turning back. I'll give them Bread of Idleness. Then she heard a voice, from somewhere beyond the Tichbornes' hedge. Faint, so that she probably misheard, because it seemed to be saying 'Black king to white queen. Checkmate.'

16

October

Our Homo erectus *ancestors spawned another monstrous burden – the*
teenager . . . Not only did women now bear exceedingly helpless babies, but
childhood also became extended. Hail the origin of teenage; another hall-
mark of the human animal . . . another distinct divergence from the apes.
HELEN FISHER *The Anatomy of Love*

In London Binnie sat in her glistening white Pogenpohl
kitchen and sipped her passiflora tea and sighed. It tasted
foul. But it was true, it did calm one . . .

Creak, creak. She won't be *in* my bloody bath.

Sip, sip. Will she?

The footsteps overhead ceased. The faint sound of a water
cistern flushed up above. The further faint sound of taps gush-
ing issued forth. As did Binnie. Knocking the passiflora tea
aside in her rage. She was up those stairs and banging on the
door of her own bathroom – from which issued the vapour of
sweetened steam – and screaming, 'Out, out, damned Claire.'

Who calmly replied, through the door, that she couldn't
use the other bathroom because Andrew's new jeans were
soaking in the bath.

And then the telephone rang. It was Ian. 'Hi, baby,' he said.
He liked to sound hip and young for her.

'Your fucking children,' she began.

Sweet little Belinda, who used only to say 'Ouch' if someone trod on her toe. Ian was shocked.

'What – Tris?'

'You know perfectly well who I mean.'

'I've booked a table at the Caprice.'

She burst into tears. 'Well, you can just unbook the sodding thing. I shall be in bed by ten and I *don't want waking up . . .'*

'It's our first anniversary, darling.'

'And it may be our last! Do you know what your daughter is doing now? Do you? *Do you?'*

Ian smiled sheepishly at his secretary and sat back to listen.

When the tirade was done, his secretary, a wise and agreeable woman whom he called Moneypenny, although she patently did not adore, or even see, the Bond in him, suggested that it might be a good idea for just the two of them to go away.

Just for one frightened moment he thought she referred to him and her and he actually felt his testicles shrink – but she meant him and Binnie.

'Good thinking, Moneypenny.' And then he shuddered. 'Better make it Sunday *and* Monday, Moneypenny,' he said, remembering the tone of little Binnie's voice. A couple of months ago he would never have believed she could sound so frightening. 'You'll just have to rearrange my Monday appointments.'

Privately Moneypenny wondered how he could have got himself into this mess. He had once had the perfect wife and an untrammelled life. The office, the business, the sum of their world together ran smooth as a nut in butter. And then this.

He cancelled the Caprice and rang All Hallows Inn in Beckingfield, where they had spent their first sinful English night together. Moneypenny scribbled him a note, 'Check they have a baby-listening service', on his pad – he did and they did – and he relaxed again. Saved by the bell, he thought.

And so a mollified Belinda, a contentedly dribbling Tristan and an Ian so entirely bound up in not cracking the eggs beneath his feet that he kept forgetting to breathe, set off for Beckingfield and a couple of nights of rekindled love.

It is a well-known fact that, up to a point, the more youthful one is, the more swiftly one's liver recovers itself. It is also a well-known fact that the three points at which this particular phenomenon displays itself to its best advantage are (1) around the age of eighteen, (2) after an all-night party, particularly an all-night party in which a wide variety of generously poured alcoholic beverages are available, and (3) after frequent vomiting. This last often being aided by a fourth consideration – that in the course of the twin meeting of youth and alcohol, and before the vomiting, there is often fitted in a colourful item called pizza.

All of these phenomena had been brought together in South Common Road, Wimbledon, on a mild Monday evening at the beginning of October.

On the preceding Sunday night, the baby-listening service of All Hallows Inn, Beckingfield, was available. But on the following day, which just so happened to be their real anniversary, it mysteriously vanished. Babies were, apparently, seasonal at country house hotels. Therefore when the season died down, and it did so at the beginning of October, there was none to be had. Tristan, being an Olympic qualifier in the tooth department, was cutting a few. The prospect of being up and down the stairs from the All Hallows famous restaurant did not excite either his father or his mother. Ian, fearful, told Binnie about the lack. Binnie, contrary to his expectations, was kind. They cancelled their second night and vowed, instead, to take a lovely, slow drive home. Thus did they and their little now eight-and-a-*half*-toothed babe set off for home early. Why push it, they both agreed. They had enjoyed their Sunday night. Why push the treat?

The night away had been bliss. Binnie was her sweet little self again. Sex had been accomplished with reasonable success after a superb dinner and a good amount of fine wine. It was enough. Domestic responsibilities lay upon them. Ian could not help thinking that they lay upon him rather more than upon his sweet little wife, who had not got out of bed when Tristan called at three a.m. And again at four-thirty a.m. But still. Something was accomplished. A state of peace between them. They set off after breakfast feeling good about the world. He kept his mobile turned off.

If Ian felt it was unfair that he should have to work so hard at the domestic arrangements and his marital arrangements, as well as spearheading the marketplace, he kept the thought to himself and wove the car lazily around the edge of the New Forest. Tristan certainly had a mighty pair of lungs on him. He could not remember either of his first two being *quite* so uncontrolled. For a moment, and *only* for a moment, he remembered how simple life had been in the old days. Focus. He was then a man of focus and concentration. And now the focus was blurred, and the concentration broken into a thousand shards of other calls on his time. He was not losing his grip, only finding it harder to hang on. He'd say one thing for the former Mrs Fytton, she knew how to organize a household. Whereas Binnie, which was one of the reasons he loved her, needed his input for everything. Even – he could smile about it now as the autumnal trees danced past the car in the breeze – even down to organizing baby-sitting. Though in this instance it was baby-sitting of a very peculiar kind . . .

For a hefty sum – and he could not believe he was doing this – he hired the cleaner to baby-sit his sodding *teenagers*. She would stay at the house on Sunday and Monday night and, with her solid Christian principles – and the hefty sum aforementioned – he felt he could rely on her to keep the wiles of his elder children at bay.

But he was – no other word for it – wrong. The wiles of his children were deeper and stronger than the ocean's tides and pulled them, irredeemably, towards having a good time. This, they both argued, was what they were *meant* to do. Having negotiated those pulling tides, their wiles were now sharper than the vixens who howled outside their absent mother's door. They had a plan.

Sunday and Sunday night at South Common Road passed well enough. The cleaner sat on the white settee and watched *Songs of Praise*, enraptured. A supper was prepared, to which the elder progeny were summoned. They came and they ate. And they went to bed. But on the Monday, somewhere around three p.m., the Christian Trisha departed. She departed never to return to that evil house. Not as baby-sitter, not as cleaner and certainly not as a woman of Christian principle up for a bit of extra pocket money.

Why was this?

This was because on rising that day, somewhere around noon, her charges, Andrew and Claire, had sought to engage her in a bit of fun. With a bowl of crisps, a couple of lagers and one of their father's lightly pornographic videos. Which they said was *The Wizard of Oz*. She had taken her place on the settee again, settled down, nibbled a couple of crisps and waited for little Dorothy to cling to Toto as she whirled away in the sky. The young woman she saw on the video clung to something quite different. Andrew and Claire, stuffing cushions in their mouths and smelling of sweet, scented smoke, turned up the volume. Trisha departed forthwith. The house, by early afternoon, was theirs.

It is amazing how much change can be wrought on a house between the hours of four and eight-thirty p.m. Amazing. Long, long after Claire and Andrew are up and grown with children of their own, and Binnie is grey and Ian draws his pension, the experience will be remembered. How, as the car turned the corner of South Common Road, Ian had a sense of foreboding. Perhaps hardly surprising since, in the distance, picked out in the headlights, he saw two staggering youths apparently kicking a ball around in the road very close to his private residence, and two staggering girls dancing along the low (fortunately) front wall of his home, possibly screaming, possibly singing, and from the upstairs middle front window saw two more youthful creatures hanging out, apparently entirely comatose. Ian did not drive into the garage but parked on the road in front of the house and suggested to the shocked, puzzled, weary Belinda that she stay in the car with their son while he, Ian, Sorted This Out.

At which point the apparent ball that the staggering boys were kicking landed with a sharp crack on the front window of the car and was observed to be – why – not a ball at all but one of the second Mrs Fytton's carefully chosen Italian brass doorknobs. At which point she felt a wholly uncontrollable wave of rage. She it was who leapt from the car and, to the twitching of curtains up and down the road, screamed obscenities at the two staggering boys and the two staggering girls (who promptly fell backwards into the pyracantha and crushed it) and shook her fist up at her bedroom window, from which the two comatose hangers-out, waking like a pair of rudely assaulted sleeping beauties, began to give as good as they got in the offering of one finger to the aggressively inclined woman below them, together with a stout rendition of 'Stick it up your arse ...'

Ian watched it all in helpless horror. He could not stop his wife because he could not leave his son. Into the house Binnie went. Ian watched her pretty little bottom gird its metaphorical loins and he felt his sense of foreboding deepen. Part of the deepening sense of foreboding was that further sexual union within his marriage seemed highly unlikely for some time after this. Another was that, if it was like this out here in the street, what the hell was it like indoors? It was as if the devil himself had come to perch upon Ian's shoulder and whisper in his ear the very terrible words, 'You ain't seen nothing yet.'

And so it was. A veil will be drawn over the scene that greeted Binnie as she entered her hallway and stepped over body after body before turning to one side and entering her once-white sitting room. Though the howl of pain could, certainly, be heard in the street. A veil should also be drawn over the sight that greeted the reeling Binnie as she made her way to the kitchen, in which, at exactly the moment she arrived, a tall young lad with a penchant for sport climbed on to her once-spotless draining board and pissed very accurately, to the sound of cheers, into first her full-sized sink and then, not at all accurately, also to the sound of cheers, into her half-drainer.

Like a phantom ascending, Belinda made her way past the

bodies that lined the stairs and up towards her bedroom. And here it was that her soul appeared to leave her body. Not because of the pair of bottoms hanging over the window ledge, still gesticulating to the garden below; not because of the several cigarettes that smouldered in her Lalique ring tray; not even for the couple clasped in an embrace of deep sleep and pizza dreams under her strangely patterned duvet that was once merely pale peach. No, none of these – appalling though they were – caused the split of temporal from spiritual in the second Mrs Fytton. But the state of her own dear once-pristine and now no more bathroom did. It was here that perhaps the marriage of that great triple alliance – a youthful liver, a goodly supply of alcohol and rather a lot of deep-pan pizza – came together in horrible fruition.

It was to no avail that the weeping Claire, swaying like a willow in a breeze, begged her stepmother to beat her for her sins. Just as well since, when the weeping Claire sobered up the next morning, she felt – on the whole – that the party had been a great success and that everything was her father and stepmother's fault for coming back early. If they had stayed away as promised, they might never have known – a fantasy brought to its knees by the need to hire the services of a cleaning contractor to put the house back together again. Nevertheless, had her stepmother taken advantage of the peach-schnapped pleadings of her stepdaughter the night before and taken a paddle to her, Claire would have got in touch with Child Line straight away, as soon as she was sober enough to tap out the number.

'I thought you liked me,' wailed Binnie.

'But I do,' said the wide-eyed Claire.

Andrew, who was found some time later flat on his back two gardens down, offered to pay for a replacement door-knob out of his next month's allowance. He was very surprised, astonished really, when his father did not exactly think that he was *due* an allowance for very many years to come. He spent the entire following day at his best friend's house, telling his best friend's mother what an appalling set of parents he had been born to and how, if he could leave home, he would. She, though sympathetic, did not offer to take him in. He went home and became even more morose when his father discovered that all – *all* – his good South African Pinotage had gone and a bottle of beautiful Napoleon brandy and that it was this, very probably, that lined Binnie's bathroom walls.

'GET RID OF THEM, OR I GO!' said Binnie.

17

October/November

One half of the world cannot understand the pleasures of the other.

JANE AUSTEN

Angela Fytton's first thought, on waking, was that the wedding anniversary was over without incident and that she had coped rather well. Her next thought was that she was eternally grateful for Daphne Blunt when she came knocking at her door.

'Thought you might like some help today.'

'It's all done,' said Angela. 'The digging.'

'I know,' said Daphne happily. 'Sam told me. I mean help with the interesting bit.'

They filled a bucket with water and seated themselves on the well to wash and pick over the finds in the sun. Daphne was very firm about the well, removing all of Angela's romantic notions. She thought it was probably sunk in Roman times, that the Celts had used it and might have decorated it, but that the structure as it was now probably dated back to the mid-seventeenth century.

'Do you think there's any water in it?' Angela asked, feeling quite deprived. Celtic sounded so much better than Restoration.

'Oh yes,' said Daphne. 'But I wouldn't go drinking it with that lot above.' She nodded at the churchyard. 'And you've probably got some bones down it already. They had a way of chucking people or livestock – preferably pigs – down wells in times of battle. Anything to foul the water. It's had its fair share of conflict, this area. You've probably even had a witch or two down there.'

She was cleaning a piece of green glass and held it up to the sun. 'So just be careful,' she said, 'with all your digging and bottling and stuff.' She laughed.

'I'd have thought Wanda was the one to be careful.'

Daphne held the green glass to her eye and studied her. 'She's got a *hus-band*. You live on your own . . . Beware.'

They continued the washing and the sorting but nothing of interest came to light.

'These bits of green glass might be from a church window. But other than that there's not much here,' said Daphne. 'No tesserae. And the bits of china are newish. This button might be old.' She flicked at the crusted object delicately with her brush. 'And these flat things are washing tallies, I think. But otherwise it's all fairly ordinary. Still, that's what life was mostly – ordinary.'

Angela felt, and looked, sad. 'I thought I might find something really old,' she said.

'If these are washing tallies then they are old.'

Angela looked at them. 'But not exciting.'

Daphne laughed. 'They were to the people who employed the washerwoman. If she hadn't had these she wouldn't have known who to give what back to.'

'You know what I mean,' said Angela. She was as disappointed as a child who asks for chocolate and gets soap.

'Oh, you never know,' said Daphne kindly. 'Things sometimes come to the surface after digging. Give it a day or two. But probably what they threw here was – well, just real rubbish. Don't forget, they had a recycling economy long before we invented it. Nothing was wasted that could be used. They were poor.'

'Maria Brydges and her husband were well off. They built.'

'But land lost its value again and again in their day. She'd have known about economy. They all did.'

Angela turned over the pile of inconsequential matter. 'I suppose I could stick all the prettier bits of china on to the outside of a flowerpot or two – make a feature of them.'

Daphne looked at her strangely.

*

Sammy Lee paused at the gate and shook his head. He stared at the two young women, remembering. Gwen Perry used to sit on that exact same spot on fine summer evenings – to shell peas or pluck a hen if the air was still – only in those days the well was loosely covered with an old plank. No regulations then, just before the war. He leaned on the gate and smiled at the girls. Silly things, showing their all. Bold, friendly, no sense of possibility. And it was October now.

'Last day of the sun,' he said. 'Make the most of it.'

They smiled back. But not the way the other one had smiled when he first leaned there. She'd smiled back with uncertainty and looked at him as if she was not sure that she should. It was where he first remembered wanting her, Gwen Perry – Gwen Hardy as was – as she sat there, the new bride, all dimples above her elbows, a true dairymaid brought up on cream, and he could see that she wasn't getting what she wanted, even then, six months in. Archie Perry was a good Christian man but he didn't have the red blood necessary. Whereas he had been tall then, fit, with black curling hair and a pleasure in just being alive. Stayed to keep the land productive, no being shot at, and with an army of Land Girls jostling all around him. So he'd smile at anyone, especially a girl on a well. And then Archie was shipped off, leaving her here, and he had helped her, like he was helping this one, only not for the same motives, not now.

He looked at the puny pair in front of him. If they'd been weaners he'd have drowned them. Gwen Perry now, she was a strong woman. Good old farming stock. You could tell by the size of her hands and her feet. Shaped for the life even at seventeen. Shaped for other things as well. He watched her go red as the haws when he touched her, but he kept his hand there. A man wasn't worried about being given away then – not like now, when you could find yourself in court like young Charlie over that barmaid. No, in those days even if she said no and you left her to it, she'd keep quiet. It was the woman's shame then for egging him on, as much as the man's for being egged. Some women just had to stand there and you wanted them. Not like these.

He smiled. She ran off that time, of course. A decent woman would. Haws bouncing in the hedgerow as she pushed past him. But he'd done keepering. He knew how to set a trail. She came back again eventually. And there was Renata, eyeing them. Pigs can't talk, he told her. And it was warm and secret in there. And she asked him to do it again. Never mind pigs – *that* was men's work. Archie's eels were never up to his wife's causeway.

'What's the joke, Sam?' called Daff Blunt.

If only they knew. 'You women,' he said. 'Should watch out for the chill. Wear a bit more.'

'Embarrass you, does it?' she called archly.

He did not bother to reply but brushed at the verge with his stick. Used to be full of elecampane around here. None now. But after the war, when that feeble husband of hers got pleurisy, she cured him with the stuff. Gwen's mother passed the knowledge on. The herbal. Like breathing. They all knew it once. Elecampane – what she called Helen's tears, pleurisy root, bit of liquorice. He could curse those women and their dribs of this and that and their herbs and cure-alls. Let him be taken, he prayed in the church. But the weak man lived. Elecampane. There was no doubt in his mind that the first girl born to them was not Archie's. Not by a long chalk.

He moved off. Gwen gone into the town. He'd miss her. Red as the haws she went that first time. Eager red, while he did the unbuttoning . . .

He looked back at the bare legs of the girls as they sat on the well. At their arms naked, at their throats all exposed. Thigh tops. Thin. And he was unmoved. No mystery, women nowadays. That day, just the size of her under her skirt made him hot. You wouldn't get a handful now. And pigs, nowadays, they were thin too. Thin girls, thin sows. Not bred to it now, not the pigs, not the women. Not bred for work or love.

After he had gone Angela said, much amused, 'Sam must be very shocked by us. I mean, Mrs Perry was so upright and proper and just – well – *good*. Like a big unshakeable tree. And here we are, half dressed and probably turning him on. Poor old thing.'

Daphne nodded. 'She wouldn't have been seen dead in shorts. Not even in the hottest weather. Imagine being covered all the time, knee to hem.'

'Not very sexy.'

'Not very sexy,' Daphne agreed. 'On the other hand, I don't suppose a proper woman like her thought very much about sex. It was just another part of rural married life. A necessity that brought them children. Orgasms were not the common fruit, then.'

Angela kept silent. They weren't exactly the most obvious delicacy around now. 'Talking of fruit,' she said eventually, 'I'm not making mulberry wine but I am going to make ale.'

Daphne smiled back. 'Of course, the *ale-wife*,' she said. 'The ale-wife was often known for brewing more than just good beer. She could be quite accommodating to the men who drank it.'

'Not this one,' laughed Angela a little wistfully. 'Well, not yet anyway.'

'Has Craig tried it on with you yet?' asked Daphne.

Angela felt herself go red as a berry. 'Certainly not,' she said.

'Poor Lucy,' said Daphne.

'Yes,' said Angela, 'she could do with a replacement.'

'Maybe,' said Daphne, rinsing the last of the finds. 'But I think she really loves him.'

'Oh, Daphne,' said Angela, 'I mean the au pair.'

They emptied the bucket and put in all the washed items. Small and inconsequential as they once were, they looked interesting in a heap.

Daphne went back to the church and Angela went down to the hens.

Some jobs were eternal. Like shovelling shit. She hoped very much, and metaphorically speaking, that it was a similar activity engaging the current Mrs Fytton right now. Wedding anniversary indeed, she thought – *wedding anniversary* – shovel, shovel, shovel.

Ian managed to calm his hissing, spitting wife by promising to telephone their absent mother.

'It's either them or me,' said Binnie, who had grown an aura of steel around her that would not have disgraced Joan of Arc.

'I agree. I absolutely agree. I'll do it now.'

From the bathroom above their heads could be heard the sound of something violent occurring in the digestive department. The teenaged hangovers were going apace.

Binnie was off up the stairs like Joan after the English. 'In my bloody bathroom *again*,' she yelled.

Ian sat down at the kitchen table, feeling weak and lost. In front of him, swilling around in various unmentionable substances on the table, was a postcard, which was largely indecipherable save for the words 'Am so enjoying . . . Fytton honey . . . Sammy is wonderful.' For a moment he looked at it quite fondly. Then his expression changed. He threw it in the rubbish bin, pushing it down among the cans. She knew very well it drove Binnie mad that she still used his name.

He went to pour himself a whisky before making the call. He needed something to calm him. He opened the cupboard. 'That too?' he whispered at the Famous Grouse. A sentiment which was echoed when he searched further, only this time it was to his beloved, wholly absent, Glenmorangie.

As Angela walked back from collecting her hops, the clouds began to assemble. Dave the Bread passed her in his van. She waved, but for some reason he looked at her nervously, waved back and accelerated. A piece of paper fluttered behind the van which she thought might have come from its open window. She chased it. It came to rest on the hedge of hazel and cotoneaster that surrounded the Tichbornes' garden. It looked like a wrapper from something, but as soon as she tried to grasp it, the wind came and caught it and whirled it up, over the garden hedge and off somewhere out of sight.

Above her head the first thunder rumbled and a spike of lightning threatened to tear the heavens apart. The air was heavy and the edge of it chill. She hurried home as the first leaden droplets began to fall.

Had she not stopped to catch the wrapper, she might have reached home in time to answer the telephone. But even as she bashed at her door with her hip, another tremendous splice of lightning broke the air, followed by a crash of thunder. There was much fury in the heavens. A lot of it seemed to be directed towards the telecommunications system in the west of England, for Angela Fytton's telephone, along with those of others around about, ceased to function. When Ian tried her again, in that vital five minutes' time, the lines were all dead, dead, dead.

Not that Angela Fytton was aware of this. She merely turned up the Aga, put on a jumper and some leggings, and sat sipping a little glass of port by the heat of the stove. Later she would make a list of all the items needed for the ale. There was much to do both indoors and out before the winter settled upon her. She strung the hops from the beams, looping them over old hooks and nails that had been there for – she was certain – generations. As they warmed themselves, they gave off a tantalizing scent, so they were quite, quite ready.

But Angela Fytton was not . . . Quite. One thing at a time, she thought happily, putting her feet up on the Aga.

Sip, sip, sip.

'The lines are all down,' said Ian. 'From storms.'

'Good,' said Binnie. 'Then maybe she's dead.'

'Oh, now wait a minute . . .' This was the mother of his children of whom she spoke, after all. He looked at his current wife in a new and somewhat unappetizing light. He could wish Angela to Timbuktu on a bed of pins, but he wouldn't want her dying of it.

'Plan A, Ian,' said Belinda, tapping her little foot dangerously. 'Plan A. Send them down to their mother's *tomorrow* . . .'

He put the Plan A to Andrew and Claire. Andrew and Claire said no. They said he was a bad father for wanting to send them somewhere so remote that the *telephone* didn't work. Somewhere away from all their friends. He heard them on the telephone in the hallway telling one of their friends that they were being threatened with *exile*. It not only sounded bad. He felt bad. He remembered his own youth. He had given parties when he was not supposed. It was all part of the pattern of growing up. True, he had not vomited all over his parents' en-suite, or piddled in his parents' double-drainer, but that was only because they did not have such things. He did not want to drive a wedge between himself and his children like their mother had done. He enjoyed having them on his side. It made up for the guilt. Perhaps they could stay if they promised to behave . . . A party – after all, what was a party?

And then Binnie rang the Christian Trisha. After which Binnie's scream of rage again awoke her sleeping infant.

Exile did seem to be the only answer. But maybe somewhere they would actually like to go . . . Not a wholly punishing exile. For had not they, through his little iniquity with Binnie, been punished enough? Maybe there was a different kind of exile. *Much* further away.

He remembered the last time they had all been so happy together. And then he had a masterplan. Somerset was very close to London. Even if he persuaded his ex-wife to take the children, there was no certainty they would stay taken.

'Binnie,' he said, holding her close. She felt like a cocked gun. 'Darling. I've had an even better idea. We'll send them on a trip to Australia. They loved it before. They'll love it again. It's their gap year. In a gap year you are supposed to expand your horizons. So they can go and expand them in Australia.'

'Won't that be expensive?'

'Not if they get a job each out there.'

She was mollified.

'When?'

'As soon as it can be arranged. I'll ask Moneypenny.'

'Tomorrow?'

'Well, I think that's a bit soon really. Er, I –'

'Not the trip,' she snapped, in a way she had never snapped before. 'Moneypenny.'

By his first wedding anniversary, it occurred to Ian Fytton that the honeymoon was, indeed, all over.

November

It rained, as Sam Lee had predicted, for days. And Angela's back did not respond well in the dampness. How, wondered Angela, had Tess Durbeyfield dug for turnips all day long and not died of it? Then she remembered. Tess Durbeyfield more or less did. It occurred to her that she was not getting any younger and that these were the very dreadful givers-away of age . . . *twinges*. She copied out Maria Brydges's recipe, put on her waterproofs and went squelching over to ask Wanda about the lavender back-rub. Sammy might not approve of Wanda, for whatever reason, but she did.

She rapped at the knocker of Tally-Ho Cottage confidently. At least she had real business to attend to. Not time-wasting. And she would surely not be kept on the doorstep in this weather.

Wanda opened the door. Just a crack.

'Come on, Wanda,' she said, smiling gamely. 'Let me in. I know all about your secrets.'

Wanda, she felt, was a woman not blessed with a profound

sense of humour. Indeed, just for a moment she looked as if she might topple over with misery. Not one for badinage, then, thought Angela. She changed to a suitable gravitas and followed her into the kitchen of Tally-Ho Cottage very meekly, as if she was treading on holy ground. A loom, vats of colour, drying garments, the smell of cinnamon, assorted coloured candles in the making. A hive of decent industry, yet picturesque as a stage set.

She handed Wanda the recipe.

'I wondered if you could make this up for me?'

Wanda squeaked something about being very busy.

'I can see that,' said Angela, trying to look round her hostess, who seemed determined she should not. 'But I'd be really grateful. Next year, of course, I shall have my own herb beds, but in the meantime . . .'

Wanda was staring at the paper. If she had looked in low spirits before, she was now looking seriously miserable.

Angela gave her another smile to buck her up. But Wanda did not buck up.

Why was this?

This was because Wanda was thinking, What the fuck is a drachm? And, I have no scruples . . .

'It was all that digging that brought on the back. Still – no reward without effort . . .' Angela touched one of the garments hanging to dry. 'You are clever,' she said. 'And it must feel *very* rewarding.'

Wanda continued to stand there looking miserably mesmerized. Angela had clearly disturbed her working day.

'Sorry,' she said. 'I'll be off.'

Wanda opened the door with, in Angela's opinion, unflattering alacrity. It reminded her of the worst of the west London women. She stood on the step, rebuttoning her waterproofs and looking out at the soggy, autumnal healer's garden. She had an idea.

'Can I count on you next spring for some thinnings from your garden and a root or two, and some strikes of this and that? I'm beginning to get the hang of herbs and decoctions and the whole process. Maybe we could work together . . .'

She was astonished to see the normally quite flushed Wanda go pale.

'Why?' she asked.

'Well,' said Angela, 'I'm learning fast.'

Wanda went even paler. Odd. Perhaps it was not done to drain the energy from another's source?

'You never know,' said Angela cajolingly, 'I might even catch you up on the weaving.'

Pale was pale, but this was ridiculous. Wanda remained mute. Very white, very mute.

'I'll call back for the rub, shall I?' said Angela.

Wanda nodded. 'Just a minute,' she said, a trifle shiftily. And she pointed at the recipe. 'Have you got any of this stuff in your garden? Mine's all gone.'

Drachm? thought Angela, later. *Drachm?*

On the way back she saw the Rudges' gardener collecting up leaves and envied them having staff.

She waved at the vicar and Mrs Dorkin and her daughter, who were just going up the Tichbornes' path, probably to discuss the famous baptism.

She called to Daphne, who was just arriving at St Hilary's and who was so intent that she did not hear her.

She suggested to Craig Elliott, who panted to catch up with her, that *he* should choose the au pair himself next time.

And Sammy Lee came along the road with four very muddy pigs, which were, he said when she asked, going on their *holidays*.

And she arrived home, soaked but happy, beginning to feel that she understood the place now and that she really belonged.

Eventually, after about a week, and late in the evening, the rain stopped for a while and a bright moon lit up the garden. Despite the chill, she put on her wellingtons and went out for a breath of air. It had been a strange day – not least because of a telephone call from her children. The first unsolicited communication between them. Usually she rang and they were either out or monosyllabic. This conversation was quite different. It was just as if nothing had happened between them. Andrew was first.

'Have you got my Fila sweater?' was his first question. 'Can I have my allowance and backdated?' was the second.

No was the answer to both.

Then Claire came on. Asking the same.

'Why isn't your father paying it?' she asked.

'Because he's paying for us to go to Australia.'

Her heart turned over. 'When?'

'Just after Christmas. He wanted us to go before but we're not budging. Have you got my green Wonderbra?'

'No' said Angela, putting aside the strange picture of herself wandering the lanes of Somerset in a laddish sporty jumper beneath which up-thrust a mighty girlish pair of tits. 'Will you two come down and see me for Christmas?'

'Can't,' said Claire. 'We might get snowed in and miss the flight.'

'You're being silly,' said Angela.

'I'm not,' said Claire laconically. 'That's what Binnie says. We're not to budge until we're on that plane.'

'Then I'll have to come up and see you. When I get back from Buenos Aires.'

'We're really broke,' said Andrew, as unswerving as if she had said back from Bognor.

'Why?'

He mumbled. She heard the words 'party' and 'Binnie' and 'bit of a mess'. And she knew. Good, she thought. *Good.*

So – a little evening air to cool the brain. She closed in the hens and then slithered up to the old orchard, where the bare trees huddled. Goodbye and keep cold, as the poet said. It could equally apply to her children. If they went to sunny Australia then her plan would fail.

Damn, damn, damn. Well, it was out of her hands. She would just have to hope for a miracle.

After a quick visit to the hives to check they had not gone the way of Noah, she told the bees. Maybe they could do something. Then she visited the two bare, dug-over circles. Spaces waiting for the artist's brush, she thought. At least if her plan failed she had all this. It was a comfort. Though nothing quite comforted the bruised spot that reminded her, now and then, that her husband resided elsewhere. If her plan failed she did not know what she would do. Take comfort, she supposed. Take comfort.

The windows of the kitchen glowed warm, the mulberry tree, which had fed the birds so well, soughed and tapped and waved its sexy arms, the hens slept, and indoors the hops dried. She was very, *very* happy here. Odd under the circumstances. It seemed that just the sight of her labours cheered her quite remarkably. She clucked an irritated cluck, not unlike her hens, and bent down to pick up that same wrapper that had whirled away so elusively over the Tichborne garden all those days ago. She read: 'Harvest Grain Baps. With added bran. The way you like 'em.' Curling her lip, she tutted once more. It must have come from those Travellers. Honestly, she thought, people just did not deserve the freedom of the countryside. Harvest Grain Baps were the sort of soft-food item they might buy. Whereas everyone else around here who knew what was what used Dave the Bread.

She took one more critical look at the bare soil and noticed a large lump. How had a lump appeared when she had dug it to the texture of Christmas pud? She went over to kick it in with her heel, but it was hard. She bent down. The earth was wet and cold and the lump slithered in her fingers. It was less of a lump, more a long lumpish rectangle. She picked it up gingerly – it did not feel like a dead rat, but it could be. It was uneven and rough to her touch, surrounded by some kind of material, as if someone had wrapped something up in newspaper. She carried it in and put it under the tap. As the water ran, some of the outer wrapping fell away. Sacking or hessian of some kind. Oily to the touch. She dried it with kitchen towel and took it back to the table. Very gradually she peeled away the covering. And the lump revealed itself to not be a lump at all but a long, thin, angular object, much rusted.

As the last piece of wrapping fell away what looked like three rusty knitting needles fell out. The rest of the find was shaped like a pair of giant tweezers or small tongs. The rust clung to the surfaces but the shape was well defined: three pronged legs – or, if inverted, arms – and a scissor-like top. About ten inches long. Whatever all of these objects were, they had been carefully wrapped before being thrown away.

Odd. She stared at them. Incomprehensible.

Through the window she could see the dim light of the church. If she found these pieces incomprehensible, there was someone who would not. She went back out into the night. This, she felt, might be an important find. Perhaps some ritual object. Maybe even Roman. She ran towards St Hilary's.

Daphne's Afghan nose went up. 'I'll be there as soon as I've put this lot away.'

Good, she said excitedly. *Good*. And, running back, she could only think, Mrs Fytton, draped becomingly across her Celtic well, holds her important Roman discoveries in her hand . . .

She waited at the table, touching the finds, feeling the sense of a thousand years beneath her fingertips.

'Well?' she asked, as the Afghan nose came twitching round the door. 'Is it Roman?'

'Roman?' Daphne smiled as she scrutinized the angular object carefully. 'Oh, nothing like that old – a hundred years, maybe two hundred, somewhere in between probably. It's difficult to date because they were still used at the turn of this century. Maybe even later. Where did you find them?'

Angela told her.

Daphne nodded and touched the discarded outer wrappings.

'They've been very well preserved. This was probably oiled hemp they were wrapped in. And these are interesting too.' She held up the rusty knitting needles.

Angela felt disappointed. Deeply disappointed. 'I thought it might be important,' she said.

Daphne looked indignant. 'Important? Of course it's important. It's a bit of history. Women's history.'

Angela looked at it. A terrible feeling of faintness came over her and the muscles of her feminine parts shrank. 'It's not to do with childbirth, is it?'

Daphne laughed. 'God, no. This is a rush-light holder. In poorer homes people made their candles from rushes dipped in mutton fat. Women and children gathered the rushes, which were stripped to their pith, then dipped, allowed to harden and dipped again and again. They were held in holders like this and lit.' She balanced it on its tripod legs. 'Only the well off could afford proper candles.'

'It wouldn't give much light.'

'Oh, they'd have two or three on the go. It was the women and children's job to tend the lights,' said Daphne. 'They burned through very quickly.'

Angela could almost see the women, sunlight dancing in their hair, skirts tucked up as they waded out to collect the rushes. 'How quaint,' she said.

'Not quaint at all. Bloody hard work as a matter of fact.'

But Angela was off again, imagining her very own rush lights lying in a picturesque pile next to the honey in the pantry. Home industries. Much more interesting than beeswax candles. That'd be one in the eye for Wanda.

Daphne picked up the three loose sticks. 'Part of a small muckle wheel,' she said, 'for spinning. In which case this holder might be as much as two hundred years old. It looks to me as if these were wrapped up waiting for mending.'

Angela yawned. It was late and these things weren't Roman. She touched the inconsequential, broken thing. 'Do you think whoever lived here once did spinning?'

She was quite unprepared for the Afghan's bark. 'Of course they did spinning,' she yapped.

Angela jumped.

Daphne did not apologize, which Angela took rather hard.

'Spinning,' she said, 'was like breathing to women. The earlier generations of women who lived here wouldn't have had any clothes to stand up in or sheets to lie down on if they hadn't spun. Medieval women could walk up to twenty miles a day without leaving their homes with distaff spinning. Even fine ladies. They were probably a good deal fitter than those wet-looking creatures in the Books of Devotions would have you think. As for cottage women, they spun all the time whether or not they were doing anything else. No John Lewis fabric department or Shepton market stalls around then, Angela.'

Angela wanted to smack her. 'I realize that, Daphne,' she said, through set teeth.

Daphne was quite impervious. 'We may mock the word spinster now, but for most families it was either spin or go naked. You think of the value of cloth in their lives, and then how they had to make it, not buy it, and you begin to see the importance of the spinster. Morning, noon and night, women sat at their spindles, rocking the cradle with their foot, directing the household to its various duties –'

'Changing the rush lights . . .'

'Changing the rush lights,' agreed Daphne. '"When Adam delved and Eve span, who was then the gentleman?" And all the while spinning, spinning, spinning. So this broken muckle wheel might well have been a tragedy. I tell you, Angela, marriage was a duty of drudgery – unless you were wealthy. If love happened it was an unlooked-for bonus. And the only safe way *then* was to become a rich man's mistress. You had a degree of autonomy and within certain confines you could come and go as you pleased.' She lifted up her long nose and smiled, very wickedly. 'With the emphasis on the former, of course.'

Angela blinked. She had never thought of Daphne as coarse.

The nose went up even further. 'Personally,' she said, 'I

always thought Nell Gwynn had it made. A little of what you fancied now and then with Charlie boy, of whom she was genuinely fond, and the rest of the time was her own . . . No rush lights and muckle wheels for her. Honestly, Angela, you do put the past into a chocolate box sometimes.'

How *had* she got to this point? The history of women used to be high on her agenda. Ah well. Life took you over, she supposed. If she wasn't careful she could end up just like Basingstoke. All present, no past. She touched the rusty object thoughtfully. 'What shall I do with it?' she asked.

'Give it to me and I'll clean it up for you.'

Angela suddenly felt very possessive. Mine, she wanted to say.

'And then you can decide,' said Daphne.

Angela made tea. Ordinary tea, as the Afghan tended to turn up her nose at herbal. While the kettle boiled she desperately tried to clear her mind of the picture of Daphne Blunt, mistress to a king, romping on a four-poster with a spaniel-wigged Charles of England. She rather envied the idea.

Daphne touched the Harvest Grain label on the table, looking at it longingly. 'You haven't got a bit of bread, have you? All mine has gone off.'

'So's mine,' said Angela. 'That's just a label I found blowing about. You know what home-baked bread is . . . So fresh it doesn't last.'

They looked at each other peculiarly, not *quite* sure what was wrong about the statement. Then they resumed looking longingly at the label and its fantasy picture of rolling hills against pure-blue skies and a landscape scattered with perfect, fresh loaves of bread of the manufactured variety.

After Daphne had gone, Angela sat thinking about the rush-light holder and imagining the cosy scene in some distant cottage as the little tapers were put into place and lit. How harmonious. How pleasing.

How sweet to be a family once more. She wondered, couldn't

help herself, what Ian was doing at that precise moment. Very probably, she thought, screwing the fragrant Belinda. Well, so what? she thought. I've got all this.

She took herself off to bed. The trouble with living in the country and getting on with things was that by the time she got into bed at night there was no time to toss and turn and plan and worry about anything, because she was far too tired and fell asleep instantly. Just as well really, with her back. She hoped Wanda would not be too long in the making of the rub.

In his Wimbledon bed Ian tossed and turned. Moneypenny was arranging the trip for the children. And even assuming they did it all on the cheap, it was going to cost a huge sum. He would have to pull himself together and get out there and earn it. It was very, very unfair that he should have all the organizational burden, as well as the financial one. And why didn't their mother make a contribution? If she would only get a proper job. After all, she'd been cushioned by him for all those years. Surely she could make a bit of a financial contribution now?

The image of her floated into his mind, surrounded by an aura of contented insanity that caused him immense irritation. He saw her standing in a garden full of blossom and bees and hens and trees, with an apron full of flowers, a pot of honey in one hand and the Glastonbury thorn fulfilling its mythology and sprouting fresh green leaves in the other, and a wide, happy, welcoming – not entirely unsexy – smile. He had a bloody good mind to go down there and give her a piece of his mind, considering all the trouble she had caused. And it was deliberate. No doubt about it. He had been a good husband, while he was her husband, and it seemed very unfair of her to turn on him like this. Very.

He looked at his little Binnie, sleeping like an angel, fast, fast asleep. He reached out to touch her but thought better of it. Life never worked out the way you wanted it to . . .

And by the way, he wondered, just what was this *Sammy* so *wonderful* at?

19

November

Real solemn history I cannot be interested in . . . The quarrels of popes and kings, with wars or pestilences in every page; the men all so good for nothing and hardly any women at all.

JANE AUSTEN

I haven't got the figure for jeans.

MARGARET THATCHER

Despite the shortening days and the dampness of the weather, Angela Fytton of Church Ale House in the county Somerset was in fine fettle as she got on with the business of home and hearth. In her kitchen and with no one to hear her or complain, she sang *con bravura*, she was so happy and busy. The hens tended to stay away during the louder operatic arias, but Sammy Lee said they went a bit down in the jib at this time of year. Not me, though, she thought. Not me. And she belted out a chunk of *Traviata* while attending to her tasks.

> A good brewer will take delight in a well-ordered cellar. Attention must be paid to cleanliness, both in the person and in the business. Observe, all cellars in the winter cannot be kept too warm, or too close or too clean. Without attention to this point the beers and liquors cannot thrive.

Wanda was in no mood for singing. Or for pouting or acting provocatively, come to that. She might have been what one sweet critic described as the worst St Joan in Christendom, never mind Huddersfield, but she thought she had got this role down here sewn up. And now this. She had just returned home from spying through the kitchen window of Church Ale House and had seen her new adversary bent over some kind of olde worlde production unit.

And she was scared.

'I can't do it any more,' she said flatly. 'Not if that bloody woman up the road is going to keep coming after me like this. And she's beginning to learn all about it herself – herbs and medicines and old wives' tales – and sooner or later she'll find me out . . .' She tapped the book open in front of her on the table: *British Herbs* by Florence Ransom. She tapped it thoughtfully and went back to reading.

Dave was in serious need of Wanda pouting and acting provocatively, because he too was seriously under threat. 'She's been asking me how to make bread – and those Somerset biscuits,' he said. 'Offering to swap recipes with her fruit ones – two hundred years old or something. I told her mine were a special handed-down mixture and she said so were hers.'

'Oh, give her the ingredients they list on the packet and let her get on with it.'

'Can't do that. She's asked me to show her.'

They both looked at each other glumly.

'She'll be wanting to do weaving next.'

'In a Miss Marple mystery someone would knock her off . . .'

They looked at each other glumly again. Wanda turned the pages of the book, wondering. Later she picked up a basket and went out. Later still, returning to Tally-Ho, she met Mrs Fytton of Church Ale House in the lane. And for once Wanda was as welcoming as she knew how.

'Lovely day,' she said, smiling broadly.

Since it was yellow, damp and raw, Angela let the bogus pleasantry pass. She peered at the basket contents. 'What are all those for?'

'Aha,' said Wanda, with thrilling mystery.

'Oh, go on. Tell me. Tell me, do.'

Wanda, taking a leaf out of yet another pantomime performance as the wicked stepmother in *Snow White*, removed a now desiccated plant from among the pile in her basket and held it up. It was tall with thick, rounded, once-fleshy stems, pale, downy leaves and yellowy-green dried flowers with faint purple stripes.

'Ooh,' said Angela. 'What's it for?'

'Hangovers,' said Wanda promptly.

She held up another tall, much more elegant-looking plant with a slender, smooth stem, reddish-purple spots, feathery leaves and umbels of seeds. 'Slimming potions,' she said quickly. 'Known since Egyptian times. And we all know how skinny they were . . . apart from Elizabeth Taylor.'

Angela was far too engrossed to point out the anachronistic, not to say entirely inappropriate, nature of the remark. Her eyes were fixed on the reddish-purple spotted plant. 'Ooh,' she said.

Wanda selected a third variety: tall and showy, with withered broad leaves and a prickly pod, half split to reveal dense-packed tiny seeds.

'Any guesses?'

'Aphrodisiac?'

'Got it in one.'

Angela preened herself. She really was getting the hang of this country life rather well.

Wanda, on the other hand, would have agreed if Angela had said 'Lumbago' or 'Halitosis'. It was all part of the psychology. She had read it in a library book the previous day. If you wait, people will tell you what it is they want from you. As a matter of fact, Wanda was beginning to think it might have been a whole lot easier if she had done things properly from the beginning. Being bogus, it seemed to her now, was just as difficult as being the genuine article. More so, since the genuine article has no cause to feel afraid of discovery. Which she most certainly did. Hence peddling this basket of nasties.

'Names?' Angela brought out her little notebook to jot

down details of the fascinating threesome.

Wanda held up the thorn apple (*Datura stramonium*, *Solanaceae*: highly poisonous. Otherwise known as devil's apple or devil's trumpet and inclined to kill, quite literally, rather than cure a hangover). 'Boosebuck,' she said very firmly.

Angela wrote it down.

Wanda held up the hemlock (*Conium maculatum*, *Umbelliferae*: a plant of evil omen, having the reputation in ancient times of being the official executioner of kings and philosophers. The only likelihood of its being useful in a weight-reducing diet, frankly, would be *after* being taken – *well*, after . . .). Wanda said, 'Thinlock.'

Angela wrote it down.

Wanda held up the henbane (*Hyoscyamus niger*, *Solanaceae*: reputedly the source of the 'soporiphic sponge' so beloved of Roman soldiers with time and spears on their hands and crucifees to deal with. Unlikely to be sexy unless shuffling off the mortal was your erotic bag). Wanda, looking anywhere but in her victim's eyes, said, 'Sweetbane.'

'Bane usually means poison, doesn't it?' asked Angela.

'Not in this case,' said Wanda very firmly once more.

'You should know,' said Angela, and wrote it down. 'How clever you are.'

Wanda rolled her eyes. She had never had anything to do with murder, beyond a review that said 'If Macbeth doth murder sleep, this Lady Macbeth murders everything else . . .' Nevertheless, she felt resolute. Her very lifestyle was being threatened. And she was sure it would be over very, very quickly.

'I'll remember those,' said Angela. 'How do you decoct them?'

Wanda told her.

She wrote it down. 'Will you help me look for them?'

Wanda nodded.

Angela thought, At last she has accepted me.

Wanda said kindly, 'But it is a little late in the season. Why not have mine?' And she handed her the swathes of plants from her basket.

Angela was touched. And said so.

Then Wanda the Craft looked up at the milky early November sun. 'Is that the time?' she said quickly. 'I must run.' She put a finger to her lips. 'Tell no one, or they lose their strength.'

'Thank you,' said Angela. 'Oh, *thank you* . . .'

Lucy Elliott sat on the end of her bed and fiddled with the zip of her black leather trousers. They were empty black leather trousers because she had not worn them since she was single. Then she could sit at a piano in them all night and not have trouble breathing *once*. In attempting to fit into them just now, she had broken the zip *twice* . . .

Her fiddling hands went hazy and swam before her eyes. The new au pair had black leather *shorts* . . . In winter. *Shorts*. Came from Finland, so she probably never felt the cold. Wouldn't feel it here either if Craig's eyes were anything to go by. He may have taken his sights off the Fytton woman, but they were now somewhere far worse. Under his own roof. He didn't even go up to town any more. Oh, why had he suddenly taken it into his head to take charge of their domestic arrangements, when he had never, ever been remotely interested before? One day he just said, 'I'm going up to town tomorrow and I'm bringing back a new girl.'

And he did. And what a girl. She would like to meet whoever gave him the idea of meddling in domestic affairs and strangle them.

She, Lucy, had to do something. She had to . . . Giving the girl a little drop of anthrax came to mind. Or sending her back to the birchy bogs, or whatever they had. But Craig wouldn't hear of her going – of course. Craig said – and he could be interpreted as being the caring husband – Craig said that she was too good, coped too well, and how clever he was to find her. He did not mention that it was the Fytton woman's suggestion that he should take charge, or that the new au pair was a discard from a north London writer whose wise wife had taken one look at her and said she could cope on her own after all.

'Lucy,' he informed her, 'my darling Lucy, you need the break.'

That was also the trouble. Apart from the leather shorts and the big everything she *was* efficient. Even the children liked her. Is there anything more depressing, thought Lucy Elliott, than a beautiful, leggy young woman who is well meaning and efficient and living in your house? She looked at the broken zip again. There was only one thing for it.

The Rudges' man from Bristol was working away in their garden and smarting from the telephone message that had summoned him down. Unlike their usual cool selves, the Rudges had left a message that was terse to the point of rudeness. Why had he not come down during the week and cleared away the leaves?

He had. He left a message on their answerphone accordingly.

They replied on his. 'Oh, now, come, come. I put it to you . . .'

But he had. He really had. The lawn had been cleared and spotless. It wasn't his fault that there was something in the ruddy countryside called *autumn* . . .

They left another message, in which they were – metaphorically – wringing their hands in despair. The amount of *leaves* you had to deal with in the country was beyond belief. They had, they said, decided that the only thing to do was to get him to fell the last of the trees. Two copper beeches that hung over their land, a silver birch (which was really annoying, leaving piles of dead matter that looked just like cornflakes), an ash and a couple of old May trees that did not really shed too badly but might as well go anyway. Besides, when the swimming pool went in, the last thing they wanted was leaves in the filter system.

Sammy watched the man working from the top of the hill. The Rudges had marked a white cross on the condemned trees, appropriate symbols of their passing. Every slice and cut felt as if it were slicing and cutting into him. One of the May trees had been pollarded to buggery, preparatory to being cut right down. And then it was lunchtime and the man turned off the machine and strolled away towards the Black Smock.

Cool for a murderer, thought the watcher on the hill, as the Rudges' man downed tools as if nothing were ill in the world. Sammy felt pollarded to buggery himself. The heart in him died a little more. If Gwen Perry had still been down there she'd have had something to say. Especially about the copper beeches, which blazed like beacons when the season turned. She wouldn't have let them go without a fight.

And then he saw something else. He saw the Fytton woman passing the Rudges' wall. He saw her peer over it. He saw her stop and peer some more. He then saw her go running faster than wellington boots might allow up to the church. And a few minutes later both she and Daphne Blunt – who was carrying a very large implement – came flying from the church, up the lane and through the Rudges' gate and with the very large implement begin beating the machine so that its ringing sound echoed throughout Staithe. But it did not, apparently, penetrate the doors and windows of Ye Olde Black Smock, where the man who owned the machine was eating his ploughman's. Sammy smiled as he saw Daphne Blunt beat at it and beat at it like a female thunder god. Whatever the machine had once been capable of, Sam thought, sighing happily, it was no more.

The vicar begged that he might be excused baptizing the Dorkin girl until after Christmas. Now, late in November, he had much to do, he told Mrs Dorothea Tichborne. Much to do.

'What in particular?' asked that lady.

'From St Andrew's Day.'

'Yes?'

'Advent, Mrs Tichborne. Advent.'

'I know that, vicar,' she said. 'But you must have a little time left over for the girl.'

The vicar closed his eyes. 'Very busy with planning the services,' he said faintly.

Mrs Tichborne closed her eyes. 'Not much planning, vicar. The services are straightforward, as in the Act for the Uniformity of Common Prayer.'

He ducked the issue of the New English version and just wished she would not put such linguistic emphasis on *the Act*.

'Choosing the hymns,' he said, even more faintly.

Mrs Tichborne opened her eyes. 'I hope there will be nothing modern about Advent, vicar?'

'Well, I had intended to teach some of the younger ones some simple tunes on the guitar . . .'

Mrs Tichborne closed those windows of the soul again. She tapped her chest so that her crucifix rattled and she warbled:

'Behold the Bridegroom cometh in the middle of the night,
And blest is he whose loins are girt, whose lamp is bright . . .'

The vicar made a strange little noise. So did her husband, sitting silent at her side.

'Horologian,' she said with satisfaction. 'Eighth century. Translated by Moultrie. We will keep the traditions. Start with that, vicar – and go on through the Hymnal. A little Luther perhaps?'

The vicar made another strange noise.

Dr Tichborne leaned forward. 'Loins are girt,' he repeated. 'Lamp is bright.' His own eyes could not have been more lamp-like in the November gloom. He touched the vicar's arm. The vicar jumped.

The vicar said to his esteemed benefactress, 'After Epiphany perhaps?'

She nodded.

Old Dr Tichborne also nodded. He said, 'After Epiphany will do, Crispin.' And he too warbled in the young man's ear:

'What star is this, with beams so bright,
More lovely than the noonday light?'

He gave the Reverend Crispin Archer a look of extraordinary yearning. 'Epiphany . . .'

'Yes, thank you,' said the vicar, breathing a little more easy. 'After Epiphany. Some time after Epiphany will do for the Dorkin girl.'

'You have given her the prayer book to study?'

The vicar nodded. Truth was he had hurled it through the letter box of the Dorkin cott and run for dear life.

'Good. Then soon she will be another new-cleansed soul shining bright in the heavens,' said Dorothea Tichborne with satisfaction. 'Oh, to be there myself, one day . . .'

'Don't let me keep you,' said her husband. But when she looked at him he was definitely looking at the vicar. Who immediately rose and left.

And once outside the Tichborne house, it was only the severity of the day that dissuaded the Reverend Crispin Archer from falling headlong into the burbling, freezing stream, with all its horrible, hell-like eels.

In her home the Dorkin girl sat with a prayer book in front of the telly, trying to make sense of the words of her coming baptism.

Dearly Beloved, forasmuch as all men are conceived and born in sin . . .

She closed the book with a snap. Blokes only, she thought. And turned up the volume on *Blind Date*. And dreamed.

20

December

*More frequently, the records obscure the work of wives. When the Grocers'
Company paid a widow 18s 4d owed to her husband for miscellaneous work,
including the provision of three garlands and nine dozen nosegays, we can
infer that the making of garlands and nosegays was actually her own work.*

SARA MENDELSOHN AND PATRICIA CRAWFORD,
Women in Early Modern England

Bad beer is often made in families where there is no
sparing of materials, for the want of management and
economy. Attention should be paid to the utensils used,
and all necessary preparations made the day before the
brewing is commenced. When all cleaning and prepara-
tion is done, fill your copper and let the water be heated
the day before, that it may be well cleansed.

Daphne held up the cleaned rush-light holder approvingly.
'It needs mending but generally it's in pretty good condition
because it was wrapped in oiled sacking. Maybe your Maria
Brydges made her beeswax candles for when there were
guests, but they were far too expensive to buy for everyday
use. Otherwise she made these. Or a servant did. I should
think the local museum would be interested.'

'Not yet,' said Angela. 'It belongs here.'

Daphne nodded and looked pleased. As if Angela had at
last understood something.

Angela basked in the approval. 'Have you ever dug up
anything really interesting? I rather liked Mortimer Wheeler,'
she added, dimly remembering a man with a dashing moustache, spotted bow-tie and teeth clamped on a pipe as he

leaned enthusiastically across some old bones on black and white TV.

'Really?' said Daphne, as if Angela had said she thought Goering was quite a jolly pilot. 'All pyrotechnics,' she said dismissively. 'Missed about a million points out of a million and two. As for Mortimer Wheeler's ladies – pah! They did all the technical bits and organized, but never, really, got any of the glory. Or rather they did, as in, "Tessa was *such* a help in the sorting and the cataloguing. Real brick of a girl . . ."'

'But he got ordinary people interested.'

'Ordinary people are *always* interested. Mostly we're digging up their lives. No, Wheeler was a reactionary old fart,' said Daphne. 'And women – well, my dear, women just did not signify. For instance, when they found one of those bog men and analysed his last meal, the technically minded boffins decided to reproduce the ingredients and cook it up and serve it. Two kinds of barley and bread, largely, made into a kind of gruel, and some herbs. The invited archaeology celebs tasted it and were deeply unimpressed. Mortimer Wheeler said it was so horrible he thought the man had died because he couldn't stand his wife's cooking.'

Angela tried not to laugh.

Daphne smiled too. 'Hil-bloody-larious. The Wheelers and the Carters and the Evanses of this world wanted winners' history. Big guns. A hoard of silver like Sutton Hoo. A tomb as fine as Tutankhamun's. A galleon as rich as the *Mary Rose*. And, of course, when it was rethought years later, they realized that the bog man's gruel wasn't some daft wife's poor culinary skills. It was bitter because it contained something to dull the pain of the bog man's death. Hanging, garotting, stabbing and having his head bashed in being a fairly painful experience.' She gave Angela an amused look. 'There are similar precedents for gentling ritual death throughout the ages. When heretics were burned, for example, the executioner would often be kind, or be bribed, usually by women – mothers, wives, sisters – and give the victim a bag of gunpowder to hold. And Greek and Roman matrons whose kin were to do the honourable thing and take hemlock persuaded the authorities to add opium to it. Otherwise the death went on for days . . . like Socrates. Poor old sod.'

Angela was still wondering which particular piece of violence killed the bog person. 'They – er – certainly wanted the bog person dead, didn't they?' she said.

'Ritual overkill,' said Daphne. 'And just the sort of knowledge that women needed protecting from. How could soft, sweet feminine ladies have any idea about garotting or stoving in a skull or slicing through the jugular while stringing the victim up? No wonder we write such good murder mysteries. We've had centuries of having the dark side of our natures suppressed. It's taken us years to be allowed to participate, even in history. Try digging in corsets, long skirts, several petticoats and the Egyptian sun. And if you did they wouldn't let you be present when a mummy was opened. You might see an ancient mummified cock . . .' She laughed. 'Or be staring at female parts while in the company of men.'

Angela felt rather protective and did not tell her that in Maria Brydges's section on the arrangement of a household, she suggested very firmly that books by gentlemen should be placed on one set of shelves, books by ladies on another.

'So if Mortimer Wheeler had found my rush light . . .'

'It would be discarded as domestic and minor.'

'But there must have been women archaeologists?'

'Not unless they were rich and prepared to be considered mad. Until this century history used, largely, to be about Big Things. You see a woman stirring a cooking pot or feeding a baby or planting a garden every day of the week . . . The little daily rituals. The ways of being. Never valued until now. And, of course, the assumption that everything was orientated towards the male. I've looked at some of those cave paintings all supposedly done by men and I've never seen a signature saying Bloke.'

Angela picked up the rush-light holder and thought how

perfect for its job it was – even though a rivet was missing – and what a pleasing object. It was beautiful even if it wasn't Roman.

Daphne took it from her and stared at it. 'I went to the Roman palace at Fishbourne to study their almost perfectly preserved mosaic floors. Which are very grand, very impressive, if a little clumsily patterned in places. Pyrotechnic stuff all right. Oohs and aahs from the walkways as the visitors toured around. And then, as I was leaving, the curator came up to me and we talked about the floors. I had seen him earlier, with a blind boy, and he was guiding his hands over a case of objects. So I asked him what they were and he showed me. And when he did, that was the moment.'

'What were they?'

'Guess.'

'Swords? Helmets?'

Daphne shook her head.

'Jewels? Tools?'

'Nope. Cooking pots, cups, tiles . . . He wanted the boy to get the feel of the different surfaces. And it was the cooking pot that did it for me. Rough outside, burnt black by the fire, and inside smooth, still with the maker's fingermarks in the smoothing. And as I held *that* item I was there with the woman who had once used it, cleaned it, stored it, used it again. I mean, don't get me wrong, I love the big impressive things – the Parthenon marbles and the Mildenhalls – and I could gaze for hours at the Delphi charioteer, of course I could. But a cooking pot is my direct line to the past. The link.'

'Like the rush light?'

'Like the rush light. Even this century the Mortimer Wheelers and the Evanses dug up a very peculiar one-sided view of the world . . . And historians wrote down only half the story. You imagine, in a thousand years' time, a Mortimer Wheeler coming along and unearthing a fifties football stadium in, say, Sunderland. What would he interpret the finds to mean?'

Angela thought. She thought about her one and only visit to

a football match, when she was sixteen and had stood with a boyfriend for one and a half hours, apart from the break, when they bought lukewarm dishwater from a van and drank it as coffee. And she thought how, as she stood there for one and a half hours watching twenty-two men kick a ball about, she could only think to herself, What the fuck is going on?

Angela Fytton, sometime wife to Ian, mother to Andrew, shrugged. 'What?'

'He would interpret the finds to mean that it was a male ritual, from which women were barred. And he would be right. And he would also be wrong. Not only would women *de facto* be excluded, but women would not want to be there in the first place. See? Not forced out, but making the choice.'

'You mean women in the fifties just weren't interested?'

'*Exactly* . . . One side of the story only. Think of poor Margery Kempe –'

Angela tried to look as if she did little else.

'Well-to-do, highly articulate, but in the fifteenth century she had to *dictate* her memoirs. And who knows how much her scribe tidied up on the way. No matter how well-to-do you were, as a woman you were seldom taught to read and write. Therefore who wrote the past down? Who observed what was important to record and what was not? Court records, church records, private family records . . . Men, not women. So you have to look at the history of women against the grain. Not necessarily what is put in, but what is left out. Not necessarily, for instance, that women were suddenly forbidden from practising doctoring and midwifery, but that they had been accepted practitioners *up until that time* . . . In order to forbid something there is usually a precedent.'

Daphne's eyes were bright and hard, but they suddenly softened. She stopped, threw back her head and sniffed through that extraordinary nose of hers. The air was rich with the scent of hops and yeast. 'You could get drunk on just the smell of that lot,' she said.

In Angela's opinion, Daphne Blunt looked quite drunk

enough. 'I'm using the original recipe,' she said. 'I've only just begun. It's almost like a ritual itself – stage after stage of it. Whoever Doll Caxton was, she was a patient woman.'

'Brewing,' said the Afghan, still sniffing. 'One of the female arts. Once. Well, let's take that as an example.'

'Yes, let's,' said Angela. Thinking that it hardly mattered whether she agreed or not. She had seen that light in Daphne's eyes once, in the matter of a wrecked chainsaw, and she knew it brooked no nonsense.

In South Common Road Ian had just come in from a particularly gruelling day being dynamic. As he told Belinda. He had also stopped off at the pub with one of his junior colleagues, a young man bemoaning his domestic fate, which he did not tell Belinda. It mattered not.

He took his baby son up the little wooden bridge to Bedford and – after a few false starts – came back down again, a successful father.

As he seated himself on the now decidedly messy white settee, with a glass of beer in his hand and his other hand tucked in the warm and sensual armpit of his wife, he made the mistake of saying 'Good day, dear?' A rhetorical question in his past life. Not a rhetorical question now.

Belinda told him exactly how it was not, nor ever had been, nor ever *would* be – until his children were gone from here. He thought of his ex-wife, yet again. And he felt rising ire. Just when he thought he had got on top of things, the spectre of Angela spoiled it all. He had another beer while Belinda put – perhaps shoved was a more accurate description – a somewhat shrivelled pizza at him.

'We could go out,' he said lamely.

'Something wrong with pizza?' she asked.

He ate. He drank his beer. He brooded.

Daphne said, 'Brewing, then. In court records when we find a woman being tried for watering down the ale she brewed – a woman, not her husband – this means that if she can be put on trial for the misdemeanour, she must have had the licence to brew in the first place. And here the ale-wife was a powerful lady. Made a deal of money, ran the local hostelry – which is why she wanted to keep in with the church. Similarly, in disputes over wills. Women did not have a disposable income because married women could not leave money – that all belonged to their husbands – although occasionally, at their behest, a sum was allowed for servants. But the bulk of the disputes were always over goods, particularly – back to the spinning – their linens. So when I get all hot and bothered about the way Dorothea Tichborne is too mean to warm the church, I remind myself that not very long ago she would have been forced to hand all her money over to her husband. At least she has the right to do with her fortune as she wishes, even if the rest of us don't like it very much.'

'Ah,' said Angela, a far-off little past bell of liberation days a-ringing, 'the personal is the historical. And going against the grain is looking for the contradiction which proves the rule.'

'Exactly.' Daphne nodded. 'Take the history of the black population of Bristol in the eighteenth century. We know there were a large number working as servants and in other domestic capacities, but unlike their white counterparts they very seldom feature in the law courts for brawling or thieving or doing damage to their masters. Which – to take it against the grain – must mean that they were not only good employees but that they lived there in harmony, were well thought of and well absorbed.'

Angela picked up the rush light. 'And this,' she said, 'what does this tell you?'

'Look at the domestic and the domestic brings out the day to day, and the day to day is the functioning – or not – of society.' She touched the rush-light holder. 'Can you imagine how many rushes were used to light a home? Can you imagine how cold the collecting was in winter – dangerous even? Can you imagine how many times each rush had to be dipped in order to make a reasonable-sized taper?' She touched it where the central rivet had come away. 'Shame it's broken,' she said, 'or you could give us a demonstration.' She laughed, wiggling that fearsome nose. 'But first find your forge.'

Angela's eyes were glowing now, just like Daphne's.

Daphne stood up and stretched. 'Time to get a bath,' she said. 'Another glorious modern invention. Oh, and I've finished the first wall, by the way. Now I'm going to start on the others. I'll let you know if I find a nude woman. You can catch me when I faint.' And she went home.

The phone rang. Angela answered it, still with a thousand years of women's history ringing in her ears, still with the image of women spinning, spinning, spinning, and getting no credit for it. Still with the thought of the rush lights and the cold, dark waters on winter mornings and the soreness of reddened, roughened hands. And sunlight playing on golden ringlets and the merry bright eyes of little apple-cheeked children.

'Angela Fytton,' she said.

'Ian Fytton,' he replied. Immediately wishing he had not. It was an old private joke.

She gave a little giggle, which sounded fairly normal to him. And then she said something which proved she was not normal at all.

'I'm really glad you rang. I just want to thank you for being so fair about my settlement,' she said. 'When I think that a century or two ago you could have thrown me out without a penny to my name and only the linen I'd woven. Well . . .'

'If you're going to speak to me like that,' he said, 'I'm ringing off.'

He waited.

'Good night, dear,' she said. And put the phone down.

Ian remained holding the receiver, considerably fazed.

'Well?' said Binnie.

'I think I'm going to have to go down and see her,' said Ian. 'She really does seem to be going mad.'

21

November/December

Now calumnies arise, and black Reproach
Triumphant croaks aloud, and joyful claps
Her raven wing!

MARY LATTER

Marry in haste, repent at leisure.

The liquor must be well stirred up the whole time and most from the bottom. As this is not brewed for keeping, three quarters of a pound of hops to a bushel of malt will be sufficient.

It was seven in the morning. The rest of the household in South Common Road was asleep. Just for a moment, as Ian gazed out of the window and sipped his tea, he wondered what it would be like to live alone. Just for a moment he thought it was probably sweet heaven. He had mixed feelings about everyone living under this roof now, even his infant son. It was all responsibility, responsibility, responsibility – and no one else seemed to be standing on their own two feet. It wasn't that he didn't love them all. He did. He felt protective of his infant son, protective of his infant son's mother. As for his two older children, he knew that this very terrible selfishness of theirs would pass; that they would go to university, perhaps scrape a degree, perhaps do well in one – and take their places as citizens of the world. Eventually. And it was the eventually that was causing the problems. It was the eventually, to coin a phrase, that was driving him nuts. Which made him think, yet again, of his ex-wife.

Observe, never bottle beer, wine or cider, but on a fine

day and let the bottles be well seen to. Use none but the best corks.

Ian sat between the chairman of the Residual Industries Board for the Midlands and a venture capitalist who drank his soup with obvious and loud appreciation. Just for one very bad moment, and transported home in his mind, Ian nearly leaned over, poked him in the ribs and said, 'Can't you do that more quietly?' before realizing he was in the Birmingham Small Conference centre, not South Common Road, and this was not his elder son eating Rice Crispies while his wife drummed her little pink nails upon the table top.

The chairman of the RIBM was very pleased with the way the meeting had gone and thought they would be finished by six. He proposed a nice little early dinner before heading off to their various destinations. Ian was about to ring Binnie and tell her that he would be home comfortably before midnight. But he did not.

The ingredients being ready, the water must be made to boil quickly, which done, the copper fire must be damped. The malt, having been previously put in the mashing-tub, reserving a small quantity, as soon as the steam begins to subside, the water must be poured upon it to wet the malt so as to render it fit to be mashed. When well mashed put the spare malt over the top and cover the tub with sacks to keep the steam and the spirit of the malt in, and let it remain two hours.

Two bad telephone calls and one truly hysterical one. About normal for one working day. Binnie rang while he was still on the train to say that Claire had arrived at the breakfast table with three extra teenagers, all of whom smoked and seemed to think that she, Binnie, was something the cat brought in. And Tristan was trying to eat his lunch within a fog of cigarettes. The new cleaner had packed and gone for good, saying she could not stay. She was on the verge . . .

Verge of what? Oh, just verge. Don't be so pedantic.

Just before noon, Binnie called again. Andrew was refusing to speak and, more to the point, refusing to move. He was slumped in front of the big television in the sitting room, watching the video of *Top Gun* over and over again. Claire said that his girlfriend (what girlfriend?) had dumped him. And all Binnie had said was that she was not surprised and why didn't he go and stay with his mother for a few days and cheer himself up? He had not spoken since. Would Ian talk to him? Ian looked apologetically at the chairman of the RIBM and excused himself. The meeting was due to start in five minutes; better now than later. Get on the phone, he said to his son, and use the Harrods account to send the bloody girl some flowers.

> Then let it mash again for the second wort in the same manner as the first, excepting that the water must be cooler and it must not stand more than half the time.

Binnie, at four-thirty – this time hysterical. A girl with a nose ring had arrived with a huge funeral wreath of flowers and demanded to see Andrew. They had been fighting and screaming at each other in the sitting room ever since. Now it was quiet. But the hall carpet was completely ruined with crushed leaves and the pollen from all those lilies and When Was Ian Coming Home?

He did not think he would be able to get back that night. The meeting would go on until eleven at least. He managed not to laugh at what he thought was a considerable display of wit on the part of his son and, with a sudden, great bubble of pleasure, said, quite untruthfully, that he had to go now because the chairman wanted him *that minute* . . . He would try to call again – no promises – next bit of meeting to be held *in camera* – no phones permitted – I love you – bye . . .

He did, he did. He did love her. It was just so good to be allowed to be invisible for a while. And besides, he did promise Binnie that he would go down and sort things out eyeball to eyeball. Not at half-past eleven at night, admittedly – but, well, when the action seems appropriate, take it there and then. It was a motto that had done him good enough service throughout his business activities. Just as well, he thought gloomily, given the amount of money his private life was costing him. How much were new carpets? How much would his student children need to stagger from bar to bar around Sydney before they found themselves a job? How much would he need to spend to appease his poor little Binnie after they had gone? It was endless, endless . . . Life was never so complicated, he found himself thinking, in the old days.

When cool, the yeast, which should be white and sweet, is added, and the liquor well stirred from the bottom with a wooden spoon, turning it topsy-turvy, which causes the beer to ferment. Be careful that the tub is not too full to work overnight.

The car was waiting for him at Bristol and the night was fine. Warm for November, said the driver. Ian took the keys and waited for the man to take his folding bicycle out of the boot and pedal away. The night is mine, thought Ian, and, feeling wicked as a schoolboy, he slipped into the driver's seat and took out a packet of Gauloise. He lit one and relished it. It reminded him of days that ran into each other, when everything seemed possible and everyone seemed, if not good, then bearable. Including himself. Wherever he and Angela went on the Continent they would buy Gauloise and play at being Belmondo and Bardot. He realized that Binnie would not even know who they were. He tried to continue thinking that was sweet. It was really. He loved the way she clung to him. Sweet. He threw the cigarette end out of the window. She wouldn't let him do that, though. He smoked another. The air in the car was thick with the smell. Just for a moment it was as if he had hit his own personal heaven after all. No one knew where he was, not a car on the road. He was tempted to drive for ever.

Angela risked taking a chill and went out to sit in the garden at midnight. She felt drunk on the air of her kitchen and her still room, with all its yeasty sweetness and drowsy malt, and was far too elated to sleep. These people surrounding her were all so good, so lovely, that she was glad to be able to prepare them a treat. They would taste the ale and they would relive with her the glory of the past in Church Ale House. And she would, finally, belong.

She was so warm from her labours that, despite the chill in the air, she wore one of Wanda's cheesecloth skirts, one of Wanda's butter-muslin tops in rosy pink, and a bandeau of pink ribbon to keep the hair from her face. Wanda had practically thrown them at her when she went to call. Her cheeks were bright, her eyes sparkled, she was tired beyond belief, but invigorated too. 'Nothing is done that is not done well . . .'

And she felt she had given today's brewing her all. She would skim it tomorrow, bottle it in four days' time and then she would be free. Time would do the rest of the work.

She leaned against the trunk of the mulberry. Frankly, she told it, what she could do with now was a bit of you know what. Well, quite a lot of it. She knew this feeling of restless tiredness and she knew that one sure-fire way of dealing with it was to give herself up entirely to the experience of being naked next to a man's naked body and letting nature take its course.

She stroked the trunk of the tree at the back, where its huge buttock shapes separated away, and she wandered around to the front, trailing her fingers across its rough bark as if it were a lover. She touched its almost non-existent swelling where the front of the trunk crotched outwards and said it didn't matter. It really didn't matter. And then she laughed and reminded the black and brilliant sky above that it was not, nor ever was, what you had but what you did with it that counted. The stars winked. They knew.

Then she put her arm around the tree again and apologized for not liking everything about it. She was thinking of the mulberries. 'But I do like your shape,' she said, by way of compensation. 'And no matter about the rest, I'll always be here for you. Let me hold you again . . .' No woman on a still winter's night could have importuned a lover more seductively.

Vague in her nostrils came the smell of French cigarettes – as if she were young again, walking with Ian and the children through French meadows after cafés in the sun. The children heavy with sleep, she and Ian heavy with love. If this was what being a country wife did for your imagination, she thought, let me have more of it . . . She wrapped her arms around that ridiculous trunk and squeezed it all the harder. Kiss, kiss, she went, feeling the rough bark beneath her lips and giggling out loud at the foolishness. And 'Oh, you lovely thing,' she told it, laughing and laughing at its coolness on her cheek.

Behind her she heard the slight click of her gate. As if someone were coming in. Or going out.

It may be tapped within not less than two months to perfection. Beer should stand in the bottles six to eight hours before they are corked. Store in a cool, dry, clean place, away from the light. Drink not before Candlemas.

22

December

*I have always thought that there is no more fruitful source of family
discontent than badly cooked dinners and untidy ways.*

ISABELLA BEETON

This was the easy time, the wintering. The hives were silent,
sleeping, no more honey, waiting for the spring. The hens had
gone on their holidays – hen holidays, not pig holidays, as she
reminded him – to Sammy's cottage, with a ten-pound note
tucked into their travelling clothes for their keep. The ale was
waiting, getting stronger, and on the shelves surrounding it
sat her summer bottlings and dryings and saltings. And, for
beauty, the frosts had come and the garden took on a sugar-
white bloom each morning, sparkling and crystal, the leaves
like sweetened glass. The torso of the mulberry tree, laid bare,
looked cold and needy, and the once-perfect soft soil of the
herb beds was packed down tight and hard as a rock.

Angela Fytton also began to pack. It was quite hard to get
her head around proper clothing. Formal attire, daywear,
decent T-shirts and jeans. But she managed it.

Only for a short while, she told the house, as she closed the
door. And then she was in her car and away from all the pleasures of rural life: her garden, her still room, the avocado suite
and all those good, good people. She would spend two nights
at Joe and Gracie's in London before getting her plane and flying to the sun. The first day and evening she would spend
with her children. If anything, she thought, was set to remind
her of how glad she was to have left London, it was likely to
be a day with those two up in town, trying to buy their presents. You paid for your pleasures.

If Ian Fytton thought that Christmas, with everything ready for the departure of his elder children to Australia thereafter, would be a calm affair, he was entirely and very dreadfully, wrong.

When the children came back from seeing their mother in London, they brought with them, as a gift for the household, a pot of Fytton honey. Which Belinda, with uncharacteristic strength, hurled across the kitchen.

'But that was our mother's honey,' they said stoutly, in unison. And reverentially they began cleaning it from the walls.

Her children had informed her that they were expecting Christmas to be a nightmare. A nightmare.

'Shame,' she said. Happily. 'What a shame.'

She made them promise that they would come and visit her in the spring, when they returned from their trip. Of the Binbag and their father the news was inconclusive. According to Andrew and Claire, both of them were complete loonies. Binnie was the stepmother from hell. And their father would not have disgraced Mr Barrett of Wimpole Street. Had they an inkling of who he was. But there was not a whisper of disharmony between the pair. Not a whisper. I have failed, she thought despondently, as she checked in her luggage. It will be me alone in that lovely place. Sad she was. So sad. But she brightened up somewhere over the Atlantic. And the reason she brightened up was that she decided, after all, that she would not paint the sewing room a tender shade of lilac. She would leave it, and every other part of that house, exactly as they were when she moved in. A lovely shrine to the past.

On landing she threw her arms around Rosa, who told her she looked well. Which meant fat. And she didn't, she really didn't, care a jot.

'Cook your own bloody turkey,' said his sweet little wife.

So he did. With no great success. And the carving of it, which had once been such a pleasure, was a mucky hell on earth.

On Christmas night, with Belinda lying rigid beside him, he began to pray. He prayed that once his children were gone to the other side of the world, all would be well again. He said this as he laid his weary head next to Belinda's upon their snow-white pillows. And he longed for – oddly – a Gauloise to place between his lips.

'No turkey, no plum pudding,' said Rosa firmly, serving oysters as a first course.

Good, thought Mrs Angela Fytton. *Good.*

Part Three

If man is only a little lower than the angels, then the angels should reform.
MARY WILSON LITTLE

Feast of the Purification of the Virgin Mary.
Derived from the lights which were then distributed and carried
about in procession. The candles of the Purification were said to be an
exchange for the lustration of the pagans. The hallowing of candles upon
Candlemas Day. The candles, having been sprinkled with holy water, were
lighted and distributed. They were considered to possess a virtue
sufficiently powerful to frighten away devils and to be a charm against
thunder and lightning. There is a general tradition in most parts of Europe,
that inferreth the coldness of succeeding winter from the shining of the sun
on Candlemas Day, according to proverbial distich – Si sol splendescat
Maria purificante Major erit glacies post festum quam fuit ante.
SIR THOMAS BROWNE

23

January

Husbands are like fires: they go out if left unattended.
ZSA ZSA GABOR

On 6 January, the Feast of Epiphany, Angela's plane arrived back in London. Despite the gruelling flight, which was spent next to a frightened little woman who had never flown before, who spoke almost no English and who wished to communicate her entire life story, a triple combination designed to lay even the most stout-hearted traveller low, she felt elated. It had been a very good Christmas.

It was also the day for the departure of Andrew and Claire, from the same airport. Amazing how easy it was to organize your life if you only had your life to organize. She just flew in from Buenos Aires, telephoned Sammy to make sure that the hens were well and that the ale had not blown her roof off, stowed her bags and cases away in left luggage, bought an English newspaper, a *pain au chocolat* and a cappuccino, and waited. It was quite simple and it was extremely pleasurable. All around her bubbled the chaos of people trying to make sense of a travelling world, and she sat, quiet at the centre of it all, reading about celebrity New Year resolutions and sipping something warm and not-quite-coffee from a polystyrene cup and picking up crumbs with her fingers. After she had done her maternal duty, she would leave the newspaper on the chair, the cup on the table, collect her luggage, collect her car and drive off to Somerset, free as air.

The party of four arrived, Andrew and Claire almost dancing with excitement – more animated than she had ever seen them – and hanging back, behind the trolley with its rucksacks and bags, was Ian, clutching a wide-eyed, sticky-chinned child to his chest. As sweet and blonde and angelic a child as any toddler could be.

Angela tried very hard not to meet that child's eye as it looked so adoringly at its father.

Ian looked harassed as he tried to negotiate the trolley, the child and himself in between the travelling crowds.

'Help your father,' said Angela to her children, commandingly. To her amazement, they did. 'And this is Tristan,' she said, tapping the baby's chin.

The baby stared at her. She stared back at him.

'I think he needs changing,' said Ian.

'I think so too,' said Angela.

Ian looked at her.

'Good luck,' said Angela.

'Oh,' said Ian.

She went over to her own children and left Ian to it. Buzzing around her head was the thought that one day by her actions, if successful, that baby would be fatherless. Followed, with more bravado than she really felt, by *c'est la guerre*.

'Oh,' she said to her own reasonably happy offspring, 'Buenos Aires was great. I must tell you . . .' And then she noticed that Claire had her Walkman headphones in and Andrew was already talking to a girl with backpack. Never mind, never mind, at least they were happy.

And the curious thing was, as she watched her ex-husband stumbling off to find the changing room, the wide-eyed baby staring at her over his departing shoulder, and hoping she had won, she was not. Happy. Nor unhappy. If this was victory, she thought, you could keep it for the generals.

Bad, thought Mrs Angela Fytton. Very, very *bad*.

When he came back she said, 'If you want to go off I'll stay with them.'

He looked at her gratefully.

She smiled at him as if dispensing much benison. He had obviously been through quite a mill.

'How was Christmas?' she ventured.

'Don't ask,' he said, shaking his head. 'Just don't ask.'

She looked into his eyes as meltingly as she could manage.

Then she took his hand in her own and gave it a hearty shake. 'Bye,' she said. 'Safe home.'

That *really* made him wince.

As if in welcome, a pair of pigeons dared the frosty air in front of her as she drove slowly along the Staithe Road. She watched them swoop over the long thatch of the Elliotts' place, its garden littered with toys, its windows papered with children's drawings, a bedraggled Christmas tree lying on its side by the gate. Onward to the Rudges' house, which, this being a Tuesday, was grey and empty, its windows like lifeless eyes, its bare-branched ornamental cherry trees empty of life. Then soar up again to perch upon the proud weather vane of the Tichbornes' house, with an upstairs window open and a lump of bedding hanging out, with the Dorkin girl lying over it and beating it in an extraordinarily lurid manner. To the west and time for one brave *loup de loup* over Sammy Lee's smoking chimney and a peck at the thatch. And from there to the church, where the pigeon pair whirled once around the tower before settling momentarily on the naked branch of the ilex in the vicar's garden, cocking their heads at the strumming of a guitar, the sound of an old cowboy love song. Away again to bounce and jounce on Wanda's washing line, which was bare of its usual sludgy-coloured, unapologetically homespun, honest-looking garments, through their garden, with its aroma of some sweet baking. And finally, finally, to hover over the garden of Church Ale House, to whoop and whirl in and out of the depressed-looking cabbage stalks, the purplish, evil-looking pods of dead broad beans, the blackened seed heads of onions, before finally coming to rest on the eaves of her own dear henhouse. She drove through the gate, disturbing the smaller birds feeding on the holly berries, and parked the car under the shelter of the rickety old outhouse.

Home.

She went immediately up to her hives. 'I'm back,' she said to their sleeping silence. She passed the closed well, the empty herb beds, the bare tree and the hedges – only the yews rustled with any faint sound at all. She looked up at the hill, down at the flat spreading Levels surrounding it, where not a cow or a sheep or a pig stirred in the frosty cold, and back to her own back door.

Bash, went her hip.

Home.

The house smelled sweet – pregnant with yeast from the ale, which sat ripening and undisturbed. The jars of honey blinked their golden eyes, the beetroots glowed like stained-glass windows, the green vegetables like treasures from the deeps of the sea, and the pickled eggs strange and sensual, pressing their smooth whiteness up against the glass of the kilners. Besides all these – something she had nearly forgotten – sat three small glass jars. Her decoctions of Wanda's herbs.

Did she need to recover from a hangover?

Did she need to lose weight?

Did she need a little drop of something to make her feel sexy?

The answer to all of these was no.

Maybe she used to need all three, but not any more. She pushed them to the back of the shelves, to gather dust for eternity. Then, like an animal returning to her burrow, she touched everything as if to put her stamp upon it all again. 'Mine,' she said to the silent stillness. '*Mine.*'

Then she turned on the immersion heater for a bath. And as she lay there, running her fingertips over the pale green velvet, she remembered Claire and Andrew's tales of Binnie and her woes. And smiled to herself. Australia. They'd be back a great deal sooner than planned, those two. You know your own children. She gave them about four weeks of youth hostels, and the general discomfort that goes with being on the road, before returning. Claire, at passport control, finally removing the Walkman headphones, talked enthusiastically about the beaches and the swimming and the barbies they would enjoy. Andrew, eyes still half on the girl with backpack (so like his father, thought Angela), talked with macho confidence about the scuba diving and the surfing parties he intended to enjoy.

They had not quite grasped the fact that two students hitting the road to Oz alone was not quite the same as two teenagers being wooed by their father and their father's new wife on a once-in-a-lifetime, all-expenses-paid, five-star family holiday. But they would. They would.

She smiled to herself as she slipped under the avocado waters of her bath and let the steamy extract of geranium soothe her dreaming skin. You didn't get much of this to the pound in a youth hostel.

In Wimbledon Binnie and Ian sat on their now even dingier white settee, surrounded by a much-stained white carpet, and gazed into the fire. They were holding hands and they were happy.

'This is more like it,' said Binnie.

Ian grunted.

'I hope they *never* come back.'

Ian tensed.

Binnie recalled that they were, after all, flesh of his flesh.

'Well, not until summer.'

Ian relaxed again.

'Middle of May at least,' he said. 'They're really looking forward to it all.'

Binnie did not care if they were really looking forward to it or if they were planning to commit hara-kiri on Bondi Beach. But she managed, just, to keep the thought to herself. One thing was for sure, *her* little Tristan would never be like them. *Ever* . . .

'Then they'll go and stay with um-er for a while.' (He never quite knew how to refer to his ex-wife.) 'Then university. It will all be fine from now on.' He smiled with satisfaction. Once a manager of people, always a manager . . .

'What was it like seeing *her* again?'

'Who, sweet?' Ian said sleepily.

'Well, you saw you ex-wife again, didn't you?'

Ian sat bolt upright and began coughing.

'It's all right,' said Binnie. 'There's no need to hide it from me.'

Ian swallowed and spoke as nonchalantly as he could. 'Mm? What did you say?'

'Seeing Angela? At the airport today?'

He breathed out. Closed his eyes again. Snuggled up to her all the more. Said through sleepy lips, 'Fine. It was just fine. We hardly spoke at all.'

'What did she think of our little boy?' said Binnie.

'Oh,' said Ian comfortably. 'She was all over him. Practically had to tear him away . . .'

'Good,' said the second Mrs Fytton. '*Good* . . .'

24

January

Giving parties is a trivial avocation, but it pays
the dues for my union card in humanity.

ELSA MAXWELL

Mrs Angela Fytton
warmly requests the pleasure
of your company at a party to celebrate Candlemas
and the making of the Traditional Ale

2 FEBRUARY, 6–MIDNIGHT
RSVP CHURCH ALE HOUSE

Another blackbird keeled over and died in the Rudges' garden. Angela pushed it gently to one side with her foot so that it lay among the winter-flowering pansies, half hidden, only its stick-like legs on view. Odd, she thought, but she put it down to the extreme cold. She delivered her invitation and heard it plop into the silent hallway, then went on her way.

The Rudges, *in absentia*, were busier than ever this New Year. The likelihood of their getting to the Ale Blessing, or the party afterwards, was – as Mrs Rudge said in her note – unlikely. They would try to make an appearance and they would probably fail. Mrs Rudge was in court, with Judge Julius Potter, appearing for the prosecution on a media high-profile case involving a giant fast-food chain and a couple of hippies who maintained that half a rain forest disappeared every time the fast-food chain opened its boardroom mouth.

Mrs Rudge was enjoying the fight, except that Judge Julius was not disposed to having women in his court in any capacity other than a minor secretarial one, or as the accused. He showed his disapproval wherever possible. Which meant that Mrs Rudge must wear Clarkes Skippies, pale stockings, a calf-length skirt and no make-up. The judge, had he been asked, would have requested that all women in court below the age of ninety-two wear a *chador*. Fortunately no one asked him. But he still managed to draw the line at being importuned in his own court by legally qualified painted Jezebels. And Mrs Rudge wanted to win. She was passionate about ecological causes.

Mr Rudge, on the other hand, could wear what he pleased, so long as it was a dark flowing garment first designed in the seventeenth century and a wig. He was prosecuting the water board for failing to give a good service; in particular, for failing to give a good service to the Fenmore Tarlocks fire brigade, who could not get enough water pressure for their hoses to quell the sinisterly unseasonal forest fires west of the Levels the preceding summer. It was argued that the lack of necessary water power was caused by the local water board's having turned down the pressure so that the leakage ratio would not look so bad, thereby saving their shareholders the unnecessary expense of replacing the worn-out system. Mr Rudge was known to be a Rottweiler when it came to such breaches of conservation business morality and it was not thought likely that a government ombudsman's whitewash would suffice to cover this one up. Mr Rudge was confident. Mr Rudge could not abide hypocrisy. Mr Rudge was sure he would win.

As the blackbird lay in the garden, slowly stiffening, a small blue pellet attached to its inner thorax, the Rudges were off at these important tasks. Whatever the outcome, like a decent international boxing match, everybody won. Win, lose or draw, they were going to reward themselves. It was from these twin mighty oaks that their little acorn, in the shape of a swimming pool, would grow.

The cat from Tally-Ho Cottage, passing through, watched Angela shut the gate. Angela watched the cat, her dugs dragging, slink over to the upturned stiff, contemplating, perhaps, a nice bit of game for her tea. Angela, not quite at one with nature red in tooth and claw, clapped her hands. 'Shoo,' she said. The cat shooed. The cat was irritated. The cat, seeking to vent its irritation on an irrational world, took the path over the back, along the hedge and up through the Tichbornes' garden. There was a nasty little snapping dog who lived there and she could drive him absolutely mental just by giving him the merest shadow of a flick of her tail from the undergrowth.

There were some, and not only the cat, who might have wished, in the weeks to come, that Angela Fytton had minded her own business in the matter of the colour of nature's dental endowments and pointed, horny extensions. But shoo that cat she did.

In search of revenge for the shoo, the cat reached the Tichbornes' garden just as Angela arrived on her bicycle and delivered her invitation into the hand – not very clean, she noticed – of the Dorkin girl, who was hovering at the back door.

'And this one is for you and your mother,' she said.

The Dorkin girl barely looked at it. She was scouring the lane with her luminous, hopeful eyes. How cold she must be, thought Angela, wearing so little in this frost. She clicked the gate shut and departed.

Unobserved, the cat slipped slowly through the shrubbery. Pimmy growled. Mrs Tichborne tutted. Pimmy barked and barked. Dr Tichborne imagined shooting the bad-tempered creature. Come to that, he imagined shooting both the bad-tempered creature and the dog. But only for a moment. What, after all, had the dog done to him?

Dr Tichborne was not a violent or evil man. Nor, as he might admit with regret, in his darkest hour, was he a courageous man. And he was having one of his darkest hours now.

He was not a courageous man – and he was having *by far* his darkest hour now, as he buttered his toast and tried not to look through the window at the young Dorkin girl. It was January, for God's sake, January. Whatever possessed her to have her chest out in the garden in this kind of weather?

As if he didn't know. As if his darkest hour was not in direct correlation to his knowing. She was out there and so was Crispin Archer. Somewhere. Golden as Helios in the faint morning sun. Either on his way to the church or on his way back from it, and she, the mammoth-fronted Dorkin, knew his every step. And worse – O fearful thought whose lucidity came suddenly, yesterday, when he saw the Reverend Crispin Archer's eyes as he watched the girl, or certain bits of her, leaning out of an upstairs window – he knew *hers*.

It cut Dr Tichborne to his very soul to see this beautiful young man throwing his private urges away on a girl with half a brain and twice as much chest as Treasure Island. He looked at his wife. She had never appeared more serene or untouched by human hand. Even her tutting was no more than the automatic response of one who knows she will, if she must, rule the world.

Dr Tichborne wanted to shout, to let all those years out in one long cry. Or hurl the marmalade. He fingered the jar. But he never would. He had never spoken to his wife above an acceptable, unaroused pitch, nor she to him. How he would love to roar like a lion. But he had only ever bleated like a lamb.

Pimmy barked for the third time. You see a cat, you don't like a cat, you react. The dog owned and expressed every emotion that his mistress did not. Dorothea Tichborne winced. Her husband winced to see it. In this morning's buttery light she suddenly looked unappealingly grey. Dorothea had never liked loud noise of any kind. Never. Which is why they had lived together so quietly.

She was poring over the ancient book of baptismal instruction. She wished the forthcoming baptism of her servant to be held as an example to the rest of the parish youth. Mrs Dorkin, who put on her pink plush hat to take tea at the Tichbornes', had remained firm. Total immersion. 'In the old days the water was taken from the well to the church. Now *that's* true repentance for you,' said the elder Dorkin with satisfaction. 'Because it's *that* cold.'

Mrs Dorothea Tichborne could see the point about the mortification of the flesh, but she disagreed about the tradition of it. The font would do perfectly well. It was a big one. Not big enough for full immersion, but you couldn't – alas – expect that nowadays. Shame. But there it was.

Mrs Dorkin had brushed the crumbs from her lap, readjusted her pink plush hat and returned home. She was not a woman to accept defeat, but then neither was Mrs Dorothea Tichborne. The font it would be. It was, after all, a Devereux font. She read on. The dog barked again. She looked up, tutted and said, 'See what it is out there, Percy, please.'

'It's a cat, dear.'

He watched, miserably, as the Dorkin girl tottered up the path in her extraordinary high heels, frontage forward, to greet the beautiful Crispin as he cycled to a halt by the wall. He watched as the vicar dismounted those adorable thighs of his, leaned over the gate, reached out his adorable hand in the frosty air and touched the loathsome girl on her foul cheek in an adorably tender way. Rage welled in old Dr Tichborne's breast and rose up like an angry bubble in his throat. He put all he had got into it. Now or never, he thought, and he yelled with a voice that had been stored deeper, even, than under a hat.

'Oi,' he cried. '*Oi.*' And he banged on the window long and hard as if both his heart and the window would break. 'Clear off! Get off! Go away! Oi, away!' He roared even more loudly. There was a rushing of wings in his head. The Angel of Rage had spoken. He banged on the window anew.

'Bloody cat,' he yelled at the Dorkin girl, for his wife's benefit. 'Bloody, bloody cat. *Bloody cat!*'

He forgot that the *sine qua non* of their marriage was to

never raise your voice. He forgot that when his wife, as Dorothea Devereux, accepted him, she begged that their married life please be as quiet and as pious as a convent. For which she would be very much obliged. She would also retain her private income.

He saw the Dorkin girl's and the vicar's startled eyes, and how they drew closer together as the gate swung away and they stared wonderingly at his frenzied window-banging. Bang, bang, bang, he went on the glass. Words he knew not that he knew came into his mouth. Good words, rich words, ancient words dredged up from a depth hitherto unplumbed. Saxon words, deep from within the historical psyche.

'Oi!' He banged again. 'You can just fuck off out of it. D'you hear? Go on – clear off! Piss off – sod off – vamoose!' This last sounding a little tame, he added, '*Bloody vamoose*,' which felt a lot better.

Then he began a little tantrumming dance of rage – something he vaguely remembered doing from long, long ago, before he had words, before someone chidingly told him not to . . .

'Fuck off, fuck off, *fuck off, I say*.'

The cat walked on impervious, now in full view. Pimmy went, quite literally, barking mad.

'Shut up,' said Dr Tichborne. And he brought his heel backwards, sharpish, on the creature's quivering flank.

It yelped.

Mrs Dorothea Tichborne tutted in a new and uncharacteristic way, a little like a hiccup.

Pimmy barked again. Pimmy yelped again.

Mrs Dorothea Tichborne again hiccuped.

It was oddly irritating. Who was yelping and who was tutting?

Dr Tichborne turned. The Angel of Rage flapped his wings and breathed fire. Mrs Dorothea Tichborne made yet another stab at a hiccup. Dr Tichborne heard the Angel, turned and said, 'And you can fuck off too, you silly bitch.'

Pimmy, being male, did not take this upon himself.

Mrs Tichborne was silent.

And then he saw through the window the shocked Dorkin girl sway and totter backwards into the rose bed, and the beautiful vicar, with those beautiful hands, reach out for her, and down they both went together. The Dorkin girl squealed like a stuck pig, and was beginning to look like one, with blood drawn upon those monstrous bare breasts.

Pimmy barked and barked and Dr Tichborne thought, above all the din behind him, that he heard the faintest of moans.

He looked around. His wife, doyenne of respectability and cream of mealtime etiquette, was slumped forward on the white tablecloth, her head in a bowl of muesli, making little bubbling sounds and moaning, in the same way that Dr Tichborne had heard many of his patients moan over the years. It was the moan of the end. He stood there wondering what to do. Even those rolling eyes of hers managed to look embarrassed at their overt activity. Do not say anything, they seemed to beg. Just go on as if you had not noticed.

What to do? What to do? He looked from the table to the window and back again. Pimmy was licking up the dripping milk. The bubbling died away, the moaning ceased, the eyes fluttered finally over their rolling whites.

What to do? *What?*

And then his heart told him. He marched past the table out into the corridor, into his study, picked up a piece of lint and a bottle of iodine, and strode into the garden. The Dorkin girl was now upright again and drawing attention (as if there was any need) to the state of her front. The vicar was showing a keen interest. Dr Tichborne brought the lint and the iodine up close and slathered it on the offending area. The vicar showed an interest in taking the job over from the good doctor, but the good doctor held on tight.

'Now get those out of the cold air,' he said, 'dear. And Mrs Tichborne seems to be calling. See what she wants.'

Then did Dr Tichborne become like the Magdalene. He knelt at the vicar's feet and tenderly administered the lint to the small graze wound revealed below the cycle clip, touching that ankle for the very first time. He remembered a voice, from a very far off, his mother's voice, and he copied it now, exalting in the tenderness. 'There, there now – brave boy – you must be a man about it. There, there now – mustn't cry. Dry those tears, little man, and I'll kiss you better . . .'

He just about stopped himself in time. Though the vicar did appear to be looking at him most strangely.

Angela Fytton, cycling up to Tally-Ho Cottage with the last of her invitations, sniffed the delicious yeasty, herby air, heard the yapping and the yelling as she parked her bicycle by the gate, and wondered.

It was probably just that cat.

Inside Tally-Ho Cottage, Wanda was making hot infused oils. At the moment a glass bowl of oil, dense with chopped rosemary, sat over a saucepan of simmering water and had done so for two hours. On the table, waiting, were a jelly bag, a large jug, several airtight sterilized dark-glass storage bottles and a funnel. This time Wanda meant business.

Seeing the new owner of Church Ale House, she smiled through the window. She was ready for her at last. Dave the Bread slid the book *Cookery for Beginners* out of sight and went on putting currants on to his gingerbread men. In the oven was another experimental batch of Old Somerset Butter Biscuits, and this time, he hoped, he had got the proportions of the ingredients right.

Wanda called over her shoulder, 'Keep an eye on the oil, Dave, while I go and let her in.'

He went to the stove, removed the lid from the glass bowl and sniffed. He'd only ever had cocaine once, at one of Wanda's theatrical parties, but the effect of what he inhaled reminded him of that giddy moment. He put his head in still further and inhaled more deeply. It gave him a remarkable confidence. He replaced the lid and went across to the oven. Out came the Old Somerset Butter Biscuits, in went the gingerbread men. The air in the kitchen smelt of sweet bakery and pungent herbs. Authentically. Which was why Wanda wished Angela Fytton to come in and see it for herself. Wanda no longer felt hunted. She had given the Theatre of the Absurd a lot of time and attention, now she was going for the new School of Realism.

She picked up a biscuit from the tray as she passed by. 'Am I glad I've learned a few real tricks. She's got a sharp eye, that one. Have me sussed in no time . . .' She bit. Crunch. 'Do you know,' she said, 'I think you're nearly there.'

She looked at her husband's eyes. He looked back into hers, as much as he was able to focus after the astonishing effect of the rosemary.

'Wanda,' he said, 'there's nothing like the real thing. Just put your nose into that lot for a moment . . .' He pointed at the saucepan. Wanda did as she was bid. 'You market that, my girl, and we'll make a fortune.'

He smiled at her, a little dazedly. But Wanda was already ushering Angela in and pointing out a remarkable bit of weaving attached to her loom.

Lucy Elliott watched her children smiling up at the beautiful goddess whose large white teeth resembled more tombstones than a graveyard. And she watched her husband smiling into those clear blue eyes that were as sunlit pools by a fiord. And, finally, she watched Angela Fytton smiling up at those suntanned cheeks that were dusted with roses, and she said, 'I'm afraid Anja will not be able to come because she will be baby-sitting for us.'

'Of course,' said Angela Fytton.

Anja smiled.

The children smiled.

Craig Elliott did not smile. He looked beyond the window, to the frost bound hill and the lowering sky beyond. Then he looked at Angela. Then he looked as thoughtful as a man could look in his own kitchen, and certainly worthy of comparison to any piece by Rodin. Finally, with just a hint of sadness about his lips, he crossed the room and placed the invitation upon the mantelpiece.

In St Hilary's she paused to look at the bench ends.

Daphne was up a very long ladder. 'I was right,' she said. 'These are the Seven Corporal Works of Mercy and those over there will be the Seven Spirituals.'

Angela handed her the invitation. She went over to the bench ends. 'Might they have done this ale thing at Candlemas?' she asked.

'Possibly,' she said. 'But more likely Easter.' She smiled down at her. 'No reason why you can't bend the truth. The Church has been doing it for years. It was pagan anyway. Why Candlemas in particular?' She returned to her brushing.

Angela fingered the bench ends. 'Oh, no reason – just an idea.'

She slipped out of the church and got back on her bike. Candlemas, she remembered from her Cambridge days, was the time when the Old Faith repurified their Virgin.

The sound of an ambulance siren split the silent air. Above her head the rooks crowed and wheeled as it roared past. She flattened herself into the side of the hawthorn hedge, which scattered its icy droplets all down her neck and into the tops of her wellingtons. And then it was gone.

Up at the vicarage it was silent and closed. The Reverend Crispin Archer was out doing his job again. A tireless young man, though strangely driven just recently. She had been trying to talk to him for several days. She had a proposition for him and she was hopeful, despite his modern leanings, that he would agree. She pushed the invitation through the door and went on her way. There was still time. Plenty of that.

Sammy was leaning over the winter pens with a stick, scratching the ears of a pig.

'Ambulance?' she said. She handed him the invitation.

He did not look up from the muddy pink and brown-spotted backs of his animals. The cold air had nipped his nose and watered his eyes. Or was it the air? His sunken toothlessness seemed more pronounced. She took a switch from the hedge and followed suit with the scratching. 'Pigs are very rewarding animals,' she said. 'Not like my hens.'

'She's dead,' he said. 'And she was the last.'

'Who?' said Angela, thinking it was probably one of his farrowers.

'Old Mrs Tichborne. Dead.'

So it was sorrow and not frost in his eyes.

'Oh, Sam,' Angela said softly. 'I'm so sorry.'

'That ambulance. Carried her off. Went –' he snapped his fingers – 'just like that. The very last of that kind. The last mistress.'

She put her hand on his arm. 'Sorry,' she said again.

He turned his watery eyes to her and rubbed a dewdrop from his nose with the back of his hand. He smiled very broadly and spat. 'I'm not,' he said. 'Good riddance. Gentlemen of the party.' He spat again.

'At every draught more large and large they grow,
A bloated mass of rank unwieldly woe;
Till sapped their strength, and every part unsound,
Down, down they sink, and spread a ruin round,'

she said softly, remembering her first journey down here.

He nodded.

'What was it?' she asked.

'Heart.'

'Poor Dr Tichborne,' she said.

Sammy looked at her, then he looked at his pigs. 'Poor be blowed,' he said. 'Could do with a few more spouses following suit.'

He rattled the gate and two of his fattest pigs came waddling over to be scratched. He scratched one, Angela scratched the other. He read the invitation and sighed.

'You asking Gwen?' he said.

'Could do.' They stood there in silence for a while. 'Did you ever use rush lights, Sam?'

He nodded. 'Hard lighting,' he said and wiped at his nose again.

'There's a forge over at Cleeve End, isn't there?'

'Fancy stuff for fancy folk,' he said. 'Play-acting.'

He did not say another word, so she left off the scratching and cycled briskly home.

Mrs Dorkin replaced the telephone and danced a jig all round the bar of the Black Smock. But she wouldn't say why. And then she carried on cleaning with a renewed vigour that took the landlord's breath away. The baptism would have to be postponed, that was all. But not for very long. No matter what happened – and it was either God or the devil looks after his own – no matter what happened, that ceremonial would still go ahead. After all, it was what Mrs Tichborne herself had wanted.

'Had wanted?' said the landlord of the Black Smock.

But more Mrs Dorkin would not say.

Later, when everything was calm, Angela slipped out into the ink-black, starry night, her boots making no sound along the frosty lane. All was dark shadows and rustlings as she made her way to the Tichborne House, as if the land were wrapping itself deeper into its winter sleep. She was right about one thing when she decided to come down here – you really could walk the lane at night without fear. The people here were entirely good. Entirely.

The curtains of the Tichborne House were drawn and all was still. Just as it should be, she thought, for a house in mourning. As she reached the gate someone swished out in front of her. She gave a little squeak. But it was only the vicar.

'A sad day,' he whispered.

'I will cancel my party, of course.'

The vicar. 'Oh, I think not,' he said. 'The good doctor wants everything to go on exactly as it was before. Indeed, he insists upon it.' And then he added, rather miserably, 'Even the baptism.'

'Older people don't like change,' she said.

The vicar looked perplexed. Truth was, his bereaved parishioner seemed to welcome it with open arms. When the vicar suggested that he discontinue the baptismal lessons at the vicarage from now on, Dr Tichborne became quite animated in his insistence. Even making light of it. His exact words were, 'One less chair by the fireside and all the more crumpet for me.' But then, death took people very strangely.

'How is the doctor?'

'Being brave,' said the vicar. 'Very brave. Immersing himself in a game of chess.'

She slid down the dark path and slipped her note of condolence through the letter box. She was puzzled, with a strange sense of *déjà vu*, to hear again the words, 'Black king to white queen. Checkmate,' before she slipped silently and swiftly away.

Safe and warm in Church Ale House once more, Angela Fytton pondered on death in the country. As one candle was extinguished another came to take its place. Or that is how she decided it would be. Candles being a feature of her life for the next few busy days.

25

January

*In poorer homes people made their own candles and rush lights from
kitchen fat. Mutton fat was preferred as it was the hardest. The thin rushes
were gathered by women and children from the edges of streams and
stripped till only the soft white pith was left, supported by one thin strip
of green rind to hold it together along its length. This served as a wick.
Such a taper would not fit the socket of a candlestick and was clasped
in the scissor-like jaws of the rush-light holder.*

MARJORIE FILBEE, *A Woman's Place*

*The tombstone is about the only thing that
can stand upright and lie on its face at the same time.*

MARY WILSON LITTLE

On the day of Dorothea Tichborne's funeral, Mrs Angela
Fytton of Church Ale House in the county of Somerset was
very busy, as she had been for several days. Secretive as
Wanda had once been, she invited no one in and kept her
doors closed. She attended the service in the church but
declined to go back to the house. Just as well, some thought,
for a very peculiar smell hung about her.

The funeral was a large one. Grand cars lined the lane and
black-clad ladies and gentlemen of quality filled the pews,
the women wearing full veils and the men wearing overcoats
made to last a lifetime. They sat, as from time immemorial, at
the front.

The Elliott family took up nearly an entire bench to themselves, with Craig put very firmly at one end and the fabulous
Anja at the other. The three children crayoned throughout,
though not, alas, on the paper their mother had provided.

From time to time Craig would bend forward and look restlessly down the length of the pew at the perfect profile displayed by someone who was not his wife. The someone who was his wife noticed this, of course. And reminded herself, pale as she was already, that she really must not eat any of the refreshments on offer at the Tichbornes' afterwards. It was either those trousers or her.

At the back of the church, where Angela chose to sit, were the lowly folk, like Sammy and Mrs Dorkin, the potman from Ye Olde Black Smock and the jobbing handymen and gardeners that attended the Tichbornes from time to time.

Two tall candles burned either side of the bier, giving off the strong, cleansing scent of rosemary. Wanda had made them. She went very pink in the cheeks with all the compliments that abounded and just about stopped Dave from handing out their business card. She had, he felt, gone very proper all of a sudden, with all this talk of truth.

A space was saved close to the front, given the grandeur of their profession, but the Rudges sent their apologies. They had to be in court . . .

Well, well. It was no matter where you positioned yourself. It would take more than the light of two of Wanda's candles to warm these walls. Whether princes or paupers, all shivered as they sat and stood and sent the last of the Devereuxs upon her way. They had held the land for generations, they had taken arable into dairy, wool into milk, laid the ploughed fields to grass and changed the nature of the landscape entirely in their time. They had hunted over it, bequeathed it, loved it and hated it. And then they had sold it. That life would be no more. And this ended life, sealed up in its coffin, was the final, sighing breath of it.

The vicar gave a good sermon on the qualities of his patronness. And he reminded the congregation about Sir Christopher Wren's memorial in St Paul's: 'If you seek my monument look around you.' In the same way, he said, with the gracious Dorothea, St Hilary's would bear a plaque saying, 'If you seek my monument feel around you,' for the place would be warm for the first time in its 600-year existence. This she had apparently whispered to her faithful, sorrowing husband, in the last moments before she died. 'Let the church be warmed,' she had said. 'And let the young people come there and play their music and be happy.'

Now that same faithful, sorrowing husband stared up at the pulpit, meeting the warm gaze of the young man who spoke. He nodded very gently at the words 'And let the young people come there . . .' Come anywhere, he very nearly shouted. But he was constrained by his neighbour, who would need, he felt, no encouragement. For next to him, in a position quite out of favour with the rules, and in a move orchestrated by her mother, sat the horrible Dorkin girl. Put there to aid him, so Mrs Dorkin unequivocally said. Stay close. Stay close.

Sandra Dorkin did so, but she was also gazing raptly at the vicar. Of the marble memorial to the father of Dorothea Tichborne, née Devereux, with its cold, life-size effigies and seven illustrative carvings of his prowess, there was now no mention.

The Devereux face, borne by the devil, stared down from the perfectly restored wall-painting and there were those among the mourners who saw it and hid their smiles, including Sammy Lee, though he often hid his smile anyway, it being without teeth. What, as he would tell the world if they made comment, had he to bother with teeth for? There was no one to see who mattered.

Daphne Blunt, who sat with Angela Fytton, feeling that a funeral was too solemn to be ignored, had kindly hung a sheet over the first of the revealed corporal works. 'To Clothe the Naked' did, indeed, display an unclothed woman, and the woman did indeed have the cast of Mrs Dorothea Tichborne about her. As Daphne leaned over and said to Angela, 'It's just as well Mrs Tichborne is sealed up in her coffin, or she might have had a heart attack.' Angela Fytton looked solemnly down at her hands.

They sang 'God Moves in His Mysterious Ways', old Dr Tichborne giving it all he had got, which was quite correct under the circumstances, everybody felt. And then Angela was free. Outside the rain poured from the leaden sky as she hurried away to make her own place in the scheme of things. Behind her the gargoyles, familiar faces on the tower of St Hilary's, sent cascades of water safely away from the fabric of the building.

Back through the door of Church Ale House she went. Bash. She removed her wet clothes and put on dry ones, covering them all over with a boiler suit found in the sewing room in a very stylish greeny grey. She then tied back her hair, rolled up her sleeves and continued her secret work. She strung a washing line across the entire width of the kitchen and pinned pegs all the way along. Then she took a large pan, put it on top of the Aga and placed into the pan yet another quantity of mutton fat. Which gradually melted. She picked up a bundle of rushes from the back door and brought them in and began to strip them while the fat slowly turned to liquid.

Back at the Tichborne house, where the Dorkins had now reverted to servant mode and were handing around the sherry and the sandwiches, Mrs Dorkin took a little extra in the way of Oloroso, for her nerves, and then summoned up the sinews.

She applied her mouth to the vicar's ear and told him of Mrs Dorothea Tichborne's *second*-to-last dying words. The very last thing that the mistress had said to her Sandra was that the baptism would be a great and holy moment in her life, and – though uncomfortable – full immersion was the only way. In the well.

The vicar repeated this to the bereaved husband. Word for word.

'*In* the well?' said Dr Tichborne, his eyes lighting up for just a second. 'As in down it?'

Mrs Dorkin, hovering, flapped her hand dismissively. 'On it, round it, down it – what does it matter?'

'Black king to white pawn,' muttered Dr Tichborne.

Mrs Dorkin took another shot of sherry. 'Would you like my Sandra to stay with you tonight, doctor?' she said. 'In case you come over all queer?'

By the end of the funeral baked meats, it was agreed that the baptism would take place as designated. That the vicar would thank Mrs Fytton of Church Ale House for her offer and be pleased to accept a drop of water out of her well for the ceremony. And as for the total immersion factor, that should be left – as a blood kin's right – to the organizational skills of Mrs Dorkin.

'You'll have to make the church warm,' said Wanda, overhearing.

'Not necessarily,' said Mrs Dorkin. 'Not necessarily.' And her eyes gleamed from a depth that was deeper, even, than the sherry bottle.

By the end of the day the Fytton boiler suit was a piebald version of camouflage gear – stiff with grease and soaked with sweat. The floor was glazed with the foul-smelling rendering and all in all it was not the fancy craft-fair experience she had anticipated. From the washing line dangled a few dozen thin tapers of hardened mutton grease. She hoped it would all be worth it. She closed the door on the proceedings and was just about to go to bed when someone knocked at the front.

'Anybody there?' yelled the slightly blurred voice of Mrs Dorkin.

Angela let her in.

'Mmm,' she said, flopping down in the parlour. 'Lamb.' And she proceeded, rather convolutedly, to put her case for taking the top off the well for the purposes of baptismal ritual.

Angela nodded. 'It would be an honour,' she said, and meant it. Though she was too weary to notice that the date set for the ceremony was the same as the one set for her own party.

On leaving, Mrs Dorkin gave Angela's shoulder a hearty squeeze. 'No reason why a woman living all on her own *shouldn't* have a Sunday roast all to herself if she wants it,' she said.

Which took the matter of the date out of her mind completely.

By the time she did rise again, and realized it, the word had gone round that Sandra Dorkin's baptism would take place on 2 February. Candlemas.

'What can I do?' she said glumly to Daphne.

Daphne shrugged. She was beginning on panel number two: 'To Harbour the Stranger'. 'Why not combine them? In fact –' she turned and pointed across to the carving on the bench ends – 'why not follow the instruction manual? The vicar will know all about the baptismal rituals –'

'I wouldn't be too sure of that,' said Angela, remembering his somewhat shifty demeanour of late.

'Of course he will. In any case, baptisms are all about lights and candles and fresh beginnings, so it will dovetail in quite nicely. And if you copy what's going on in those carvings – well, it'll be . . .' She stared up at the roof beams, as if for inspiration.

'Be what?' asked Angela.

'A nice thing to do.'

It was with a light heart, therefore, that she set off to collect a very particular item from Cleeve End smithy. Play-acting, indeed. Sammy Lee could be too sour sometimes.

When she came back she put her precious package down on the grease-soaked kitchen table and went straight round to the vicarage, where she got quite soaked all over again since the vicar took so very long to open the door to her. And even then he only opened it a crack at first. Just for a moment she thought he was not going to let her in. But once he saw who it was he seemed very pleased. Inordinately pleased. He virtually yanked her inside.

Ten minutes later she left, feeling very pleased herself. A combined baptism and Blessing of the Ale, with all due accord to Mrs Dorkin's wishes, was just right.

'It will be a unity, vicar,' she said.

'Cool,' he said. 'And do call me Crispin.' He looked less imposed-upon than relieved. 'A burden shared is a burden halved,' he said.

'Something for the whole community.' She nodded.

'The more the merrier,' he agreed.

Old Dr Tichborne walked past, whistling and looking very jaunty.

'He's being so brave,' said Angela, on the doorstep.

'He certainly does seem to be stepping out a lot,' agreed the vicar. And he waved.

So did she.

If she were not so wholly well disposed towards the kind old man, she could have sworn he glared at her with something approaching murder in his expression.

On then to the Dorkin cott. Mrs Dorkin was all for it. It would, she felt, give her daughter an added stardom. And it would also mean that she did not have to either make, supervise or distribute the baptismal feast. A boon for the servant classes.

And thus it was agreed.

And thus the whole community looked forward to the joint celebration of the Blessing of the Ale and Sandra Dorkin's baptism. With full immersion.

26

January

Witchcraft was hung, in History,
But History and I
Find all the Witchcraft that we need
Around us, every Day.
EMILY DICKINSON

It was extraordinarily hot in Australia. Even if you went to the beach and drank and drank and drank, it was still too hot to ever get cool. And beer was not cheap. The youth hostel in Sydney was Oh Just *Bad*, and sleeping on people's apartment floors was not much better. Unless you wanted bar work, there was nothing to do to earn money, and the bar work was no good because they wanted you to work the hours when you wanted to be out with your friends. So there was nothing for it really but to get rid of your thirst by having a few beers. Do the barbies on the beach. And check into an hotel. As Claire said to Andrew, it was hardly likely that if Binnie and their Dad were here *they'd* be staying in a youth hostel. So why should they? And Andrew, who had suffered the mortification of being called a pale-skinned pom by the first girl he tried to chat up, agreed.

So they checked into the Harbour Hotel, worked out that they could manage to live there fairly well for two and a half more weeks, and rearranged their flights home accordingly.

It seemed appropriate that they should keep the date of their return a surprise for their father and Binnie. They did, however, telephone their mother, who agreed that it was a very good idea. Who then rang them the following day to tell them that it was a terrible idea. And who rang a third time to tell them to be sure not to tell their father that they had let her in on the secret of this possibly good, possibly terrible, idea.

'If Mum didn't like the idea,' said Andrew, 'she would have sent us some money so we could stay on a bit longer.'

'I think she's broke,' said Claire, when she rang off.

'How come?'

'She's making her own candles.'

It was Binnie who took the phone call despite its coming through very early in the morning. Ian was in the shower; Tristan was still asleep and she did not want him woken. So she pottered down to the kitchen, collected the phone on the way and spoke into it in a low voice as she crossed to the kettle. She could even afford, in her new springtime, to be sweet and civil to her stepchildren.

'Andrew,' she said, 'how are you?'

Pause. Binnie listens. 'Good,' she says. 'Good. And Claire?'

Pause. Binnie listens. 'Good,' she says. 'Good. And what's the weather like there?'

Pause. Binnie listens. 'Yes – it's raining in London too. But at least where you are is warm.'

Pause. Binnie listens. 'I thought it was summer over there.'

The kettle begins to steam. Still Binnie potters about getting teapot, mugs, milk, with the telephone tucked safely under her little ear. She is safe. So she thinks. Until she asks, 'Well, where are you, then?'

Pause. Binnie listens. She laughs a cracked little laugh.

Her husband, father of this Andrew, this Claire, comes into the kitchen just as her cracked little laugh goes an octave higher. She stands there, in front of her husband, who is also the father of her blood child, and she clutches the milk carton to her chest while she silently hands to this man, husband and father, the telephone. He, taking it, looks at her face and thinks she must have had a very rough night, which is strange, because for the last few weeks or so they have both been sleeping like babies, as indeed has the baby.

He speaks into the telephone tentatively. It could be anyone. But it is only his son.

'Hi, Andy,' he says. 'How're you doing?'

He places his free hand on his wife's little shoulder and rubs it gently in a gesture of complete solidarity and tenderness. He had no idea that the advent of his older children had affected her so much. Why, even though they are thousands and thousands of miles away now she looks half mad with fear and her face wears that crumpled look.

'What's the weather like there?'

A small sob escapes from Binnie's throat. Ian feels the vibration of it in his hand. But his hand is now stilled, glued to the spot just above his wife's collar bone. Then he squeezes so that she gives a little yelp.

'Where?' he asks quietly into the telephone.

'Heathrow,' says Binnie automatically. 'They are at Heathrow.'

Above them the sweet, seeking wail of their son begins. A new day, a new dawn.

'Get on to that witch,' spits Belinda. 'This is all her doing. And if she isn't there, keep trying until she *is* . . .'

'Who?' says Ian. But he knows who.

On the telephone, still in his hand, still at his ear, his son is saying querulously, 'So will one of you come and get us or what?'

'What?' says Ian, and switches off the phone.

It is to no avail. Come they will. Ian departs for work – he has to or empires will crumble. Binnie remains in the house for just as long as it takes to have a bath in her own little bathroom, dress herself, dress her child and get out. Although they now have a new one, it is not a cleaning-lady day, so she locks the door behind her and goes off to the zoo. Perhaps there will be some explanation, some comfort, in the behaviour of the apes?

She weeps with rage, vexation, frustration and bile. She

thinks of the former Mrs Fytton in her rural retreat, full of peace and quiet, and she begins to get a sense of having been stitched up. Who can say why she should suddenly think this, but she does. She knows that there is no justification in the world for she, Binnie, to say to her, Angela, You must have your children to live with you. They are no more her children than they are Ian's. That is equality. She is stuck. She looks at the birds in the beautiful white aviary, trapped. And she knows that nothing will ever be the same for her or Ian or Tristan again.

She turns to go home. Wishing with all her little bruised and weary heart that when she first saw Ian she had not fallen at his feet. Wishing that she had simply leaned over and patted his hand and said a friendly goodbye – and gone, resolutely, on her way. Instead of thinking that he was attractive, rich, vulnerable and would be easy to remove from his marriage. And that she was fed up with waiting for an available Mr Right to come along. And wishing that there had never been such a thing in the world to drive her to it like the ticking of her biological clock.

Baby Tristan waves to the birds and makes noises indicating that an ice cream is in order, despite its being the last day of January and freezing. Binnie pushes the stroller towards the café with damp, bowed head. Whatever is coming, she thinks, come it will. She sees her life stretching forth as a single parent after all. Hellfire and damnation, she shrieks inwardly, she might as well have gone for the IVF and saved everyone a load of bother.

Claire said that the only way to get in was to break in. So they did.

Thus did Binnie arrive back with the sleeping Tristan to find a howling gale blowing through the house from the conservatory where Andrew had broken a pane of glass. And her two suntanned stepchildren in the whitish sitting room eating crisps and watching TV and wonderfully uncritical of there being no thought spared for their arrival. One thing you could say about these two teenagers was that they did as they would be done by and were forgiving and without expectation in the matter of people being organized. To go out and forget to leave a key was just the kind of thing they might do themselves. And there was no harm done.

Binnie, being of a different opinion, took to her bed, tucking Tristan up beside her and thinking that he could stay there with her in future and that Ian could get into the cot every night. That might make him see sense about his horrible, horrible children. She then threw the boomerang, the gift of her stepchildren, across the room violently.

Fortunately, it was another failure, and it did not come back to her.

Now Belinda, who once asked nothing from life but the chance to be cared for by a husband, and who was perfectly prepared to cede liberation for the net gain of a place in the maternal pantheon, decided to have one more go at putting things right. So she rallied. And here she was, mid-rally so to speak, sitting on the settee trying to look relaxed and commanding and in control. That last was very important, because she had been somewhat out of control these last few days and it was quite a frightening experience. Largely the out of controlness manifested itself in an urgent and recurring desire to wring her stepchildren's necks, closely followed by a bursting into frustrated tears because she was not allowed to. So, at considerable expense, and wishing to see her own son grow up and not from the wrong side of prison bars, she went to see a counsellor.

The counsellor told her that if she wanted to preserve her marriage and retain the father of her child's goodwill, she must get some kind of solid foundation of understanding going between the interpersonal dynamics of the situation. Binnie took interpersonal dynamics to mean the opposite of strangling, so she listened to the advice. And now here she was, and here they were, and she was about to put it into practice.

'Sit down,' she said very nicely, indicating the chairs.

The pair, slightly nervous, did so.

'Drink?' said Binnie. She had the drinks tray on a table in front of her with ice and lemon and glasses, so there was no fussing. She poured them a vodka. Grown-up drink for grown-up occasion, she thought. And, just as she replaced the cap on the bottle, from above came the wail of little Tristan.

'I'll go,' said Claire.

She brought him down. He stopped wailing and beamed around the room at everyone, pleased to be part of the proceedings. Andrew made goo-goo noises at him, which sent him off into paroxysms of chuckling. Binnie wondered, when she looked at them all behaving together like this, whatever it was that made her so full of murderous intent.

She said, 'You know sometimes, when they are in love, people like to spend time on their own together.'

Two pairs of very surprised eyes stared at her, with a third pair that simply looked.

'Y-e-e-s,' said Claire.

'We all need our space from time to time, don't we?'

Andrew said, 'I was going to ask you about that.'

Now we're getting somewhere, thought Binnie happily.

'Can I have a double bed?'

Binnie went on sipping. This, she felt, was slipping away from her as she sip, sip, sipped. She just made the faintest of noncommittal noises. It seemed the best way. 'Umph,' she went, and waited.

'So that Elly can stay.'

It dawned. This was not some unimaginable trial sent by the gods. This was her stepson Andrew on sparkling form. And Elly was a poisonous creature who viewed the entire house and its contents with eyes of green glass.

'And Claire?' she said. 'Perhaps you'd like your boyfriend to move in with you too?'

'Oh no,' said Claire, with complete derision. 'I haven't got one.'

Andrew looked at Binnie very kindly. 'I wouldn't,' he added sweetly, 'mind if it was only a futon actually. After all,' he said with urbane reasonableness, 'this is my house too.'

It seemed strange to him. After all, it was a so-called responsible adult, his very own mother, who had pointed out the veracity of that statement. And now here was another of the so-called breed going ape-shit at the very suggestion. Jeezus! Life was a minefield when all the adults surrounding you were nuts.

'Er – isn't it?' he added, with quiet confidence.

Which, oddly enough, though she did not know her root-stock, touched a part of Binnie that was entirely and absolutely peasant. At the mere thought of some spotty little fuck-wit suggesting that he owned a share in her estate, she went – as she was to tell the counsellor the following day – ape-shit. It occurred to her that the likelihood of herself being a single parent and Tristan growing up without benefit of a loving dad about the place was increasing. Unless she embraced the alternative scenario, which was of Tristan growing up with a loving dad, two adoring half-siblings and a dribbling idiot for a mother.

And so ended Binnie's serious talk, grown-up fashion. With Claire and Andrew shaking their heads at the unbelievable madness of grown-ups and their stepmother in particular – and with Binnie tucking little Tristan up and then going back downstairs and having three vodka slammers in a row. Or possibly four, five or six.

By the end, if she could have seen to dial, she would have dialled the number of That Witch. As it was, she had a couple of stabs at it and got a hotel in Bannockburn, followed by the talking clock.

'You know,' said the counsellor, 'they do not sound so bad. I myself had teenage stepsons who stole from me, set fire to my car and put a card in a telephone box saying I gave good head.'

'I do not,' said Binnie, 'pay you to tell me your problems.'

Belinda decided, in that good old-fashioned way, to take her baby and go back to mother.

27

Candlemas Eve

Isn't there any other part of the matzo you can eat?

MARILYN MONROE, ON BEING SERVED MATZO
BALL SOUP FOR THE THIRD TIME IN A ROW

Where do you go to get anorexia?

SHELLEY WINTERS

It was two weeks since the funeral of Mrs Dorothea Tichborne and apart from one particular incident when old Dr Tichborne was found very much the worse for wear outside the vicarage at two in the morning and brought home by the potman from the Black Smock, an incident which the entire community thought quite pardonable, life was calm.

These were the last of the dead days – the last of the silent world of winter before the hints of spring should be seen. Shivering bees buzzed around the Christmas roses and hungry pale-grey pigeons huddled together on rooftops. The mornings were raw and the days were scarcely drawing out again, but they were – and little peepings of green all around made the world that lived above ground renew its hope. It felt like a time to have a celebration, a party, a happy ritual – and all those things were about to take place in St Hilary's and Church Ale House and garden on the following day.

Angela gave the piano tuner a glass of ale which he said was the best thing he had drunk for a long time.

'Seems like you'll be having quite a party,' he said, looking around the parlour. 'Very festive.'

When he drove off he hit the gatepost.

*

In Tally-Ho Cottage the scent of oil and ginger and cinnamon hung like a warm blanket over the proceedings. In the kitchen Wanda packed the last six of her small bottles into the last of her six wicker baskets and handed them to Dave the Bread. 'Prunes in the High Street will take three,' she said, 'and two go to my private customers at the Taunton Vale Building Society. And one to the manager of the Co-op. You'll be going in there anyway to get your bread.'

Dave put on his cap, picked up the baskets and shook his head. 'No need,' he said. 'Biscuits are done. And I should be able to bake before we go.'

Wanda stood up. 'You're never going to risk doing the bread yourself?' she said, in admiration.

'If I get up early enough,' he said, 'I should be able to manage it.'

She removed his silly cap and ran her cinnamon-scented fingers through his hair. 'If you get up early enough tomorrow morning,' she said, 'there'll be time for more than just baking...'

Lucy Elliott passed out in her bedroom. Down she went, crump, on to the floor. She was *determined* to get into those leather trousers by tomorrow and had managed to not eat anything for nearly two days. Needs must when the devil drives, she told herself, every time she set down a meal for the children, or cleared away their plates without picking up the scraps and shoving them into her mouth. (*Why?* What was it about cold baked beans and dry toast crusts that compelled one to eat the things instead of tipping them into the rubbish bin?) Anyway, no one had noticed that she had not eaten and now here she was, up in her bedroom, about to try the things on again and then – pouf – her head went all swimmy and she needed to sit down and then everything went all black and...

Craig Elliott tutted with irritation. He had been struggling with the imagery of Dorothea Tichborne's final moments, as told to him by the Dorkin girl, and the imagery of death is a very delicate thing for a writer, so the last thing he needed was his wife to start moving the furniture around. He had been toying with the idea of renting a little place on a regular basis in London and now he was convinced. Being so near and yet so far in the proximity of Anja was torment for the free artistic spirit in him. And the Fytton woman was entirely busy with her silly party so she no longer had time for him, and as if that were not bad enough, now even his wife could not keep the domestic arrangements quiet. And he had just got to the upturned eyes, the Gothic colours, the stillness and the dribbling too . . . and the sound of the milk going plink, plink, plink. Not easy to construct prose delicately around something like that.

He got up from his desk, strode down the passageway to their bedroom and opened the door. He was about to speak quite curtly when he beheld his wife lying, eyes upturned, greeny-white and still as marble and giving a pretty good impression of the imagery of death upon the floor. The shadow of Dorothea Tichborne's final moments came back to him. A terrible punching sensation hit his solar plexus. Little Lucy – his wife – his helpmeet in all his needs – mother of his children – warmer of his bed – rock upon which everything was built. Was dead. What would he do now? Without her? He fell to his knees, sobbing.

Old Dr Tichborne, coming out of the gate of the Elliotts' house around lunchtime, patted Craig Elliott reassuringly on the arm. 'Better luck next time,' he said.

Which Craig Elliott felt was very peculiar.

'Your wife will need monitoring, but there is nothing wrong with her. Nothing at all. Bit on the thin side, of course. But strong as an ox. Sorry.'

Craig Elliott was not taking any chances. He telephoned a specialist in London. He would take her there next week. He ran back indoors to check that she was still alive.

*

The doctor himself was feeling a mite less strong than he expected after last night. Last night was supposed to be wonderful. Crispin came around with his guitar and some of his CDs. Old Dr Tichborne set out the chess pieces and banished the Dorkin girl, saying that even he knew how to make an omelette. And the beautiful vicar presented him with a bottle of mulberry wine. Though he would have preferred a nice Chablis, he partook of the gift, blessed as it was by the young god's hand.

It being a cold night, the vicar accepted a glass immediately, saying it was only fruit. And then another. He was, he said, knocked out by it. The vicar then helped himself to a third and started playing his guitar. Very loudly. He then put on one of his CDs and played along with it, even more loudly, had one more ruby glassful and began singing very loudly too. He showed little inclination to eat the omelette, and even less to play chess, since at one point and giving a particularly hearty swing with the guitar he swept most of the pieces off the table and on to the floor. He then looked at them, said, 'Well, isn't that just like life . . .' and burst into a wild rendering of something that sounded like 'Achy-Braky Heart', so that Dr Tichborne retired from the room wounded and had to stand outside the door for some time wondering how to regroup.

As he stood on the wrong side of his sitting-room door and listened to the Reverend Crispin Archer apparently yodelling, he was not sure what to do next. He had lived for many years, more than forty, in a relationship of peace and quiet and harmony. Was he, he wondered, going to give all that up for initiation into the mysteries of physical love with a guitar-twanging, boot-stamping, spurs-jingling, God-bothering cowboy?

Only fruit indeed. In the end he had politely shown the wild-eyed vicar (still beautiful, still beautiful, but Oh So Dangerous . . .) the front door, watched him stagger off, spurs a-jingling, and spent the next hour sitting alone and playing his Ashkenazy Chopin études very quietly in order to calm down. And the really frightening thing was that he had seen the beautiful Crispin this morning and the beautiful Crispin was scarcely affected by the excess. A little green about the gills, but upright and functioning. A young liver. Youth. Old Dr Tichborne could never keep up with that. He was torn. Yea, verily, he was torn between the spasm and the what's-it, the bit in between – where the shadow fell . . . Perhaps it would all be revealed to him in due course. But in the meantime – what to do, what to do?

The Rudges left a note for their gardener asking him to tell Mrs Dorkin and Mrs Fytton that they would try to get back for the Sunday celebrations. If their cases moved along quickly they might just do it. Mrs Dorkin and Mrs Fytton doubted this very much.

Meanwhile the gardener set up his machine again, still unclear why the previous saw was so wantonly damaged. He blamed the Travellers, naturally. And now they had gone. So presumably all was safe again. And down came the pollarded tree. Angela Fytton, being a kind woman, and seeing how cold he looked, invited him in for a quick half of warmed ale. Which became two not-so-quick ones. When the gardener went back to the Rudges' garden his machine, inexplicably, would not start. A vital part appeared to be missing from the motor. But then again, he could not be quite sure, since his sight also seemed to be missing a vital part. He went to lie down. And very nearly got hypothermia. The copper beeches remained to tell their tale for yet another week.

Unaware of their gardener's fate, in Bristol Mrs Rudge bought some Sparsofen to sprinkle on the pure, bare soil of the garden. If the slug pellets were the hors-d'oeuvre, the Sparsofen was the dessert. That'd give any hungry, slimy creature a headache if it ventured out for a quick snack in the coming weeks, she thought with satisfaction. She nipped back into court. The case against the great big fast-food chain was going really well.

Mr Rudge was also doing extremely well with the water board. Curiously enough, during the case, he had received his first cheque as a shareholder of the very same company. 'Good', he thought, banking it. For, if asked, he would point out that as in life so in jurisprudence. One is talking about the law, not justice.

The following morning the Dorkin girl stood on the top of the Mump and lifted up her own two mumps to the wintry sun. I am the new goddess, she said to the sky. Which was approximately what the vicar said to her as he fairly pulled her out of her bedroom window last night and bedded her in the straw in the old barn at the back. He smelled of fruit and he intoxicated her. How could she resist? Not that she had the slightest intention of doing so. It was not in her nature to resist. She was a nice, warm, friendly, compliant girl – only just a bit more compliant with some than with others. The vicar was also very compliant and warm and friendly – though perhaps nice was pushing it. 'You are the new goddess,' he said, and he called her his little mulberry as he ripped away at his clothes. But he changed his mind when he ripped away at hers and she lay beneath him in the moonlight. 'Or the devil incarnate.'

Mrs Dorkin, washing the floor of the Black Smock, smiled and sang to herself. Her daughter was a sly one. Slipping off into the night like that. She had seen the low lights behind the drawn curtains of the Tichborne house and heard the soft piano music on the night air. That was where her Sandra had gone. Two in the morning it was. He wouldn't be much trouble to her, being so old. It would be a dream come true. And tomorrow's little effort should just about clinch it. If her favourite film star, Raquel Welch, could do it, so could her Sandra. Even if the weather was a bit cold at this time of year . . . Thus, a little muddled, but *she* knew what she meant, a smiling Mrs Dorkin went on washing floors.

Sammy Lee baked a ham for the proceedings. And wondered

whether or not he would need to put his plate in. All depended, he said to the beautiful, succulent pink haunch as he drew it out of the oven. All depended on who was coming to the feast.

Daphne Blunt removed the sheet from 'To Clothe the Naked' and stood back to admire her handiwork. 'To Harbour the Stranger' was now finished too. And that would have to do until the ceremonial was over tomorrow and she could begin on the others. It was a slow process, letting the walls yield up their lessons in love and humanity, and it would not do to rush it.

28

Candlemas

At night any illumination must be artificial and in places where no artificial light is available people have to go to bed at sundown. From the pure vision point of view, a certain standard of illumination is necessary if comfortable working conditions are to be achieved. Where there is either too much or too little light, there is a marked falling off in working efficiency and this applies to housework as much as any other kind of work; there is also the danger of permanent injury to the eyesight.
'The scullery is in an awkward position, it's against the kitchen and makes the kitchen dark.'

FROM CHAPTER XIV, 'LIGHT TO SEE BY',
MASS OBSERVATION'S *People's Homes*, 1943

In Wimbledon the house was dark and silent. While Binnie and Tristan were in Wales, Claire and Andrew were staying with friends. Ian had sat them down, said, 'Watch my lips,' and told them that if they so much as set foot in South Common Road until he said that they could he would disown them for ever, drive them to Somerset and leave them there for good. It seemed that even they had finally reached the furthest point on their behavioural compass. They agreed.

Moneypenny, who valued the peace and quiet of her job, and who knew that the peace and quiet of her job was threatened by the boss's domestic upheavals, did not think it was a very good idea *at all* to leave Belinda Fytton in Wales. Especially not with her mother. A mother being a partial sort of an individual. Belinda Fytton must be collected forthwith. 'Will you go by car?' asked Moneypenny.

'My wife drove.'

'Will I ring to arrange the train tickets?'

'You can leave all that to me.' Said with a smile of deprecation. Quite understandable since he had not arranged his own travel, apart from one strange requirement for a car in Bristol, since the advent of Moneypenny.

She gave him a most compelling look. 'Very well, Ian.'

At Church Ale House, at ten minutes to five, all were assembled and ready to make their way to St Hilary's. They stood in the foursquare hall and were not allowed to look in the parlour because all of Angela's preparations were to be a surprise. As she looked around at the party standing wrapped against the cold, a unity with their torches and lanterns and nipped raw noses, and in her house, she was reminded of the very first time she crossed this threshold and how she knew no one. She felt remarkably cheered by the thought. You had to keep faith with people and with friendship. You had to continue to believe. After all, as she said to Mrs Dorkin, people are all we've got. Mrs Dorkin nodded her pink plush several times, but her eyes said she was on a different planet. The only time she came to life was when the Dorkin girl flatly refused to remove her cardigan. Mrs Dorkin whipped it off quicker than ninepence and tucked it into her bag. Still, she seemed to look at the stars. Indeed, it was remarkable how intent and absorbed and grave each of the faces in the party looked. Not one snigger, not one giggle, not even from the plastic biker jackets, who came to see.

The fair maiden with the flowing locks and the swirling cloak and the flagon of ale would, of course, be the Dorkin girl. Daphne had borrowed a suitable container from the local museum and this was filled for blessing in the church. After the blessing each would drink a little from it and the rest would be returned to the main brew, first touched by the lips of the assembled faithful, so that the blessing could spread into every particle . . .

Remembering therefore the light that you bring us,

We beseech you to bless this honoured Ale.
Medicine of life, Earthly benefit of Sacred Burgess.

Angela gave the flagon-bearer one of the gooseberry-green velvet curtains to slip around her shoulders and beneath it she wore the white surplice of fine linen and lace which Dorothea Tichborne, who had, it seemed, been *remarkably* conversational with everybody at her demise, bequeathed from her marriage chest for the event. The stitching might be local but the lacework was Chard and it was not less than a hundred years old, for there was a bill for its mending from Staithe dated 1899. The Dorkin girl told her mother that she wished to wear this lovely garment over some warm winter underwear. An unholy state of things which her mother deplored with a stout clip round the ear.

The vicar, torn between desire and humanity, said either way would be right in the sight of God. Everything is in the sight of God, he reminded himself, and tried not to catch, for the umpteenth time, the Dorkin girl's winking eye as the front door was opened and they slowly filed out. What, he wondered, *what* had happened in between his leaving Dr Tichborne that night and arriving back at the Manse? And was what he *thought* had happened merely a dream? As it had been countless nights before . . . She winked at him again. Her wink indicated that the dream point of view was unlikely. In more ways than one he wished he could remember.

Sammy would carry the symbolic sack of barley, though Angela Fytton packed most of it with newspapers. She did not want another death on her hands. But his jaws looked sadly shrunken. If only he had put in his teeth.

The Elliott boys were carrying the lights, which the sensible Anja contrived from small oil lamps furnished by Wanda. These were lit on Angela's pathway and began to glow and bob like a pair of dancing glow worms. The boys were immensely impressed with their central role in the proceedings and their innocent faces became old as time with the intent and glow of concentration. And, perhaps, with the proposed trip to the panto in Bristol and an overnight stay at an hotel. Their first night away from their mother – which made it even more exciting. Their mother looked upon them with a sad little smile. It was just as well, she murmured to her husband, that they were so independent – for who knew? Who knew? Then she cast down her lashes and shaded her eyes and her expression became quite impossible to read. Though the curve of her mouth was definitely on the upward side. Craig Elliott pulled his wife's shawl tighter around her shoulders against the cold.

Dr Tichborne held the circle of bread, baked by Dave and decorated with dried bog myrtle and hops by Wanda. This was her own invention but she was getting quite carried away with all this knowledge and some of it was bound to burst out in the wrong place occasionally. The bog myrtle (*Myrica*), so she discovered, was believed by the ancients to confer the power of detecting witches; and as if that wasn't enough, it was also said that if the leaves crackled in the hands the person beloved would prove faithful. So bog myrtle on the bread it was. It crackled like billy-o in Dave's hand as he placed it on the crust. For which she was, of course, most grateful. And a leaf stuck itself to Angela Fytton's sleeve and remained there throughout the ceremonial, about which Wanda, the only one to notice, said absolutely nothing.

'As darkness leaves the land we light the way of this Good Ale made by our own hand and ask for blessing of it. May it keep sweet until the last of it be drunk.'

Daphne had simplified the text, muttering words like *Didache* and *Apostolic Tradition* and *Hippolytus* with just a hint of a curl of getting even on her lips. 'Much better,' she said, handing it to Angela. And it was. Even the biker boys read audibly from their word sheet and they only shoved at each other in mild and harmless reflex as they gazed at the girl in the gooseberry cloak.

'Look kindly on this gift as we place it in Your Holy House.'

And so saying, they all set off from Church Ale House at ten minutes to five precisely.

Ian drove all the way across the Clifton Suspension Bridge and took the dark, winding road towards Tintern and the wife that he loved and the little boy that he adored. But when he reached the old abbey, he stopped. He thought. He got out and lit a Gauloise and looked at the beautiful, moonlit ruins of the ancient place and the bare winter countryside rolling away from him. He was not expected anywhere again tonight. No one, anywhere in the world, had a call on his time. It would serve the lot of them right if he never came back at all.

But then what? As a little boy he had once lost his mother's hand in a crowd. Just for a moment he had that feeling again. Excitement and fear. Part of him wanted to explore, but the other part – the greater part – wanted to rush back to that comforting grip and be safe and secure. Apart from anything else, he muttered to those eerie, moonlit arches and the rooks perched above him on the shadowy half-walls, apart from all that, he wouldn't know where to begin if he was left on his own. He was not brought up to it. It was not his function.

One thing was for sure. If one wife could be down in the countryside making pickles and honey and drinks or whatever it was she was going about, all done up in her aprons and rolled-up sleeves, and baking and being self-sufficient and putting on weight and not needing him at all . . . As per bloody usual. And if the other wife could just get on a motorway and drive to her mother's with his son and not need him because she had all the support she needed from the Under Milkwood relations, if . . . if . . . Then where was he in all this? Nowhere. No-bloody-where. He might just as well begin all over again with somebody else. And if he might just as well begin all over again with somebody else, why not stick with what he had already got? Either way it was the same.

He certainly did not want to be alone. He did not want to go home at night to an empty house and eat from an empty fridge and sleep in an empty bed, like David Draper did now. Apart from the washing machine, there was a dishwasher and an ironing board (more complicated than a Rubik's Cube) and an iron apparently designed by nuclear physicists, requiring an extensive knowledge of the properties of matter (silk, rayon, wool – how would he know?). He could make a computer do anything he wanted, but he could not – and he *would not* – learn how to service himself too. He made a lot of money. Let someone else be paid to do it for him. He needed looking after. He deserved looking after. He ought to go right on down to his wife's parental home and drag her back by the hair, saying 'Ug!' and beating his chest all the way.

As it was he smiled at the thought, finished another cigarette, flicked the stub into an arc of sparks in true Bond style, took one last look at the Gothic scene, returned to the car and drove straight back along the dark, winding road, over the Clifton Suspension Bridge again. Away from his little, adorable, troublesome wife. Too late to do anything about anything now because of Tristan, of course. But nevertheless, he drove.

Below him the moonlit water looked like a sheet of milky silk. Made him go all sensual just to look at it. Must be the tobacco and the memories of France. He put his foot down and the car decided to show what its twin turbos could *really* do. And over the border into Somerset he went. Doing 115 miles an hour.

Along the lane the procession came, through the lych-gate, up the church path and through the stout oak doors, with the gargoyle of the ancient Devereux above them, dry-mouthed and grinning in pain.

The church was full of light. Wanda had set out sixteen little novelty table-top braziers (in boxes of six dozen from the Taunton cash and carry) to line the flagstones of the aisles, each with a scoop of her ginger (circulatory stimulant and cleanser of poisons) and cinnamon (circulatory stimulant and effective against the common cold) oil warming pungently in its nest. And she had, after all, taken Church Ale House beeswax to make a pair of enormous candles that burned with the remains of the funeral candles, on either side of the altar steps. The scent of rosemary hung above the scent of ginger and cinnamon, and all this, combined with Daphne Blunt's two Dimplex radiators, contrived to make the air in the church warm and intoxicating. Even old Dr Tichborne, waiting cold and peevish in the porch for the vicar to enter first, began to mellow as the scent came swirling about him.

The Dorkin girl visibly relaxed as she came first through the oak doors. Her erectile tissue was finding it acutely difficult to do anything but become very erectile indeed, but in here all was warm and welcoming. She looked up. Well, warm and welcoming apart from the pictures on the wall, one of which looked suspiciously like her old mistress bearing a forked tail and burning in hell. Fear clutched her not inconsiderable breast at the thought. If old Mrs Tichborne was burning in hell and she so pious, what future was there for a sinner such as herself? She caught up with the vicar and looked at him for hope, but the vicar cast down his eyes and looked away. Again. She was foxed by his behaviour. After all, he had seemed to enjoy it so much. She winked once more but he was as stone. For the first time the Dorkin girl suffered the faintest stirrings of the feeling that she had been used.

Craig and Lucy Elliott walked slowly behind their sons. For a moment Lucy Elliott forgot that she was an invalid, and as such incredibly precious to her husband, and nearly giggled at the sheer bright joy of the whole thing, and the pride of a mother seeing her children perform. But she kept up her grave pace and let Craig's arm support her as they slid into a pew and he tucked her coat very firmly around her knees. After all, she really might have died. And then what?

Mrs Dorkin, who whipped off the green velvet curtain from her daughter's shoulders and would have consigned it, together with the cardigan, to her bag if there had been room, was glad of the candles and the braziers and the immense wall-light that cast such shadows. It left little to the imagination about what her Sandra had on under her shift. Or not. She stole a glance at old Dr Tichborne as he slid into his front pew. He certainly seemed riveted by something happening up ahead.

The vicar, in a rather fetching shade of pink, owing to Wanda's discovery that the rosadea berry (*Pinko deofloris*) provided the dye for the vestments that it was once obligatory to wear on this occasion, stood with his arms outstretched to welcome his flock. Behind his golden head the light above the wall-painting made a halo all around him and the shadow of his body glimmered through the rosy garment. He looked like an exotic butterfly, or an illumination in an old manuscript. Sandra Dorkin sighed.

Dr Tichborne was thinking, Love the pink, but he was also thinking that when all this was over, and the party endured, he could creep off to the quiet of his house again and read Trollope and put on his Chopin and admire from afar, because to admire from afar was, it seemed, the more delightful of life's options, and the simple, enduring temptation of being the grass beneath young Crispin's press-ups, so to speak. He might have another go at seducing the god-like creature. Or he might not. Oh, what a conundrum. Oscar Wilde, he now understood, had got it absolutely right when he said that the two greatest tragedies in life were not getting what you wanted and getting it. It was in this new spirit of understanding that, as a gift to himself on the decease of his good lady wife, he had purchased a set of more powerful binoculars.

Dave had thought long and hard about what to wear before participating in the ceremonial and he decided that the church was really no place for a baseball cap. Wanda made him a little roundel of beaded felt which everyone admired, and even Sammy said he would purchase one if one were available. Since they cost tuppence to make and were quick as a wink, it was a silver lining now that the profit from the bread was reduced. The Lord taketh away and the Lord giveth, thought Dave, bowing his head in the flickering light.

Everyone settled, silent and expectant, into their pews. The vicar played 'All Things Bright and Beautiful' and Wanda picked out the descant until Mrs Dorkin, feeling a little like the mistress of ceremonies with her daughter up the front like that, leaned over and nudged her and told her in a loud whisper that she was going wrong. Very wrong *indeed*. She readjusted the pink plush and sat with her back very straight, as she had seen Dorothea Tichborne do, and from behind, for more than half a century.

It was a short while after passing back over the Clifton Suspension Bridge and taking a last look at that milk smooth silvery expanse beneath him that Ian passed a stranded four-wheel drive, this year's model, with an RAC man bent over its open bonnet and two huddled individuals sitting inside. Had they but known where the speeding car was heading, they would have thumbed a lift. Weekending in the country, thought Mr and Mrs Rudge, was proving less enchanting than it had once seemed. And the neighbours never, really, became friendly . . .

Ian sped on, those turbos going like jets from a James Bond movie.

'God's gift of good husbandry – hops, malt and barley. God's gift of good husbandry here in this ale. Here is the light in the darkness of winter. Here is the gift that will bring us to spring. All gifts are God's gifts, our hands but the making. We thank you. We thank you. God's gift and good husbandry here in this ale.'

'Good*wifery*,' muttered Angela.

But only Daphne Blunt heard. 'Oops,' she said. 'Sorry.'

Sammy smiled to himself as he kept the sack firm across his shoulders. He'd seen it all before, the rituals, the needs, the hopes and the dreams, all bound up in this one little building. What he wanted was the true blessing of the ale. And that was to drink it. Pub and church. Two centres of the communal universe. And if anyone had the sense, they'd make them the hubs of their universe too. Not, though, in Sammy's private opinion, anyone of the male gender wearing an earring. But that was his private prejudice. Which he kept, as one should all private prejudices, very properly to himself.

Angela Fytton, standing in the pew at the front, felt a hand brush her arm and a warm breath in her ear. She very nearly jumped out of her skin as a familiar voice said, 'I hoped you wouldn't mind if I came . . .'

She turned and saw that it was Mrs Perry, and she thought that such a good and noble country woman completed the sense of continuity. 'No,' she said. 'No. Not at all.' And she slid along to make room for her. She saw that Sammy, looking up, was also pleased. He immediately put his hand up to cover his smile.

If the time of the open-air baptismal proceedings was set at half-past five in the hopes that the February evening might have warmed up a little, it was a foolish hope.

'I have no idea what's going to happen,' Angela told the newcomer in the pew beside her. 'None.'

Mrs Perry looked comfortably unfazed. 'I am a great believer in leaving everything to fate,' she said, and she cast down her eyes.

They stood and sang:

'Little drops of water, little grains of sand,
Make the mighty ocean, and the beauteous land.'

Mrs Perry smiled. What will be will be, the smile seemed to say.

*

When the Blessing of the Ale was over and the candles safely snuffed, the braziers doused, the lights switched off and the Dimplex radiators unplugged, the processors made their slow way back to the Fytton garden and the Fytton well, shutting the door of the church and leaving the gift of the little warmth they had made behind them. On the wall above the paintings of the naked woman and the shunned stranger taken in, the Virgin smiled down from her elevated place among the angels. *She* looked like no one except herself and the devils were cowering at her feet. And if behind that smile she was puzzling why there should ever be a ceremonial for her purification after the birth of her son, since she had got it on the best authority that he came directly from God and entirely bypassed the naughty human, sinful bit, well, she was not, for another thousand years or so, prepared to say. Not until she had ironed out the question of gender with the Authority anyway.

Angela picked up the gooseberry velvet and tucked it around the Dorkin girl's shivering shoulders. But she seemed not to notice. She was rosy-cheeked and staring very firmly at the vicar as he slung his guitar over his back and swirled off to lead his flock towards her coming redemption.

'I'm going to be born anew,' she said delightedly, 'in the light of innocence.'

'Ah,' said Angela.

There was something, she thought uncomfortably, about participating in a baptism that made her think of innocent little babies (*not* the Dorkin girl) and how they needed, if possible, their fathers. But what of love, she asked the stars – what of me and my love? Silence.

It ever was thus. Stars may twinkle all they like, but they have no conversation at all.

It also occurred to her, take this event for instance, that she was doing quite well down here on her own.

29

Candlemas

Brevity is the soul of lingerie.
DOROTHY PARKER

Past the holly hedge, through the gate, up towards the well. Yes. Here, at last, Mrs Fytton of Church Ale House in the county of Somerset felt she really belonged. Though there was no doubt that the sense of belonging held around it an outer edge of sadness and loss. She might have been doing pretty well on her own, but it was hard to contemplate it being like that all the time . . .

When the procession arrived in the garden of Church Ale House Mrs Dorkin took full command and Mrs Fytton was perfectly happy to let her do so.

Earlier in the week Mrs Dorkin and Mrs Fytton, accompanied by the potman from the Black Smock, had visited the well to remove the cover and when this was done all three of them peered into its dark depths. Mrs Dorkin held up half a brick and dropped it. After what seemed an eternity there was a faint splash.

'Long way down,' she said. 'You leave it all to me. I know what to do all right.'

So Angela did.

Now the party followed, weaving their way through her garden, past the henhouse, round the mulberry, past the hives and skirting the empty herb beds, coming to a stop by a circle of four buckets, placed around the open well, each containing water and each, rather incongruously, bearing the legend FIRE.

Angela did not like the look of those buckets at all. Not at all. Two upturned torches were placed nearby, giving light. The Dorkin girl had the curtain wrapped around her as the vicar stepped forward to begin the ceremonials. It was then that a fundamental flaw was spotted in the proceedings. No godparents had been designated. Mrs Dorkin, hot on the physical set-up, was a little shaky on the spiritual. The vicar, having had his mind elsewhere, let slip the hour. And Mrs Dorothea Tichborne, who might have thought about that side of things, was now six feet under.

In memory of his wife, Dr Tichborne was hastily asked to stand, and agreed because he could hardly refuse. Daphne Blunt volunteered and was accepted, since, although not at all religious in the ecumenical sense, she had a strong interest in churches. And Angela Fytton was asked and also agreed. It was, indeed, a moment of triumph. Now she, like her vegetables, had put down a root.

'But we must have a candle,' said the vicar, 'to welcome her as a new light.'

The Dorkin girl said 'Oh!' in nervous rapture. And Dave the Bread held on to his little beaded hat and ran the short distance back to the church to bring one.

My bees, thought Angela happily. Mine.

The baptism continued.

The Reverend Crispin Archer managed to keep himself within the sight of God and never erred in his duty. The Dorkin girl attempted at every opportunity to attract his glance with her eyes, and she did this by winking first one, then the other of her own, or by crossing them in what was meant to be an expression of profound connection, or rolling them, so that the Reverend Crispin Archer was in no danger of being seduced, but in great danger of feeling sick with the visual upheaval. But then it came to the point when the water was required.

The vicar dipped a tentative pair of fingers in one of the buckets and shivered. But Mrs Dorkin was not happy with the arrangement.

'The complete washing away of sins,' said that good lady

with absolute conviction. 'As agreed. In the name of the old mistress.'

If anyone heard her mutter 'and on with the new', they were far too cold to consider it. She handed a bucket to the vicar and one each to the other godparents. The vicar blessed all the buckets and, putting two tentative fingers into Dr Tichborne's bucket, swiped them over the Dorkin girl's willing forehead and felt that was more than enough.

Not so Mrs Dorkin. She stepped forward, took hold of the velvet curtain and whipped it off her daughter as if it were a dust sheet and her daughter a settee. The Dorkin girl stood there shimmering in the moonlight in the soft white robe. A Rembrandt Bathsheba in a shift, trembling, molten and looking rapturously at the Reverend Crispin Archer. Who, it seemed, was also undergoing a touch of the trembling, molten and rapturous himself.

Mrs Dorkin seized the moment and, taking the vicar's bucket, upturned it over her beloved daughter's head. And with a smile of invitation she encouraged old Dr Tichborne to do the same. The beloved, meanwhile, stood there, speechless and, in truth rather than metaphor, frozen to the spot. As was everyone else. Dr Tichborne, who felt that on the whole it was women who were responsible for all the sins of the world, followed suit as indicated with tremendous satisfaction, holding up his bucket like a flaming sword and slinging its contents with more force and accuracy than might have been considered seemly in his appointment as godfather.

The word FIRE on the side of the bucket seemed even more inappropriate.

The shivering Dorkin girl rediscovered her lungs. And gave a yell of righteousness that would not have disgraced St Catherine on her wheel. But unlike that good and pious lady, the Dorkin girl looked every bit the fantasy made flesh of any garage mechanic's dream. Fine old linen has a way with wetness in that, when soaked, it will display all its fineness of weave in a clinging transparency.

'Raquel, eat your heart out,' Mrs Dorkin was heard to mutter, forgetting in the excitement of the visual success that discretion was the better part of mother.

Yes, indeed. Beneath her pink plush Mrs Dorkin stared in satisfaction. At first. But the satisfaction rapidly gave way to an altogether different emotion. Possibly closer to rage. Little about the Dorkin girl's body was left to the imagination and it was a fair guess, from the way the fabric clung like a second skin to her generous contours, that she was not only a very bonny girl in her own right, but that she was a very bonny girl who had been fructiferous in her own right too. Probably around nutting time .

The vicar stared, having lost his voice and his memory regarding where he was, who he was and what his duty. But even he knew a fructiferous female when he saw one. And a vague memory stirred – along with several other parts of his anatomy – that he had seen it all before. But *how*?

Mrs Dorkin continued to stare. Old Dr Tichborne did not stare. Exclamations of horror abounded. But no one moved. Angela, in her first act of charity as godmother, picked up the curtain, threw it round the shivering girl's shoulders and led her very quickly indoors.

Behind her a babble of voices indicated there were strong arguments for the ceremonial to conclude. Mrs Dorkin, in particular, was of the view that it should conclude with the girl actually being sent *down* the well and preferably with a bucket tied round her neck.

The vicar opposed (a very relieved vicar opposed, it must be said, for even if what his memory hinted at was true, and even if miracles still happened, the beautiful curves of that belly before him were more than twenty-four hours old), saying that they would conduct a proper ceremony on the morrow, in the church, with the Dimplex radiators on, and all were welcome. 'For your daughter cannot be married in the church,' he said, 'if she has not been baptized first.'

'But who will she marry, vicar?' asked Mrs Dorkin, all forlorn, fully aware that Old Dr Tichborne might be a bit senile but had attended enough women in an interesting condition to know what was what. The point here was, who was who? And that was that.

The biker boys slipped away into the silence of the shadows and ran on the soft heels of their trainers all the way home. Everybody else, in need of warmth and sustenance, trooped back through the garden into the welcome of Angela Fytton's kitchen, where already the Dorkin girl was sipping a hot ale and eating a ham roll with pickled cabbage and wearing one of Wanda's more Arctic-orientated creations while seated on a chair by the Aga.

Angela looked up and smiled a welcome as they came in. Frankly, if no one else was going to react to the shocking occurrence, she wasn't. The Dorkin girl herself seemed to have a very forgiving nature. Beside her the large candle still burned. She had grabbed it on the way, her new light of innocence, hers by right.

'I told you I wasn't sure what was going to happen, Mrs Perry,' she said. 'But I am glad that you came.'

And then Sammy Lee sidled over, almost shyly, and smiled at Gwen Perry, and Angela was surprised to see that he now sported teeth. He must keep them in his pocket. His voice was oddly tender too. More tender than she had ever heard him, even when addressing his pigs. 'Didn't see your other half in church,' he said to Gwen Perry, and touched her hand.

'You don't see everything, Sam Lee,' she said. But her eyes looked very tender too, Angela observed.

'No Archie?' said Sammy, looking all around him.

'No Archie,' agreed Gwen Perry. Her voice, with its Somerset burr, was soft as old velvet.

Ale was poured. The dark fluid gushed and foamed into the glasses and each – no matter what their other concerns – raised their drink and gave a toast: 'To the ale and to the coming of spring.' Which, according to Daphne Blunt, was more or less the correct thing to say. Then Dr Tichborne looked into the vicar's eyes and the vicar looked into the Dorkin girl's eyes, and Mrs Dorkin looked into the eyes of all three of them until she nearly went giddy, hoping to instil a sense of propriety or, as she put it to herself, doing right by my Sandra.

Craig Elliott looked into Lucy Elliott's eyes and Lucy Elliott managed to make her eyes look slightly cloudy, as if tinged with a little death. Anja had long since taken the children home. Lucy Elliott thought about Angela Fytton's piano and flexed her fingers. She might even play a little later, if encouraged.

Dave the Bread looked into Wanda's eyes with admiration and she looked into his with admiration, and if they could have done a dive under the kitchen table and given immediate and physical vent to their silent tryst, they certainly would have done so.

Daphne Blunt looked up and around at the curves and lines of the ancient kitchen and she thought, and would have said though nobody asked her, If these walls could speak . . .

Angela went over to the answerphone, which was winking. It was the Rudges' message to say they had just broken down and they would not, sadly, be able to make the party after all. At which no one was at all surprised.

'Fill your plates and fill your glasses,' said Angela Fytton. And they did, over and over again. The ham was eaten, with Dave's good bread. And Angela's pickled beetroots and shallots – the ones she had drooled and cooed over as little miracles back in the summer, sweet, dear things – were most savagely devoured. Her preserves were complimented and the pickled eggs, strange things, were pronounced exquisite and who-would-have-thought-it, and also began to disappear. That's nature for you, thought Angela Fytton again, but this time with satisfaction, red in tooth and claw. And as she surveyed her Great Success, she wondered, with a little frisson, how Ian would fit into all this now . . . And she thought, but only for the fleeting glance of a shadow of a mote of a glimmer of a glimpse, that he might not. But *she* did. She looked around her again and smiled with happiness, she did, she did, she did . . .

'Getting the hang of it now,' Mrs Perry said to Dave, of his bread. Dave looked slyly at Wanda, who was busy – between bites of her pickled egg – chafing the Dorkin girl's wrists and ankles and backs of knees with her ginger and cinnamon oil.

'Now,' said Wanda, 'you can do this whenever you feel the chill and it's perfectly harmless. And if you feel sick I can make you some ginger pills, which will help. But on no account, *no account* –' she wagged her finger at the girl – 'must you take wild yam during your pregnancy.'

The Dorkin girl gave a passing fair impression of one who was willing to be persuaded against.

'Nor vervain, nor wood betony, nor excessive amounts of thyme . . .'

The Dorkin girl nodded in wide-eyed accord as her fourth pickled egg went down.

Mrs Dorkin felt obliged, somehow, to take up the duties of barmaid. It was one way of getting as much of the drink inside herself as she wished, without drawing attention to the fact. And she wished a great deal of the stuff to be inside her. She had been cheated of her victory. And she thought she might have known it. Her class would never rise. She looked around for the two spotty lads in their biker jackets. Which one was it, she wondered? She took another drink. It scarcely mattered. Sandra, she thought mournfully, was sunk.

Angela Fytton looked around the room and smiled. Yes, she thought, congratulating herself. Yes, I can stand alone. And she congratulated herself all over again, thinking, You wait until they see my grand finale.

30

Candlemas

I did not have 3,000 pairs of shoes. I had 1,060.

IMELDA MARCOS

In Claire and Andrew's opinion, one thing was sure. Living down south with parents had got to stop. What with their mother in some remote bit of the country keeping hens and going undeniably crazy and wanting them to go and live with her and go crazy too, and their father up in London acting like a gaoler while his new wife – who had once been so nice – *also* seeming to have gone crazy, finding the slightest thing – the very slightest thing – they did upsetting. It was doing their heads in. What was a party, for Chrissake? What was a bit of spilt beer? When sweet little Tristan (whom they both agreed that they loved) made a mess, everyone smiled. When they made a mess, the roof blew off. What the bloody hell the solution was, neither of them knew, but they were of the opinion that never mind the parents going mad, *they* would be bananas by the time September came if they didn't do something about it. But what?

And then Claire, her mother's daughter, had an idea. And when she had an idea, no power on earth could stop her putting it into practice there and then, immediately, right away and – if her French GCSE was anything to go by – *tout suite*. Andrew booked the tickets and a hotel, since he had something left on his credit card. Which is why they were in the late train heading north and reading their university prospectuses. Their eyes gleamed. The life of a student looked even better in the reading matter than they had heard it was from their friends.

'Something will happen,' said Claire firmly.

And Andrew agreed. Meanwhile they would just have to sleep on somebody's floor.

The ale was slipping down a treat. Lucy Elliott was requested to play the piano for the assembly and she – after a glass or two – agreed. It was time, Angela Fytton observed, for them all to go into the parlour.

Mrs Dorkin, silently considering the possibility of having another go at the good doctor herself later and who had been very busy and generous in her barmaiding line, refilled everyone's glasses one more time and in they trooped.

'Don't switch on the lights,' said Angela, as she turned the handle of the door and ushered them in.

All was darkness except for the bright flames from the fire. Craig settled his wife on the piano stool and stood by her side as if by being there he could protect her from all ills. Mrs Angela Fytton lit a taper and, very proudly, and with much ceremony, though she blinked frequently from seeing two of everything, managed to light one after the other of the rush lights pegged about and bedecking the room. The last one to be lit was on the mantelshelf, in the old rush-light holder which the Cleeve End blacksmith had repaired. 'So much for play-acting, Sam,' she said smugly. Which came out as something like 'Shoshplacting, Sm.'

She blew out the taper, looked around her room very happily and said, 'History is reborn,' even more smugly. Which came out as something like 'Sisterybor.' She gave Daphne Blunt a happy smile. A very happy smile. Daphne attempted to say something, but for the life of her she could not quite form the words. She did not, in fairness, look quite as happy as her friend.

'The celebration of the Virgin's Lustration,' said Angela Fytton, slurring but game, and gesturing around the room at the little lights. 'From the pagans . . .' Somebody let out a delicate little belch and Dave the Bread hiccuped. Angela took this to be agreement. Fit in? Of course she did. She did, she *did* ... And Ian would too. Thus does well-brewed beer warm the mind.

Then Lucy Elliott began to play Chopin, very, very beautifully.

Old Dr Tichborne, seated in a padded velvet chair, smiled beatifically at the music and scarcely saw that his Crispin had, so to speak, crossed the floor. Who would have thought that little Lucy Elliott could play so handsomely? What did he, old as he was, care for guitars and hand-clapping when he could listen to such as this in his house for ever more and love and yearn from afar? A decision had been reached. He could play chess with the Reverend whenever he wanted (and without benefit of mulberry wine): a hand could be brushed against a hand, a smile smiled into eyes that would smile back – who needed more than this when all his life he had never had so much? No, he said to himself, looking out of the window and up at the moonlit Mump and its stark green curve. It wasn't everything by a long chalk. Whatever 'it' was. He thought, somewhat thankfully, that he would never know now. Best way really.

Daphne Blunt continued to look unimpressed at the lighting arrangement of pegged tapers hanging about the room. She stared at the rush-light holder and, for some reason, perhaps the ale, perhaps not, tears filled her eyes, though whether tears of sorrow or anger who could say. Her proud hostess assumed it to be strong emotion at the sight of something so simple being used again, history being brought alive, and smiled contentedly. She focused enough to see a tear, then another, course down the side of that Afghan nose. Some well of deep emotion. And Amen, she thought. Although, then again, it could be the slight and rising smokiness of the room.

Ah well. Mrs Angela Fytton felt extremely proud of her achievement. Rushes picked and stripped by her own hands. Rushes dipped in mutton fat and turned until they were of the correct, thin shaping. How long it had taken her. She had read her way through three whole novels while doing it, for you must wait for the mutton fat to harden fully each time before another coating can be made. *That* was commitment. *That* was determination. Why, looking at the line of little flames she knew for certain that she could do or make or grow anything. She was independent, free, completely self-sufficient. Such was good husbandry. She was sure Maria Brydges would be proud of her too.

She peered at all the faces assembled to see how their rapture was faring. She peered harder. She had to peer even harder, for the faces were becoming even more hazy – dim even. Behind her someone coughed. Then another. More coughing broke out. Someone stood up and a chair overturned. Glasses were hurriedly emptied, more coughing, even more difficult to see. And then Angela realized, suddenly, that the room was filling with mutton-fat smoke, that the rush lights were sputtering and spitting and quite noxious in their smell, and that everyone was leaving the room and rushing out into the corridor past the little roundel, back through the house, into the kitchen and out into the night – gasping and choking in their quest to get some air. Plates of food lay abandoned on the table or were scattered on the floor, half-empty glasses lined the route to the front door – the piano ceased and the room became intolerable with the smoke and the smell. Angela Fytton too fled.

Sammy Lee, who had earlier persuaded his old love to follow him into the garden, heard the word 'Fire' as he snuggled his ancient chin into the warm folds of Gwen Perry's comfortable bosom out by the hives in the moonlight, and immediately abandoned his delights and stumbled back to the house. Through the window he could see a flashing and a flickering, and without a moment's hesitation he raced, so far as his knotty old legs could race, back to the well, picked up two of the buckets still waiting in their innocence, and ran indoors with them, upending them over the rush lights and dampening everything from the velvet curtains to the left-over food to the little bowls of burning, scented oil. The rush lights ceased immediately and the air was filled with the nauseating smell of old mutton, damp fabric and pickle juice. He checked that all was safely out and then left the room, closing the door behind him and shaking his head at the folly of it all. Only in the kitchen did one candle rekindle itself. The Dorkin girl's, made by Wanda, supplied by the bees and of good honest wax.

Gwen Perry took his arm. They understood. They understood and they did not, at all, approve. Rush lights . . . they said to each other. *Rush lights*.

'It was the same with those terrible biscuits of hers,' said Sammy. 'What's wrong with digestives?'

And they hurried away up the hill.

The vicar and the Dorkin girl and the Dorkin girl's mother made a voluble trio as they staggered their way towards the Dorkin cott.

Mrs Dorkin was all for putting her daughter out, away, off – all for sending her to the crossroads, to the fields, to the Mump itself to hurl herself into the darkness if she chose. And the vicar was trying to get a word in edgeways about the possibility of his taking her in.

Mrs Dorkin merely snorted. 'I should have thought she's been taken in quite enough, vicar. I should have thought from the look of her you could see how much she's been taken in . . . She's been taken in so much, my Sandra has, she's started coming out again.'

But the Dorkin girl was smiling to herself and suggesting, not too politely, that her mother put ye olde sock in it. What did she care now? For she had the vicar's arm around her waist. Or what was left of that part of her anatomy nowadays. She knew it was her mother who had been taken in. By old Dr Tichborne. But if there was one part of her anatomy she *had* learned to keep shut it was her mouth. She did not say what was on her mind, which was binoculars.

On they walked, away from the foul smokiness of Church Ale House.

'Funny, all that smoke,' said Mrs Dorkin. 'I remember rush lights in the three-day week. You don't go out of your way for *them*.'

'I think,' said the vicar, forgetting that his hand was where it was in order to offer support and letting it, instead, caress. 'I think it was some kind of exercise in humility.'

'Don't approve of exercise,' said Mrs Dorkin. 'Makes you stringy.'

She sighed. All those years of not letting Sandra go swimming or ride a bike. For what?

'No,' said the vicar, confused. Though in one particular he was clear as a bell – and not confused at all. He kept his happy hand exactly where it was.

Craig Elliott was relieved to get Lucy Elliott out of the poisonous atmosphere. She coughed rather sweetly, a little like La Dame aux Camélias (she was still weak, poor thing), and clung to him as they walked. 'You played so wonderfully,' he said. But it came out oddly. So he decided just to think the rest, which was, Don't die, Lucy, over and over again. He felt strangely emotional. Don't die, Lucy, he thought. Or I shall die too. For where should I be without you? And, as he told the stars while their footsteps rang out along the lane, I am not *drunk*.

But Lucy was very far from death. She was so far from death that she almost broke into song. But since, for some extraordinary reason, the only song that came to her lips was *circa* 1905 and charged the listener with the command 'Hold your hand out, you naughty boy . . .' she felt it best to keep it to herself. Women should, she now understood, have a little death now and again. Craig had been giving women a little death now and then for as long as she had been married to him, and now she was having one of her own. She knew what

311

her husband was thinking. She knew it was, Don't die, Lucy – and that he meant it with every breath in his body. Apart from any emotional considerations, if she popped her clogs he'd have three children to look after and a great deal of inconvenience, and *then* where would the magnum opus be? She leaned into him again, making a little pale oohing sound and hiding her smile in his lapel. She was smiling because she remembered what she was wearing. Her black leather trousers. Perfect fit.

Old Dr Tichborne was not at all sure what had happened. But since the music stopped and the vicar departed in such a hurry, there was nothing more to keep him in that velvet chair with something hot and smelly spitting all over him, so he slipped off home. Slipped seemed rather an appropriate word, since on the way he found some new aspects of the lie of the lane to negotiate, and several branches along the road had definitely extended themselves further in order to bump him one. Quite often he found himself pursuing the way home along the cracked and frosty ditch instead of up on the road – which was odd – and once or twice, for no apparent reason, he became entangled in the hawthorn hedge. Picking off the bits and looking up at that spangled darkness above him, he wondered why it seemed that the very stars themselves tonight were racing in the heavens. Swirling in the firmament. Art and beauty. To admire from afar yet never to possess. Perfection. He remembered the beautiful, flowing music tonight. He remembered the extra-strong binoculars recently purchased. Pity of it was that he had no one to hide them from, now that Dorothea was no more. It took, he thought, some of the relish out of it. Perhaps he wouldn't get rid of the dog. A little company was no bad thing.

Wanda and Dave the Bread hurried along the frosty distance laughing and laughing and laughing, though they were not entirely sure why.

'We're weaving our way home,' said Wanda, exploding with more unladylike guffaws, so that her husband felt obliged to take a large handful of her nether flesh and press it warmly. Which had the immediate effect of upending them into the ditch and into an interesting heap that should have comprised two, and was in fact three. Old Dr Tichborne was about to climb out of the ditch for the very last puzzling time when he received visitors.

'Hello,' he said.

'Hello,' said Wanda conversationally.

And in the way of all good and genuine neighbours, they hauled Dr Tichborne out. And then helped him home. From where he then helped them home and Wanda, having seen the light as much as any Evangelist, said she had nothing to hide and that he must come in and see her macrame snoods. Which he declined, feeling he had eaten enough. So that they felt obliged to see him home again, and he them, until after some confusion between the parties as to who lived up which path and through which door, they parted company and went in to sleep it off.

'Woman's a fool,' said Wanda as she climbed into her bed. 'She could have made candles from her very own beeswax. Or bought them –' she yawned with great satisfaction – 'from me.'

But Dave the Bread was already asleep, and crowing in his dreams for all the compliments his baking had been given. He still, though unaware of it, wore his hat.

Only Daphne Blunt remained, hunched in the cold, waiting by the gate, the smoke-induced wateriness gradually turning to a glitter in her eyes. Mrs Angela Fytton, a little less secure about being of Church Ale House in the county of Somerset, knew she was there but for some reason did not wish to join her. At that particular moment, she rather wished she had not moved anywhere. Particularly not to the same neck of the woods as Ms Blunt.

'Sorry,' she said forlornly.

'You know what you've done, don't you?' said Daphne. 'You've made a mockery of the whole thing. You've made the whole thing into something out of *Country Life* meets the Rural Dream. Free rush-light holder with every floral flounce . . .'

'Yes,' said Angela.

'The house is fine. The garden is fine. The hives, the hens, the apples, the mulberries – even the *ale* is fine. Just. A true tradition. And you were quite right. It brought us all together. A sense of community. And now you've mocked it. We don't need rush lights, Angela Fytton. And rush-light holders belong in a *museum* . . . thank God. And we certainly don't need someone to come along and tell us how *good* we all are.'

Mrs Angela Fytton mumbled something along the lines of meaning to donate the thing to the local museum the very next day . . . But Daphne Blunt was not to be mollified. Angela found it peculiarly sobering.

'We don't need rush lights, and *that* is what we should be celebrating. No women and children struggle home wet through and weighed down with their burden nowadays. No women and children cut their fingers to pieces stripping them down. No women and children have to tend the things constantly so that they don't go out . . . That was not a tradition, Mrs Fytton. *That was a burden and a necessity*. And making the holder into a mantelpiece fancy. Oh, please . . . What will you do for an encore, Angela? Construct a gibbet in the garden as a feature and hang a few effigies of witches from it? You could even sew bells on their feet to frighten away the crows.'

Angela Fytton put her hands over her eyes as if to hide the words. She knew they were true. She hoped to God she didn't go blurting out that she'd read three bloody *novels* while doing it . . .

'Did they really cut their fingers to pieces?'

Daphne waved her hands in an irritated gesture. 'Oh, forget it. Fortunately we all drank so much that no one realized the silly sentimentality of it all.'

'I just think people are so much better down here. Traditional.'

Daphne Blunt rolled her eyes. 'If you are going to live in the country, you'll have to abandon sentimentality. Honour its past by all means, but don't, for God's sake, try to re-create it.' She stopped suddenly. She too put her hands over her eyes. 'Do you know,' she said, 'I think I've got to go and lie down.' With which she turned towards the sparkling road that led to her home. 'One thing I will say,' she offered faintly. 'That ale was bloody good.' And off she went.

Angela, very close to tears, called after her, 'But what shall I do? It's such a mess.' She felt this was correct both in the physical and the metaphysical.

To which Daphne Blunt shrugged, winced and replaced her hands to her head. 'Just be good yourself. That's all you can do. And redecorate, of course. Start living in the place. It's not a scene in a play, or a book, or a poem, my dear. It's real life. Forwards, not backwards. If there's one thing those women needed like crazy, it was progress.' Her voice was growing very faint. 'Good night,' she called. 'Good night.' Which came out, roughly, as 'Gntt.'

But one drunk can always translate for another. Angela knew exactly what had been said to her, of course. And she watched her friend go (and sometimes two of them) until she turned the curve in the lane and was out of sight. What had Maria Brydges said? 'Take the good from the past ... And add the benefices of the modern world?' And Sammy was right. Anything else was play-acting. She was going to have a very big headache in the morning, one way and another. A very big headache. And she felt so alone.

She went back indoors, passed by the kitchen table, once scrubbed and now covered in discarded food and drink, and entered the parlour. Miserable, forlorn, unhappy place. She heard the chimes of St Hilary's clock strike midnight.

Damn, thought Mrs Angela Fytton. Got it wrong. It was something of a new feeling.

And with the foul smell lingering all about her, and wishing very much indeed that she was not so alone at that precise point in the proceedings, she sank down into the velvet chair and burst into tears. Which ceased only momentarily when she thought, for one foolish moment, that she caught the scent of Gauloise cutting through the foul mutton air.

31

Candlemas

I've married a few people I shouldn't have, but haven't we all?
MAMIE VAN DOREN

*There's nothing like a good dose of
another woman to make a man appreciate his wife.*
CLARE BOOTH LUCE

Binnie, tear-stained Binnie, had fallen asleep in front of the television, which now showed nothing but a white flicker. Binnie's mother looked at her sleeping daughter and her sleeping grandchild and shook her head. Binnie's mother knew very well the old adage that if you sow the storm you reap the whirlwind. She knew, being a Celt, originally from Pontypridd and therefore more pragmatic than many, that romance was Welsh rain, Scotch mist, Irish dew and English drizzle. It evaporated. Always.

So she prodded her sleeping daughter, who woke up and blinked her eyes and she said to her, 'You must go back home and make the best of it. And get that silly idea that it's easy being single and with a baby and on your own out of your head.'

Binnie blinked again, for this was a complex sentence to deal with when one has just woken up. But she got the gist.

'As husband's go,' said her mother, 'he's a good one.'

Perhaps she was right, thought her daughter. After all, her mother had been married to her father for thirty-three years and they seemed to get on well enough, so she must know something.

'Do you really think so?' she asked.

Her mother nodded.

So Binnie steeled herself. 'I'll go home tomorrow,' she said. 'Though if he's such a good one I don't know why he hasn't come for me.' She stroked her little boy's cheek.

Her mother looked at the scene and pursed her lips. 'If you go home and be civil, you can have quite a happy life. You don't, and someone else snaps him up . . . Like you did once.'

Binnie kissed her baby's head. The maternal lips pursed anew. Welsh pragmatism, sprung from the caves of the Celts, told her that unless someone brought home the bacon, you had to go out and get it.

'I shall never love him again, Ian,' said Binnie firmly.

'What's love got to do with it?' said her mother. 'Try affection. It's easier.' She tucked the quilt around her grandchild's sleeping head and then helped her daughter to bed. 'And if you want romance you can always get it from a book, or go to the pictures . . .'

So Binnie went off to sleep again, prepared to get up and pack and go back to Wimbledon the next day. Just for now, though, because it was late, she would not ring her husband. Let him stew for another night all alone and wondering up there. He'd be worried out of his skin. And that was *something*, she supposed.

Was there a star in the sky, he wondered, amused, and did it hang over a chicken shed? Here he was, back once more, and the only house in the whole place that had a light on was his ex-wife's. He smiled fondly, for he always doubted she would fit into the country life. Up with the lark and to bed with sun was not the way he remembered life with Angela Fytton. Just for a moment he felt a catch of breath in his chest at the thought of what he had lost. And then another catch in his chest at what he had gained. It was a conundrum. Quite a painful one.

He parked some way back and walked along the glittering road, enjoying the freshness of the air, the sharpness, the silence, the stars, and smoking his Gauloise, inhaling both its scent and the scent of the crackling night. So what if he had crept off last time? This time he would knock on the door – despite its being midnight – and ask if he could come in and be welcome in the warm-looking kitchen or the inviting sitting room which he had glimpsed through the windows last time. And whoever she had been making love to that night could take a walk. He squared his shoulders, ready for the fight. He needed to talk to somebody and his ex-wife was the somebody. Mrs Perfect. Call off your dogs. You have done what you set out to do. My marriage is wrecked. Couldn't you have got things wrong *just once*? So now what? He wanted to ask her. *Now what, superwoman?*

He smiled to himself rather a nasty little smile, rather a nasty little smile tinged, though he would not acknowledge it, with jealousy. He might even surprise her in bed with whoever he was. After all, it was too cold tonight to be doing it under a bloody tree. Even for her. He flapped his arms like a frustrated crow as he surveyed the pleasing sprawl of Church Ale House – all this bucolic bliss and getting everything right down here too. He could not help himself. He had to say it. It's just not *fair* . . .

I'll give her bucolic bliss, he thought. He was about to knock when three things happened. One, he smelt the very strong whiff of something scorched and soaked and not at all pleasant. Two, he heard a woman crying. And three, when he pushed at the front door it was open. So he went in. And he tiptoed down the corridor towards the sound. He trod on a glass and broke it, and nearly tripped on some cutlery and a plate. Odd.

He felt strangely moved. He had heard his new wife crying piteously several – no, many – times of late and the sound had eventually not moved him at all. But this touched his heart. This sound was new. This sound was the sound of his ex-wife, Mrs Perfect, weeping copiously. Ian Fytton was surprised to find that his first, his very first, thought was,

Perhaps he has abandoned her . . . Which was oddly cheering, though not very kind. He composed his face as he arrived at the door of the room from which the sounds came and he turned the handle and he went in.

Angela, midst howl, sniffed. There was that faint scent of Gauloise again. Above that other smell, the vile odour of her failure. The scent of the French cigarettes made her want to be held very, very tightly and comforted. It came, she thought woefully, from a land called comfort.

The smell was *nauseating*. He had expected the house to exude the odour of comforting, delicious, desirable things. And not only was the smell foul but the place was fouled too. The inviting little sitting room looked like a scene from a disaster movie, with upended plates of food and glasses of half-finished drinks spilling over the tables and dripping from the mantelshelf. A velvet curtain lay in a puddle of water and an upturned chair, its covering soaking wet, was legs up on its side. Above all this, strung around the room, pegged from a washing line, hung scorched-looking tapers, blackened, bent and forlorn. He wondered if it was the new rural drug scene. It had an air of old hippiedom about it, with all candles hung about and bunches of leaves suspended from the beams. Dope could sometimes smell a bit ripe, but this . . . Perhaps it was Satanic? Jesus, not his Angela! What had he done? His ex-wife, face buried in her hands, did not look at all like a woman who had embraced either dope or the devil. He approached, very quietly, unsure what to do with the weeping woman who had once been his mate.

'Angie?' he said softly.

She looked up.

'Angie?' he said again, approaching her now as if she were some sort of lunatic animal in pain. He held out his hand. 'Angie?'

She focused. Her crying ceased. And then began again,

with renewed vigour. 'I am such a failure,' she said over and over again. 'And don't call me *Angie*.'

But Ian Fytton took heart. For what he saw was that his ex-wife was – to put it kindly – not entirely sober. She reached out a feeble hand and clutched his. She was languorous in her misery. Soft and pliant, temptingly vulnerable. Which gave him, the ex-husband in question, a certain frisson.

He sat beside her, keeping hold of her hand, feeling strong. And he asked her to explain. She produced a series of sounds and gulps and cries and peculiar incantations which told him nothing. And she clung to him, smelling of something beery and smoky and hot, making a fairly reasonable stab at accusations of his abandonment.

'I did come,' he said, stroking her hair. 'I did come, once before.' Indignation rose in his breast. 'But you were having it off with someone in the garden.' Two could play at the game of accusation, after all.

'I most certainly was not,' said his ex-wife, with a surprisingly clear verbal rally.

'You most certainly were,' he said. 'You were up against that big tree out there and you were really going at it . . .'

He spoke with such conviction that Angela began to wonder if she *had* forgotten a moment like that. She attempted to call her muddled, fuddled brain to order. She began to feel quite bucked. Maybe she had. Good, she thought vaguely. Good.

'You were wearing pink,' he said. 'Not a lot of it and it was certainly a chilly night. You sounded, from what I heard, quite warm enough . . .'

She remembered. She had been making the ale. That was all. She was innocent. Nevertheless, there was something in his tone of voice that made her disinclined to enlighten him. You can stew, you bastard, was what she actually thought, but even in her cups she knew better than to come right out with it.

'I wanted to discuss our children,' he said righteously, 'but it was hardly the moment, given what you were up to.' He looked stern. She liked that. Stern. And then a very serious and wonderful thought occurred to her which she just could not keep in.

'Were you jealous?' she said.

'Yes,' he said.

They both stared at each other, very surprised.

And then she realized, as someone in their cups can sometimes realize a profound and difficult truth very easily, that she was both glad that he was here and sorry that he had come. That she had much to give up as well as much to share. And that this was the moment of no return. Synthesis. Reunification, she thought. All I have dreamed of, she thought. And then, for some extraordinary reason, she remembered Berlin.

'Look where reunification got them,' she said.

'Who?' said Ian.

'The East Germans,' she said. 'Of course.'

'I take your point,' he said carefully. If she wanted to discuss politics, then why not? If she didn't, then he had an overwhelming urge to carry her off to bed. 'In what way the East Germans?' he asked.

'All that glisters is not gold,' she said. 'Curate's egg. Good in parts.' She put her arms around his neck. 'You give up as much as you gain.'

'In Berlin?' he said, hoping he was still on the right track.

'In reunification,' she said, taking a few stabs at the word before finally settling for an approximate version.

He was still attempting to follow.

And, with a great deal of strain, two phrases did finally stand out from the crowd: 'Don't go ever. Don't go. Well, not yet.'

He brought her some water. 'Come on,' he said. 'I think you ought to get into bed.'

Angela looked up from weeping. 'Only if you'll come with me,' she said.

He looked suitably torn between morality and desire. Whatever the morality of it all was. Why not? Binnie wouldn't know.

Nobody would know. And anyway, in a manner of speaking, this was still his wife.

He whispered into her quivering ear. She blinked. He whispered again.

'Oh, speak up, sod it,' she said, with a touch of a completely new Angela about her. But she lay herself back against him very sweetly.

So he said it once more. 'Do you want me to get in it too, or just on it?'

'What?'

'The bed.'

And she nodded. 'Assolutly,' she said.

They bathed together in the avocado bath, lit by moonlight and a beeswax candle. When Ian pulled the velvet curtains to keep out prying eyes, she yanked them back again. 'No one can see us,' she said. 'We are invisible.'

'This is what I wanted,' she said as they held on to each other and creaked their way along the moonlit passage.

Ian opened the door of the sewing room, out of curiosity. 'You haven't done much to it yet,' he said, not as a criticism but as a statement of fact.

She stopped for a moment and gave him a searching look. Her eyes were dark and unreadable in the shadows. 'No,' she said, and quickly closed the door.

'What a lovely room,' said Ian, looking around in the moonlight. 'I like it.'

As she turned down the white piqué bed cover she smiled. 'So do I.'

She supposed she must thank the mulberry tree. For if it had not existed and if Ian had not mistaken what was going on in the garden on that previous night, then what was going to happen between them *tonight* would have happened too soon. She would not, quite, have known her own mind. Reached her synthesis. And she did and had done both now. Nothing is yours for all time. You have the use of it for a while before you pass it on.

'Don't go' and 'Not yet' made perfect sense.

Better by far, she thought, slipping in beside that dear and familiar body with its mind and manners that she had trained so well – and which, she supposed, had probably trained her so well too – better by *far* to do it this way. After all, what was good enough for Nell Gwynn was good enough for her. Better to be a happy mistress than a harrowed wife.

'Don't go' and 'Not yet' would suit everybody perfectly. Except, perhaps, Maria Brydges. But she wasn't here any longer. Was she? And she couldn't be expected to get *everything* right.

Epilogue: April

Vice is nice
But a little virtue
Won't hurt you.
FELICIA LAMPORT

Angela Fytton felt she had paid the price. The stinging suggestion about a gibbet had finally shed the light of her own lustration. Her very own Candlemas.

She took the rush-light holder to the local museum, who were pleased to keep it. In a display case. Where it belonged. With a prettily scripted ticket explaining that it was donated by 'Mrs Angela Fytton of Church Ale House'.

And she had the Celtic well resealed and never again mentioned the idea of dressing it to the vicar. Who, in any case, had quite enough to do with the dressing of a new baby, which was more wriggly than any eel.

She put Maria Brydges's diagrams aside and drew up a list of the herbs *she* wanted, including heart's-ease and love-ache, because you never knew when they might be required. And she spent a very happy springtime going between her vegetable bed and her herb beds, and when she was not doing that she wallpapered and painted and made the inside of the house her own. You did not, she found, need to alter the fabric of a place in order to shape it. It was, she realized, quite bogus to live in another woman's shoes. Except, she might wickedly speculate, Eve's. So she wore her own. And she sang as she went about her work and was very, very happy.

She tiptoed around Daphne Blunt very carefully these days, and if they talked of such matters at all, they talked of the paintings in the church, which were nearly complete.

'Consider this,' said Daphne, standing back to look at her work. 'Consider that the tenets of goodness upon which the Christian faith, and most other faiths as well, including our secular one, is based are the qualities held to be inherent – now even *genetically* inherent – in women. Odd, isn't it, then, how little we have gained in terms of power in those places?' And she turned back to the last section of the wall, saying, 'Much to do and much to learn, still. Much.'

To tend the sick, to feed the hungry, to give drink to the thirsty, to clothe the naked, to harbour the stranger, to minister to prisoners, to bury the dead:

These were the Seven Corporal Works of Mercy. In each one, Dorothea Tichborne's face was clear – lying on a sickbed, holding up an empty bowl, receiving a cup of water, standing naked and shivering, knocking at a door, standing behind bars and, finally, lying on a bier.

The painters had their own way with revenge.

To convert the sinner, to instruct the ignorant, to counsel those in doubt, to comfort those in sorrow, to bear wrongs patiently, to forgive injuries, to pray for the living and the dead:

These were the Seven Spiritual Works of Mercy. In which the Tichborne face could be seen as a sinner, as ignorant, as a doubter, as one in sorrow, as one who is wronged, as injured, as sick but alive, as dying or dead.

Revenge, thought Angela Fytton, did not necessarily have to hurt anybody. Revenge, thought Angela Fytton, could simply be a balm from within. As was that medieval painter's. Revenge could be exacted without hurting any of the parties concerned. Especially an innocent child. But she did not say this to Daphne. In case she asked her why.

It was an even playing field between her and Belinda now. And everybody got what they wanted. Ian was a bit confused at first, which was understandable, given that he seemed to have sprouted two wives. But his capacity to love expanded to embrace both of them. And he soon saw the benefit. And Angela, who had never countenanced the illicit in her life, let alone sharing the man she loved, took to it like hens to sweet breadcrumbs . . . Not the food of life, of course, but a little bit of something very pleasant on the side. Freedom was no longer just another word for nothing left to lose, freedom was choice.

'But I love you,' Ian said. 'I want to stay with you.'

'And I love you too.'

And then he thought. And he said, 'But I also love Belinda.'

To which his ex-wife, though he was expecting an explosion, responded with a nod. 'And Tristan, you love him too?'

'I do, I do,' he said, suddenly feeling that twist to his heart. She could not help but add, 'And all Tristan's lovely, adorable, intellectual teeth?'

Her ex-husband looked at her for a moment. And immediately felt a surge of something requiring immediate gratification. He put his hand out to touch her.

'And our two?' she said. 'You also love them.'

He growled. 'Possibly.'

She removed his hand.

Confound lust.

'Definitely,' he agreed.

And also celebrate it.

'Why change the habits of an entire planetary history?' she said, being quite convinced, having seen what she had seen of the birds and the bees, not to mention the hens and the pigs, that the male member was never made to be faithful. Well, not yet. How could it be with several thousand years of genetic programming behind it? But what it could learn to do, as the female of the species had learned with its own particular brand of genetic promiscuity, was to be *discreet*.

Later she picked up the bog myrtle leaf that had fallen from her sleeve to the floor and gave it to him to hold. It crackled, of course.

And thus it was that Angela Fytton discovered it was perfectly possible to become Mistress Fytton of Church Ale House but without the ringlets and the sprigged muslin and the mulberry tarts, of course.

And what of her offspring?

'Get your feet off that settee,' demanded Claire Fytton. 'And wash up those mugs. They're festering.'

A skinny girl with freckles and a boy with an inadequate moustache leapt up as if they had been stung. This was not the usual behaviour they expected from a student flat.

Andrew Fytton, coming into the room behind his sister, made way for the pair as they scuttled off down the corridor towards the kitchen.

It was such a responsibility being the owners of a student flat. Or, if not exactly the owners, because their father and their mother were, then the subletters of same.

'We've got the electricity bill,' said Andrew Fytton to his sister. 'I'll divide it by four and add theirs to the rent.'

'Good,' said Claire Fytton, '*good*.'

Her brother nodded. Something caught his eye and he frowned. He got up and paced across to the window. 'Bloody curtain pole's coming down again,' he said. And he went off to get a screwdriver.

'I've told you before,' he called to the boy with the inadequate moustache, 'when you pull the curtains, do it *gently*, for Chrissake.'

The boy with the inadequate moustache shrugged. 'Sure,' he said. 'Keep your hair on.'

'Up yours,' said Andrew mildly. And returned to the curtains and their pole, quite expertly.

After the fixing of which, and the ritual by Claire of the inspected and passed mugs and kitchen sink, the four of them went out to sample the delights of studenthood in a northern town. Where smallish flats on the perimeter of existence were remarkably (as Ian commented to Angela when they visited the place) cheap.

'Clever of them,' he said.

'*Very*,' agreed Angela.

'Did you notice,' said Claire to Andrew as they walked along the windy streets, 'that Dad and Mum held hands when we came up here?'

'No,' said Andrew.

'Better not let Binnie know,' said Claire.

'Know what?' said her brother.

When her children came to visit they approved of Ye Olde Black Smock and little else, but they were kind enough to allow that while *they* might not find Church Ale House a desirable place in which to live, their mother did, and parents – perhaps – had rights. If not to full-blown happiness then to a certain degree of equilibrium.

Whenever her ex-husband visited her, Angela thought there was nothing so pleasant as being a mistress to a man to whom you had once been married. You know everything about him. He knows everything about you. Even that little bulge just above the top of your knickers that would be quite difficult to introduce to anyone new. An ex-husband finds such things, and holds them, and speaks of them as familiar delights. And then, just as one is thinking his little ways are becoming irritating, and he is thinking the same of you, it is time for him to leave and go back to his one, true wife. And his delightful, many-toothed son.

Belinda is also happy. And as for the extra mortgage taken out concurrently by Ian and his ex-wife in the name of housing their children, why, it is nothing compared to the peace and quiet and pleasure that Binnie feels now that she is, once again, mistress of her own life. And she is doing the little bit of dentistry necessary to pay for Ian's share of it with a willing,

willing heart. Because she is happy. Quite possibly, in time, she will be happy enough to think of a little brother or sister for Tristan – another little brother or sister for Claire and Andrew. But – she shivers – perhaps not *quite* yet . . .

And Angela Fytton has long since put the memorandum book of the redoubtable Mrs Maria Brydges to the back of the bookshelf for occasional reference only. And she continues to make her own mistakes from time to time. For it does not do in this life to be seen to be too clever by half. Angela Fytton is now a pragmatist, not a country dreamer. She knows that a woman must learn both to swoon, when swooning is required, and to shin up a ladder and fix the roof when that is also required. Her task in life is to be sure not to do the swooning bit when she is *up* the ladder. Get that right, baby, thinks Mrs Angela Fytton, and you too may find yourself saying to your hives one night that life, on the whole, is Good.

Very good.

Addendum

The Rudges, of course, had to leave. They simply could not bear the vandalism prevalent in the community of Staithe.

Why, whatever might the local miscreants not do to their swimming-pool filters and suchlike when they were away? Let alone those nasty, omnipresent leaves. So they moved on. Somewhere else. Maybe to a village near you.

Select Bibliography

Bishop, Frederick (late cuisinière to St James's Palace, Earl Grey, the Marquis of Stafford, Baron Rothschild, Earl Norbury, Captain Duncombe and many of the first families of the Kingdom), *The Wife's Own Book of Cookery* (1856).

Although several of the recipes and pronouncements on a well-run household come verbatim from this book – a happy find which, of course, reflects its times and predates Isabella Beeton by five years – the memorandum book of Maria Brydges is wholly invented.

Filbee, Marjorie, *A Woman's Place* (Ebury Press, 1980)

Fisher, Helen, *Anatomy of Love: A Natural History of Monogamy, Adultery and Divorce* (Simon and Schuster, 1993). Very regrettably now out of print.

Glob, P. V., *The Bog People* (Faber and Faber, 1969)

Mass Observation, *Report of People's Homes* (1943)

Mendelsohn, Sara, and Crawford, Patricia, *Women in Early Modern England* (Oxford University Press, 1998)

Miles, Rosalind, *The Woman's History of the World* (Michael Joseph, 1988)

Ody, Penelope, *Home Herbal* (Dorling Kindersley, 1995)

Plath, Sylvia, *Ariel* (Faber and Faber, 1965)

Ransom, Florence, *British Herbs* (Penguin Books, 1949)

Somerset: The Little Guides (Methuen, 1949)

Street, A. G., *The Gentleman of the Party* (Faber and Faber, 1946)